SECOND CHANCE

THE CHRONICLES OF FREYLAR

- VOLUME 1 -

by

Liam W H Young

First edition printing, 2016

ISBN 978-1-78280-777-3

Copyright © Liam William Hamilton Young 2016.

All characters appearing in this work are fictitious. Any resemblance to real persons, living or dead, is purely coincidental.

All rights reserved. No part of this book may be reproduced in any manner without written permission except in the case of brief quotations included in critical articles and reviews. For further information, please contact the author.

Cover Illustration Copyright © Liam William Hamilton Young 2016, moral rights reserved by Hardy Fowler.

A catalogue copy of this book is available from the British Library.

Printed and bound in the United Kingdom by Biddles.

www.thechroniclesoffreylar.com

ACKNOWLEDGEMENTS

Foremost, I would like to thank Nigel Winter for his own literary endeavours and his continuous wise council, both of which inspired and motivated me to write this book.

Thank you to Hardy Fowler, an exceptionally talented digital artist, who created the amazing cover art illustration for this book which beautifully renders the world I envisaged, for which I am extremely grateful.

I would like to thank Matthew Webster enormously for meticulously editing this book, and also for his boundless advice on this project – his welcome enthusiasm was extremely motivational.

Thank you to Mark O'Shea for his advice on copyright law, and to Julia Raines for her invaluable proofreading.

I would also like to thank Kevin Forster for advising me on the correct use of medieval weaponry. Lastly, thank you to Kai Zammit, a talented filmmaker, who inspired me with his short film 'Peacekeeper' – I appreciate being permitted to use the term 'Peacekeeper' in this book.

I dedicate this book to my loving wife Emma and to our wonderful son Tristan.

This book started life as project 'Night-Night'; an endeavour which I commenced whilst sitting beside my son, who had great difficulty sleeping at night. My presence comforted Tristan, helping him to doze off, and whilst he slowly drifted away each night seeking fresh adventures within his dream world, I set myself the challenge of creating a world of my own.

To Amy,

Thank you for the support, it's really appreciated.

P.S. you're doing a grand job managing the dark sunny side.

Ethan Young

TABLE OF CONTENTS

ONE Rain

TWO Farewell

THREE Light

FOUR Rebirth

FIVE Air

SIX Revelations

SEVEN Confrontation

EIGHT Purpose

NINE Nocturnal

TEN Dust

ELEVEN Scorn

TWELVE Endurance

THIRTEEN Sanctuary

FOURTEEN Advance

FIFTEEN Serenity

SIXTEEN Gambit

SEVENTEEN Restless

EIGHTEEN Deception

NINETEEN Contact

TWENTY Despair

TWENTY ONE Retribution

TWENTY TWO Reflection

DRAMATIS PERSONAE

ONE
Rain

The early afternoon July heat was oppressive. He had never actually seen a desert, not first-hand at least, but if he had surely the metropolis' heat trap, courtesy of its monolithic office blocks and polluted sky line, was not entirely dissimilar to such conditions. No doubt fanciful thoughts, for he knew little beyond the hardships of living life on the edge. Desert voyages were for the middle classes looking to get away from their mundane office lives, or those affiliated with legendary expeditions in the fantastical books he read, not for the easily forgotten waifs of the city's Shadow class. He was Shadow class; an undesirable by-product of the government's inability to reduce the welfare gap between those with and those without, of which he was firmly the latter. Despite his bleak social status, he was clothed in someone else's unwanted garb and was not so gaunt as to look ill, therefore, in his world at least, all was well, relatively speaking.

With the sun only just beginning its inevitable descent towards the western horizon, straying from shade was not desirable. Neither was moving, not in the near unbearable heat. So he sat quietly, patiently, as the sun made its journey across the bleached sky. Occasionally the tyrant would fade temporarily from existence, as it played second fiddle to its cloudy companions, introducing a touch of chaos to the ephemeral shadows cast by the broken canopy of the park's secluded wood in which he retreated from Apollo's wrath. The opaqueness of the meandering clouds and their increasing number suggested to him that the heat would not last the night. This notion pleased him immeasurably. The thought of sleeping once more in sweat drenched dirty clothing did not; the constant itching maddened him. Those in his position were not privy to the luxury of a clean hot bath; the best he could realistically hope for was a dip in the park's reservoir, though this was rarely an enjoyable experience - the vast body of dark water was always icy to the touch. He was rarely able to visually penetrate its calm mirror sheen surface, thus there was no accounting for what laid beneath. On several occasions he had disturbed the remains of decomposing fish which had invariably rolled over revealing their one swollen semi-recognisable good eye; they would stare intently at him whilst he washed himself or his attire. Other times his toes would brush up against submerged foreign objects; this would set his imagination alive with undesirable thoughts. Everything below the surface had a silky glaze, perhaps caused by algae or silt, rendering his sense of touch useless. It was best not to try and understand the true nature of such things since his vivid imagination often distorted fact, twisting it into nightmarish fiction.

Labelling it a park failed to do it justice, so most did not. More often it was referred to as the Wild. A more accurate description would have been humanity's tribute to mass landscaping, all neatly packaged within the confines of the surrounding urban sprawl of towering concrete, glass and steel. It was intended to be a retreat for the occupants of the metropolis, but it meant so much more to him. After five years of residency, he now considered the Wild his home. During the darker times of his life, before fully settling within the heart of the metropolis' artificial wilderness, he had leeched off the streets for a while. Prior to that he was shunted between a series of children's homes, but at age eighteen you were considered a capable adult and so the system closed its doors on him. He was homeless; albeit a capable homeless adolescent. According to the previous generation, the number of people living life on the streets was once negligible. So few were the numbers that local charities were setup to try and help manage the isolated cases. During the closing years of the last decade those numbers swelled uncontrollably, largely due to ineffective government policies. The unrealistic cost of education further increased and the severe downturn in unskilled work continued to be eroded by relentless automation as industry advanced the process of streamlining. Work therefore, was sparse. If you lacked money, both education and work were largely unobtainable. Those born into low income families were destined to struggle. Those who had no parents to care for them, including himself, were destined for a life outdoors; he was nothing special in this regard. As work became increasingly unobtainable, financial pressures increased, people lost their homes and the annual statistic for abandoned children rose. Time marched on and the number of unfortunates, later classified by the government as Shadow class, reached threatening levels. Those who the system had failed were shunned by a society which simply did not care enough to solve its darker problems. This dangerous mindset gave birth to unethical policies and agendas set in motion by those in power, chief amongst which saw local Peacekeepers tasked with moving the Shadow class out of the metropolis; a forced exodus endorsed by an uncaring society choosing to burry its head in the sand by pushing the problem elsewhere.

As he sat in the shade, waiting out the worst of the sun's cruel caress, his thoughts drifted back to those awful days of the Exodus. Never before had he witnessed the forced relocation of so many people from their homes; these were invariably little more than shanty constructs, poorly erected and often located in undesirable districts within the metropolis. Some groups within the Shadow class, family units mostly, had moved into the dilapidated buildings of the historical boon years, all of which had been condemned by the government. When businesses moved out, members of the Shadow class unlawfully moved in. This further agitated government officials tar pitting their plans for redevelopment; initially, no one had the stomach to forcibly evict struggling families with no place to go. In time, the political landscape changed. The other classes became increasingly vocal on the matter, sometimes even violent following renewed agitation by the media. Eventually the overwhelming majority came to view the Shadow class as little more than vermin. To this day he struggled with the concept of human vermin. Nonetheless the term came into being and social interaction between the classes changed, disturbingly so. Unrest became viral, people on both sides were scared and reports of rioting started to surface. The government had thus far failed to resolve the matter of the Shadow class. With a major crisis imminent, officials claimed they were forced to implement a less humane solution; the Exodus. In the space of a single month the Exodus - or Rout as many called it - was manifest. Spearheaded by what seemed like a legion of Peacekeepers, the metropolis was swept clean of its human vermin. The operation was surgical, though horrifying in its implementation. Curfews, a bought media and tightly controlled dissemination of information had the other classes believe that the Shadow class was escorted to a new district, well beyond the metropolis' perimeter, where its members could start over. The word 'escorted', however, had no place when Peacekeepers crashed through the already smashed windows of homes with stun rifles; these devastating weapons delivered rounds which released a cocktail of neurological disrupters into the human biological system. Those hit by stun rounds had their motor functions taken away from them within seconds. They fell where they once stood, temporarily paralyzed yet still fully aware of their lot. Once neutralised, the victims were forced to stare in mute horror as they witnessed their loved ones being lifelessly turned over onto opened black sacks before being zipped up wholly within. The same abhorrent fate would then befall the watchers themselves. The month long operation was methodical. Age, gender and disposition were irrelevant; none of these things mattered. The only relevant criterion was social class. If you were Shadow class then you were stunned, bagged and loaded into windowless boxy carriages trailing lightly armoured transports; these swiftly redeployed Peacekeeper teams across those districts which fell within the legalised remit of the Exodus. Even now, three years since that awful time, he recalled vividly the silent screams etched forever into the faces of those never to be seen again. He was no parent himself, but he remembered thinking during the Rout that those who were must have died inside as their children were taken from their still life arms. Sometimes infants were stolen, spirited away to lead new adopted lives, cared for by the apex classes with influence enough to legalise such abhorrent actions. Arguably, these were the lucky ones.

The remainder of the Shadow class simply disappeared; at least that was the general perception, though he knew better.

His limbs felt heavy now and his breathing was deep. The incessant heat seemed to drain energy directly from him, yet gave nothing back. More clouds gathered defiantly on the horizon, darkening as their ranks swelled; a war for supremacy of the heavens seemed inevitable with neither side ready to back down. His gaze drifted towards the sun's assailants; had they come to finally liberate him, or instead to impose their own form of tyranny - one meteorological dictator for another - he mused. Still, the prospect of rain fall would be more welcome than slowly being cooked from up high. As he pondered the answer to his own question, the Exodus returned to the fore of his thoughts once more; indeed it never really left him - a result of psychological trauma others would more often say, which he likened to scarring of the mind. He recalled the colossal number of transports as they left the metropolis en masse, enough that the column resembled a tarnished silver serpent as it slid its way out of the metropolis beyond his view and into the unknown. He had never ventured further than the outer perimeter of the metropolis, thus his knowledge of what lay beyond was limited to the distorted information disseminated by both the government and the media.

On a few occasions he had tried to access the metropolis' Infonet to further his knowledge of the events surrounding the Exodus, however the system's tight moderation and class level access offered little substance; sensitive data was no doubt restricted to the apex classes. Of course he had never used his own biometric key to access the system, not after the Exodus at least. To do so would have no doubt broadcast his location to the authorities, besides, he no longer possessed his own bio-key. Once the Shadow class realised that the various government authorities were using their bio-keys to track the origin of their data access, there was little choice but to forcibly remove the implants thus severing their access to the Infonet. Losing access to the Infonet crippled their ability to coordinate their ranks; this was a necessary handicap to avoid giving up their whereabouts. The procedures themselves were often rushed, sometimes even botched affairs, carried out by whoever happened to be standing in close proximity at the time. Some had little choice but to operate on themselves; the ugly scar on the fore of his right arm was testament to his own novice knife work.

As his mind continued to rehash the past events of the Exodus, he wondered why so few had lacked the cunning to evade the Peacekeepers. He did not consider himself to be particularly intelligent, but he was certainly quick and a born survivor; a nomadic childhood had taught him those skills well, yet there was definitely more to it than that. For as long as he could remember, his disposition had been one of dogged determination. He strived to achieve whatever he set his mind to, never giving up, never quitting. It was his personal trait, it defined him. Some viewed this behaviour as bloody minded stubbornness, and perhaps it was. Despite his critics to him it was a useful tool, one which allowed him to continue moving forwards. More importantly, it allowed him to survive the Exodus.

Almost the entirety of the Shadow class' members had clung to the metropolis like suckling infants, unable to separate themselves from the architect of their own demise. Not him. Many proclaimed him foolish to seek a life beyond the streets, claiming that it was unwise to stray too far from food sources and the protection of others in the same situation. He viewed things differently, however, and preferred anonymity to be his ally. To him it was naive to think of the Shadow class as a means of protection. They were barely able to get by, let alone offer protection against a common threat. Crowds were often seen as intimidating by others. They drew attention, the unwanted kind. In his mind the best play for the Shadow class was to disperse, go to ground and maintain a low profile until the time for coordinated action was right; congregating only made them vulnerable, placing them firmly under the spotlight of current affairs. Despite his doubters, he remained unperturbed. As soon as he was able to do so, he moved on. His end game was to survive independently outside the metropolis and away from its sham politics, but in the interim, the Wild would be his training grounds.

Subconsciously he felt the temperature drop, followed by the feint touch of sporadic drops of rain on his exposed skin. Slowly his strained gummy eye lids parted allowing the fading light of day to dance across his retinas. As he began to consciously register the light, his surroundings started to blur into being. He blinked rapidly several times to sharpen his vision; this was more a reflex action as opposed to his sluggish brain instructing him to wake up. His vision cleared and there was a moment of tranquillity as his mind struggled to reorder itself, then he was awake. In a heartbeat he was bolt upright, albeit sat squarely on his backside.

'Shit!' he announced, to an unseen audience, as it finally dawned on him that he had succumbed to the heat's lethargic embrace and fallen asleep.

What time was it he wondered? How long had he laid asleep, vulnerable and exposed?

'Garr, you can be such a moron at times,' he proclaimed, scolding himself. 'The Peacekeepers probably deserve to drag your stupid arse away!' he continued, verbally flagellating himself.

It was late afternoon, that much was obvious. Apollo had finally lost the battle above and now Thor looked set to take his place in the heavens. The rain fell randomly; singular heavy droplets here and there, a sign that a deluge was about to ensue. Looking up, the once bleached sky had succumbed to a sheet of angry dark grey. It would not be long before the phrase 'drowned rat' became rather apt. He needed to find shelter and fast. He had not endured the last five years in the Wild by being careless and lacking forward planning, though given his recent unscheduled mid-afternoon siesta he reconsidered the fact. Nonetheless, fortunately he was also quite cunning. Because of these characteristics, and his self-imposed exile into the Wild, many had nicknamed him 'Fox'. Most of nature's gifts had died out after successive global conflicts which saw over seventy percent of the planet decimated across a century of hell, according to the historians. Many species were rendered extinct due to the destruction of their habitats; only the scavengers survived, though unfortunately this also included humans who had been the instigators of the apocalypse. Urban foxes were also counted on the short list of those surviving species. They were often seen slipping between the cracks of the metropolis, tracking down and surviving on the scraps left in the wake of an over-indulgent society; indeed it was relatively easy to do so, provided one was accepting of lowering their standard of living. Whilst freshly disposed perishable goods and castoff consumables made living possible, it was by no means an enviable way of life. Still, the foxes did not seem to care.

He sprang to his feet and immediately broke into a sprint. Without consciously giving it any real thought, he headed towards his nearest survival cache. He had eighteen such caches strategically located throughout the Wild; part of his monthly routine involved maintaining these caches to ensure their effectiveness in the event that he needed to call upon their aid. The caches themselves consisted of emergency medical supplies, field rations and essential items, such as clothing, all tucked securely within camouflaged waterproof bedrolls. All of the caches were well concealed; some were hidden within areas of dense natural growth, within the Wild's central wooded area, whilst others were buried beneath false walkways or turf-covered short wooden planks masking hollowed out sections of earth he had painstakingly excavated. The particular cache his body was now instinctively directing him towards was tied to the upper branch of a tree; he cursed the fact that the imminent heavy rainfall would make climbing the venerable giant all the more difficult.

As his speed increased so too did his recklessness; the number of scratches along his exposed arms and across his face multiplied as he brushed up against the surrounding thicket with careless abandon. His heart pounded like the rhythmic beat of a drum, hard enough that he felt sure that it sought to escape from his chest, as he bounded his way through the undergrowth. All around him the light was seeping away as the density of the canopy grew and the sky became ever darker.

'Fine...just don't piss on me!' he panted, as he briefly glanced up.

The darkness did not concern him for he had spent much of his life embracing it, though light on the other hand both exposed and drew attention to him. Living within a society which abhorred his kind, it was better, in his mind at least, to remain unseen. A good soaking, however, was not desirable.

The wood rapidly opened up into a small natural clearing; it was as if nature's other subjects had purposefully made way for the some twenty metre tall behemoth which now towered before him. He likened the surrounding organic growth to rank and file troops giving way to their lord commander, but in reality the enormity of the tree's root structure had probably kept the interlopers at a distance; that and the lack of light its enormous canopy permitted to contact with the ground. He slowed his pace considerably upon breaching the perimeter of the clearing, though continued to maintain enough momentum, as he lined up his approach. Approximately a metre and a half from the base of the giant, he leapt with all the force he could channel through his right leg whilst bringing his left knee up. Twisting his body mid-flight, he planted his left foot into the tree at a forty-five degree angle to the trunk where he found grip; the rain had yet to slicken the aging bark. Driving his foot down, releasing the tension in his knee, he straightened his left leg, launching himself up and to the right. Arms outstretched he grabbed hold of a lower branch immediately hauling himself up, aided in part by his upwards momentum, then hooked his right leg over it, securing his elevated position. Resting momentarily, he fought hard to slow down his breathing whilst he assessed the vertical path that lay ahead.

It took him a good few minutes to scale the next seven or eight metres of the tree, though he had no need to ascend any further as he spied his prize tied to an overhanging branch easily within arm's reach. Upon reaching up the heavens opened splattering sheets of heavy rain across the canopy; the deafening noise was akin to the sound of hail bouncing off a perspex roof. He had to work fast, for as thick as the tree's leaf cover was, it would not be long before the weight of the rain forced its way down upon him. With his left hand he swiftly untied the length of electrical wire which secured the cache to the branch, while supporting the weight with his right hand. Once the cable was free, he tucked it hurriedly into his left trouser pocket before lowering the cache cautiously with both hands down to his chest.

'Got you!' he said, relieved as if finishing the chapter of a book, though his words were barely audible above the cacophony of sound the rain beat out across the canopy.

Quickly he unfastened the outer straps of the bedroll and unravelled it so that it lay unevenly across several close knit branches, the density of which had increased markedly with his ascent. When he first scouted the tree some years back, he chose it as a viable cache site knowing it would double up as an elevated bolt-hole of sorts. It was by no means perfect when he first made the climb, though over time he had bent, lashed together and interlocked many of the tree's branches to create a more suitable platform upon which he could lay firmly supported, albeit not very comfortably. He often preached to himself and others that it was never unwise to plan ahead. Now, with his past exploits finally coming to fruition, his beliefs were firmly vindicated. With great care he unzipped the side of the bedroll whilst mindful of his footing on the network of branches which were already becoming slick with rain. Once opened, he eased his body inside the waterproof cocoon careful not to disturb its contents which had clustered within the foot of the bedroll. Reaching down with his left arm he fumbled the items until his fingers touched upon the smooth cylindrical length of a glow-tube. Grasping the end of the tube, he brought it up to his chest and began to rapidly shake the translucent acrylic cylinder until the contents reacted; a green light began to emanate softly from within, slowly building in intensity until he could make out the items resting against his feet. The rain was coming down hard now and so he used the bedroll's inner zip to seal himself almost entirely within; he purposefully left a gap the size of his foot to allow fresh air to penetrate his shelter.

It was only now that he realised just how wet through his clothes were as they clung to his skin. He wrestled with his sodden t-shirt, within the confined space of the cocoon, before eventually managing to pull it over his head and free from his body; there was a spare, still part folded, at the bottom of the bedroll which he promptly changed into.

'Yes, you'll do nicely!' he said, whilst gently nodding in agreement with himself.

Next he examined his worn trousers. They were castoffs also, which he had salvaged from a refuse site several months back. Fortunately his trousers had managed to escape the worst of the rain and as such he chose to leave them to dry of their own accord. It was then that he momentarily thought about eating, though his appetite had left him as of late – probably a result of the heat.

Discarding the thought as quickly as it had manifested, his attention turned to the dull ache in his arms. He was used to running and so his legs were holding up just fine, though it was not often that he hauled himself up gargantuan trees in a hurry thus his arms felt the wrath of his rapid ascent. The alien light of the glow-tube revealed no cuts on his arms which was a small blessing, just a lattice of minor scratches which reaffirmed his hasty journey through the Wild's inner sanctum. Regrettably, his eyes locked their gaze once more on the scar running along the fore of his right arm. His bio-key was gone, but the unattractive scar, marking its removal, looked uglier than usual under the green light of the glow-tube which exaggerated the shadow line of the scar tissue making it all the more prominent. Determined not to let his mind stray back to the events surrounding the Exodus, he closed his eyes and tried to bury his thoughts. All that remained was the sound of the rain as it continued its relentless assault on his shelter, though there was something calming about the rhythmical sound it produced. He adjusted his body to fit the unconventional mattress then lay still whilst listening to the rain which continued to hurl itself at the ground. After a short while his eyelids began to feel heavy. Slowly he began to drift away, content to shut off the world around him, secure in the knowledge that he was safe in his human nest.

TWO
Farewell

She did not perceive herself as an authority figure, though her powers of scrying had swiftly elevated her through the ranks of Freylars's warrior caste. The Blade Lord himself had called upon her talents time and again to help avert the dangers visited upon their domain, yet despite her growing powers she had not foreseen the ill fate which had befallen Lothnar's scouts that cycle. She told herself repeatedly that it was not possible to foresee every facet of the future laying in wait, though her heart still ached with a pang of guilt which she struggled to absolve. The future was an amorphous, sometimes fickle, creature; its path so easily altered by the actions of others. It was a fool's errand attempting to foretell the future in its entirety, though nearly all with the ability were ensnared by the allure to attempt such foolishness at some stage in their lives. The promise of being able to fully predict an individual's fate was rapture, however, this dangerous path also lead to undesirable outcomes for the scrier, such as obsession, megalomania and even despair. She was counted amongst the most talented of her kind; this was largely due to an indomitable self-discipline which allowed her to fully control her ability. Many succumbed to a path of self-damnation through loss of control, whilst others suppressed their ability for fear of losing that control. On extremely rare occasions those Freylarkai with the ability to scry, who had fallen irrevocably from the light entirely, were run through with a blade; these dangerous and unstable Freylarkai could never be allowed to live in such a state of turmoil. As she closed her distance on the Cave of

Wellbeing, her thoughts continued to dwell upon the casualties Lothnar's scouts had sustained. Most of The Blades he led on the reconnaissance mission had made it back alive; albeit tired, bloodied and mentally exhausted from their ordeal. Lothnar himself had chosen to keep his own counsel since then, remaining strangely absent. Sadly, however, one of The Blades did not return – at least not in her entirety.

Alarielle was a fine warrior, pure of heart and well on her way to achieving the rank of Blade Mistress. The untimely release of her soul was tragedy enough, but for one's soul to be torn from its moorings and denied passage to the Everlife, as was her fate, was truly abhorrent. The Narlakin responsible for the atrocity yet lived; worse still it trapped her soul within itself, preventing her ascension, thus dooming her essence to an eternity of torment. Whilst Lothnar was able to wrestle Alarielle's body free from the nightmare horror, he did not possess the means to free her soul from its grasp. When Alarielle left Freylar, mission bound for the Narlakai borderlands, she was a vibrant idealist who radiated an infectious optimism which permeated those around her. When she returned, it was only her physical body that did so; her soul, the essence that was Alarielle, was lost. Lothnar and his scouts were hit hard mentally by the ordeal. Losing any Blade in battle was a painful reminder of the risk fraught lives they led, but to lose such a bright star tested their resolve. When Nathaniel learnt the news of his daughter's fate, he was utterly devastated. She recalled the moment, with perfect clarity, when The Blade Lord himself delivered the hammer-blow in person; in that singular moment Nathaniel's legendary calm demeanour shattered explosively. Captain Ragnar, also in attendance out of respect for The Teacher, was forced to use his unrivalled might to wrestle the hysterical grief-stricken Freylarkin to the ground. She had wept the first time she witnessed Nathaniel's heart break when scrying the outcome of delivering the awful news, watching the scene play out for a second time, with Nathaniel pinned to the ground by the Captain, was far worse.

Dull light emanated from the cave's entrance and for a brief moment she stood at the threshold transfixed by its welcoming embrace. She had no need to cast her gaze into the cave's recent past to know that Nathaniel remained inside; he had not left his daughter since his request to transfer her body to the Cave of Wellbeing, as was his right being a master renewalist himself. Nathaniel had been holed up in the cave for many cycles now, according to his peers. Whilst permitted to join the cave's custodians, The Blade Lord was not prepared to allow Nathaniel to remain there indefinitely.

'Marcus, with respect, Nathaniel is still grieving for his daughter,' she had said earlier that cycle within the queen's council chamber, 'His recovery is not something that can be rushed.'

'I appreciate your view on this matter Kirika, however, I will not risk his prolonged mourning evolving into something far sinister!' he had countered. 'It warms me to see you finally stand your ground and hold firm to your beliefs within this council,' he continued, 'I encourage you to do so more frequently when commanding The Blades, however, you are still young in your role of council member. This matter is one of Freylarkai security over which I have authority.'

The Blade Lord's words would have stung if spoken from the lips of another, but not when he voiced them. Marcus was a natural leader; his demeanour was one of power and authority, yet she had never known him to be intimidating. His warm smile and calming voice quickly won over his audiences time and again; she was no exception.

'Nathaniel is the whetstone upon which The Blades hone their keen edge,' he proclaimed, 'I will not endanger their lives by affording him the chance to give into despair. You yourself have witnessed that possible outcome.'

Marcus paused momentarily, allowing his words to permeate her, before making his will known. 'I need The Teacher back Kirika...I need you to help him find his way back.' he said with commanding authority.

It was only then that she realised just how enraptured by his commanding presence she had become; she felt like a Blade Aspirant once again, holding onto Nathaniel's every word back in the arena.

'Very well,' she conceded, 'Though he is not exactly approachable in his current mental state. How do you propose I bring him back?'

'Just be with him Kirika. Your compassion for others serves you well, as it has always done in such delicate matters. Remind him that the rest of us still exist, and get him out of that bloody cave before he loses his own soul.'

A silent moment of understanding passed between them, then she replied, 'I will do what I can.' before gently nodding and turning towards the closed door of the chamber. Before she could complete her turn fully, Aleska, who had remained silent during the exchange, gently touched her left arm.

'Kirika...please bring him back to us,' she said emphatically, though her watery eyes betrayed her true concern for Nathaniel's fate.

Smiling weakly to Aleska in return, she slowly nodded once more before departing the council chamber for the Cave of Wellbeing.

The past became the present once more as she woke from her brief reverie. Drawing in a deep breath, she exhaled slowly before dipping her head slightly to avoid impacting her head on the cave's naturally low entrance. Sheepishly, she stepped forwards into the violet glow of the cave's sanctum whilst steeling herself, as best she could, for what was to come.

Her eyes quickly adjusted to the subdued light allowing her to fully appreciate the entirety of the vast space before her. The cave itself was clean and dry and the air was naturally cool and soothing. Crystals studded the walls of the cave radiating soft light which illuminated the space with a mixture of mauve, violet and sapphire hues. She immediately understood why the renewalists brought the wounded to such places. The cave's ambiance was one of tranquillity, indeed it helped greatly to calm her own jangled nerves. Making her way towards the centre of the space, she detected the sound of trickling water. A narrow stream cut diagonally across the exposed bedrock floor as it traversed its uneven path towards a natural fall somewhere in the distant gloom. Long stone waist height plinths spaced at even intervals lay perpendicular to the perimeter wall of the cave; all were vacant save for one which supported a single female Freylarkin. Slumped untidily adjacent to the plinth was Nathaniel, instantly recognisable by his long straight white hair which now hung loosely, partially obscuring his hunched shoulders, as he sat with both knees drawn underneath his chin. Clearly Nathaniel had seen her enter the cave, though he seemed to stare through her vacantly as she continued her meek advance towards him.

As she closed her distance to within five paces Nathaniel chose to break his silence; he spoke in a strained cracked voice, not even bothering to look up. 'So...HE sends Fate Weaver to do his work for him does he?'

'Marcus is concerned about you Nathaniel,' she said, 'As are we all,'

'Then where is he?' barked Nathaniel.

'You know very well that had Marcus visited you in person, Nathaniel, you would have set your wrath upon him!' she said, as if scolding an Aspirant.

'Then why are you here in his stead Kirika?' he said, losing some of the venom in his voice.

'Of all those you have diligently trained, I needed your combat training the most. I see you, still to this cycle, looking out for me, guiding me, even in my new role of council member. I do not believe you would turn me away as you have done others.'

Without giving him pause to respond, Kirika dropped to his side mimicking his own pose. 'Now then,' she said, softly sliding her arms around his waist whilst resting her head gently on his right shoulder, 'Let me help you.'

It was early; the new dawn had barely broken in for the current cycle. He sat with his back to the base of a tree. The cycle's first light began to meekly filter its way through the cloud covered sky. He had not slept much that night; the unexpected flash storm had woken him during the early hours. From there on in he was doomed to remain awake, unable to suppress the bleak thoughts fighting to be heard within his head. Leaf litter lay scattered everywhere which was unusual for the season; the storm had literally come from nowhere. All of the usual signs, which aided him in predicting the coming of such adverse weather conditions, had not made themselves known prior to its sudden arrival. It was as though someone had released the storm from a box, only to shut it away once more shortly thereafter. It was a curious phenomenon, one which he had never witnessed before. Still, the rapid deluge had been good for Freylar; everything smelt fresh again, as if renewed, and all around sparkled as the morning light danced off the lingering droplets which clung to the flora and fauna.

    Absentmindedly, he slid a throwing knife out from the sheath strapped to the underside of his left arm. Deftly, he placed the blunt edge towards the palm of his right hand with the point towards the base of this thumb which he slid on to the flat of the blade. Swiftly he arranged his fingertips in a vertical row along the opposite flat of the blade griping it firmly. Drawing his right arm back, just past his ear, he immediately snapped his right arm horizontally forwards releasing the knife at full extension. Light momentarily flashed off the blade as it flew straight some twelve paces through the air, whilst completing a full half turn, before striking the trunk of an opposing tree; the knife embedded itself horizontally, quivering momentarily, protruding from the rough bark adjacent to its sister blades each of which were evenly spaced apart in a straight line. As his right arm subconsciously moved towards his left to draw again, he suddenly froze as subtle changes in the surrounding environment alerted him to the presence of another.

'You know,' he said out loud, 'You really should give up trying to sneak up on me like that brother. Even with my back to you and my thoughts elsewhere, I can still detect your ungainly arrival at least thirty paces away.'

From well over forty paces to the rear of his position came a deep audible growl. Slowly, he heard Ragnar rise to his full height, no longer bothering attempt at concealing his large frame. The sound of long bounding strides followed shortly thereafter, headed directly towards him. Upon approaching his position Ragnar rapidly slowed his pace to a halt. After his brisk jog, Ragnar's long tousled red hair bordered on dishevelled. It reminded him of his own, though he favoured shoulder length; more practical to maintain when scouting the borderlands. His own hair was also naturally brown in colour, suitable for his line of work. Ragnar would never settle into the role of a scout. His movements lacked grace, patience was not amongst his virtues and he would have to do something about that mane of his. Though as a battlefield warrior Ragnar had few equals; perhaps only Thandor, The Teacher or The Blade Lord himself. Ragnar was also an accomplished light bringer, very useful, especially when battling the Narlakai. He was forced to crane his neck back to behold the entirety of his fellow Paladin. Ragnar cut an impressive physique, though that was hardly surprising given the Captain spent most of his time burying the smile of his enormous axe into the wooden practice targets which littered The Blades' combat arena.

Drawing the fingers and thumb of his right hand across his long beard, Ragnar boomed 'There will yet be a cycle when you will not see me coming Lothnar!'

'When that time finally comes, my soul will have already departed for the Everlife.' he responded with a wide smile.

For a moment Ragnar looked as though he was ready to explode with wild rage, then, slowly, a smile formed across the stern features of The Blades' Captain who broke into a deep guttural laugh the sound of which reminded him of thunder echoing through a deep valley. Partially bending his right knee, Ragnar offered an arm which he clasped tightly around the forearm before being hoisted abruptly off the ground to face the red haired giant; he was by no means short, but Ragnar towered at least a head taller than himself.

'You feel lighter than I remember Loth, the borderlands not feeding you right?' Ragnar said with a childish grin.

'Your witty camaraderie has been sorely missed brother. As much as I take pleasure in roaming free across the borderlands, it can be a rather lonely affair much of the time. Tell me, what is new in Freylar?' he said inquisitively.

'Well, your recent concerning report of Narlakai movements for a start!' replied Ragnar.

'Oh yes, that.' he responded, suddenly looking past Ragnar to the neat row of knives still protruding from the tree opposite.

Ragnar followed his gaze. A moment's silence ensued between the two as they paid their respects to those former Blades no longer counted amongst the living. Ragnar was the first to break their silence.

'You tried your best to save her brother. Taking your frustrations out on a tree will not alter her fate.'

'I have seen you fell entire trees after undesirable mission outcomes before,' he said.

'True enough, and I cursed the Everlife too on occasion, for taking its harvest early...none of which changed anything. Fate is what it is.' said Ragnar in moment of reflection which took them both by surprise.

'Kirika might disagree with you there my friend.' he replied.

'That she may, but Fate Weaver's kind needlessly pursues a fruitless endeavour. A Freylarkin's fate can never be fully manipulated despite their interventions.' said Ragnar in his characteristically defiant manner.

'Well, regardless, that thing still lives and it traps her soul within its miserable self. That is a fate I could have averted, I know it!' he said, as he slipped past Ragnar towards the opposing tree where he began to wrestle the knives free from their perforated target.

'If you could have killed the beast without endangering the souls of the others Loth, then you would have done so. You were ambushed and they knew well to target Alarielle who was your sole light bringer. Remaining steadfast against a foe with both superior numbers and a prominent tactical advantage would have seen the release of all your souls.' said Ragnar before continuing. 'You were foolish to waste time rescuing Alarielle's body.'

'Do you think I do not know that?!' he snapped, turning sharply to face Ragnar, unperturbed by the obvious size difference between them.

'Answer me this,' he said in a more controlled manner, allowing his momentary spark of anger to dissipate, 'When was the last time one of us was burned on the pyre?'

'Too long brother,' Ragnar replied immediately, holding his gaze firmly.

'Indeed. The Narlakai desiccate the bodies and devour the souls of their prey. They leave nothing for families to honour. Worse still, they rob their victims of passage to the Everlife. I could not allow that Narlakin to deny Nathaniel proper farewell to his daughter; it would have haunted me for the remainder of my time amongst the living Ragnar.' he proclaimed.

Ragnar took in a deep breath as if ready to quell his words, but instead released a heavy sigh before nodding slowly; a sign of affirmation. Having reached a mutual understanding, Ragnar raised a firm left hand which he placed upon his shoulder.

'Come then. Let us build that pyre for The Teacher so that both he and the rest of us can pay proper respect to Alarielle.' said Ragnar. 'Perhaps after we can recount happier times over a drink and a roaring fire?'

'Nothing would please me more - except the warmth of a female of course,' he said smiling weakly.

'Ha, I thought you would have sated your appetite for lust whilst sharing body heat with another during those nights under the open sky. Clearly you are more vigorous than I ever gave you credit for!' replied Ragnar as he rocked him gently with his left hand. 'Come now, we need to get moving. Marcus has asked that we convene with him mid-cycle to discuss your latest report in detail. That leaves you little time this morning to track a female Freylarkin who will reciprocate your desires.'

Ragnar slid an oversized left hand round his back and gave him a mighty pat, the force of which set him into a steady stride; they began their trek back to the arena where he would reacquaint himself with his brothers and sisters.

THREE
Light

He woke abruptly to the sound of an almighty crack of thunder. For a brief moment he lay in a state of confusion unsure as to why his back ached as much as it did, and then his brain expertly slotted everything back into place reminding him of his current predicament. He pushed his rough hands up to his eyes and began to rub crusted rheum from their corners, then slowly he dragged his hands down the length of his face and across the stubble slowly amassing along his jaw line. Morning ritual complete, he was now ready to reassess the outside world and the dangers it might present him. Turning his head slowly towards the gap in the bedroll, a flash of lightning lit up the sky. Almost immediately another deafening clash of thunder echoed out across the Wild, following in the wake of the sudden light.

'Close to the eye...or perhaps in it.' he whispered to himself.

Slowly he shifted his body weight and rolled on to his side allowing him to peer through the gap in his artificial cocoon; the rain had subsided, though only to be replaced by a warm light wind. Casting his gaze into the void, he spied a curious ethereal glow which seemed to emanate from beyond the perimeter of the clearing. Initially he assumed the source of the light to be artificial; no doubt originating from somewhere in the distant metropolis. He quickly discredited his own theory though, as he regained his bearings. The eerie glow seemed to originate from deeper within the Wild's central wooded area, therefore, how could it be artificial he questioned. He had combed every square metre of the Wild over the years; there was nothing out there of note, only the abundance of artificially engineered wildlife, and to the best of his knowledge he was the Wild's sole permanent human resident. Another brilliant flash of lightning illuminated the wood once more. For a brief moment it resembled an over-exposed image which played havoc with his imagination; he fancied glimpsing everything from malformed humans to mythical many-headed hydras lurking amongst the trees. An increasing number of other-worldly images continued to flood his imagination when suddenly it dawned on him; the last blast of light lacked its musical score entirely. An unexpected twinge of pain near the base of his spine quickly abated his enthusiastic imagination; his back ached badly now. The practicalities of sleeping in a large tree clearly needed reviewing he thought to himself; he desperately needed to stretch out his back. It was then that the notion of temporarily abandoning his elevated bolt-hole surfaced to the fore of his mind. It was certainly not his finest idea, though the prospect of shaking out his stiff back was an allure he could not resist.

Grabbing the glow-tube from within the bedroll, he reactivated its strange alien glow once more. He placed one end of the cylinder in his mouth freeing his hands for the task of descending from his temporary abode, which had sheltered him from the worst of the rain. It did not take him long to work his way down through the network of branches before he was able to drop to the mulch strewn ground with ease; the sleep, albeit uncomfortable, had done him good it seemed. Immediately he stretched out his back which was a welcome relief, then he grabbed the glow-tube from his mouth with his left hand holding it at arm's length to better illuminate his surroundings. Disappointingly, the glow-tube proved largely ineffective in the open as the surrounding darkness swallowed its meagre light with ease. It did not matter though. He had spent many years in the shadows, embracing the essence of his social class, using them as a means of avoiding detection. Trained to work with minimal light, his pupils dilated quickly allowing him to make out the rough contours of his surroundings.

Casting his gaze about once more he spied the same alien light which he had first glimpsed through the gap in the bedroll, though it was diffused by the intervening thicket. While silently debating his next move, the wind made its call known as it whistled through the trees rushing up against him; the wind seemed to be picking up strength. Then, without warning, a third flash of light ruined what little vision he enjoyed. The last of the light deregistered across his retinas a few seconds later, fading what should have been to black. Instead the distant light had intensified significantly, aiding him to see more clearly. Allowing his curiosity to prevail over better judgement, he squeezed the redundant glow-tube into his right rear trouser pocket and made his way to the edge of the clearing. For a fleeting moment he considered retreating back to the safety of his lumpy wooden mattress, but the unknown origin of the light continued to pique his curiosity. Breaching the perimeter of the clearing, he began picking his way through the thicket towards the light. The wind seemed to strengthen with each step, causing the trees to rustle in unison as they defiantly stood their ground. Over the wind's increasing howl, a fresh sound became audible; it began as little more than a faint bassy echo. Closing his distance to the light, the clarity of the sound sharpened identifying itself as the distant bark of a dog. Undeterred he pressed on, guided by the ever-present light and the now incessant barking which began to cut an audible path through the wind.

He grimaced as another brilliant flash lit up the area, this time virtually blinding him due to his proximity to the source. He was compelled to halt his progress until his vision righted itself once more. The barking had stopped at least, though instead there was now a whining, or perhaps whimpering, coming from the direction of the light. Standing his ground, whilst struggling to regain his sight, the wind buffeted him with enough power to force him to lean into it to maintain his balance; the elements seemed intent on preventing him gaining further ground. Regardless, he would not be denied the chance to sate his curiosity. Angling his body further into the wind the instant his sight came good, he channelled renewed strength through his calves driving his body forwards. The light was so bright now, as though a flood light had been turned on immediately in front of him. He had little choice other than to raise his hands to block out the worst of the light's blinding assault. Without warning, the light imploded causing a sonic boom to ring out across the wood; immediately he went deaf, except for a painful high-pitched tone in his ears which refused to abate. Similarly, the wind rapidly lost all momentum causing him to stumble to his knees. Instinctively he raised his hands to his ears as if somehow the action would alleviate the pain, which it did not. He began to feel incredibly hot as a wave of heat surged in his head, causing him to shake uncontrollably, whilst the pitched tone continued to drill through his brain. His mind fogged up and all sense of balance escaped him. He slumped on to his side, writhing on the damp floor, whilst the excruciating pain in his inner ears screamed with agony as the pitch reached its crescendo. Mercifully soon thereafter, the sound began to quickly recede; it was then that he realised he was involuntarily holding his breath. As though resurfacing from several minutes under water, he immediately gulped a mouthful of air before slowly exhaling trying to regain some measure of control over his breathing. His brow was soaked and his medium length brown hair was slicked to his forehead. Still trembling, he quickly righted himself on to a pair of shaky legs whilst trying hard to avoid any sudden head movements. His head throbbed, but at least the sound had receded almost entirely now. Regaining his balance, he tried to blink his vision back into focus desperate to understand visually what had just happened. Blurred at first, his sight slowly returned once more. The light had all but burnt itself out now, though there was still enough for him to make out the bizarre scene unfolding before him.

The distant barking had come from a dog; it was a dishevelled looking thing, probably a stray, a fellow survivor no doubt. It plodded unsteadily in loose circles, directly ahead of him, in what appeared to be a state of confusion; the animal was likely struggling to recover. He knew little of canines, but the dog appeared to be a breed of bull terrier. The animal was a solid lump of muscle with fierce looking eyes. It was covered in old lacerations which had healed badly leaving ugly scars across its body, not entirely dissimilar to the one on his right arm. This was not the sort of domesticated pet one kept in their home. It had either been poorly treated or actively gone looking for trouble; either way he did not suppose it had a friendly disposition, towards humans at least. To the left of the dog, approximately ten metres from where he stood, was something he could not even attempt to categorise. In appearance at least, it was a dull luminous sphere of pulsating light which floated roughly a metre off the ground. The sphere looked to be composed of multiple lattice layers each rotating in different directions which allowed an inner light to weakly pass through when in alignment; the effect gave the object a transient look. Random arcs of light leapt from the sphere contacting with the ground and surrounding wildlife. These arcs varied in length, anywhere up to three metres long, and appeared to slowly discolour those areas they contacted. It suggested to him that the sphere drew energy across these arcs; each new arc appeared to reinforce the sphere's inner light further illuminating the surrounding area. It seemed to be feeding, or perhaps healing, itself.

    Finally shaking off its confusion, the dog resumed its barking which it directed firmly towards the alien object. As the light intensified the dog barred its discoloured teeth and issued a series of lunges and withdrawals against its amorphous opponent which it clearly perceived as a threat. A succession of fresh arcs leapt from the sphere momentarily striking the dog causing it to whine in return. This hostile behaviour served to further antagonise the animal, which began to close its distance, as opposed to forming an effective defence. Judging by the scene playing out before him, he surmised that he had stumbled into the second round of an ongoing conflict between both parties. The sound wave released earlier by the floating orb, although certainly effective, had clearly left it weak and thus vulnerable to attack. It occurred likely to him that precious time remained before the agitated canine fully realised its tactical advantage and closed in for the kill; he needed to split the pair up before the conflict escalated further.

Attempting to communicate with the sphere was likely a fruitless endeavour. Instead, he focused his attention on the dog; its prevailing survival instincts were probably limited to hunger and fear, the latter he could make attempt at manipulating to his advantage. Dropping to a crouched stance, he ran his fingers across the ground until they contacted with something of substance.

'That'll do.' he said snatching at a decent sized lump of orphaned bark which he quickly hurled in the general direction of the animal.

The bark landed just short of the dog breaking up a little as it hit the ground with a dull thud. The dog glanced at him for a second, unrelenting in its barking, before turning its frenzied gaze back towards the sphere.

'All right then, let's do this the hard way you stubborn animal.' he said quietly to himself as he stooped to grab another projectile.

The second shot was a stone, half caked in mud, which he skittered between the dog's legs. This provoked a more promising reaction as the dog backed up a little reassessing its opponents. Still barking ferociously the dog rapidly yanked its head between the sphere and himself, undecided as to which target warranted the worst of its wrath.

'Back off!' he yelled, as he took a step forwards towards the animal looking to increase his threat level.

The dog backed up slightly, as if momentarily startled, before beginning a series of lunging feints. Though previously unsure how to tackle the alien sphere, the dog knew full well the process of running down a human; its stance was now a prelude to that outcome.

'Shit!' he whispered, realising the inevitable; that single moment of doubt, wasted on a profanity, was all it required for the dog to affirm its single-minded charge.

The canine rapidly bounded towards him. Knowing full well that he could not hope to outrun the animal, he raised his arms ready to lockup with his opponent in an attempt to take the edge off the impact. Instead, the dog changed direction subtly as it left the ground. It veered to his right, just below his guard, catching him flush along the bottom of his rib cage. The force of the impact knocked the wind out of him sending him spinning to the ground as the dog followed through, over-running him. Upon impacting the ground he felt the glow-tube in his back pocket crack open, spilling its contents, before his momentum rolled him unceremoniously on to his front. Face down in the dirt, he gasped for air like a fish out of water. Pain shot through the lower right of his rib cage, though he was unable to cry out in pain for want of breath. Nonetheless he had been in his share of fights over the years, prior to settling into the Wild, and knew well the importance of remaining upright in a fight. As such, he quickly forced himself back on to his feet whilst instinctively bending his right arm pulling it in close to apply pressure to his injury; the dog's attack had broken the skin just below his ribs. The wound felt wet and warm, a sure sign that he was bleeding. That was unimportant now as he watched the dog circle back ready for a second charge, all the while struggling to find his breath. He had to slow his opponent down. Right arm still pulled in, he started running straight towards the dog. At first it pulled back, unsure how to react, then, dropping its head slightly, it began a fresh charge directly towards him. Prior to contact, he swerved down the dog's right flank before rapidly decelerating into a tight turn to face his opponent. With his left hand he pulled free the electrical wire still jammed into his left rear trouser pocket. Deftly he grabbed the other end of the cable with his right hand and twisted it once around both, then pulled it taught between the two forming a simple garrotte. Weapon readied he ran straight towards the dog, which now lacked the distance to form an effective counter charge. Instinctively it reared up on its back legs, ready to lunge with teeth fully bared; the dog's bravado, however, had foolishly exposed the full length of its neck. Fuelled by adrenaline and an unshakable resolve, he crashed into the animal almost butting heads with it upon impact as he drove forwards with his attack. His superior mass allowed him to force the dog further back on its hind quarters, pushing its open maw to the side. Seizing the opportunity which presented itself, in one fluid motion he brought the wire up and under the animal's exposed neck before looping his left arm round its head closing off the weapon's deadly embrace with astonishing alacrity. Before the dog could turn its stinking maw back to his neck, he pulled hard on the wire causing the animal to yelp in pain; its legs immediately gave out sending it crashing to the ground in a crumpled heap. Still clutching the wire, he was unceremoniously dragged down on top of the animal. He fell awkwardly onto its left side, contacting with the right of his torso, grimacing as he released a sharp groan of pain. The dog took the worst of the impact, however, as his dead weight crushed against the animal pinning it to the floor. It released another loud yelp then thrashed its hind legs wildly as it sought to desperately escape. The dog's frantic movement, coupled with the agonising pain spearing through the lower right of his torso, saw his right hand falter, releasing its grip on the garrotte; sensing the tension in the weapon fade, the dog redoubled its efforts and managed to drag itself free from underneath him. Immediately it was upright and limping unsteadily on its legs. Circling tightly a few times attempting to nuzzle its left side, it then came to an abrupt halt a few metres opposite him with its head bowed low regarding him with an uneasy silence.

'Go...now!' he cried out to the injured animal, raising his left arm with authority directing its line of retreat. 'Go!' he screamed for a second time.

Defeated, the dog lowered its head further. It turned sharply away from him before retreating into the wood out of sight.

Using his left hand, he applied pressure to his injury which was bleeding notably now causing his t-shirt to stick to the wound. He would not be climbing back up to his elevated bolt-hole now, he thought to himself amusingly. Clearly not wanting to be excluded from his private joke, the heavens opened; droplets of rain broke across the back of his neck signalling the opening salvo of yet further torment. The timing was beautiful, so much so that he could do nothing to stop himself from painfully chuckling in despair. The adrenaline pumping through his body was fading fast now, revealing the painful extent of his injuries. The true pain was no longer being masked; now he felt the full agony of the damage inflicted upon him by the canine's initial charge. He surmised that one of the dog's teeth had torn open the wound during their first exchange of blows. Given the general state of the animal's mouth and the discolouration of its neglected teeth, the wound was almost certainly infected. He needed to reach another of his caches fast so that he could sterilise the wound, though the closest was buried on the other side of the wood. The likelihood of successfully dragging his broken form to the cache site seemed slim. He allowed himself to roll gently onto his back. Staring vacantly into the broken canopy above, he lay still gathering his composure whilst assessing his limited options as the rain started to beat down on him.

Except for its tendril like arcs, the sphere had remained stationary for the entire duration of the fight; only now did it start to move. Glancing down the length of his body, he witnessed its arcs suddenly dissipate like a broken circuit. The sphere promptly began moving silently towards him maintaining a constant height above the ground as it passed gracefully through the air. Fear told him to run, or at the very least to make attempt at doing so, though awe and his infernal curiosity compelled him to stay. Besides, the alien entity might react badly to sudden movement; that was the pitch his curious mind sold him at least. As the sphere floated serenely towards him, he realised that the rain literally had no impact upon it; the rain simply ceased to exist upon contact with its alien surface. In complete contrast, his clothes were now soaked through and clung to his skin uncomfortably. Water rolled down his face, dripping off his chin, to the extent that he needed to blink repeatedly to clear it from his eyes. At least the water might help to clean his wound he thought, trying to find a silver lining to his grim predicament. Soon the sphere was hovering directly above the end of his feet where it came to rest. The time for withdrawing was now past; he was committed to the encounter, whatever the outcome.

Despite being much brighter now, the Sphere had not yet reached blinding levels; he was able to stare into the void of its light, as though gazing into a fire lost amongst dancing flames. It was a comfortable feeling which helped to distract him from the ever present pain in his side. A singular arc of light then slowly began to emanate from the outer shell of the sphere. It extended cautiously towards his left hand which he continued to hold firmly against his wound to prevent further blood loss. Gently the arc contacted with the back of his hand prickling the surface of his skin before retracting ever so slightly. There it remained, poised, as if waiting for him to move his hand. Reluctantly he did so, choosing to indulge his interrogator's patience by sliding his left hand away revealing the full extent of his injury; watery blood continued to leak from his torn skin further staining his sodden t-shirt. The arc extended just enough to brush against his wound where it lingered for a moment. He felt its familiar prickle once more whilst it, presumably, made an assessment of his condition. Once satisfied, the arc receded slowly within itself. Resuming its movement once more, the sphere traversed the length of his body, whilst maintaining its constant altitude, then came to a sudden halt directly above his head. There it lingered, ominously, for what seemed like several minutes until he decided to break the silence.

Lifting his head, whilst trying to form a weak smile, he said, 'With respect, I don't exactly have the time...'

Before he could finish his words, a stream of arcs launched from the sphere contacting at varying points across his face and upper torso. He felt his head immediately drop back down, then without warning his back arched violently and his limbs went taut as though a current of electricity had been shot through his body. His world went silently dark.

'What the...' were the unimaginative words he attempted to form, though there were none; he had no mouth with which to voice them!

Indeed he had no physical body at all, he just...existed. Somehow, someway, he was conscious of the familiar world around him, though his perspective of that world had been drastically altered. He was no longer in physical contact with his environment; no longer did he reside in a form made of flesh and bone. Instead, he existed in a sort of non-corporeal transient state. Immediately his consciousness shifted to a state of panic and confusion. He could not run, scream or even cover his eyes for he had none; there was no way of escaping the horror of his current torment, or rather none that he knew existed. Unable to think clearly, his focus was broken entirely. Thoughts, far too many to process, raced through his conscious chaotically colliding into one another. His mind, if he still had one, was ready to explode.

'*Calm now.*' commanded a voice, though there was no sound.

The voice was instead more of an impression, or perhaps an understanding, which suddenly penetrated his non-being.

'What's happening?' he questioned, again without sound, anxiously awaiting the other presence to respond.

Whilst awaiting a response, his conscious regarded his physical body which lay beneath him; a ruined saturated form which continued to leaked watery blood due to the damage it had sustained. It seemed to him at least, that his conscious floated directly above the head of his motionless body. The body he once lived in.

'Am I dead?' he pleaded, 'Is this death?'

Again there was no response. He could sense his panic rising.

'What the hell happened to me?' he thought.

'*Calm now,*' commanded the familiar presence once more.

'How am I supposed to remain calm when I'm floating above my own lifeless corpse?' he snapped.

'*The Guardian is not floating,*' said the voice, '*I am,*'

'Where am I?' he replied.

'*You are within me. Your vessel was damaged, so I released your soul,*' it replied matter-of-factly.

Initially he was stunned, or perhaps instead paralysed with confusion, by the direct remark. As his conscious slowly began to accept the bizarre state of affairs, his feelings rapidly altered from those of bewilderment to raw anger which he directed towards his self-proclaimed benefactor.

'What right did you have to cast my mind adrift like this?' he said vehemently.

'*You aided me and those souls I nurture. Your vessel is broken, therefore I released your soul,*' it responded flatly. '*Your soul was destined for the Everlife. Do you wish a new vessel, or should I insert your soul back into its broken original?*'

There was no empathy from the presence, it simply stated what it perceived as fact and offered him a choice. With a measure of control returned to him, he began to clear his mind and think more clearly. Whatever the presence was, it did not strike him as capable of lying. Besides there was nothing further it could gain from him, regardless of his decision; he had already aided it.

'*Decide now,*' it commanded in the same monosyllabic tone.

'That's an enormous decision, I need time to think!'

'*Decide now,*' it repeated.

Possibilities started to race through his conscious. Whilst his physical body had seen better days, surely it could be saved he questioned. Still, there was always the possibility of a bleed out whilst stumbling around in the dark. Furthermore, there would be no one in the Wild to assist him at this hour; moreover, accepting assistance would likely expose his presence to the Peacekeepers. That dog was also still out there; would it vengefully track him down and score an easy kill? But then what did another vessel entail he wondered; he could end up trapped in the body of some other waif, or worse.

'*The Guardian must decide now,*' it repeated once more.

'OK! I've made my decision' he hastened, 'Though why do you refer to me as The Guardi...' he tried to respond, but before he could finish conveying his question to the presence the world went silently dark for a second time.

FOUR
Rebirth

On a subconscious level, she felt the crick in her neck increasingly agitating her long before she opened her eyes. Nathaniel was no longer by her side, though he had propped her up neatly against Alarielle's plinth. It was hard to approximate the time of day given the static hues within the cave. Secluded from the outside world and its countless affairs, she began to understand how time had little meaning in the renewalists' private sanctuary. Nothing seemed to change within the Cave of Wellbeing; it was the epitome of tranquillity. She appreciated more so now the ease of which one could lose their self to its calming influence. Rising to her feet, Kirika began to run through a series of stretches, most of which had been drilled into her by Nathaniel in person. Repeating the well-rehearsed series of movements, her gaze shifted towards Alarielle's body which lay serenely on its plinth. Even with the release of her soul, her physical body continued to draw the attention of those in attendance; a common trait amongst light bringers, all of whom radiated an inner glow which permeated their skin. It was therefore hard to lay eyes upon their broken forms when finally defeated in battle; to witness such vibrancy laid low in a bloody mess by Freylar's would-be destroyers was always hard to bear. Still, that was not Alarielle's fate. Though her body had suffered various wounds and abrasions during the attack on Lothnar's scouts, Nathaniel himself had personally restored her body to perfect health. Regrettably, he could do nothing to restore her soul; gifted as the Freylarkai were, not one amongst them possessed the ability to bring a soul back from the Everlife. Though some misguided Freylarkai fancied they could commune with the released, Kirika had never actually met a Freylarkin who could successfully contact the souls of the Everlife. For an accomplished scrier, focusing their second sight upon a body devoid of its soul was always an unsettling experience. Her kind was used to picking up flash imagery of past and future events from those they came into contact with. Lifeless corpses, however, were like bottomless holes in the fabric of reality. They were vacuous things, cold and unnerving to behold; little more than hollowed out remains of their former selves. Scrying Alarielle's body revealed the same nothing which always sent a chill up her spine, thus the Freylarkai burnt the bodies of those whose souls had passed to the Everlife.

'You narrowly missed a hell of a thunder storm Kirika,' echoed Nathaniel's distant voice from the mouth of the cave.

'Storm?' she said inquisitively, as she turned to face her former mentor. Nathaniel was now leaning against the rock face beside the cave's entrance. Arms folded across his chest, he looked almost preternatural as the light from outside the cave framed his white hair.

'I do not recall any signs of a storm prior to entering this place,' she replied as she took several steps towards him. 'Was I asleep for that long?'

'Ah, so Fate Weaver does not see all then?' he replied with a wry grin.

'Well at least you have regained some of your humour, even if it is at my expense.'

The sad loss of Nathaniel's daughter had eroded part of his welcoming spirit, though he looked more at ease now as if a great weight had been lifted from him. He still looked drawn and thin as a result of his prolonged mourning and self-inflicted malnutrition, but the Nathaniel she knew was slowly returning to the fore; yet he would never be the same. The Teacher she once knew was lost forever, however, something good still remained.

'I am glad we had the opportunity to ta...' he began to reply, before his gaunt face suddenly drained of what little colour it still retained. His expression was that of a Freylarkin run through with a well sharpened blade; his jaw had dropped and his eyes looked abnormally wide as they stared intently past her.

'Nathaniel, what is the matter?' she said concerned, though he did not make any attempt to respond.

Slowly she turned, following the path of Nathaniel's unbreakable stare. Prior to turning around fully, her peripheral vision detected that something was not as it should be. In no way was she prepared for what her physical sight regarded next. Alarielle's body no longer laid flat on its plinth, instead the entire length of her back was arched. Her rigid limbs were splayed out in an awkward pose, it seemed impossible that they could support her weight alone given their bizarre configuration and her elevated back. Fluid streamed from the corners of her mouth, as though her stomach was rejecting its contents, and her fingers appeared dislocated. Kirika screamed as she witnessed the horror unfold before her, though it was not the physical sight which caused her distress.

Pouring forth from Alarielle's once empty body came a wave of discordant images which assaulted her second sight. Each flash image was more harrowing than its predecessor, made more so by their unfamiliar composition; towering habitats composed of glass and metal, alien bodies stuffed into black sacks, grubby skylines, mobile armoured constructs churning up foreign soil, infants taken from their parents, people cutting themselves with small blades, black warriors with exotic ranged weapons. All these images and more laid siege to her mind threatening to overwhelm it. A lesser-talented scrier would have likely succumbed to a seizure; their mind crushed by the weight of what she was witnessing. Kirika, however, possessed a supreme mastery of her ability and did not falter. Forcing her emotions and sense of reason to one side, Kirika allowed the images to wash over her mind. The temptation to analyse each image was immense, though she knew well that to do so would cause her mind to buckle in the wake of total incomprehension. With tremendous effort she relaxed her conscious further still allowing the images to slide through it, as light would traverse a pane of glass. Trying hard not to fixate on any of the images, one in particular lingered causing her concentration to lapse. It was a ball of pulsating light, though its surface was made up of several insubstantial layers each in motion sliding beneath the other in opposing directions. The intensity of the ball's light increased when the holes in the layers momentarily overlaid; the effect of which was hypnotic. Fixated now on the ball and its ephemeral light, the strain on her mind's eye began to increase once more. Again she started to scream, unable to look away from the alien images which started to overwhelm her mind once again. The ball then altered its form, extruding multiple tendrils each composed of light. It seemed to do this in defiance against some form of animal which clearly threatened it. Next there was a brilliant explosion of light which momentarily blinded both her physical and second sight. The pressure on her mind was now immense; pain shot through the front of her head towards its core causing her to retch. She had to disengage before her mind fractured from the attack. Summoning all her will, she forced the building pressure back down and erected mental blocks to shield her preternatural sight from the worst of the light. Nonetheless the images still came at her, unwilling to relent, though her perception of them was now blurred as she managed to soften their impact. The clarity of the images continued to recede, however, one last montage burned into her mind. She was now grappling with the ball's attacker, strangling the life from it, and then the ball itself was upon her. Next she witnessed a male alien corpse up close bleeding out in the rain, then finally...nothing. As abruptly as they had started, the images suddenly ceased, releasing their hold over her mind. The sudden disengagement jarred her physical senses causing her to momentarily lose all sense of balance. Nathaniel was there to break her fall as she dropped to the floor in a disorderly fashion.

'Alarielle!' she heard Nathaniel cry weakly.

'No!' she said bitterly, struggling to form the syllable as aftershocks of pain continued to stab at her forehead. 'That is...not Alarielle.' she continued, 'There is most definitely a soul within Alarielle's body, but it does not belong to your daughter!'

His back still ached; he should never have slept in the tree. That particular cache site would need relocating he reaffirmed himself. As if in sympathy the back of his head also now ached, so too did his fingers. Slowly he opened his eyes to an unfamiliar ceiling; he seemed to be staring at the roof of a cave or perhaps some other rocky enclosure.

The air felt cool and the strange soft light at his periphery carried a similar sentiment; he felt calm, yet also confused. Recent events quickly returned to the fore of his mind; what the hell happened, he wondered. In the background he could hear a voice, though its sound was muffled. Then, without warning, his world abruptly came alive as nerve endings and senses throughout his body flared into life.

'...a soul within Alarielle's body, but it does not belong to your daughter!' came the voice once more, this time in perfect clarity.

'Who are you?' followed a second voice which had a venomous edge to it.

Physical life returned to him now. He could work his fingers again; instinctively he felt the smooth hard surface upon which they laid. His toes also responded and he could feel his chest heaving as his respiratory system processed air once more. He had returned to the physical world, though it felt different somehow. Something had changed.

Quickly he sat up placing his hands to his side for support; he was surprised at how easily his stomach muscles pushed his torso vertically upright. There was no pain in his side, indeed there was no wound where there ought to have been one. His gaze drifted towards his right hand which was firmly pressed down on the stone surface; its fingers were long and slender, not the dirty calloused things he remembered. They seemed to radiate a warm ochre glow, as did the rest of his exposed skin. These were not his fingers. Moreover, this was not his body.

'Answer me! Who are you?' thundered the second voice, this time loaded with aggression.

'I...I err...where am I?' he said fumbling his words due to both confusion and the unfamiliarity of his own voice which now had a feminine tone to it.

There were two humanoid figures opposite him, though both were clearly of a different species. Their forms were lithe and their facial features somewhat elfin in appearance. They had ears which were both tapered and had ridges along them. Their fingers were slender, like those he now possessed, and their eyes glistened like precious stones against the gloom of what was clearly a large cave. During his time in the metropolis, those of the Shadow class with whom he kept company often speculated about what manner of human creatures survived beyond the safety of the perimeter. There was plentiful talk on the subject from mutants and other freaks of nature, to beings that had potentially evolved; he wondered if the latter rang true for his newly acquainted interrogators.

'You are in the Cave of Wellbeing. My name is Kirika and this is Nathaniel,' said the female humanoid, rising unsteadily to her feet aided by her companion whose arms supported her delicate shoulders. 'That body you inhabit is not your own; you know this I presume?' she continued in a firm, yet calm, manner.

Kirika rocked unsteadily on her feet and raised her right hand to her temple, massaging it as her violet eyes twitched occasionally; she seemed to be suffering from random pangs of pain from some kind of mental trauma. Her loosely curled purple hair ran half way down the length of her back and encompassed an elaborate waterfall braid which she wore elegantly; the choice of style seemed understated, to him at least, but it gave her a formal look in conjunction with the fitted gown she wore. Nathaniel, her male companion, appeared to be much older and in contrast possessed straight long white hair which hung unbound just above his shoulders. Nathaniel's eyes were tiny silver orbs fixated intently upon him; coupled with his white hair and pallid skin, Nathaniel had an almost vampiric preternatural look about him.

'My own body was badly wounded whilst defending a...' he said, before pausing to find the right words. 'I was in a fight with a dog, which was attacking an entity made of light,'

'The ball of light you mean?' Kirika interjected.

'How could you possibly know that?' he replied, clearly taken aback by her knowledge of the event.

'Because I saw it,' she said flatly. 'Just now I used my ability to scry Alarielle's body expecting to find nothing, though instead I was assaulted by images of your past,'

'You're telling me you can recount someone's past!'

'In a fashion yes, you seem surprised.' replied Kirika.

'Well...yes I am. I don't recognise this place or your kind.'

'We are Freylarkai.' she said. 'You are in the domain of Freylar. Surely you recall how your soul came to inhabit Alarielle's body?' Kirika enquired.

'Not entirely,' he said. 'I saw off the entity's attacker and in return it gave me a choice.' he continued. 'The alien entity proclaimed that my soul was destined for the Everlife, therefore it took mine into itself. It referred to me as The Guardian and offered me a new vessel.'

'And so you stole my daughter's body!' barked Nathaniel.

'What?!' he said looking straight into Nathaniel's piercing silver eyes. 'This Alarielle you both mentioned, this body...belongs to your daughter?'

'As if you did not know,' snapped Nathaniel. 'Return my daughter's body to me now thief, or I will release your soul for a second time this cycle!' demanded the Freylarkin who moved swiftly past Kirika towards him.

He still retained his quick reflexes deftly swinging his legs towards Nathaniel, though his lower body strength was left wanting when sliding off the stone plinth which caused him to land unsteadily on his dainty feet. The dimensions of his new body were unfamiliar to him; he struggled to maintain balance whilst seeking to adjust to his lithe new form.

'Nathaniel wait!' cried Kirika. 'Do not allow emotion to dictate rash action, you taught me that lesson too, remember!?'

'This thing invaded the body of my daughter!' cried Nathaniel.

'Not intentionally,' pleaded Kirika, 'Please, let us hear its story in full before passing final judgement.'

'How can you ask this of me Kirika?' replied Nathaniel whose glare remained fixed on his unsteady stance.

'Because Alarielle is gone!' she cried. 'You have been holed up in this place almost ten cycles since your daughter was tragically lost to us in battle Nathaniel. She will not be coming home. Your soul knows this. Now your heart must accept the miserable truth of it.'

The direct nature of her words cut Nathaniel to the bone, though not in a malicious way. Moreover, it was the finality of her candour which shattered the last of his vain hopes. Immediately Nathaniel dropped to his knees, buried his face in his hands and began to weep uncontrollably for his loss. Kirika's words signalled an end to his mourning; now Nathaniel wept his last remaining tears for his daughter.

The anonymous entity of light had cast him into a new body, in a place unfamiliar to him, and his first action was to mock a grieving father; he needed to right this wrong. Summoning every ounce of strength he could channel through his newly acquired legs, he willed his alien body forwards unsteadily like a marionette worked by a novice handler. He stumbled a metre short of Nathaniel and collapsed to the ground; instinctively Nathaniel thrust his arms forwards to break his fall. His entire body was shaking, whether this was due to his lack of motor control or stress he could not tell. If there was ever a time to find the right words, now was surely that time.

'I have wronged you unforgivably,' he whispered, 'There are no words for my transgression. Take your daughter's body from me. I have no entitlement to it. I do not deserve it.' he continued, allowing his head to drop submissively.

Slender calloused hands cupped his lower face then raised it level with Nathaniel's watery silver eyes. Nathaniel held his head firm whilst he looked him straight in the eyes; he felt the Freylarkin's glare bore into his soul searching for anything short of truth. Nathaniel's grip was absolute; escape now was not an option. If Nathaniel so desired, he could sever the vertebrae in his neck with ease. Time passed, slowly, all the while his body continued to shake against his will. No further words were required; silence was now their preferred method of communication. The silence would reveal all to Nathaniel and within it his fate, be it absolution or quick passage to the ever-live. As he continued to lock gaze with the father of his own body, the grief etched across Nathaniel's face and the despair in his eyes began to take root in his own soul. His heart began to ache realising fully the renewed sorrow he had visited upon Nathaniel. Uncharacteristic of his hardened emotions, his eyes began to water causing him to blink heavily. Tears started to patter down his cheeks and Nathaniel's saddened visage blurred.

'Enough,' whispered Nathaniel. 'Though it is difficult for me to lay eyes upon you and accept your words as spoken, nonetheless you speak the truth of it.' continued Nathaniel in a cracked voice.

'My anger should not be directed towards you, I know this now. Your soul has answered me honestly, and in doing so has provided your affirmation.'

Nathaniel slowly eased the pressure of his hands then withdrew them entirely. Swiftly, Kirika approached his right side where she dropped to her knees gracefully and slid her arms around his waist.

'Thank you,' Kirika said softly, 'This is the moment you come back to us Nathaniel.'

Nathaniel smiled wearily then raised his left hand to Kirika's shoulder, grasping it with assurance.

'What is your name?' asked Nathaniel patiently.

'My name is Callum...or at least it was.' he replied, wiping the remaining tears from his eyes. 'Though I no longer know who, or what, I am.'

'Callum,' replied Nathaniel, 'That is an unusual name, certainly not one native to Freylar. It sounds male.'

'You would be right in your assumption,' he confirmed, before casting his gaze downwards allowing his sight to fully appreciate his new physique. 'These are new!' he said light-heartedly, returning Nathaniel an awkward smile.

'Oh my,' said Nathaniel, now fully realising Callum's predicament. 'Perhaps any questions you may have regarding such matters are best directed to Kirika eh?' he said, following with a thin smile of his own. 'We are a pair, are we not?'

Kirika rose to her feet and promptly extended a hand to both of them, 'Come, let us get out of this place and see what fate has in store for you both. This place has served its purpose.'

FIVE
Air

'I find it difficult to accept that humans cannot take to the sky,' said Nathaniel inquisitively.

'Believe me, I don't,' he cried, trying hard to keep his sight fixed on the murky horizon. Whilst Nathaniel had ensured him that the Freylarkai were only capable of short periods of low level flight, hurtling at speed little more than three metres above ground level was more than enough to unsettle his stomach. The only time he had ever left the ground was when free running across the metropolis at night, aside from climbing the occasional tree. This, however, was very different. It was not so much the height which caused his anxiety, but more the rapid pace of their journey.

'Could we not have simply walked!?' he blurted out as the trio banked hard into a series of tight bends which snaked through a tree line causing his stomach to sink even further.

'This is the fastest way to queen Mirielle's council chamber,' said Kirika quickly glancing in his direction, 'It is best we make haste for her counsel now, before dawn breaks.'

He knew this to be the best course of action; the last thing he wanted was to be spotted by every Freylarkin in the domain whilst being dragged across the sky. That said he had no wish to discover the contents of Alarielle's last meal either. Nonetheless the trio were making good time, though his arms were now starting to ache where both Kirika and Nathaniel pulled him firmly in tow. When Nathaniel first proposed the method of travel, he was unable to stop himself from staring mutely at his new companions in sheer puzzlement. The Freylarkai, visually at least, did not seem to possess the necessary physical attributes to obtain lift. This assumption, however, was quickly proven to be incorrect when Nathaniel unfurled a set of seemingly ethereal wings which grew outwards from the Freylarkin's upper back on demand. The wraith-like constructs were magnificent, as though moonlight had been captured between two panes of glass cut into long geometric shapes. He likened them to those of dragonflies, which he had read once existed before the various global conflicts had scoured his world clean of life, though they seemed proportionally shorter in length. Kirika's wings were shorter still, yet they had slightly more depth to them and were a translucent shade of violet. Both sets were paper thin and seemed impossibly delicate to him; he had no doubt that they would be easily ruined if not for their spectral nature. When in motion their wraith wings beat so rapidly that they became little more than blurs of coloured light which left short light trails in their wake. They seemed an impossibility of nature to his logical mind, yet here he was being hauled through the air at break neck speed by beings possessing such gifts.

'How do they work?' he had asked, desperate to understand the science behind the magic before abandoning the solid footing of the cave.

Kirika had laughed childishly replying, 'Your question is rather like me asking you how your arms work. They just do.'

'But science has explained the inner workings of the human body; ligaments, muscle tissue, electrical impulses, bones. All these things work in unison to make an arm function.' he had replied factually.

'I do not understand your words Callum,' Nathaniel had responded whilst exchanging a puzzled glance with Kirika. 'Perhaps you could explain what this science is which you speak of?'

'Well...perhaps that's a discussion for later.' he replied; it seemed likely that his new companions would further compound his confusion for some time yet.

Their rapid flight felt more like a dance to him as they wove their way towards their destination. Occasionally his feet would brush against the surrounding canopy as the tree line rose and fell. Whilst they skittered across the woodland below he tried to make out his surroundings in the dim light of the coming dawn. Ordinarily he would have been entirely comfortable in the gloomy pre-dawn light; however, the laws governing the physics of his newly acquired body were content to stunt his visibility in low light.

'How is it that you can both see where you're going?' he cried, 'I can barely see five metres in front of me.'

'You are a light bringer now. Those with your ability do not share the embrace of darkness, as Kirika and I do; instead they repel it.' answered Nathaniel factually.

'I see...or rather, I don't.' he said humorously, to Kirika's personal amusement.

'You ask a great many questions Callum,' replied Nathaniel, who seemed oblivious to the irony. 'Whilst I find your eagerness refreshing, all will become known to you in time.'

Against the backdrop of the dim sky, both Kirika and Nathaniel appeared as little more than blurs of trailing soft light as their wraith wings continued to beat at impossible speeds. His own skin too contrasted against the last of the retreating darkness; its ochre glow gently permeated the pale lose robe which clothed him. Everything seemed so surreal to him. Was he dreaming, or perhaps this was all some crazy wonderland his vivid imagination had conjured up to occupy his mind whilst his physical body bled out from the dog attack. Maybe he had actually died and this was some kind of elaborate afterlife. These questions and more caused his head to ache. Nathaniel had asked him to be patient, and yet he did not want to wait for the answers he sought.

Without warning they banked hard leaving the tree line which opened out into an enormous vale. Both sides of the vale were cordoned off by a series of low level mountain ranges; the lower level peaks flaunted verdant coverage due to the encroaching flora rising up from the vale below. As if announcing their arrival, the sun gingerly edged above the horizon to the far end of the depression causing the first true light of dawn to break across the magnificent landscape which burst into colour before them. Light danced across a wide meandering river which ran the length of the vale flanked either side by an abundance of verdant wildlife. The majestic nature of the vale was truly breathtaking; by contrast his old home, the Wild, seemed like a poor cousin in comparison. He felt his legs rise above his head, threatening to finish off his stomach, as they began their rapid descent into the heart of the vale before them. If indeed the alien sun rose from the east, then they had entered the vale from the north-west for which he was eternally grateful; whilst still coming to terms with the physics of flying at speed a few metres above ground level, the notion of diving head first down the side of a mountain did not appeal.

'It seems that the domain of Freylar welcomes you with her warm embrace.' said Kirika gesturing with her free arm towards the sun's light.

'This place is magnificent!' he said in complete rapture. 'Do you both live here, in the vale that is?'

'Indeed we do,' replied Nathaniel. 'See the forest dwellings either side of the river? That is where those who live within the vale make their homes, myself included.'

'Do you live amongst the forest dwellers too Kirika?' he asked.

Kirika seemed to blush at the question; her pale pink skin took on more colour than normal, now clearly visible to him in the morning light. Indeed he noticed that the light had enhanced his own skin tone as well; the light of day had wrought an energising affect upon his physical form causing it to come alive, as though fully waking from slumber.

'Kirika is newly appointed to the ruling council of Freylar, as such her title necessitates that she resides within the inner sanctuary. It is an honoured privilege, so I am told.' said Nathaniel casting his characteristic wry grin in Kirika's direction.

'Oh how you delight in playfully taunting me Nathaniel. You had the same opportunity as I did. You do still recall, in your venerable age, the time you chose to shun the council do you not, Teacher?' replied Kirika playfully, having recovered from her injection of colour.

'Ha, venerable now is it?' replied Nathaniel. 'You know well that I am not suited to a life of governing and politicking. My soul will be released of its duty with blade firmly in hand, not through boredom sat in some stale council chamber.' he continued, defiantly.

'At the very least you could feign interest by making your home within the grounds of the arena, as is your honoured privilege.' she replied, as though lecturing him.

'Despite being charged with instructing The Blades, my place will always be at the sharp end of both battle and life.' Nathaniel said thoughtfully. 'I could never be parted from the people.'

Their speed began to taper off. Looking at both Kirika and Nathaniel this appeared to be due to growing exhaustion on their part; Nathaniel had warned him that the Freylarkai could only sustain flight for short amounts of time, now that limitation was making itself known.

'Are you both ok?' he enquired politely.

'Sustained flight takes much out of a Freylarkin, though we are almost at our destination. Look there young Callum, see the arena in all her glory!' said Nathaniel inclining his head towards the south, whilst clearly displaying signs of over-exertion.

They had moved over to the river now and were moving fast upstream. Despite having lost some of their initial altitude in addition to speed, they were nonetheless still travelling at a significant pace; fast enough to manifest ripples across the surface of the river in their wake. Momentarily distracted by the light reflecting off the surface of the crystal clear water below, he then followed Nathaniel's gaze towards the southern ridgeline. Projecting forth from the base of one of the many verdant slopes along the mountainside was an impressive raised platform, semi-circular in shape. Its curved perimeter was outlined with an ostentatious low level wall spanning its length, whilst opposite tiers of stone seating cut directly into the slope overlooked the almost crescent shaped amphitheatre.

Walkways and outbuildings flanked the tiered seating and colourful banners with unfamiliar elongated diamond-like heraldry spiralled down from their fixings above which arched forth from the mountainside. Whilst the arena cut an impressive sight, its glory melted away in comparison to the magnificence of the towering construct that grew out of the rock face immediately above it. Ensnared by the awe of what his peripheral vision was registering, his gaze was quickly drawn further up the mountainside in sheer wonderment of what he was now witnessing. Over shadowing the arena was a structure, somewhat akin to a citadel, which grew out from the exposed rock and extended upwards towards the sky daring to defy the laws of gravity. The structure glistened in the dawn light, as though made from highly polished cut granite, and seemed impossibly tall given its slender build. It had three immensely tall towers each topped with a conical sapphire roof and dotted with windowed openings at random intervals; one of the towers even bent half way up its length at a forty-five degree angle before promptly straightening once more, as though proudly displaying an intended kink in its eloquent design. The base of the citadel was equally slender though it teemed with many more windowed openings, well beyond the combined quota displayed by the three towers.

'That's incredible!' he proclaimed. 'How is it that the Freylarkai are able to construct such impossible architecture?'

'The shapers,' replied Nathaniel breathing heavily now, 'Their craft is responsible for such achievements.'

'But how do they create such wonders Nathaniel?' he enquired, desperate to understand how such feats were even possible given there were no notable signs of industry within the vale.

'The shapers are able to enliven all that is,' replied Kirika.

'I don't understand,' he responded.

'You will when you see their ability with your own eyes Callum. Queen Mirielle is herself a shaper, the most powerful in Freylar no less. It was she who created the Tri-Spires.' explained Kirika.

'That's...,' he said before breaking off in thought. 'There's just so much I don't understand. I thought perhaps Freylar existed beyond the perimeter, yet the wonders I have already seen defy the physics of my world. This place...simply cannot exist within my world.' he mused.

'I am afraid that I do not fully understand your thoughts Callum,' replied Kirika with a strained voice. 'Nathaniel, I need to stop now.'

Kirika's face was now flush with exhaustion; their journey had clearly drained much of her energy. Nathaniel nodded in understanding, clearly appreciating the need to cut their flight short. The trio banked sharply to the south leaving the glittering river behind them, before promptly setting down just beyond its south-side bank in a less wooded area of the vale. Despite falling short of their destination, they had covered a significant amount of ground; he estimated that the walk to the base of the arena would take less than an hour, provided they did not drag their heels. He hoped dearly, however, that his entourage had no intention of making its way to the summit of one of the citadel's impossibly tall spires.

It was only now that he realised just how much strain had been exerted on his arms despite their short flight. He rubbed the length of his arms with the palms of his hands, trying to ease their built up tension. They were slender delicate looking things which, to him at least, seemed easily broken. Though his original body was notably lean, his new form appeared quite dainty in direct comparison. He was not the only one suffering from their rapid journey either. Kirika was still flushed in the face and breathing hard, whilst Nathaniel worked hard to slow his own breathing; tiny beads of perspiration had broken across their foreheads glistening like morning dew. The Freylar were truly blessed with wondrous abilities, however, those abilities had their limitations. Now that they were on firm ground once more, their wraith wings retracted through their clothing, back into their bodies as easily as they manifested. Perhaps in time he would fully understand and master the ability himself, he mused, still rubbing his strained arms.

'Alarielle's body...' Nathaniel began, before correcting his own words. 'Your body I mean to say, has weakened through immobility and thus that is why your arms ache more than they should.' he explained.

'Could be the early stages of muscle atrophy,' he suggested.

'Again I am afraid that I do not understand your meaning Callum, though perhaps I can cure your ailment for you.' replied Nathaniel who seemed to be breathing more normally now. Kirika, however, was still struggling to regain her composure.

He was now able to regard his companions fully in the morning light. Nathaniel, though clearly older than Kirika, had a somewhat regal look about him. Despite his thin build and drawn appearance, Nathaniel's posture was resolute. He wore a fitted sleeveless tunic made from dark leather-like material. A belt was pulled tight around his waist, into which was tucked a sheathed blade approximately two hands in length; more of a secondary weapon he thought given its compact design. Nathaniel's exposed arms were well defined, completely at odds with their slender form, and played host to a plethora of scars along their outer edge; these were the arms of a veteran who had likely seen countless battles and skirmishes in his time. Nathaniel caught him eyeing the scars and let slip another of his wry grins.

'My scars pique your interest?' said Nathaniel inquisitively.

'I apologise. I did not mean to stare.' he replied slightly embarrassed.

'No need to apologise,' replied Nathaniel, 'Ask your question, for I know now that you have one, your inquisitive nature demands it.' he continued with the same wry grin.

'Kirika referred to you as Teacher, then you yourself mentioned that you are charged with instructing The Blades who I assume are a military order. Presumably you possess great martial skill, indeed the build of your arms suggests to me that you are agile yet deceivingly strong, therefore I find the frequency of the scars on your arms curious. Furthermore, your scars were the result of minor wounds, nothing grievous.' he explained. 'I believe, therefore, that you allowed these to happen?'

Nathaniel remained perfectly steadfast; his only movement was that of forming a thin wide smile across his face. Kirika, however, seemed surprised by his level of perception and the well-constructed framework for the basis of his question.

'They are more than simple scars Callum.' said Kirika who had managed to slow her own breathing down now and was thus able to speak more easily. 'Each is a critical lesson learnt by a Blade Aspirant,' she continued, 'That one below his left wrist was my lesson. Nathaniel is a master renewalist and could heal his scars at any time, but instead he wears them to remind us of his tutelage. Their ever-presence continues to save many a Freylarkin's soul from early release. They are a stark reminder of the dangers The Blades regularly encounter.'

'I'm still somewhat confused,' he replied, 'May I ask how you learnt such an important lesson given the wound was inflicted upon Nathaniel and not yourself?'

'We were sparring in the arena. I naively thought that I had the better of Nathaniel, having landed that cut, so I pressed forwards my assault bypassing his guard...or so I believed.' she said. 'In point of fact Nathaniel had allowed me to step through his guard deliberately, further fuelling my adolescent bravado. With his free hand, which I failed to take note of, he knocked my blade cleanly from my right hand then grabbed my wrist and used his superior strength to pull me in close.'

Kirika then paused to fix Nathaniel firmly in sight. The unexpected interlude was uncomfortably silent with neither making the slightest movement. His curiosity burned within, desperate to hear the end of her account, though he dared not interfere with their silent commune.

'His blade then cut across my neck.' she said flatly, punctuating her words with a subtle widening of her violet eyes.

'You're kidding right!? You mean to tell me that Nathaniel slit your neck?' he quickly replied, clearly shocked at what he was hearing.

'Correct. I cut across the side of Kirika's neck and allowed her to experience fear, dread and terror, all in that singular moment, as her life blood gushed from the wound.' said Nathaniel turning from Kirika's icy stare to better study his interrogator. 'Induction into The Blades is not something that should be taken lightly. Few have the stomach or the nerve for it Callum. It would be negligent of me to allow those Freylarkai not up to the task to progress beyond the rank of Blade Aspirant. They would endanger not only their own lives, but also those of their brothers and sisters, whom they would ultimately fight alongside.' said Nathaniel. 'I healed Kirika's wound after the realisation in her eyes screamed to me that she had accepted her inevitable release. Only then is the lesson truly learnt. In truth, I did not expect her to return to the arena after that cycle. I was wrong.'

'I will never forget that lesson, of which Nathaniel's scars are a constant reminder,' said Kirika thoughtfully, 'Indeed the lesson was two-fold. Firstly...never allow your opponent to bait you! Secondly...life is fleeting.'

There followed a long period of silence between the three unlikely companions after Kirika's final words on the matter. She appeared to enter a state of self-reflection as though rehashing past events in her own head space. Nathaniel, however, continued to study him as though trying to solve a complex puzzle which had no obvious starting point. Ignoring the scrutiny of his newest benefactor, he began to survey the vale in more detail now. They had touched down in a wide clearing within the woodland clinging to the south side of the river. The air was crisp and invigorating; not polluted with the stench of industry as was the Wild. Above, the few clouds present were quickly dissipating and all around the unseen native animals began to make their voices heard. Yet despite the post dawn idyllic feel of his new environment, everything seemed to be slightly out of place as though a great disturbance had recently passed through the vale. Snapped branches had been cast awkwardly to the ground and an abundance of leaf litter was strewn haphazardly all around. The river was running fast, riding high along its banks, and the woodland canopy rustled gently in a fading breeze.

'A storm passed through here I assume.' he said breaking their prolonged silence.

'Indeed,' said Nathaniel still assessing him, 'It passed over the Cave of Wellbeing as if to announce your arrival, before making its way across the vale. It was a frenetic one at that. I was fortunate to have witnessed it.'

'The forest dwelling Freylarkai will be up soon, probably assessing the damage wrought by the storm,' said Kirika returning to her normal self. 'We should therefore press on now before we are noticed by them.'

A well-trodden path led out of the clearing in a south-easterly direction towards the distant arena. He hoped that his controversial question had not stunted conversation for the remainder of their journey; there was still ground to be covered. They would need to move quickly to avoid unwanted attention now that the cover of night had abandoned them.

'Let us continue then, this time on foot,' said Nathaniel, with another of his characteristic wry grins, 'And best you use that hood of yours.'

Marcus leaned casually against the arch of the window in his personal chamber, whilst half sat across its sill looking down on the vale. The view from the Tri-Spires never failed to impress him, regardless of the season. Watching the world pass slowly by, from his unique vantage point, gave him clarity of mind and the quiet solace he required to develop strategy pertaining to matters of Freylar security for which he was entirely responsible. He enjoyed a close relationship with queen Mirielle on account of his rank, one which he hoped would eventually blossom into something beyond discussing matters of domain security. Mirielle relied heavily upon him for the continued defence of Freylar; a responsibility of the utmost importance which tolerated no failures. Lothnar's latest written report, delivered by Sky-Skitter ahead of the Paladin's mournful return, was yet another concern which his ever broadening shoulders would bear. The report highlighted numerous Narlakin movements across their borderlands in addition to the ill-fated attack on Lothnar's scouts; such activity was both unusual and without apparent explanation. Typically the Narlakai were driven by instinct, known to attack opportunistic prey in small skirmishes; he had never known them to possess cunning enough to implement an ambush. This was a disturbing recent development in their behaviour; either the Narlakai intellect was evolving or something, perhaps even someone, was manipulating them. Given their new-found tactical awareness of the abilities possessed by members of Lothnar's scouts, Marcus was inclined to believe that the latter was true and that someone was directing them. If his assumption was correct, then a dark shadow would likely threaten Freylar in the fullness of time; that scenario could not be allowed to come to fruition. He made a mental note to have Kirika attempt to scry this possible outcome, though without access to a captive Narlakin, determining the likelihood of his theory would be near impossible.

Looking down on the vale his thoughts turned once more to that of Nathaniel's wellbeing; the loss of Nathaniel's daughter had been a devastating blow to the veteran. Nathaniel had witnessed many horrors during his service to The Blades, but none which cut so deep as the loss of one's own daughter. He remained unsure as to whether Nathaniel would endure such personal loss for a second time, though perhaps the surrogate parental relationship with Kirika would allow her to wrench Nathaniel's soul free from the abyss threatening to drown it in despair; losing The Teacher, if only in spirit, would be morally devastating to The Blades, especially now. That said, Kirika was a shrewd politician. He tried to assure himself that she would indeed find a way to bring Nathaniel back to The Blades. Very few could resist her feminine wiles; Ragnar being one of the few, though the Captain's apparent immunity stemmed solely from a profound dislike of scrying in general rather than any personal animosity towards Kirika.

Whilst lost in ever deepening thoughts, his stomach groaned due to lack of nourishment. He had developed a nasty habit of not eating properly when troubled; both Mirielle and Aleska had pointed this fact out to him on numerous occasions. Absentmindedly he raised his left hand opening its palm widely then, with a flicker of thought, a small cluster of berries leapt from a wooden bowl sparsely occupying a plain writer's bench sat adjacent to the wall on his left. The berries catapulted forth with enough force to leave their former resting place rocking a circular motion on the bench. Once in flight the berries arced through the air landing neatly in the clasp of his hand. Slowly he devoured each of the berries in turn, all the while casting his gaze across the landscape below. Most of the forest dwellers were not yet up it seemed, though it was difficult to tell for certain given the density of the canopy below. A few Freylarkin gathered along the southern edge of the river bank, of which most were washing garments and subsequently laying them across the bank to dry under the morning sun. Others appeared to be engaged in conversation, whilst another seemed to be frantically running here and there. Drawing his sight back towards the base of the Tri-Spires he saw three Freylarkai walking briskly towards the base of the arena. At such distance his sight offered little definition, though despite the lack of visual clarity he immediately recognised the lead traveller; the straight white hair and resolute posture was a sure portent that The Teacher had returned. Logic dictated therefore that the purple haired Freylarkin adjacent was Kirika, but who then was their companion taking up the rear he wondered. Raising his open hand again, another cluster of berries raced towards the palm of his left hand propelled by unseen forces. Once more he caught the airborne fruit without sparing them a moment's notice.

'Who is that?' he questioned whilst leaning forwards to better his view.

Their companion was clearly a light bringer, that much was obvious by the unmistakable tone of their exposed skin, yet he could not determine their gender. The Freylarkin was also stooping which made it hard to draw any conclusions from their height. He or she had raised the hood of their robe making it harder still to identify the mysterious third wheel; it was still early, why would someone choose to conceal their face at this hour he wondered. His stare intensified as the trio drew slowly closer. He could not put his finger on it, yet something was not right with the scene playing out before him. The stranger's build came slowly into focus suggesting they were female, however, their movement was awkward; an old injury perhaps, but then surely a renewalist would have seen to such. There was nothing feminine about their enigmatic companion's advance; indeed the stranger carried themself more akin to a male. The mystery of the stranger's unknown identity was now dominating his thoughts; those of Narlakai troop movements were no longer an immediate concern. Something about the stranger was hauntingly familiar, yet their demeanour was completely alien. He felt sure he had seen the Freylarkin before.

'I know you,' he said aloud once more, as if conversing with himself.

Another cluster of berries flew into his hand replacing their predecessors; the need to solve the stranger's identity was fuelling his new found appetite. Without warning the stranger stumbled forwards like a marionette cut from its strings. Kirika doubled back lending her arm which the stranger readily took righting them self. As the stranger rose to their full height, the hood of their robe receded slightly revealing a partial glimpse of their face proper which was framed with dark red hair.

'That...cannot be,' he said bemused by what he saw, 'Alarielle?'

SIX
Revelations

The walk to the Tri-Spires had taken far longer than he had anticipated, though without access to a traditional means of determining the time he could not be sure exactly how long the journey had taken them. The Freylarkai seemed to use the sun's position in the sky along with their body clocks to approximate the passage of time, the accuracy of which seemed unimportant to them. Despite their simplistic approach to measuring the passage of time, the inhabitants of Freylar did acknowledge the concept of a complete day which they referred to as a cycle. What was certain is that he was the cause of their slow passage. Although able to control his new body reasonably well, all things considered, its unfamiliar dimensions thwarted any attempt at finesse; he was clumsy. He had stumbled numerous times during their slow ascent from the river and cursed his inability to carry out the simple task of walking without issue. Nathaniel had encouraged him to be more patient with his new body, yet he was frustrated by his failure to quickly re-acquire basic motor control of his legs.

Upon finally reaching the arena, despite still being relatively quiet, there were those who lived in the neighbouring Tri-Spires who had woken early and were busying themselves with their duties. The increased Freylarkai activity demanded they quicken their pace; fortunately he had since developed better control of his legs and was able to coordinate their movements more assuredly. He made sure that the hood of his robe was pulled close and kept his head lowered to avoid prying eyes, all the while Kirika and Nathaniel assumed forward flanking positions to better obscure his profile. They snaked their way through the alleys and outbuildings surrounding the perimeter of the arena; he had no recollection of the path they took, though more importantly speed was their ally now. In the background inquisitive voices could be heard over the distant clash of occasional sparring blades. Those Freylarkin who witnessed their quick passage were clearly surprised to see Nathaniel's sudden return, but even more by his mysterious companion being ushered towards the Tri-Spires. No one made any attempt to confront Nathaniel; his rank amongst The Blades, coupled with his recent loss, kept the sparse onlookers at bay.

When they arrived at the base of the Tri-Spires towards the rear of the arena, he afforded himself the brief luxury of looking upwards. The spires were impossibly tall feats of architecture and were made from cut granite. Their construction seemed somewhat organic, as if grown rather than a product of industry. The Tri-Spires were imperfect constructs completely irregular and non-uniform, yet beautiful despite their obvious flaws; he had never before witnessed such alien architecture, the sight of which was truly magnificent. The base of the Tri-Spires was equally organic in design and resembled a warren which had grown from the surrounding rock face with all its exposed windows, few of which were still shuttered suggesting that the majority of its inhabitants had woken. His stomach felt uneasy again, though this time nerves were clearly to blame. It was completely uncharacteristic of him to be nervous; however, he was completely overwhelmed by recent events and far removed from his comfort zone. Now the thought of meeting Freylar's queen made him feel anxious.

'Please don't tell me we've got to walk to the top of one of those spires,' he said, unsure that his legs were up to the task in light of their poor ascent from the river.

'Walk no, but we will be ascending the central spire.' said Nathaniel with another of his grins.

'Do I even want to know how?' he replied with a furrowed brow of bewilderment.

Nathaniel chuckled aloud, then said, 'Do not look so worried Callum, rest assured that Kirika and I will escort you to queen Mirielle in one piece.'

'One piece you say. Is that after you're required to use your skills as a renewalist to reassemble me I wonder?' he said smiling for the first time since commencing his walk in the bizarre wonderland of Freylar.

Kirika momentarily broke her composure laughing childishly once more as Nathaniel continued to chuckle. After their shared moment of amusement had passed, the trio promptly resumed their journey by entering the base of the citadel. Once inside they wove a complex path through its polished granite tunnels passing a host of private quarters and communal areas as they swiftly made their way. Eventually they passed through a small antechamber guarded by a single Freylarkin sentry who allowed them to pass unquestioned. He was starting to fully appreciate the level of authority his companions held over the domain of Freylar and its inhabitants; whisperings aside, thus far no one had made any attempt to question their intentions. How easy would it be to breach the spires if one were able to adopt the appearance of a high ranking native he wondered, for surely such things were possible in his new fantastical world?

The chamber beyond was larger than any he had thus far glimpsed within the citadel. It was completely absent of any furnishings and had a high vaulted ceiling, again grown from the surrounding granite. Spaced around the room in a large half-moon arrangement were numerous waist height pedestals each cut cleanly across the top exposing large individual colourless crystals half buried within. Another voiceless sentry stood watch in the centre of the room regarding them with interest as they entered unchallenged. Like the antechamber before there were no windows; the only source of dull light came from a single large sapphire crystal which hung on a silver chain from the highest point of the ceiling, directly above the sentry. The highly polished granite walls caused what little light the sapphire weakly emanated to shimmer as they crossed the chamber towards the central pedestal.

'That crystal up there,' he said tilting his head back slightly, 'I saw similar crystals along the tunnel walls and in the Cave of Wellbeing.'

'We call them Moonstones,' said Kirika, 'They are used heavily throughout Freylar as a source of light.'

'Come, we can discuss Freylarian architecture and aesthetics later,' Nathaniel interjected politely, 'Word of our arrival will have likely reached the inner sanctuary by now. Queen Mirielle will be expecting us.'

Nathaniel promptly strode towards the central pedestal nodding courteously to the sentry in passing. He stopped just short of the pedestal and offered his right hand to Kirika who readily accepted it.

'Callum, take my hand,' said Kirika, 'And please do not ask me why, just trust me.'

'I do trust you Kirika, until you give me reason not to do so,' he replied, taking her hand as requested.

After linking hands with one another, Nathaniel pressed his free hand to the side of the pedestal's exposed crystal. Suddenly he felt light on his feet, as though gravity was somehow slipping away, then a stark shiver ran the length of his back. Like coloured inks running down a canvas, his surroundings started to fall away. The effect was slow at first, so that when he glanced towards Kirika her body appeared to be elongating, then it rapidly accelerated until his surroundings resembled little more than a stretched blur of fast moving light. His body lurched at the sense of displacement and he felt stomach acid rising up his oesophagus, though before anything further came of it the displacement came to an abrupt halt as everything snapped back into focus. They were no longer in the same chamber, yet Nathaniel still cupped his free hand around what appeared to be the same crystal, half protruding from an identical stone pedestal to that which he had seen in the previous chamber.

'What...was that?' he said trying to regain his composure.

'That was a Waystone activation.' said Kirika. 'We use Waystones to immediately transport ourselves between locations.'

Nathaniel withdrew his hand from the crystal's colourless surface, then turned towards him in search of further amusement. 'Do not let the queen see you looking like that young Callum, you will need your stomach for when she questions your arrival here in Freylar.'

'My floundering in this domain of yours clearly amuses you Nathaniel.' he responded flatly.

'Please, do not take my words to heart Callum. In truth, I find your reactions refreshing. Your arrival here has given me welcome distraction from darker thoughts, which could so easily manifest when laying eyes on you.' said Nathaniel. 'I see great potential in you Callum. Remember that.'

'You will find your feet before long, of that I am certain.' said Kirika looking to further soothe his wounded pride. 'The queen likely awaits, let us not keep her waiting further.' she continued, beckoning to a pair of arched solid wood doors just beyond the pedestal.

The doors opened smoothly of their own accord as they made their approach and beyond was a large chamber full of wondrous exotic constructs. The chamber itself was almost entirely circular, less the space occupied by the adjoining Waystone antechamber, suggesting they were some way up the central spire. To their right was a magnificent gnarled tree made from the same polished stone as the spires themselves; its upper branches twisted and turned inwards forming a complex network resembling a giant nest. The tree's branches were entirely leafless; instead hundreds of small crystals hung from its naked branches suspended by thin silver chains. The tree had an angelic look about it; light from a large arched window opposite refracted through the sea of crystals, casting an amorphous design across the curvature of the wall behind the tree further enhancing its splendour. Staring in awe at the tree's magnificence, his thoughts returned to the alien sphere responsible for his rebirth in Alarielle's body.

'My tree fascinates you I see. Perhaps it reveals hidden meaning to you.'

Immediately he turned his head forwards, keenly aware that he had allowed his attention to become distracted by one of the many surrounding works of art. Embarrassed by his lack of focus, he felt a sudden wave of heat rush towards his cheeks and pricks of sweat formed across the back of his neck. Before him stood two Freylarkai; a male and a female, both of whom exuded unquestionable leadership and authority. The male stood a few paces before his female counterpart and was the perfect Freylarkin specimen; his hair was close shaved, further emphasising his well-defined facial features, and his exposed limbs displayed well defined musculature. These characteristics, along with the Freylarkin's impressive height, accentuated his commanding presence; this was a Freylarkin who had clearly served extensive time amongst The Blades and was a born leader destined to command. His right hand rested lightly upon the pommel of a large bastard sword, which hung from his waist, and he wore a fitted silver muscle cuirass embossed with an immensely intricate design similar to that of the tree which had distracted him moments earlier. His semi-naked arms were clad in leather vambraces, outwardly lined with linked silver plating, and he wore a short dark split skirt made from armoured scales with silver rivets; perhaps a trophy from a past conquest worked into a functional garment by Freylar's artisans. The Freylarkin had first nodded respectfully to Nathaniel as they entered the chamber, then proceeded to observe him silently with piercing slate-grey eyes seemingly at odds with his charming smile and relaxed stance.

'This is Marcus, Blade Lord and commander of The Blades. He is tasked with the security of Freylar.' said the female Freylarkin as she took several steps closer coming to rest at Marcus' side. 'I am queen Mirielle, but you are not Alarielle.'

Mirielle's voice was a commanding one, though far from hostile. Indeed it was warm and inviting as was her general demeanour. She stood, perfectly calm, dressed in a plain white fitted sleeveless gown accompanied by a thin silver cord circling her waist. Mirielle needed little in the way of ostentatious finery to affirm her regal status; she wore a delicate silver wreath-like crown which was enough to set her aloft from Freylar's general populous given her captivating presence. Much like his own ochre skin, Mirielle's too radiated an inner light though hers was a soft white glow which seeped through her marble like skin. Her eyes were pupil-less - looking at them was like staring into a white abyss - and she wore her straight white hair in a complex double rope braided bun which revealed the length of her neck. Mirielle's grace and beauty was astonishing. She possessed an ethereal quality, as if composed entirely of soft light.

'Apologies for my earlier distraction,' he said hoping to quickly regain any lost favour. 'I have never seen such extravagant and intriguing works of art before. Nor have I ever stepped inside one.' he continued, gesturing towards the polished stone wall of the spire.

'There is no need for an apology. I find your candour refreshing. Most would rather bend their knee and stare vacantly at the floor than review my works.' she replied smiling warmly, before taking several more steps closer to broach the heart of the matter. 'So, Alarielle who is not Alarielle...what are we to make of you?'

'I was hoping that you would be able to offer me some insight on the matter.' he replied.

'Perhaps I can, however, first you have a tale to tell.'

They had been standing for some time now, listening attentively to Callum's detailed account of his arrival in Freylar. She had expected Callum to display signs of nervousness whilst in attendance to queen Mirielle and The Blade Lord, as she would have done in his position. Instead their new companion was resolute in his story telling, and remained steadfast when assaulted by the seemingly endless questions which ensued. She continued to stand patiently as she observed the proceedings. She watched silently as Mirielle took stock of all that had been said, whilst pacing gracefully around the chamber allowing her fingertips to whimsically brush across her extravagant works as she passed. Time passed during which nothing further was said whilst Mirielle continued her silent contemplation. Eventually she altered her course towards Callum, coming to a stop several paces in front of him.

'There is something I wish to show you, though your eyes will not see the truth of it in their current state.' said Mirielle rather cryptically. 'I ask now that you trust me implicitly.'

She watched curiously as Mirielle approached Callum and pressed the tips of her fingers to his temples. Callum made no attempt to evade her touch; instead he took a single step forwards, entirely accepting of the unknown fate which would follow. Pulses of light ran down both of Mirielle's slender marble like arms, further enhancing their natural soft glow, as they raced towards her fingertips. Upon contact with Callum's temples, he let out a sudden cry of pain then dropped to his knees pressing his hands firmly to his eyes.

'The pain will not last, neither will the gift I have temporarily given you.' said Mirielle.

'What have you done to me?' replied Callum through gritted teeth.

'I have enhanced your physical sight, albeit for a short time, so that I can show you the answers you seek. Come, rise and take my hand.' continued Mirielle who offered her hand freely.

Mirielle's actions were entirely unexpected. Rarely had she seen the queen act in such a forthright manner; both she and Nathaniel adjusted their body weight subtly in light of the ordeal, uncomfortable at what they had just witnessed. Marcus, however, maintained his relaxed stance and continued to fix his gaze on Callum, analysing his every move. Callum lowered his hands revealing the same pupil-less look in his eyes as were characteristic of Mirielle's own. Callum rose unsteadily on his feet whilst taking Mirielle's hand.

'My vision is...I can see beyond the physical, like tunnelling deeper into the essence of reality,' said Callum excitedly spinning his head, reviewing the world around him from an entirely new perspective. 'This is incredible. How long will this ability last?'

'Not long. Shapers, including myself, can manipulate soul-less objects to the extent of our own individual prowess, though imposing our will on that which has a soul is a different matter entirely. Permanent manipulation of a soulful object requires a shaper to give up part of their own being...indefinitely.'

'May I ask what it is you sacrificed for this gift?' replied Callum.

Her expression became anxious, and she knew it. Whilst he was obviously fascinated with the subject matter, these were personal matters which one did not typically enquire about when in attendance to their queen. She glanced towards Nathaniel who looked similarly concerned; clearly he too was troubled by Callum's boundless curiosity and the undesired response such personal line of questioning might incur from their ruler.

'You may, though not this cycle.' replied Mirielle with an increasingly warm smile.

Mirielle's unexpected response drew a raised eyebrow from Marcus, who until now had remained perfectly still. She watched curiously as Mirielle lead Callum towards the chamber's single arched window, before inviting him to sit on its wide sill. Mirielle chose to stand, and fixed her vacant gaze upon Callum, studying his every action.

'Look to the sky and tell me, what is it you see?' enquired Mirielle.

Callum promptly turned his head towards the sky. At first he appeared completely nonchalant, as though his new eyes had failed him revealing nothing of note. Slowly his expression adopted a look of confusion. She looked on as Mirielle continued to study Callum closely, whose mind seemed to be churning silently in thought.

'What is it you see?' asked Mirielle inquisitively once more.

'This cannot be,' he said unconvincingly, to no one in particular.

'Yet you doubt even your own words. It called you The Guardian. It said that you aided it...it and the souls it nurtures. Look again Callum, tell me what you see.'

'You imply the impossible!' he replied vehemently.

'Why is that Callum? Is it any less improbable than your arrival here in Freylar, foretelling one's future or shaping objects with thought alone? Perhaps the science which you spoke of during your account is simply unable to provide the clarity you so desperately require? I ask you again Callum, what do you see?'

'I see the entity Mirielle, the same sphere of light which transported me to Freylar! Its moving lattice layers crisscross the sky, or rather that which lies beyond revealed by this sight you have given me. How is this even possible?' he questioned, pressing his hands to the side of his face.

She gasped at his words, unable to hide her shock. The Freylarkai gave no thought to what lay beyond the sky. It was vast, limitless even; no one questioned its boundaries, or even cared, yet now all that had changed. Had she witnessed first-hand a world beyond her own through her second sight? The Freylarkai's blissful ignorance was being stripped from them with mere words. She felt so small, insignificant even. The chamber began to spin and she felt light headed as profound developing thoughts on the revelation breaking before them swarmed her mind. Even Marcus shifted uncomfortably.

'Tell me, what lies beyond the sky of your home world Callum?' asked Mirielle, pressing her line of enquiry.

'The Universe,' replied Callum factually.

'And this Universe, what lies beyond it?' Mirielle continued.

'I...I don't know. I've never really thought about it.' answered Callum.

'Your people surely believe in deities, do they not?' enquired Mirielle.

'...not exclusively, but yes, some of them do.' replied Callum.

'As is true of the Freylarkai.' replied Mirielle, prior to pacing the chamber slowly once more. 'Callum these eyes of mine allow me to see so much more, as well you now know. When I look at you, I see more than just a Freylarkin. You are very different, so much more than the rest of us. Your soul is...unique.'

Mirielle paused for some time, allowing her words to permeate those in attendance, before continuing to develop her audible thoughts.

'I believe that you once walked with our own deities.' proclaimed Mirielle.

She gasped again as their queen's words caused a mixture of shock and awe to ripple across the chamber's intimate audience. If Mirielle's conjecture was indeed true, then they all owed their continued existence to Freylar's newest arrival. She continued to feel giddy; she needed fresh air and time to consider their queen's massive assumptions. As a member of the ruling council of Freylar she had been privy to a great number of secret truths, none of which came close to carrying the same crushing weight as this recent revelation.

'I apologise,' said Mirielle rather abruptly, 'Please, all of you, forgive me. I have often wondered what lies above us. My enhanced sight only leads to more questions, not the answers I hoped would be revealed.' she continued. 'This personal curiosity of mine has waited long enough; it can wait a little longer. More pressing is what to actually do with you Callum, now that you are here. You need a place to stay.'

'She...sorry, HE, can stay with me.' said Nathaniel rather hastily.

'Nathaniel, it warms me to see you with us once more,' replied Mirielle. 'Whilst I respect you enormously, do you believe that my granting of your request would in fact be wise?'

'I understand your reservations, queen Mirielle.' replied Nathaniel. 'Alarielle is gone, she will not be returning to me. I know this now, and indeed I accept it. Callum's body is the same one I raised from birth. The same one I renewed after the ambush. It was my daughter's body. I cannot simply turn my back on it, despite the uniqueness of the situation and the future emotional pain it may cause.'

'Very well, if you are certain Nathaniel, then I charge you with familiarising Callum with our way of life. See that he adjusts to the change, for there will be no going back for him.' replied Mirielle. 'Kirika, please help Callum adjust to the other challenges that await him.'

Mirielle's unusual request aided her to shift her focus back to local concerns, for which she was secretly thankful. Callum would require schooling in the feminine arts; a matter entirely beyond Nathaniel's grasp. She fancied her role as that of an older sister and smiled given the challenge ahead.

'As you wish Mirielle, however, if you are to move forwards Callum, then we cannot call you by that name.' she said.

'Agreed.' said Mirielle. 'There will be confusion enough, let us not compound matters. Do you have a suitable alternative you would like us to use Callum?'

'Err...no, I suppose I don't. Not off hand at least.' replied Callum.

'Rayna,' said Marcus, finally breaking his silence, 'That is what we call the morning sun as it breaks across the horizon. This morning's was particularly beautiful. Freylar chose your new name for you, fitting as it is for a newly resurrected light bringer.'

She was a little taken back by Marcus' decree, though it was a good strong name and entirely appropriate. She could do no better herself; indeed she rather liked the name having warmed to it almost immediately. Surprising was that a male Freylarkin forged by The Blades and destined to command could produce such creativity on a whim. Her overwhelming respect for Marcus continued to surprise even herself; it was near impossible to find fault with The Blade Lord. Marcus' ascension to the role, following the loss of his predecessor, had been a glorious occasion; one which had wrought a renewed solidarity amongst her brothers and sisters. She was a mere Aspirant at the time and recalled vividly how their new commander had stoked the fire in their hearts in the wake of their collective mourning.

'A fine name,' said Mirielle, 'Callum, do you object?'

'I do not.' replied Callum before continuing. 'This morning has been rather overwhelming for me. I clearly have an awful lot to learn. I thank you all for your acceptance, in particular yourself Nathaniel. Whilst I never knew Alarielle, I gather from the high regard everyone held her in that her loss was devastating. I will work my hardest to ensure that I do not tarnish her memory through my future actions. This I promise.'

'Callum, since your rebirth, you have shown complete respect for the legacy of my daughter. You already do her credit.' said Nathaniel in a humbled voice.

'Then it is agreed. Rayna you will be named as such hence forth. Nathaniel, Rayna is your responsibility now. Kirika will offer her services as necessary.' said Mirielle ending the matter. 'Regarding all that has been spoken and theorised here this cycle,' she continued, 'Clearly this information is potentially volatile, though it cannot be contained. Its profound nature will inevitably see it pass down to the wagging tongues of Freylar. Therefore...I encourage this.'

'Mirielle, are you certain the Freylarkai are ready for...a revelation?' said Marcus flatly.

'Far from it, however, the information will have less impact if disseminated slowly. Sow the seeds, instigate the rumour, and allow the populous to fill in the blanks. We will refine their thinking over time, by which point they will be more amenable to...your revelation.' replied Mirielle. 'The nature of Rayna's arrival in Freylar is not unlike a stone already cast into still waters. The ripples will spread. We cannot prevent this, though we can soften their impact.'

'Very well, I will set events in motion to that end.' said Marcus. 'Rayna, I am afraid that you will likely meet resistance from a number of Freylar's inhabitants. Not all will be as understanding as those in this room. Are you prepared for that eventuality?'

'No, I'm not. But I do not turn from life's challenges, despite the pain they may cause. I move forwards...never backwards.'

'Good. You will need that strength of mind. Your determination will serve you well.' said Marcus. 'I have a meeting with my brother Paladins and sister Valkyries of The Blades highest order. Nathaniel, I would like both yourself and Rayna in attendance.'

Nathaniel nodded politely at Marcus' request. She was unsure as to whether Nathaniel personally agreed with Marcus' decision to throw Rayna to the wolves so soon, though Kirika knew well the merits of picking the location and time of one's battles; even if they were round a table. The decision was bold, and it would rob potential opposition of valuable time to formulate counter arguments of any real substance. She knew Aleska well enough to know that her mentor would be sympathetic to Rayna's predicament, and Thandor would likely be indifferent about the entire matter. Natalya would likely take a pragmatic view of the facts as presented, though Ragnar and Lothnar both had potential for explosive confrontation. She silently hoped that Marcus' speculative faith in her new sister's mental fortitude was not misplaced.

SEVEN
Confrontation

'That...body thief dishonours your daughter's memory Nathaniel!' said Lothnar vehemently. 'Alarielle's body should have been burnt on the pyre, as is customary for all fallen Blades. Instead your prolonged mourning has allowed this *thing* to invade what was rightfully hers.'

'Stay your tongue Lothnar or I will cut it out!' cried Nathaniel standing up abruptly, knocking his wooden chair to the floor with a loud bang which echoed around the sparsely furnished subterranean chamber.

'Enough! Both of you!' said Marcus, bringing his clenched fist down on the large oval table before them. 'Nathaniel, sit back down. Lothnar, show him the respect that he rightfully deserves!'

Marcus had forewarned her that some of the Freylarkai would react poorly to her arrival in Freylar, now that prophecy was playing out before her. Rayna felt obliged to add her own voice to the raucous debate – perhaps heated argument was a better description for it. When she finally mustered up the courage to speak, she noted Thandor, sitting to her left, suddenly shaking his head as if to suggest that her timing was poor. Biting her tongue, she pursed her lips in silence as those of greater import argued her lot. Rayna resented being unable to defend herself, but she was new to the Freylarkai and had yet to prove her worth; her words would carry little weight with her doubters as it stood, though perhaps in time that would change.

'Marcus, with respect brother, you expect us to believe that this interloper was some kind of guardian over Freylar! The very thought of it makes me laugh.' boomed Ragnar.

Ragnar had taken up position adjacent to Marcus who, as lord commander of The Blades, sat at the head of the table. To Ragnar's left sat Lothnar, whose barely contained rage boiled fiercely on the surface, then Natalya who rolled her eyes clearly unimpressed by the lack of decorum on display. Given their lower rank, or in her case complete lack of, both she and Nathaniel clustered at the bottom end of the oval. Thandor, Aleska and Kirika made up Marcus' right flank. Kirika sat opposite Ragnar with a stern look about her. Rayna was not entirely sure what to expect from Freylar's highest military echelon prior to the meeting, though she had not expected the level of animosity currently being displayed. Whilst she assumed that their individual military prowess or political aptitude was unrivalled, there were a number of strong personalities at odds within the group. She understood well now why Marcus had been selected to give them the cohesion they so badly needed. Fortunately their meeting took place in an earthy subterranean chamber, beneath the arena and far from prying eyes; at least below the surface they could vehemently debate contentious issues amongst themselves without tarnishing their public image.

'Your queen asks you to! Kirika has validated Rayna's account. As fantastical as it may sound, her past is what it is whether you choose to believe it or not. But in any event, that is the party line and you will follow it Captain.' Marcus decreed.

'Bah, your faith in Fate Weaver's abilities is your weakness Marcus, she does not see all!' retorted Ragnar.

'And your loathing for Kirika is tiresome brother.' replied Marcus. 'Each of you has mastered your own unique ability. You are all unrivalled in your field and that is why you sit at this table. Collectively we shield Freylar from those that would see it in ruin, though we cannot maintain that goal if we continue to bicker amongst ourselves. The situation is as I have explained. I do not expect you all to like it, or indeed to agree with it, but you will do as I command. I will not see the Freylarkai divided by Rayna's arrival here. If Nathaniel can find it within himself to accept Rayna, then each of you will do so as well. I am not asking you to like her, or even to respect her.'

'So be it Marcus, but know that I will do neither. I find her presence here abhorrent.' said Lothnar ferociously.

Silence followed Lothnar's scathing proclamation. Few appeared to have the stomach to further attempt to sway his loathing opinion of her, and those that might have done so seemed to have given up any hope of trying to bring Lothnar around. Ragnar too appeared to be put out by her arrival in Freylar, though at least he tempered his dim view of her. Reason and logic begged her to leave the situation well alone, but switching bodies had done nothing to abate her determination when faced with unfavourable odds. Rather than allow herself to drown in self-pity, no matter how well deserved, Rayna called upon her fighting spirit; she possessed strength of mind which allowed her to challenge those who would see her laid low. Her face took on a stony expression, and her breathing deepened as she steeled herself for what was to come. Before making her own voice known, however, she offered Thandor a courteous glance seeking his silent approval for her imminent oral tirade. Thandor reciprocated, nodding slowly in agreement; that was all she needed to begin her verbal assault.

'If there is nothing further of note regarding this matter I would like us to move on to discuss Lothnar's latest report which deeply concerns me.' Marcus said looking to dissolve the poor aftertaste of Lothnar's closing words by introducing an alternative subject.

'I would like to be heard now,' she said matter-of-factly, much to the piqued interest and concern of those present.

Slowly she rose from her chair, deliberately causing its legs to scrape loudly across the stone floor. She stepped close to the edge of the table and leaned over it as far as her supple body would allow planting both her hands flat on its surface. Slowly she raised her head ensuring that her eye line had Lothnar firmly fixed in sight. Natalya leaned into her chair and folded her arms, eager to observe what was to come next. She purposely paused, before giving voice to her thoughts, allowing the tension in the chamber to heighten. Then, narrowing her eyes, she glared intently towards Lothnar before parting her lips.

'It is clear to me that you loved Alarielle, but that you lacked the conviction to make your feelings known to her before her untimely release,' she began, ignoring the audible gasp from Aleska. 'Do not think that I will be a willing target for your regret, or that I will absolve your failings simply because I inherited her body.' she continued, before pausing once more for effect. 'I do not ask for your respect Lothnar. Instead, I will earn it!'

Once more silence descended on the chamber, allowing her words to take root amongst those present. She had half expected Lothnar to boil over entirely and erupt into a verbal rage, but instead he remained perfectly calm with an almost vacuous look in his eyes. She could not tell if her words had lanced through his heart or whether Lothnar was simply ignoring her, though she remained steadfast and continued to fix him in her sight in anticipation of his response. As she awaited Lothnar's response, the tension through the muscles of her arms started to build as the strain of her body weight bearing down on them gradually increased. Realising this, she fought back the dull ache gnawing away at them determined not to show any signs of physical weakness; to do so would undermine the conviction of her words. Despite her efforts, she could feel her arms begin to tremble as the strain through her weakened muscles took its toll. Despite her difficulty she would not back down, not until Lothnar had at least acknowledged her words, though the weakness in her arms refused to go unnoticed as they continued to tire. Lothnar spared a lazy glance towards her left arm before returning to her unrelenting gaze; he was no doubt aware of the strain on her newly awakened body. She fully expected him to exploit her disadvantage as she continued to lean across the table unyielding in her stance, yet Lothnar issued no response, nor did he make any attempt to move; he seemed content to watch her struggle until, that is, her arms began to shake uncontrollably. Slowly Lothnar reached forwards with both of his hands and grasped the sides of her trembling arms, steadying them before drawing in close to her face.

'See that you do.' said Lothnar coldly. 'Have your Teacher over there train you. Come winter, you and I will meet in the arena and I will test the strength of your conviction girl.'

'It's a date.' she replied, offering him a curious half smile.

Lothnar returned her gesture with a deep "Humph" then promptly ended their exchange with, 'The rest of this meeting does not concern you, or The Teacher. Leave us now.'

Lothnar released his grip on her arms, which she quickly withdrew. It was a welcome relief as the strain in her arms promptly dissipated. She lingered for a moment, smiling at Lothnar, as she took his measure then turned slowly to walk round the back of her chair towards Nathaniel who was now on his feet. Glancing one more towards Thandor, she detected a weak smile from the enigmatic Paladin who continued to sit silently with his arms folded neatly, observing the proceedings. She offered Thandor a respectful nod, then fell in line behind Nathaniel following him towards the chamber's Waystone stationed at the far end of the room.

It was early afternoon. The warmth of the sun was now at its fiercest, making its presence felt fully, as it burned down across the vale. The walk back from the arena, down the slope of the southern ridgeline towards the river, had been far easier than the ascent earlier that morning. Aside from the obvious aid of gravity, her leg muscles were now much stronger in light of their renewed use. She paid the price for their abrupt reawakening, however, as they persistently ached; as did most of the newly invigorated muscles of her new body. Neither she nor Nathaniel had spoken since their departure from the arena. The information Mirielle had shared with them weighed heavy on her; the revelation dominated her thoughts, as it bubbled incessantly at the fore of her mind, refusing to abate. Despite the majestic beauty of the vale fighting its hardest to compete for her attention, she found it difficult to focus on anything other than the sphere of light. Was it even possible for an entire world to be contained within the body of an entity? Indeed where did it all end, she mused trying hard to comprehend a concept well beyond her mental grasp. She had wanted to understand the nature of her traumatic arrival in Freylar, yet the pursuit of this knowledge had led to more questions which would likely remain unanswered.

'Well...that could have gone better.' said Nathaniel breaking their silence. He paused for a moment before continuing, 'Rayna, are you listening to me?'

'Apologies Nathaniel, I was in another world.' she replied.

Nathaniel laughed heartily before replying, 'Indeed you were, for the second time this very cycle no less. You have barely set foot in Freylar and already you have left your mark; indeed you have incurred us both a challenge with a Paladin. I am unsure as to whether I should applaud your efforts, or instead reprimand you for your defiance in the face of one well beyond your station.'

'He challenged me Nathaniel.' she said. 'You do not need to fight my battles. I am entirely responsible for my actions and will be accountable for them.'

'No, the challenge was issued to us both.' he replied. 'Lothnar was not schooled by me. His martial prowess is entirely self-taught. I am fortunate enough to have earned both respect and loyalty from my students, of whom Marcus was my greatest protégé. I never instructed Lothnar, or Ragnar for that matter. Therefore I do not share the same bond with them as with my students, past and present. I have often felt that it is this bond which they resent, hence their low opinion of me.'

They were closing on the location where they had first made landfall after departing the Cave of Wellbeing. During their earlier flight Nathaniel had spoken of his decision to live amongst the people. Now she would meet those very same people for the first time; she wondered if they would react as sourly to her presence as some of her earlier critics. Still, the Paladins and Valkyries were privy to the raw facts; these Freylarkai would receive that information at a more manageable pace whilst she played the role of the enigmatic new arrival. With that goal in mind, she drew her hood up once more, concealing the majority of her face. She would stride confidently alongside Nathaniel, leaving a trail of gossip and intrigue in their wake. The forest dwellers would likely draw their own conclusions, based on the little knowledge they gleaned first-hand from her mysterious unannounced arrival.

'That bridge downstream is where we will cross the river.' said Nathaniel pointing westwards.

The scars across Nathaniel's arms were more prominent in the light of the early afternoon sun, causing her to fully appreciate the level of commitment he afforded his students throughout their studies. He was clearly extremely protective towards them and was prepared to go to great lengths to ensure their continued wellbeing, despite the inevitable dangers they would encounter. As they walked single file alongside the southern edge of the river bank, Rayna saw civilian Freylarkai up close for the first time since her rebirth. A handful of female Freylarkai were meticulously folding garments which she presumed had been laid out to dry earlier that morning. Several of the workers turned to face her as she and Nathaniel approached; clearly they recognised Nathaniel, though it was evident that they were not entirely sure what to make of her presence. The nearest onlookers began to whisper amongst themselves, and the gossiping soon spread through the remainder of the congregation. She afforded herself a little smile; it was a first, amongst many that day, being the talk of the town. Nathaniel paid the rumour-mongering no heed and continued his course towards the bridge; she followed him diligently despite the public spectacle they had clearly become. As they passed the female workers, the idle gossip became more verbose as her spectators regarded the particulars of her form; in particular the colour of her hair which she deliberately failed to fully conceal behind the hood of her robe. Regardless of the speculation, she and Nathaniel crossed the aging timber bridge without pause. They then proceeded promptly towards the forest dwellings where Nathaniel made his home, in relative isolation from the politics of the Tri-Spires.

The dwellings were more extensions of the forest, as opposed to structures looking to suppress nature's claim over Freylar. The organic design of their construction suggested that shapers were the architects of their genesis. The trees of the forest had been enhanced, or rather abnormally enlarged, such that their trunks were wide enough to enclose entire rooms. Many of the trees seemed to merge into one another forming larger structures; presumably family dwellings, or instead intended for commerce. Some leant their branches towards another, forming external shelters for storage and livestock, which she had no realistic hope of identifying. Other dwellings seemed to exist above the forest floor composed entirely of branches which had been twisted, weaved and interlocked to form organic walls adorned with multiple species of plant life in full bloom. Yet despite their altered appearance, the dwellings complimented the surrounding forest further adding to its enchanting beauty. Aside from well-trodden paths which ran between the living structures, the forest appeared completely unspoilt by the presence of the Freylarkai. The forest dwellers had managed successfully to integrate their lives with the forest without denying any of its natural splendour.

Nathaniel continued to lead her along a series of dry mud paths, deeper into the forest and away from the worst of the sun's rays, which somehow managed to spear down through the increasingly thick verdant canopy above; the rays lit up everything in their wake, revealing tiny airborne insects and rendering plant life in dazzling colour. She felt childlike again, touching everything in her path and eager to investigate everything she saw. Even the caress of the surrounding flora and fauna was alien to her; soft and inviting, completely at odds with the coarse spiny wildlife of the Wild which she had become accustomed to.

'That one there is where I live,' said Nathaniel pointing to a modestly altered tree further along the path. 'I will get you settled in and find you something to eat. I think you have had enough excitement for this cycle.'

'You're right of course, but everything here is so new to me. I hunger to see more.' she replied.

'We will sate your appetite for new experiences tomorrow Rayna. Remember, this is new for me also. The vigour of youth has long since abandoned me, and not just physically. I need time to assemble my thoughts. I must decide the best course to further your knowledge, and you need to give some thought as to your role here in Freylar.' lectured Nathaniel.

His words struck a chord with her, pushing thoughts of the sphere to one side – albeit temporarily – as they approached Nathaniel's home, which would also be her own for the foreseeable future. She had not previously given any thought as to what she would do, now that she had arrived in Freylar. Certainly there was no going back at this stage; her original body was likely already in full rigor back in the world she once knew. Besides, that mentality was entirely uncharacteristic of her; the notion of going backwards never appealed to her. Always move forwards, that was her way. Still, Nathaniel had cut straight to the heart of the matter and was right to do so. Regardless of how the Freylarkai coexisted, be it through exchange of goods and services, currency or respectable ethics serving the good of the race, those she had briefly encountered since her arrival seemed to have purpose in their lives. She would need to find a path of her own to follow in this new life she had been given. She could ill afford to sit around idling away, particularly so given the challenge laid down by Lothnar.

'Here we are,' said Nathaniel. 'It may not be as ostentatious as those dwellings within the inner sanctuary, but it serves me well. There is space enough for you here too Rayna.'

'Thank you Nathaniel,' she said. 'I owe you a great debt.'

'You can return the favour by forcing Lothnar to work up a sweat in that arena.' he replied smiling wryly.

'I will do more than make him sweat Nathaniel. I intend to see to it that Lothnar feels the ground on his back when the time comes.' she said quietly, as though making a sincere promise to herself.

Nathaniel raised an eyebrow at her remark then narrowed his eyes slightly as he regarded her silently. He seemed to be assessing her, though for what reason she was unsure. Nathaniel had indicated that the challenge was issued to them both; perhaps he was already considering her potential for combat. Or maybe he was bemused by her audacious attitude towards an authority figure with an overwhelming upper hand. Still, she enjoyed a challenge; at least that is what she told herself, as the magnitude of the undertaking suddenly solidified in her mind under Nathaniel's visual scrutiny.

'And I intend to see to it that your lofty intent is made possible.' he proclaimed. 'But for now, let us settle on acquainting you with your new home.

'Are you certain that you wish to go ahead with this Loth?' said Ragnar with a genuine look of concern on his face.

'Do not try to talk me out of the mission brother. Marcus speaks the truth of it, we need more information before The Blades can move on this.' he replied as he continued to meticulously fold items of clothing he had selected for the journey ahead. 'Besides, I am able to move more freely along the Narlakai borderlands without an entourage slowing me down and drawing unwanted attention.'

'So be it brother. It frustrates me having to wait like a chained animal. If Marcus commanded it, I would join you gladly with axe in hand.' replied Ragnar in his characteristic brutish manner. 'Instead Marcus has me performing...administrative duties.'

He could do nothing to prevent his outburst of laughter at Ragnar's words. He was astonished that Ragnar even understood the concept of administration. The thought of Ragnar sitting behind a bench managing the affairs of The Blades and reviewing troop deployments made him laugh heartedly. Ragnar was a warrior; all one needed to do was give him an axe and direct him towards the enemy, and yet his martial prowess was also a curse. Aspirants, Novices and Adepts held Ragnar in high esteem; he was an inspiration to the order. Lothnar had fought alongside Ragnar many times, and on the field of battle Ragnar was nothing short of devastating to the enemy. The tireless swing of his axe eagerly released the souls of his adversaries; few could oppose Ragnar in battle for any length of time, unsurprising then that respect from his brothers and sisters made Ragnar an ideal authority figure for The Blades. If Ragnar marched into battle, so too would his brothers and sisters, regardless of their morale. Ragnar's presence in the field was reassuring, second only to the presence of The Blade Lord. When both Marcus and Ragnar fought side by side, The Blades were utterly steadfast; none would falter and each would fight to the fullest of their capabilities. Whilst Ragnar had not actively sought captaincy of The Blades, he could never refuse a direct request from Marcus; The Blade Lord had a way of selling the impossible. Besides, very few of the Paladins and Valkyries possessed the required disposition to inspire, as Ragnar did, on the front line. Though each of them was revered by those of lower rank, it was Ragnar who emboldened entire regiments steeling jangled nerves ready for the charge.

'I am glad my misfortune amuses you Loth!' boomed Ragnar.

'Calm brother. The rare entertainment is well received, more so given my lack of a decent bed for the foreseeable future.' he replied.

'Ha, you could sleep in shit if you had to. The land is to you, what air is to the rest of us. Besides, you always complain that the beds here are too soft.' said Ragnar.

He grinned whilst nodding agreeably. Ragnar was rough around the edges and often quick to antagonise, but he had the measure of their Captain and as such was able to push the boundaries of their friendship. Both he and Ragnar enjoyed a strong relationship; one akin to that of two blood brothers he supposed. He always enjoyed their camaraderie; it was one of the few reasons he even bothered to return to the Tri-Spires. For the most part he was content to leave the politicking and management of the domain to those with a taste for such things; his soul yearned for more than power and career progression. He craved the excitement of living life on the edge, not knowing when the next meal would present itself and whether his skill was even sufficient to reap it. His was a life of continuous adventure. Aside from his friendship with Ragnar, there was little left to draw him back to the bosom of Freylar – the tragic loss of Alarielle had seen to that.

'Perhaps, if I am fortunate enough, I will cross paths with that *thing* which defiled Alarielle's soul, release her from torment, and bring you back a trophy for your bench.' he said, playing on Ragnar's misfortune a while longer.

'Indeed I hope you do. But do not go looking for trouble little brother. Avenging Alarielle is not the mission. We need you back.' replied Ragnar.

'You mean you will get bored if I do not return?' he said, grinning once more.

'Ha, something like that. Now be gone Loth, before you start to well up on me.'

Instinctively they grasped each other's inner right arm with their hand before parting ways. Farewells were never longer than necessary between them. Both knew their role and each did what was asked of them. They would meet again, of that he was sure; neither one of them was ready for the Everlife just yet.

As Ragnar made his way to leave, the Captain suddenly broke step and moved aside, allowing Aleska to cross the threshold into his chamber. She exchanged a courteous nod with Ragnar, who then promptly left after a brief moment of hesitation. Despite being his senior, of many passes, Aleska was still a capable adversary and not to be taken lightly. She had mentored Kirika alongside Nathaniel, and in doing so had become notably fond of The Teacher. Whilst Nathaniel instructed Kirika in the art of physical combat, it was Aleska who honed the young female Freylarkin's mind. Being a scrier herself, Aleska was perfectly suited to the task of developing the skills of her eventual successor; a responsibility which she had readily accepted when it was proposed by Marcus. As the passage of time marched on, Aleska's ability to scry had waned. Yet despite her fading ability Aleska continued to remain a valued member of the ruling council, though many believed she would step down once Kirika came into her own. He had a great deal of respect for Aleska, and all that she had accomplished in service to Freylar, though like Ragnar he too held a general loathing of those with the ability to scry. Perhaps the word loathing was unjustly harsh and entirely unsuitable; a sense of distrust was probably more appropriate.

'Aleska,' he said acknowledging her with a courteous nod of his own.

'Lothnar,' she replied. 'So, how have you been keeping?'

'Please, with respect, forego the pleasantries Aleska for you did not come to my chamber to make idle conversation.' he said cutting straight to the reason for her unexpected presence.

Aleska smiled warmly then took a seat at the foot of his bed, adjacent to his newly folded pile of clothing. She paused for thought, clearly unwilling to be rushed by his curt statement.

'I suppose not.' she said, finally acknowledging his proclamation.

'You are here to defend Nathaniel's honour I presume?' he said sardonically.

'Nathaniel's honour requires no defence, nor do I attempt such. He can defend himself. He requires no aid from me.' she replied calmly, unwilling to allow his words to rattle her.

'Ah, so it is the body thief then?' he said vehemently.

'She has a name Lothnar. Kindly use it.' said Aleska, still maintaining her cool demeanour.

Despite the passage of time etched across her features, Aleska still cut a fine figure; she clearly looked after herself and still practiced occasionally in the arena, though she no longer possessed the vigour that only youth can truly offer. Much like her strength Aleska's once violet long hair had faded almost entirely now, giving it a tarnished silver look overlaid with a subtle violet hue which acted like a pearlescent coating.

'You want me to go easy on her, is that it? Is this why you are here enquiring about my wellbeing?' he said scornfully.

'Indeed quite the opposite, in point of fact, for you play the part of the grieving secret lover well.' replied Aleska.

'Ha, so you are here only to mock Aleska. I thought your venerable rank had taught you better than that.'

'Not to mock. I am here to request a favour of you Lothnar.' said Aleska quietly as she placed her hands neatly in her lap fixing him with her steely eyes.

'Which is what exactly?'

'I ask that you maintain your pressure on Rayna, and that you continue to harbour your hatred of her.' explained Aleska.

'What is this hidden play of yours now Aleska, reverse psychology perhaps? Do not think me so easily manipulated by your words.' he replied curtly.

Again Aleska paused for a moment in light of his terse response, no doubt considering her next words carefully; she was an accomplished wordsmith and regularly advised Marcus on public announcements. Often she played with political fire, rarely ever being burnt in the process. Though her usefulness on the battlefield was now limited, in the political arena she was nothing short of deadly; a true mistress of the art of subterfuge.

'I appreciate that you are wary of scrying and the validity of information divined through such ability. With that said, you cannot dismiss its potential usefulness. Kirika is young and her ability runs rampant. Kirika sees too much, too quickly, which can both confuse and place great strain on a mind, however, in time she will hone her ability. I am not Kirika. My second sight no longer sees as frequently as hers does, however, when I see...I see with clarity.'

Once more Aleska paused, in the same manner as a storyteller might to keep the listener wanting more. He was now that listener; Aleska had piqued his interest and he wanted more from her.

'What is it that you have seen?' he asked, seeking to expedite Aleska's words.

'I have glimpsed Rayna and the great feats she will achieve in service to The Blades, if driven to do so.' replied Aleska. 'That Freylarkin's soul is not of our domain Lothnar, nor is it of our world. She is as Mirielle proclaimed. I believe that Rayna will blossom into greatness, given the right impetus. I need you to be the force that drives her.'

Aleska seemed sincere in her delivery, yet he had been deceived by her tongue before. Whilst she never, to his knowledge, lied outright, Aleska had a way of manipulating the course of any conversation to suit her own agenda.

'Tell me. Why should I care whether or not she...blossoms, as you so eloquently put it?' he replied.

'Because I believe that she will bring you that which you seek.'

'And what is that?' he said, raising an eyebrow.

'Vengeance!' said Aleska.

EIGHT
Purpose

It had been several cycles since Rayna's controversial arrival in Freylar. At that time queen Mirielle had been very specific, tasking her with the job of schooling Rayna in the feminine arts to help facilitate the changes demanded by her new body. She had gladly accepted the opportunity to play the role of the elder sister, though she had yet to commence her tutelage. She sold herself the notion that Rayna would require a few cycles to settle in first but, in truth, self-doubt over her suitability for the role had gotten the better of her. Ever her own worst critic, she often hesitated when faced with new challenges and uncertain outcomes. Reliance on scrying was partly to blame; through Aleska's teachings she had learned to rein in her ability for situations that warranted it most. Now she needed to learn to cope with the unknown as well as any other. Dealing with her own self-doubts was part of her development, apparently; of course she knew that her sponsors were right in this. Her walk through the heart of the forest, however, had done little to ease her concerns. Unlike Nathaniel, she was no longer of the people. Rarely did she leave the confines of the Tri-Spires and its neighbouring community. Both her studies and service to The Blades kept her close to the inner sanctuary; she had little cause to venture into the heart of the vale. Now that her work had demanded that she return to the place of her childhood, she felt a wave of nostalgia rising. Yet despite her fond reminiscing, it was evident that time away had rendered her a stranger amongst the forest dwellers; most of the forest's native inhabitants who witnessed her passing regarded her with suspicious eyes, attempting to discern the true motive behind her sudden return, for it was clear to them that she was far from homesick. As she steered her course towards Nathaniel's residence, the number of eyes on her back increased along with the whisperings. It seemed apparent to her that Rayna's arrival had already set tongues wagging and that her own unexpected presence would likely further fuel the rumours. Still, this was after all Mirielle's intent; to allow the people to piece together the facts at their own manageable pace, unlike the hammer blow dealt to her brother Paladins and sister Valkyries below the arena. She felt uncomfortable under the watchful eyes of the gossiping half-hidden amongst the trees, though she would likely feel even more so reacquainting herself with Rayna in light of her tardy visit. Still, there was no delaying the matter any further; she increased her pace and in doing so sought to escape her secret audience. She soon arrived at Nathaniel's tree, stopping abruptly in front of its narrow solid wooden door. Before she could raise a single hand to knock against it, the door swiftly opened as if of its own accord. Nathaniel stepped into the dull light of the forest and ushered her quickly inside before promptly closing the door behind them, hiding them from their onlookers.

'Make yourself at home Kirika.' said Nathaniel eagerly.

Nathaniel's appearance was notably improved since last they had spoken. The gaunt visage of a Freylarkin she found mourning in the Cave of Wellbeing had entirely gone. His cheeks had filled out slightly and he had a spritely vigour about him. It was heart-warming to see her mentor full of purpose once more.

'I had hoped that you would visit us sooner. I am certain that Rayna has questions which...she would rather put to you for answers.'

'I am so very sorry Nathaniel.' she replied, giving away nothing of the actual reason for her delayed visit.

'You are here now, for which I am grateful.' said Nathaniel. 'I believe the enormity of the changes she faces are now fully realised. She will need a great deal of help from both of us if she is to successfully integrate with Freylarkin society.'

'I understand.' she said, 'Though, where is she Nathaniel?'

'In her room, at the top of the stairs.' he replied. 'You should go see her. I am sure that Rayna will be pleased to see you.'

The compact downstairs living space of Nathaniel's residence was functional, though it lacked any real design flair. The space was little more than a place to rest and contemplate. To the right of the door were two large rocking chairs, stationed by a small window, adjacent to which were numerous piles of books. A cursory glance suggested that most were battle doctrine, though there were a few standout surprises. Despite her long-standing relationship with her arena mentor, she had never once had cause to visit Nathaniel at home. She had always assumed that he would choose to live in modest dwellings, as was indeed the case, though discovering that he was the owner of several books of classic poetry came as a surprise. She considered that they might have once belonged to his late wife, who was tragically released of her soul during Alarielle's traumatic birth, but surely such treasured keepsakes would not be permitted to collect dust amongst the seemingly disordered piles. The temptation to scry the truth was almost irresistible; however, she considered the use of her ability for matters of personal curiosity to be intrusive. More importantly, such self-serving actions were amongst the first steps on the road to ruin for any scrier. Unless she found the courage to broach the subject with Nathaniel directly, his potential interest in the literary arts would likely remain a mystery to her.

'Not quite what you had expected eh?' said Nathaniel suddenly.

'I am sorry Nathaniel, my eyes clearly betray me. I did not mean to pry.' she replied hurriedly, embarrassed that her gaze had been caught lingering.

'No need to apologise.' he said. 'When you eventually find the confidence to ask me such questions Kirika, I will answer them. But for now at least, you should go see Rayna. She has not slept well these last few cycles. Memories of her past keep resurfacing. Perhaps you can help her with your ability.'

'I understand. I will see you shortly Nathaniel.'

Nathaniel laughed gleefully before replying, 'I very much doubt that you will. She asks a great many questions.'

Absentmindedly, he gently rubbed the fresh scar on the fore of his right arm; it itched insatiably and had done so since the back alley procedure several months back. It was a stark ever-present reminder of the abhorrent ethical change society had wrought upon itself over the last few months, ultimately climaxing with the Exodus. He slid smoothly between those dark recesses of the night unwilling to be swallowed up by the many lights of the metropolis, ensuring that his movements were fluid at all times. Melting between the shadows, he moved swiftly through emptied streets; swept clear by the Peacekeeper-enforced curfews. Infiltrating the metropolis was a dangerous move, though he had little choice; having not eaten in days, his stomach groaned tirelessly as it threatened to feed on itself. Food was sparse in the Wild, more so with the onset of winter. Now he was forced to scavenge the streets once again in order to satisfy his growing hunger. Fortunately, the passing years had taught him where best to look for sources of free food within the metropolis; these were plentiful provided one was happy to lower their expectations of quality. Typically his harvests came from corporate waste management sites, a relatively risk-free endeavour if timed correctly. Distributors would often discarded unsellable stocks of perishable goods in the late afternoon, however, with the introduction of rigid curfews and frequent Peacekeeper ground patrols, infiltrating the metropolis undetected had become a dangerous sport. Since he only dared to attempt such foolishness under the cover of darkness, he was forced to delay his entry into the heart of the metropolis until sundown. At such late hour, waste management sites would be on full lockdown meaning he would have to resort to other measures. Attempting a break in, or trawling through public bins during the dead of night, was undesirable given the current number of boots on the ground patrolling the metropolis. If he was spotted, he too would quickly find himself at the business end of a stun rifle, followed by a one way ticket out of the metropolis; a fate whose particulars were still largely unknown to him. Those members of the Shadow class escorted from the metropolis during the Rout never returned; they simply vanished, along with any sign of their existence. Only memory kept the events real in his mind, yet each harrowing account left a deepening scar across his mind. History was once again being written by the victors and his kind had no place in the archives. Their disappearance would likely be explained by a freak viral outbreak targeting the Shadow class exclusively; propaganda would therefore regard them as vermin, both contracting and spreading plague. Despite the miserable social forecast, he continued his silent advance slipping unseen along vacant streets and across roads where the darkness still claimed supremacy. His knowledge of the neighbourhood served him well, for frequent Peacekeeper patrols demanded that he continuously adapt his chosen route. It would not be long before he left the relative safety of the derelict former business district, once home to the Shadow class. The darkness would quickly recede from the ubiquitous light at the heart of the metropolis. Fortunately he needed only to penetrate the outer layer of the urban core. There he would find his sanctuary amongst the middle classes under Kaitlin's benevolent protection. Regardless of the late hour, he knew Kaitlin well enough to know that she would still be burning the midnight oil whilst continuing to relentlessly devour the entirety of the knowledge contained within her public library. Though physically printed media bordered on extinction, there were those – especially within the apex classes – who still enjoyed thumbing through the pages of a good book; he was no different. It was his love for physical literature which had drawn him to Kaitlin's library during his nightmarish tour of the metropolis' children's homes; she was the library's primary curator. It was there that he found solace and, more importantly, a life-long friend in

Kaitlin. She did not judge one by their designated social status; she accepted him for who he was as an individual, not as a social class stereotype. Their shared interest in books saw their friendship blossom over the years; even after his difficult decision to relocate to the Wild, he still made frequent pilgrimages to her sanctuary. Now though, he needed Kaitlin's aid for entirely different reasons.

Shortly after leaving the old business district, he came close to colliding with a young woman as he approached the end of a long terrace of dilapidated office units. The scared woman ran frantically past him as he neared the junction at the end of the street, clearly unaware of his presence. He reacted instinctively by throwing himself into the shadows of an adjacent office unit pressing his entire body flat to the cold hard ground. He glanced up to see the woman stumble into the wall of an opposing building as she lost her footing whilst mounting the pavement at speed. She hit the wall hard, bouncing off it like a rag doll, then collapsed to the floor in an untidy mess where she remained, perfectly still. Given the speed of the collision, he was unsure as to whether or not the woman was still conscious, though his question was soon answered as she began to slowly and unsteadily pick herself up off the floor. The dishevelled waif was completely exposed by strip lighting along the side of the wall which lit up the section of pavement she had fallen upon. Even at a distance, the stark white light allowed him to make out patches of blood smeared down the right side of her panic stricken face. His quick visual assessment noted that she wore nothing on her feet and that her clothes were grubby and worn. Her long black hair was matted and she looked impossibly thin. This woman, whoever she was, had the unmistakable stain of the Shadow class upon her; she was one of his surviving kin. Abruptly, the woman turned her head awkwardly to her left then began to stagger forwards. The sound of running boots thumping against the road followed; muted at first though quickly building to a crescendo. Before the woman could recover from her dazed state, the unmistakable whine of a stun rifle echoed down the street. The shot hit its mark sending the woman back to the ground as her legs immediately gave out from underneath her. Her head struck the ground as the weight of her body pulled her down, and her limbs splayed out across the pavement in awkward positions. Shortly after her body came to rest, three Peacekeepers rapidly entered view. One had their weapon still sighted on the woman whilst the remaining two pulled up alongside her prone body. With efficiency bred solely from repetition, the two Peacekeepers unravelled a black sack which they laid on the pavement adjacent to their victim. Showing zero compassion, the two members of the unit rolled the woman's lifeless body on top of the sack then hurriedly stuffed it wholly within. The sack was then zipped shut, completing the successful capture. One of the Peacekeepers then raised the back of their forearm to the mouthpiece of their head gear and reported the capture; the hunt was over.

    His head screamed at the sight of the atrocity unfolding before him. Rage caused his muscles to tighten and the adrenaline racing through his system fuelled his desire to end the lives of the three law enforcers. The desire to kill was entirely vengeful for he was not normally that way inclined; misery and pain were prevalent throughout his life, but rarely did he venture to that dark place. His want for retaliation threatened to overwhelm all reason and logic, as a deepening hatred flooded his thoughts; fortunately, however, his need to survive was greater. Pragmatism blunted the edge of his vengeful rage; what realistically could he in fact do against three armoured Peacekeepers, aside from give them another target? He was agile, fast enough even to out-run them, he fancied, but even those traits would likely not allow him to evade the skills of trained marksmen. They had numbers, technology, weapons and an open battlefield across which to gun him down. Doomed battles were not his style. Instead he swallowed both his pride and anger before trying to slow his breathing, then cautiously he pushed himself further back into the dark embrace of the adjacent building. Now that the attention of the Peacekeepers was no longer distracted, he needed to better conceal his presence if he wanted to continue evading their detection. As he lay perfectly still in the darkness, a muffled noise emanated from somewhere close by; he struggled to identify the sound at first, though he likened it to someone calling out to him. Again the sound came; it was definitely a voice, the tone suggested that of a female, though its origin continued to elude him. A third time the voice called out to him, this time much louder. It sounded like a name being cried out over a raging wind. One of the Peacekeepers turned their head to stare directly into the black abyss which enveloped him; his heart began to race at the thought of being detected. Whoever was calling out to him now threatened to expose his position; he cursed the poor timing of the voice. Once again it shouted out the same unfamiliar name to him.

'Shut up!' he whispered angrily.

The Peacekeeper was now moving quickly towards his position, weapon raised and pointed directly into the void concealing him.

'Shit!' he cursed, realising the inevitable.

The sound of his heart thumped loudly in his head, like someone banging on a door. Likely scenarios raced through his mind, most of which had a poor outcome. He still had the darkness at his back, which gave him an edge, and a fresh shot of adrenaline coursing through his body giving him the impetus he so desperately needed. With preternatural speed he pushed himself off the floor and straight into a low sprint down the remaining length of the building, the dying shadow of which masked his movement. Before the Peacekeeper could react to his ephemeral position, he altered his trajectory abruptly charging headlong towards his would-be hunter. The familiar whine of a stun rifle round splitting the still night air flanked his left ear, narrowly missing its mark. Stooping low under the Peacekeeper's guard he grabbed the underside of the firearm, using his momentum to drive the butt of the weapon up and into the protective head gear worn by his attacker.

'*Rayna!*' the voice screamed.

Nathaniel had informed her that Rayna was in her room, yet despite calling out to Rayna a number of times there had been no response. She briefly considered that perhaps Rayna was sleeping; she could always come back later, the coward in her reasoned. She loitered uncomfortably outside the room for a moment, undecided about how to proceed. When she eventually motioned to knock she hesitated, again unsure if it was best to disturb

Rayna. In her mind's eye she pictured Aleska, Marcus and Nathaniel regarding her disapprovingly; each of them waiting for her to show conviction in her actions. She knocked several times on the door. There was no response. On impulse, which surprised even her, she pushed the door wide open rather abruptly then took several confident steps into the bedroom. Rayna was sat upright on a plain wooden bed staring towards the room's only window; at a glance Rayna appeared to be asleep, yet her unblinking eyes were wide open and her pupils dilated. She quickly walked over to Rayna and crouched directly in front of the dreamer. There was no reaction from Rayna to her presence whatsoever. She grabbed Rayna by the shoulders and shook her, gently at first then more aggressively, though she would not be woken.

'Rayna!' she shouted, unsure how else to rouse Rayna from her waking dream.

Almost immediately Rayna woke up; she was clearly dazed and confused, unsure as to what had transpired, and sat wide-eyed in bemusement. Nathaniel had heard her shout and promptly run up the stairs to investigate the cause of the alarm.

'What is the matter?!' said Nathaniel with a look of concern.

'Rayna was having a waking dream which I have since woken her from. I am sorry for alarming you Nathaniel.' she said.

'It's ok Nathaniel,' said Rayna, at last reorienting herself, 'I am awake now.'

'Very well, I shall give you both some space.' he said, gently nodding his head. 'I have a few errands to run and maybe gone a while.'

She returned Nathaniel's smile and with that he left the room, closing the door as he went. Alone now with Rayna, she immediately became very self-conscious once more; Nathaniel seemingly had no issue leaving Rayna in her care, yet she had no plan of action and no precedent to draw from to aid her with the task at hand. Again she began to question her suitability as apprehension started to cloud her thoughts.

'I'm glad that you came.' said Rayna breaking the silence.

'As am I, though I regret that I did not visit you sooner.' she replied. 'Nathaniel told me that you have been having trouble sleeping. It seemed to me, just then, that you were experiencing a waking dream.'

'Memories of my past keep resurfacing and I am unable to shut them out.' replied Rayna.

'These memories you are recalling, are they entirely familiar to you?' she asked.

'No. Each one reveals a new element.' replied Rayna thoughtfully. 'It's as though the dreams start on familiar paths which I have already trodden, however, each then spirals down a new dark route entirely unfamiliar to me.'

She was loathe to use her ability for a second time on Rayna given the overwhelming nature of their first engagement, however, Nathaniel had suggested that she might be able to use her ability to help; she was not about to let her mentor down. Steeling herself, she began to prepare mentally for another dive into Rayna's disturbing past. The initial attempt had overloaded her senses to near breaking point with brutal alien stimuli, however, this time she would be better prepared and far from complacent; the previous encounter had taught her that lesson well.

'Are you ready to trust me a second time Rayna?' she asked.

'Of course Kirika, but what are you...'

'Hush now.' she said cutting short Rayna's insatiable curiosity.

Opening her second sight, she allowed the harrowing events of Rayna's past to stream through her conscious once more. Again the ferocious assault on her mind threatened to lay waste to her mental fortitude, however, her previous experience had taught her the value of allowing Rayna's past ordeals to flow harmlessly around her; like water passing around a rock in a stream, causing only minor erosion. As the images slid past the periphery of her mind, she maintained a watchful eye for the events of Rayna's waking dream. As though summoned, the specific images she sought raced to the fore of her mind eager to reveal their unattractive presence. Again she bore witness to the merciless black-armoured warriors, with their savage ranged weapons, as they relentlessly hunted across an unfamiliar landscape. This time their target was a single unkempt female who unsuccessfully attempted to outrun their grasp. The outcome of the pursuit made her shiver, though she was careful not to linger on the details of the grim encounter lest she be pulled down by the weight of the sorrow her preternatural sight revealed to her. Moving on she regressed further into Rayna's past attempting to isolate an instance of the ordeal beyond that of the dream world. Again images of the original instance were eager to make themselves known upon request, this time, however, the scene ended rather differently. Having obtained that which she sought, she quickly severed the link to Rayna's past forcing the alien world to vanish from her second sight.

The world she knew quickly reasserted itself. She was back in the bedroom. Rayna remained sat opposite; her lips moved rapidly but the sound from Rayna's mouth was muffled, as though shouted from behind a wall. Her limbs felt heavy and she struggled to maintain her balance as the last of the alien fog receded from her mind. All of her senses then abruptly re-engaged as the transition from Rayna's past back to reality completed its course.

'Repressed memories, these are what you are recalling through your dreams.' she said emphatically.

'I don't understand.' replied Rayna with a puzzled look. 'Why is it I'm experiencing repressed memories?'

'It is not uncommon for traumatic memories to become subconsciously locked away by the mind. Those darker memories which you have unknowingly buried are now resurfacing.' she surmised. 'From what I have thus far glimpsed of your troubled past, I assume that your previous existence was one of survival. Your mind likely blocked access to the more harrowing events you experienced so that you would not become disturbed by them.'

'Yet, I have witnessed far more disturbing events not withheld by my mind.' said Rayna.

'Perhaps, but did those events incur the same emotional burden?' she replied.

Rayna turned her head away and stared absentmindedly at the floor. She dipped her head causing her hair to separate partly concealing her face from view, though the soft glow of her ochre skin refused to be masked; it gently lit the nearside of her dark red hair which made it flicker vibrantly like a deep flame. Rayna possessed an enviable raw beauty; it was easy to understand how Alarielle had attracted so much attention from the male Blades – which was to her advantage in the arena. Those born during the height of summer invariably radiated the same invigorating inner light as Rayna, characteristic of all light bringers, yet Rayna's light was brighter than most; even now as she sat ruefully on the edge of her bed.

'You're referring to the guilt I shoulder as a result of my decision.' said Rayna meekly.

'There is no shame in your decision.' she replied. 'Every great leader must recognise when to fight and, more importantly, when not to. You know well the outcome of that futile conflict.'

'But there is always hope.' said Rayna turning to face her once more.

'Sometimes a fool's hope.' she countered.

'Perhaps, or maybe you attempt to absolve my guilt. Besides, I'm no leader Kirika.'

'Not yet. But in time you could be.'

It was late afternoon when he finally returned; his errands had kept him far longer than he had expected. Still, it would do Rayna good to spend time with Kirika, he thought as he took the last few steps to his front door. Slipping past the door quietly, he caught both Rayna and Kirika completely unaware of his presence. The downstairs living space had been superficially cleared; chairs were pushed close to the edge of the room along with the piles of books he had lazily allowed to clutter the floor. In the centre, Kirika was standing just behind Rayna; both had their back to the door and were oblivious to his silent observation. Kirika was in the middle of instructing Rayna on the correct grip of a short sword, which they had removed from its natural resting place under the window.

In truth he had forgotten entirely about the weapon, having inadvertently concealed its existence behind piles of literature; seeing it now painfully reminded him of his loss.

'That sword belonged to Alarielle, it was one of her practice blades.' he said flatly causing them both to turn their heads towards him clearly startled. 'Please put it down.'

Rayna started to respond but Kirika quickly cut her short.

'Nathaniel, I am sorry, the fault was mine. I did not realise.' she said apologetically, blushing through her words.

Nathaniel grinned wryly before replying, 'There is no need for an apology. I only ask that you put the blade down as it is not the correct weapon for Rayna.'

Attentively Kirika returned the blade to its unofficial home amongst the books. He turned his attention back to Rayna who stood resolutely before him; he acknowledged the positive change in Rayna's demeanour. For the last couple of cycles she had been partially withdrawn, or perhaps lost was a better assessment, though this had done nothing to reduce her insatiable appetite for complete understanding. She had not been the same defiant Rayna who refused to break under Lothnar's wrath on the cycle of her rebirth, nor had she been the unflinching interloper held accountable to their queen. Now, Rayna's gritty determination had resurfaced, seemingly in the short time she had spent with Kirika. It warmed him to see the Rayna he had first met make herself known once more. Through Kirika she had found purpose again, even if the catalyst was learning to wield an inappropriate weapon in a cramped living space. He realised then that Rayna needed constant stimulation, as a plant would require light in order to grow. Confining Rayna to their home since they returned from the Tri-Spires was a mistake, he realised that now. It was time to guide her along a new path and see where that decision led them.

'Why are you wielding a blade in our home Rayna?' he asked inquisitively.

'You asked me to think about my purpose here in Freylar Nathaniel. I have had time enough to contemplate your words and have made my decision.' replied Rayna.

'That is good to hear. What is it you have decided?' he enquired.

'I have decided to enlist with The Blades.' Rayna proclaimed.

On hearing her words his wry grin morphed into an entirely selfish smile. Her decision was not entirely unexpected, yet its affirmation was most welcome. A small part of him had been concerned that Rayna might take on a passive or supporting role within Freylar; few of which he would have been able to assist her with. Rayna's decision to become a Blade Aspirant, however, sat extremely well with him; he could assist her with training, and in doing so would likely strengthen the bond between them.

'You honour my daughter's memory Rayna, but you will forge your own path, along which I will guide you.' he said, nodding agreeably. 'Kirika, perhaps you would join us for dinner? There is a great deal to discuss.'

NINE
Nocturnal

Four cycles' hard walking and a series of short flights across Bleak Moor had brought him to this; the Narlakai borderlands, beyond which laid the nightmarish hell that was Narlak proper. The land ahead of him was bleak and cracked as far as the horizon. Nothing survived here unless it was an apex predator or, like himself, moved unseen. The Narlakai were nightmare horrors, reminiscent of amorphous black clouds out of which writhed gangrenous tendrils which tethered prey, dragging it back to the source for desiccation. They left nothing behind of their victims save for withered, empty husks; the Narlakai did not have the stomach for Freylarkai hair and skin, though everything else was consumed. The soul was always the first component to be devoured, as was the case with Alarielle, then followed a darkening of the skin as internal workings and fluids were drained from their victims. It was a miserable way to be released; the victims' souls were rendered unable to pass on to the Everlife since they remained trapped within the predators themselves. The Narlakai lived long, far longer than the Freylarkai who typically enjoyed two hundred passes; to be trapped by a Narlakin was a harrowing fate. Whilst it was possible to destroy the horrors, thus freeing any souls trapped within, it was near impossible to distinguish the Narlakai apart since each looked as grotesque as the last. He knew that, realistically, locating Alarielle's soul would not be possible; this bitter knowledge hurt him the most.

That morning he had slept long into the cycle, building his strength, preparing him for the night ahead. Now he would become nocturnal for the duration of the mission, as was characteristic of the Narlakai. Fortunately, having been born during the height of the winter season, his night vision served him well on such sorties. At dawn the Narlakai retreated into the cracked earth away from the hurtful rays of the sun, though come dusk they spread like a plague wind across the land. Each measured two paces in width and nearly three in height when at their fiercest, but they were semi-gaseous creatures ever changing in form. Coupled with the length of their tendrils, it was almost impossible for a Freylarkin to fly over one unmolested, but they had their weaknesses too. They burned away like ash cast into a strong wind when exposed to intense light, and were slow to move; only their whip-like tendrils possessed any form of agility. In order to track their ponderous movements he would need eyes on them; this was not possible during the waking cycles. Since they left no discernible tracks, he would need to spy on them through the void of night, when they were predominantly active, to gain any meaningful insights regarding their movements. Yet there was too much ground to cover for a single Freylarkin alone. He would need allies and he knew well those he could turn to for help; his lupine brethren would answer his call.

Before he could commence scouting Narlakai movements, however, he first needed to inform The Blade Lord of his location. For this he required the willing and able assistance of a Sky-Skitter. The black, sleek corvids were common throughout Narlak and made their homes amongst the black twisted copses, which dotted the uninviting landscape, one of which he spied less than two hundred paces from his location; with any luck a Sky-Skitter nest would be present. Altering his course, he promptly headed towards the copse in search of his first ally. Once his message was sent, he would turn his attention towards his lupine brethren to enlist their aid for the task ahead.

The copse was black, like burnt wood; the perfect camouflage to go unnoticed in such a bleak and hostile environment, since it effortlessly melted into the background as just another blot on the landscape. He approached the thicket with caution, sliding his right hand towards the sheath strapped to the underside of his left arm. Slowly he eased one of the knives from its home in readiness; with so little cover throughout Narlak it was unlikely that the copse would be devoid of inhabitants, most of which would no doubt be hostile. Unwilling to prove him wrong, two sets of yellow eyes promptly winked into being from the depths of the copse. Although small at first, the eyes quickly grew in size as their owners closed the distance to his position. Both were fixed intently upon him, refusing utterly to blink; they were hunter's eyes, stalking their prey. He recognised their shape, colour and the way in which the eyes subtly moved as they assessed their target. Remaining steadfast, he slid the knife back into its sheath then strode confidently towards his onlookers all the while fixing them with his own unflinching gaze. Upon reaching the edge of the thicket, he rose to his full height and stood resolute before the hunters. For some time the eyes held fast; they maintained their position in response to his bold move, which was no doubt unexpected. Most would have run, only to be caught and torn asunder, but he knew better than to attempt to outrun the pair. To remain unyielding, despite his numerical disadvantage, was to command respect. To flaunt confidence was to suppress any stench of fear his attackers might seek out. He had played the game before, many a time in fact, and was yet to lose; he had no intention of bucking that trend. The eyes continued to regard him from the darkness of the copse, yet they were unable to detect any weakness in him; this was a fight his audience did not relish. Time continued to pass. Their battle was a silent one, played out in the mind without ever exchanging physical blows. The wounded did not survive long in Narlak, thus its predatory inhabitants were careful to choose their battles wisely. Winning only a minor victory was to court the release of one's soul by scavengers lying in wait to finish off the scraps; a minor victory was no victory at all, not in Narlak. Hunter assessed prey, and prey slowly became hunter. Finally, concluding their business, his would-be attackers slowly revealed themselves proper, with their heads hung low in respect, before lying down submissively in front of him entirely accepting of their unknown fate. Both were adolescent dire wolves with fur darker than a winter's night, experienced in the hunt yet short in the tooth. Either could have laid him low on a good cycle, but neither had wanted to test that theory; they had been taught well by their pack leader. Better to concede to a potentially superior foe and seek mercy, than to risk debilitating injury trying to defy unfavourable odds of success. Playing the role of the dominant alpha male, he stared at the pair intently for some time feigning a measured response to their downcast demeanour. Although he had no intention of bringing any harm to the pair, he needed to ensure that his dominance over them was unquestioned. Once he was satisfied with their complete obedience, he used his ability to open a conduit between his mind and theirs.

'I am Lothnar, your new master. Stand before me.' he communicated telepathically to the pair.

Immediately both dire wolves stood to attention. With their minds still linked, he could interpret their obvious confusion at being in communication with a Strider; a concept they used to label the Freylarkai. Although their minds were less evolved than his own, they were nonetheless still capable of basic thought, which meant he could converse with them on a rudimentary level. His previous dealings with other breeds of lupines meant that he already possessed adequate understanding of their mental architecture to be able to issue them with basic commands. Moments prior to their confrontation he was a single scout, let loose along the borderlands. Now he commanded two dire wolves. Twenty cycles from now, he would run the entire pack.

'Kirika is this really necessary?' asked Rayna for the third time since they arrived at the Tri-Spires that morning.

'Yes, now keep still.' she said, slightly impatiently. 'It is important that we get this right. You are not Alarielle and the people need to understand that. You cannot continue to roam Freylar in her past attire. Besides, is that how The Guardian would dress?' she continued with a smile.

'Oh please, stop with The Guardian thing already. I fought a dog and ultimately lost.' countered Rayna in her characteristic playful manner.

Rayna had a way of cutting to the heart of any matter with inoffensive plain talk; unlike herself, carefully measuring every decision, then questioning her actions long afterwards. Rayna was quick to decide and resolute in her decision making. She envied the simplicity of Rayna's head on approach to life, and hoped that that infectious demeanour would influence her in adopting a similar attitude going forwards. Marcus had often encouraged her to speak her mind more frequently, and to impose her authority over the lower ranking Blades, though she often felt uncomfortable doing so. It was high time she stepped out of Aleska's shadow and played a more prominent role on the council; perhaps spending more time with Rayna would bolster her own confidence.

'Regardless of your own perception of the events, the Freylarkai have already started gossiping and most have interpreted your arrival very differently. Some, dare I say, even revere you!'

'Larissa, please tell me that you don't believe this nonsense?' asked Rayna imploringly of the room's third occupant.

'All I know for certain is that if this new dress of yours is to look the part, then you need to remain still...Guardian!' mumbled Larissa sternly whilst struggling to maintain her bite on a number of dressmaker's pins.

Larissa was renowned amongst the inhabitants of the Tri-Spires for her mastery of the art of dressmaking. Larissa had insisted, therefore, that nobody but herself would tailor new attire for Rayna. She had gladly accepted Larissa's offer and was adamant that Rayna cast aside all ties to Alarielle in order to ensure that the public, and Nathaniel for that matter, did not confuse the two. Rayna's demeanour was entirely different to Alarielle's, therefore she had decided that Rayna's clothing would follow suit. Alarielle was ever the optimist, hopeful that all would right itself in time. Rayna, on the other hand, had lived a traumatic life, evidenced by what she had already witnessed first-hand through her second sight. Yet despite the personal hardships suffered, Rayna's determination had seen her overcome adversity; her new appearance would reflect that same determination and in doing so wrong foot her doubters. Moreover beauty was a weapon itself, often capable of distracting the beholder. It was foolish to blunt weapons of subterfuge if one clearly possessed them; she knew well this power of distraction, though she often lacked the confidence required to maximise its true potential.

'Mirielle entrusted me with such matters regarding your personal development, therefore on this particular occasion you have very little say over the matter.' she said with a beaming smile and a quick raise of her eyebrows, emphasising the futility of Rayna's protests.

'Oh very well, fine. Just don't make me look like a pretentious little girl blinded by current fashion trends, OK?!' conceded Rayna, defeated by her complete lack of immediate support.

'Believe me, that is far from what I have envisaged.' she replied somewhat easing Rayna's obvious concerns. 'I am aiming for a bold, sassy and unyielding look. You will distract weaker minded opponents, whilst ensuring that those more experienced realise that you are not to be taken lightly.'

Rayna groaned in response; she was clearly uncomfortable with the dress being tailored for her, not surprising given her abrupt change of gender. It was hard to think of Rayna as a male, though there were numerous signs within her mannerisms which told tale of her past. She wondered how she herself would have coped with such radical change; likely not nearly as well as the would-be Blade Aspirant standing before her now.

'Far be it from me to question your better judgement Kirika. Besides, I'm hardly qualified to comment otherwise.' said Rayna, before smiling weakly.

'I suppose not.' she replied, still smiling warmly. 'Larissa is the best dressmaker in Freylar, she will not disappoint either one of us.'

'Well, I might make an exception just for you Rayna if you do not stop fidgeting.' said Larissa, whose voice still mumbled behind a mouthful of dressmaker's pins. 'Now keep still else I may decide to stick one of these pins into you!'

'Larissa informed me that the first of your new dresses will be ready tomorrow morning. We can stop by early before you commence your training in the arena.' said Kirika tugging mercilessly at her dark red hair.

She sat in front of a plain wooden dressing table to the side of her bed, looking at the stranger staring vacuously back at her from the dresser's mirror. Since her arrival in Freylar this was the first time she had really taken stock of her new appearance. Kirika fiddled with her hair, attempting to discern the perfect style to compliment her new attire. It was a strange experience; no one had ever waited on her before. She had always been entirely self-sufficient, except on the rare occasions when she bit off more than she could chew. Looking now in detail at her new face, nothing remained of the Callum she used to be. Her once hazel-green eyes were now a deep brown-orange and her eyebrows, previously thick dark brown, now traced thinner dark red lines. The hard jaw line she had known all her life had been completely softened and her new dainty ears tapered and sported ridges. There was nothing familiar about the female staring back from the tarnished mirror. Visually, the person she had once been was now entirely lost to her, replaced by the face of another. Whilst those now closest to her had been supportive of her inherited form – after the initial shock of her arrival at least – Lothnar's words still occupied space in her mind, reminding her of the stark truth; she was a body thief, and no amount of kind understanding words would alter the fact. She had claimed ownership over the body of another, a fact that still sat uneasy with her. She supposed that in time others like Lothnar might become more accepting of her predicament. Perhaps she would even find solace as Alarielle's inadvertent successor.

'There, that is the one.' said Kirika, having finally settled on a style for her hair. 'You do not see many side pony tails in Freylar, yet it creates a flattering finished look.'

Kirika continued to comment on her handiwork, and muttered something about a braid, though the words seemed muffled and distant. Her thoughts returned to the darkness clawing incessantly at the periphery of her mind; repressed memories Kirika had called them. Whatever their definition, they preyed on her distraction, waiting for such times to launch their continued assault on her idle psyche. As she continued to stare blankly into the mirror she felt her new reality slipping away, allowing her dark past to return to the fore, bringing with it fresh heinous acts of human barbarism.

Remaining concealed, within the shadow of the dilapidated office unit, he watched the three Peacekeepers scornfully as they chatted loudly amongst themselves, bragging over their newly captured prey. Occasionally one would kick the lumpy black sack laid across the pavement on which they were gathered; he presumed this to be the marksman who had downed the panicked woman. All it would take was a rifle and three rounds to right the injustice playing out before him, yet he had neither the weapon nor the likely skill required to wield it effectively. Instead, he had only his hatred and that alone would not see the vengeance, which the prone woman so rightly deserved, exacted. It was some time before one of the familiar windowless boxy carriages finally rolled into view, and all the while the three huntsmen continued to gloat amongst themselves. The same masked individual needlessly continued to stick his boot into the prone body of the woman cocooned within the sack. Each dull thud of the Peacekeeper's boot made his stomach churn in disgust, further increasing his choler. The dark place which he so desperately sought to evade clawed at the edge of his mind, intent on flooding his thoughts with murder and death. The darkness craved retribution, yet gave no thought to the consequences of such action. He imagined mercilessly strangling the masked assailant's neck with the raw strength of his hands, crushing his larynx whilst savouring his death whisper. Then his thoughts turned darker still, as he caved in the officer's mask by repeatedly pummelling it with the unforgiving heels of his hands. He imagined smirking sardonically as fluids drained from the extremities of the expressionless mask. Before his mind could stray further into the realm of evil, the sack suddenly began to twitch violently as if to suggest the woman within was experiencing spasms or convulsions. Ordinarily the neurological disrupters contained within each stun rifle round were sufficient to facilitate total capture of one's target, however, he had seen instances before where the effectiveness of the toxin had been reduced or even negated entirely; whatever the cause of the woman's reprieve, she was clearly coming round and in pain. For a brief moment the three Peacekeepers seemed somewhat caught off-guard by the unexpected turn of events; it suggested to him that perhaps none had encountered the scenario before. The marksman was the first to react by unshouldering their rifle. In a single deft move they pulled the butt of the weapon in close to their right shoulder, sighting down the length of its black metal barrel. The hunter was primed and ready to unload a second round into the woman who was obviously unaware of her assailants, sacked as she was. Before a shot could be fired, the Peacekeeper who reported the capture slid his right hand across the top of the barrel of the marksman's weapon. The intervening Peacekeeper then gently pushed down on the weapon, prompting an abrupt look of contempt from the marksman; he supposed the woman's masked benefactor held authority over the others. But was this indeed an act of mercy he wondered. The woman had already sustained several injuries, both from her initial impact with the adjacent wall and from the malicious boot of the marksman; perhaps the true act of mercy, therefore, was indeed to stun her a second time. He had stared into the unblinking eyes of stunned victims before and recalled well the anguish of those blank stares he had played witness to; perhaps one still felt pain in their paralysed state he thought angrily. Regardless of the facts unknown to him, the question was quickly rendered moot as the one-time benefactor pulled a silenced hand gun from its holster strapped to their left thigh, then proceeded to shoot the woman three times in the head region. Immediately the body of the cocooned woman went slack, her life coldly snatched from her in a mere instant. The other Peacekeepers nodded in turn to one another, signifying that the action they had just witnessed was acceptable to them. This sickened him further, causing his thoughts to descend entirely into darkness, as he continued to lie on the cold hard floor. His muscles tightened and a fresh shot of adrenaline flooded his system, beckoning him into action, then his stomach groaned painfully once again reminding him of his original purpose in the metropolis. Shortly after the heinous crime the summoned carriage rolled slowly into view, tasked with its regular purpose of relocating members of the Shadow class. Breaks squealed as the boxy mobile prison lazily slowed to an eventual halt, ready to receive additional cargo. Thick metal doors to the rear of the container swung open violently, disgorging two heavily armoured Peacekeepers. Each was armed with a shock rifle; cruel weapons designed to pacify targets whilst simultaneously making an example of them. These awful instruments were pure terror weapons; their primary purpose was to dispel mobs, which they achieved by passing an electrical current through their victims causing their bodies to violently spasm. This served as a stark warning to onlookers, whilst completely neutralising their targets. He had seen such weapons used before and recalled the characteristic clenched teeth and streaming tear ducts of their victims; some even bit through their lower lip, or worse still sheared their tongue clean off, as the excruciating agony of the electrical current discharged by the shock rifles caused them to bite down hard. Despite her obvious death, the armoured Peacekeepers trained their rifles on their objective as they assessed its threat level. Satisfied that the corpse would offer them no resistance, both shouldered their rifles then dragged the body of the dead woman between them, towards the back of the transport, holding her at either end. The middle of the sack scraped along the floor like sandpaper. With zero compassion they tossed the black sack into the back of the transport; it made a muffled thud upon connecting with the interior of the vehicle. Each then mounted the vehicle in turn before slamming the solid metal doors behind them with crude finality. The sound of the doors slamming shut echoed around the empty junction cutting through him, jarring his very being. The awful sound signified an end to the woman's uncaring fate, and with it etched the travesty forever in the dark recesses of his soul.

Rayna flinched abruptly. Startled, she lost grip on the comb she had been using; it clattered across the wooden floor noisily. Rayna's face was pale, even for a light bringer, and tiny beads of sweat had started to appear on the nape of her neck. Her composure was entirely wooden, as though all traces of her personality had been stripped away revealing the stark foundations of Rayna's very being.

'Are you OK Rayna? Did I pull too hard?' she asked, concerned that perhaps she had been a little too rough with her hair dressing whilst absentmindedly caught up in the moment of an amateur would-be stylist.

'I err...experienced another repressed memory. Actually, it was a continuation of the last one.' said Rayna.

She saw colour slowly return to Rayna's face; the initial shock of her traumatic reverie was passing, allowing her true self to return to the fore. It was always disconcerting to see a light bringer in anguish, for the soft glow of their ochre skin was always the first thing to diminish.

'How bad was it?' she asked out of concern for Rayna's wellbeing.

'Enough that I would happily choose to forget it, given the choice. It would seem that your earlier diagnosis of my condition was unerringly accurate.' explained Rayna.

She sighed in response; she had hoped that, having identified the reason for the episodes, perhaps they would slowly relent – particularly now that Rayna was consciously aware of what was happening to her. Sadly, this appeared not to be the case. If anything, the episodes were increasing in their frequency. She considered that perhaps Rayna's body was looking to expel the evil deep-rooted recollections of her past, as though trying to fight off an infection or a foreign substance which did not belong.

'How am I supposed to get past this Kirika?' asked Rayna imploringly.

'That, I do not know. I know only that you will...in time.' she replied, offering the reflection in the mirror a weak smile as she pressed her hands reassuringly to the side of Rayna's arms. 'Perhaps the silent voices of your past need to be heard now, maybe only then can you truly become free of them.'

'Or perhaps their cacophony will drive me to despair.' replied Rayna, dejectedly.

Despite identifying the probable cause as to why Rayna was being haunted by her dark past, she possessed no means by which to prevent the episodes from occurring again. They had lain dormant, silently following their host from one life into the next. Now they wished to be heard, and would not do so quietly. Rarely did she feel such helplessness, but this was the past; it could not be undone, only endured. Time was ever the great healer, however, and in time Rayna's mental wounds would mend. Although their scars would never fade entirely, the impact of her past demons would soften with the distance that only time could bring.

'Your determination will see that you endure them. Only then will you be able to shed the last vestiges of your former life which still cling to your soul.' she reasoned.

'But I don't want to endure them Kirika. I'm concerned that they will have had a negative effect on my soul by the time they have run their course.'

'Yet you have experienced much adversity throughout your former life, which you vividly recall. How is it that you managed those events without drowning in despair?' she asked flatly.

Rayna considered the question intensely for a while, then stood up abruptly and turned to face her. Rayna's colour had returned fully and she looked as though a great mental weight had been lifted from her. Rayna had the same defiant look about her which she had observed beneath the arena during the altercation with Lothnar prior to his recent departure.

'I took the raw emotion of those events and used them to fuel my determination to succeed.' proclaimed Rayna. 'I've been angsting, needlessly, over my forgotten past. As of tomorrow, when I step into that arena for the first time, I will once again channel my darker emotions and bend them to my submission; I will fashion an invisible blade from them, a wraith blade, and use it to best my opponents.'

She beamed at the sudden uplift in Rayna's demeanour. Her words had reignited the fire within Rayna's soul which had dwindled since their return from Larissa's; she had stoked that fire and in doing so the raw determination of Rayna's being had surfaced to the fore once again. This was the Rayna she admired, the one who would silence the venomous tongues of her doubters. Yet there was more to her joyous smile than the simple satisfaction of contributing towards Rayna's mental resurgence; her words had given another true impetus, and in doing so had bolstered her own self-confidence. If she could continue this trend then perhaps she could indeed step out from Aleska's shadow.

TEN
Dust

It was first light when they reached Larissa's. Kirika had been adamant that they make an early start so as not to keep Nathaniel waiting; she got the impression that to show The Teacher a lack of respect in the arena, was to court his wrath. She had no intention of falling short of what was expected of her, especially during her first time in the arena, so she kept pace with Kirika as they hurried towards the Tri-Spires. She had loathed the prospect of turning up for her first cycle of combat training neatly turned out in new attire, however, Kirika had made her thoughts abundantly clear on the matter. Recognising the futility of debating the subject further with her scrying mentor, she had reluctantly conceded the point hoping that Kirika was indeed correct in her assessment.

Upon arriving at Larissa's, neither Freylarkin wasted any time dressing her in her new outfit. Kirika busied herself adjusting buckled leather-like straps whilst Larissa made a multitude of minor adjustments to her new dress, ensuring it drew in correctly round the back. She felt immediately uncomfortable in her new outfit, though not in the physical sense. Instead it was more a feeling of embarrassment due to the amount of skin the dress exposed, yet she was assured by Kirika of its benefits. The ability to distract an opponent's attention, no matter how briefly, combined with less restricted movement would serve her well. She could appreciate the logic behind Kirika's reasoning, though she was certain those were not the only criteria for her chosen look. Kirika was also right in that she needed to put some distance between herself and the memory of Alarielle; if she was to become a citizen of Freylar in her own right, she would need to sever ties with her lingering ghost. Regardless of Kirika's motives, the dress was comfortable enough. In time she would learn to feel more at ease with her appearance, besides she had more pressing concerns over the length of her dress. This would be the first time that the Freylarkai public would see her fully as her reborn self; there would be no hiding who or what she was.

'Perfect!' said Kirika with a beaming smile across her face. 'As always Larissa, you outshine all others in your trade.'

Larissa stepped out from behind her and moved to stand alongside Kirika. There Larissa paused for a moment to view her work fully before passing any kind of judgement over her labours. She felt like the main exhibit in an art exhibition, being carefully scrutinised by her viewing public. Larissa was analysing the minutiae of her new dress, reviewing every detail, assuring herself that it was free of any flaws. It was some time until Larissa moved to speak, ready to pass final judgement over her latest work.

'Yes, I believe we are done here.' said Larissa finally. 'I have your precise measurements now Rayna, so you will be able to collect the remainder of your garments eight cycles from now. Should you need any alterations then please visit me again. You are always welcome.'

'Thank you Larissa for both your patience and skill.' she said. 'I appreciate your efforts, even if perhaps my body language says otherwise.'

Larissa smiled in response to her candid words then nodded in affirmation. It struck her that a Freylarkin of

Larissa's disposition appreciated honest praise as opposed to the faux jubilations of those following the latest fashion trends, all eager to discard their own individuality in the pursuit of apparent normality.

After the fitting they said farewell to Larissa and headed immediately for the arena. The enormous structure was surrounded by a maze of outbuildings and alleys; this proved to be no challenge for Kirika, who deftly navigated them through the network of vendors' stalls, food stores, armourers and other such structures, all of which began to burst into life as morning continued to break. They picked their way through the outlying structures of the arena. Her ears burned with interest as she caught fragments of the audible babble of their onlookers. Each change of course brought with it a renewed tirade of gossip; everyone, it seemed, stopped to pass judgement on them – her in particular – whilst they snaked their way towards the arena. Alarielle, outworlder, Rayna, The Guardian, thief, deity; all were words she frequently picked out from the background chatter whilst struggling to keep pace with Kirika's swift progress.

'Continue down this path and you will enter the arena via the west gate.' said Kirika before coming to an abrupt halt.

'You mean you're not coming with me?' she asked, suddenly feeling quite nervous.

'Sadly I cannot. I have duties to perform which I have neglected these past few cycles.' said Kirika. 'I have enjoyed our recent time together, though I must return now to the Tri-Spires.'

The prospect of being abandoned to discover her fate alone within the arena left her feeling vulnerable. Since arriving in Freylar, she had been shepherded by Nathaniel and Kirika who had been her ever-present entourage. Now the inevitable moment had come when she would be required to stand alone and prove her worth. Taking a deep breath, she steeled herself for what was to come and summoned forth her unrelenting determination to succeed. The current cycle would herald the first of many trials to come. Now was her time to achieve something meaningful with the new life she had been gifted; a second chance.

'Get up!' he shouted.

He scraped his boot towards the Aspirant, kicking grit and dust from the arena floor into their now matted hair. He had no desire to mock Rayna's efforts, however, the simple truth was that she lacked experience and needed to be up-skilled within a short timeframe in order to meet Lothnar's challenge. He had therefore decided that intensive training was the key to developing Rayna's abilities quickly; her fierce determination would either see her rise to the enormous challenge or it would falter, like the dying embers of a used hearth. Ordinarily he found the technique fruitless, though with Rayna's disposition, being as it was, and elements of Alarielle's former muscle memory, the chances of success increased dramatically. Besides, time was not their friend. Lothnar would mean to test Rayna this pass at the Trials; that left them with only two seasons for training. It was not enough time to complete Rayna's training, and yet it would have to be. Rayna would be required to train every cycle until that time. Hers was a difficult path ahead, but Rayna was his student and he would not abandon her to tread that path alone. If Rayna failed, then he would fail with her. He hoped, with all his soul, that they would make the journey successfully, and in doing so earn the respect they both deserved.

'Get up,' he shouted for a second time, 'Pick up the weapons you so carelessly dropped.'

Slowly Rayna pushed herself off the arena floor; a thin line of blood dropped from her mouth onto the ground as she raised her head. Rayna's lower lip was split open where he had struck her cleanly with the flat of his wide practice blade. The blow was not hard, but enough to give Rayna cause for thought once she recovered from her bewildered state. Rayna's dress was already attracting a fine layer of dust; an improvement he thought. When she had first entered the arena that morning he was momentarily caught off guard by her raw appeal unleashed; Kirika had known exactly how to reinvent his former daughter, providing Rayna with her own unique visual identity. She was dressed in a knee-length, dark red, halter-neck dress, over which she wore a long, fitted, low-cut, sleeveless military jacket of earthy green hues which complemented her hair. The dress was pleated from the waist down, allowing freedom of movement. A pair of long buckled boots rose above her knees and her arms were almost entirely bare, though a good set of vambraces would easily remedy that. Kirika had chosen well; Rayna's tailored combat attire would lend itself well to the light armour he had in mind for her. Now, though, her appearance was ragged, as sweat glistened across her ochre skin causing her fiery red hair and dust from the arena floor to cling to her body. It was a good look, in his opinion at least, and one which appropriately complimented her raw determination. The art of distraction, which Kirika had obviously engineered with

Rayna's selected attire, was not lost on him; her brother Aspirants would find her a tough opponent to manage.

'How am I supposed to defend myself if you do not show me how?' said Rayna in a strained and riled tone.

'Good. More questions. A positive sign, suggesting that you are not done just yet.' said Nathaniel sardonically. 'Now, pick up your blades. Your worst mistake was releasing your grip on them. If you think you are ready to face opponents unarmed, you are sorely mistaken.'

He had selected two matched blades for her, believing them to be a good fit for her disposition. This was a dangerous decision, since it completely opposed the stance his daughter had favoured, with shield in hand. Rayna was not Alarielle though, and forcing her to fight against her body's natural inclination, in addition to her opponent, was not wise. The trade-off, however, was that she would sacrifice balance and, more importantly, some of her body's muscle memory conditioning. Despite these undesirable losses, she would gain access to a greater number of attack and defence options; this would help increase her unpredictability and reduce her opponents' ability to read her in battle. Rayna was a quick and decisive thinker, capable of responding in unexpected ways. She reacted well to changing circumstances, thus he felt confident training her in a more unorthodox style of combat. If she was to entertain any hope of lasting in a fight against Lothnar, she needed to be unpredictable. Rayna could not hope to rival the martial prowess of a Blade Paladin, at least not in the time available to them. This was therefore her best option, in his mind, but he needed to develop her skills fast.

'You still haven't answered my question.' said Rayna as she righted herself fully before turning to reclaim her practice blades.

As Rayna carelessly began to turn away he rapidly broke into a sprint directly towards her, with astonishing speed, like an arrow released from its bow. He contacted with Rayna's back, driving his shoulder in hard, launching her forwards a good couple of paces before she crashed awkwardly onto the floor of the arena. The ambient sound of clashing blades partially abated, as Blades of varying rank close by temporarily ceased sparring to observe Nathaniel's latest sermon. Rayna had hit the ground hard, and for a time appeared not to move at all. A single Blade Aspirant, named Anika, sparring closest to Rayna's point of impact moved to assist, though he quickly raised his left hand denying her the chance of offering compassion to her fallen Blade sister. He studied Rayna's prone body intently for signs of breath; it was not long before her torso began to heave heavily again.

'You will learn the lessons I teach, in the order in which I practice them.' he proclaimed. 'Never turn your back on your opponent!'

Rayna slowly rolled onto her back. She lay there silently for a moment, before quietly laughing to herself. Anika promptly turned to face him with a confused look, failing to comprehend why one would find being knocked to the ground in such a brutal manner amusing. Nathaniel chose not to respond to either Aspirant; instead he continued to fix his scrutinising gaze upon Rayna.

'At least I didn't drop both of my practice blades this time.' said Rayna light-heartedly, interrupting her own personal amusement.

'Hold onto that humour of yours. You will need it.' he retorted.

Rayna rose once more to her feet. Her right cheek had taken a hard knock and was already beginning to swell. The vibrant dress Rayna had entered the arena with was now covered with grit and dust from the arena floor, yet her unkempt appearance had done nothing to diminish the fire within her. The hard stare of Rayna's eyes cut directly into his soul, confirming that he had succeeded in agitating her fiery determination. It struck him then that Rayna thrived on being downtrodden. Attempts to subjugate her only fuelled her desire for vengeance, yet he observed that Rayna also possessed restraint. Rayna was happy to endure his sermons, so it seemed, whilst using the opportunity to study both his craft and his behaviour. Rayna's eyes had betrayed her motives, a painful lesson he would eventually teach her. For now though, he was pleased with Rayna's initial progress. Ordinarily he chose not to begin his teachings in such a harsh and brutal manner, but time was against them and Rayna needed rapid motivation; besides she was good for it, she was a survivor and she would endure. Slowly Rayna retrieved the weapons she had dropped earlier; this time she made a point of keeping him within her field of vision whilst collecting her abandoned blades. Having retrieved her weapons, Rayna advanced towards him stopping abruptly a few paces short of where he stood. Her lower lip was still bleeding from the earlier fall.

'May I ask what weapons these are, and more specifically why you selected them for me?' asked Rayna.

'That is a falchion.' he said pointing to her left blade. 'Typically one would not fight with two of these weapons, though you are quick to react which will lend itself towards this unconventional arrangement.'

'I don't understand Nathaniel,' replied Rayna. 'I will already be at a significant disadvantage when I receive Lothnar's challenge. Why seek to handicap me further with unconventional battle doctrine.'

'Look around you,' he said, offering a brief glance towards the other low ranking Blades sparring throughout the arena. 'What is it you see, or rather more importantly what is it you do not see?'

Rayna breathed deeply, seeking to regain some of her composure, before surveying the arena as asked of her. He watched with interest as Rayna methodically studied her fellow Aspirants, attempting to detect the abnormality of which he cryptically spoke. After reviewing them each in turn, she directed her gaze towards Anika who had yet to resume her sparring since Rayna's last encounter with the arena floor. Rayna's gaze lingered for some time, becoming more intense the longer she observed. Anika began to fidget uncomfortably; she was clearly nervous being the subject of Rayna's prolonged study.

'What is it you see?' asked Anika in an uncertain tone, unsure as to whether she had committed a faux pas.

'Variation in armaments, specifically a complete lack thereof.' replied Rayna turning to face him once more.

'Good.' he replied. 'At least you can observe, if not fight.'

Rayna ignored his condescending response to her successful observations. Instead she pressed her line of questioning, eager to understand his reasoning.

'You believe that if I fight differently to the other Aspirants, I will have an advantage.' suggested Rayna.

'Nearly all Blade Aspirants and Novices are trained to wield a sword and shield, in addition to being instructed in the use of a bow. There are few exceptions to this. Adepts further their studies and are permitted to indulge in the use of other armaments should they choose to do so. Typically when one reaches the rank of Master or Mistress, a Blade will have settled on one or two weapons, subject to their ability, disposition and personal preference. The use of dual falchions is exceptionally rare and to my knowledge no current Freylarkin actively practices the technique. Although I did not instruct Lothnar, like all The Blades he too spars in this arena albeit less frequently. His typical opponents therefore, are those whom you see before you.'

'So I am to fight in a style unfamiliar to him?' she asked.

'Correct. You cannot realistically hope to match his martial prowess in the time available to us, so we must adopt a different strategy...something unexpected.' he continued. 'You have experienced a life of hardship prior to coming here, relying on your determination and ability to adapt in order to survive. You react well to changing circumstances, and that is how you will fight. You will fight reactively; using one blade to turn your opponent's, thus creating opportunities. When attacking, you will be feinting to draw your opponents in for the reaction and riposte.'

Raya paused for thought. Rather than simply accepting his judgement, she considered all he had said carefully; she was a different breed to the somewhat mindless, though willing, Aspirants he was typically charged with. In a way Rayna reminded him of Marcus; efficiently considering the facts presented and the best logical course of action.

Marcus made decisions swiftly and was resolute in doing so; he worked on the principle that it was impossible to make correct decisions each and every time, and so he did not waste time trying. Marcus made strong decisions and The Blades followed their Blade Lord diligently, irrespective of their personal feelings. Few ever challenged Marcus. Typically only members of the ruling council, Ragnar and he himself dared offer counsel to the contrary on the rare occasions it was actually required. The Blades held a deep respect for The Blade Lord. Although Marcus still had many tens of passes left in him, Marcus had often confided in him that he needed to identify a suitable successor who could be groomed as his eventual replacement. Finding a worthy successor, however, would be an extremely difficult task. In order to lead The Blades effectively, Marcus believed strongly in doing so from the front line; Marcus was not a back-seat commander, though such practices placed The Blade Lord firmly in the firing line. For that reason Marcus had insisted that he be ever vigilant in the search for a suitable candidate, one capable of succeeding him when the time eventually came. He hoped dearly that such a time would never come to pass, though he was not blind to the fact that all things changed in time.

'Very well, I see the wisdom in your counsel. Now, how about you show me...Teacher...as opposed to further motivating me through hardship.' replied Rayna. 'I can't very well react to your movements if my face is all bloodied up.' she continued before spitting a small amount of blood onto the arena floor.

He smiled warmly in response to Rayna's brazen outburst; in truth he had expected this moment to come some cycles later, if indeed it were to come at all. Most of his Aspirants were timid things, more often than not frightened into silent obedience by his reputation as a harsh task master in the arena; some even referred to the arena as his proving ground. Since the release of his wife's soul, his daughter and the arena were his only true sources of happiness. He was dedicated to the proper upbringing of his daughter and the correct training of his Aspirants, Novices and Adepts. When a Blade in his charge finally attained the rank of Master or Mistress, and concluded their training under him, they tended to follow their own path – though most remained loyal to him and his teachings thereafter. He found it hugely rewarding helping his students to develop their combat ability and watching them grow, until the cycle finally came when they would come into their own as true defenders of Freylar and forge their own reputations according to their future endeavours. With the untimely release of Alarielle's soul, there was now a massive void in his world. He no longer felt as he once did. Part of his soul had become numb, lost forever along with his daughter. For the second time, his world had been drained of colour in a single instant, yet before him now stood another who could paint it vividly once more. Rayna was clearly not his daughter, and Kirika's influence over Rayna's appearance had punctuated that fact, but despite this he still felt something paternal manifesting in his relationship with her. Still, he could not allow for such feelings to interfere with Rayna's training and development. He would train Rayna hard, as he had with his own daughter, perhaps even more so given the unique circumstances.

'I see no need to beat you down further at this time Rayna,' he said. 'I can see that you are now ready to commit to your studies. Come close so that I can attend to your face.'

'There is no need. I will wear my lessons as do you those of your students.' she replied, pointing the sharp end of her right falchion towards his exposed left arm.

'You will do no such thing, for there is no need. I will not have Kirika's efforts wasted on my account. You will need your feminine wiles if you are to fully exploit Lothnar's weaknesses.' he said.

'That particular skill set is entirely alien to me. It is one I am not keen to practice I can assure you, however, having been on the receiving end I can appreciate the merits of having the option available.' replied Rayna.

Rayna stepped towards him, though she maintained her grip on both falchions as per his earlier lesson. She was a quick learner; Rayna's ability to absorb and retain information would aid their cause significantly. Whilst he possessed great patience with his students, the prospect of not having to repeat himself appealed greatly. He raised the tips of his fingers to her swollen face, touching them against her lip and right cheek where the damage was greatest. The blood trickling from her split lip had begun to coagulate around the wound and her cheek was bruising nicely, with blood spots beginning to permeate the broken skin. The wounds were superficial; intended more to annoy than cause any real pain. Repairing such wounds scarcely required any effort on his part, though he was always thorough in his work and as such treated each wound with the same degree of attention. Over the passes he had learned to control his ability masterfully, however, it was not always so. During his youth he had shouldered the burden of several mishaps, and even lost a number of grievously wounded patients who were beyond his level of skill at the time. It was a painful period of his development, one which taught him well the lesson that not all souls could be saved; he was no god of life and death, nor would he ever be. There would always be wounds too severe, even for his ability, to mend. Likewise, there would always be enemies whose skill would surpass his own. He knew his limits, more importantly he respected them.

'You will experience a burning sensation, though it will quickly pass.' he said.

'Burning? Why would...' Rayna replied, commencing a fresh line of enquiry before her words were abruptly cut short by the pain he had pre-warned her of.

Rayna twitched and groaned as the broken skin of her cheek renewed itself promptly at his command. He needed only to visualise the wound re-growing and knitting itself back together in his mind before it was actually so. The only remaining evidence of there ever having been any wounds to Rayna's face were the spots of blood on her cheek, which he wiped clean with the back of his right hand. The coagulated blood on her lip fell to the ground of its own accord, losing all purchase on the freshly renewed skin of her lip. Once again the ochre skin of Rayna's face began to glow softly, signalling the successful completion of his work. He brushed the thumb of his right hand across the renewed skin of her lip, ensuring that no irregularities were present, after which he withdrew his hands, folding them across his chest. Rayna pursed her lips then bit her lower lip gently, confirming the absence of any pain. She twitched her right eye too, again looking for signs of pain which were no longer present.

'That's incredible!' said Rayna.

'Many Freylarkin possess an ability, all of which are impressive in their own right.'

'So you're saying that not every Freylarkin possesses an ability?' Rayna asked.

'Correct.' he replied. 'Some have speculated that all Freylarkin have the potential, but that not all have learnt to manifest their inherent ability.

'So...I will have to learn how to manifest those of a light bringer despite Alarielle's previous capability?' Rayna questioned.

'In all likelihood yes.' he replied. 'Though do not concern yourself with such thoughts just yet. For the time being at least, you have more pressing concerns, such as how to wield those weapons of yours.' He smiled wryly before continuing, 'I am not referring to the dual falchions you hold either.'

Rayna smiled at his remark, clearly appreciating the dryness of his humour. Although Kirika had put some distance between Rayna and his daughter with a new look, Rayna would always possess certain characteristics which would forever remind him of his loss. Seeing her smile again caused a brief pang of pain deep within his soul, reopening the recent wound. He tried hard not reveal his inner pain, though on a subconscious level he believed that Rayna was keenly aware of the hurt she inadvertently inflicted upon him. If she was, she chose deliberately not to reveal her insight.

'Kirika will see to that aspect of my training I'm sure. Nathaniel, it is time now that you show me how to use these.' Rayna said extending her arms holding both falchions before her.

He remained perfectly still before Rayna, taking the measure of her one more time. 'This might just work.' he mused to himself.

'Indeed.' he said aloud. 'Let us begin.'

ELEVEN
Scorn

Their efforts to herd the Narlakai without being noticed had clearly failed; far from an unexpected scenario with Lothnar poking his nose around the borderlands. She cursed herself for not being able to get an exact fix on his current whereabouts, though she was confident that in time she would. Sky-Skitters subservient to Lileah's telepathic influences had alerted them to his presence; it was only a matter of time before her scrying of the airborne creatures would reveal one destined to lay eyes on his future whereabouts, which in turn would allow them to predict his movements. He would not elude their detection for long. Venturing alone across the borderlands would be his undoing. He was always too sure of himself, and the arrogance of his solitary incursion into the Narlakai borderlands proved it. To his credit Lothnar was the best scout under Marcus' command and his telepathic prowess was impressive, though his ability fell short of Lileah's own; he could do little to avert a future that she herself would help manipulate into being. She was the future's one true mistress. How pathetic that the ruling council of Freylar hunted her kind; hunted those scriers seeking to push the boundaries of their ability. How dare that bitch Mirielle decree that the development of Freylar's scriers be both stunted and closely monitored? The queen's sanctioned scriers were permitted only the briefest glimpses of both past and future; she refused to abide by restrictions imposed through fearful ignorance. Pleading for the legitimised use of what was rightfully hers to use, as she saw fit, was beneath her. She would not be dictated to by one in power looking to restrict and control her own ability. That defiance had cost her dearly. She looked scornfully at the menacing bronze mechanical claw which protruded from her left wrist where once a beautiful slender hand had been. The fully-functioning prosthetic was ornate, the result of exquisite workmanship and had far surpassed her expectations when she first had it commissioned many passes ago. And yet it was a mechanical horror, fashioned from tiny bronze gears and miniature pistons working tirelessly in unison allowing her to manipulate the curved blades which made up the claw's prosthetic's digits; it had no place being her substitute hand. The process of bonding the claw to the flesh and bone of her stump had not been an easy one, indeed the rogue shaper employed to carry out the task had warned her of the pain she would experience during the shaping. More than just simple pain, she had been forced to endure searing agony throughout the process; even her self-scrying had failed to adequately prepare her for the torment she would suffer. Still to the present cycle the flesh around the top of her wrist screamed in pain with each new twitch of her bladed claw. Rather than fight it though, she embraced the pain her claw's continued use inflicted upon her. The hurt became an ever-present reminder of what she had lost, fuelling her desire to end the one responsible for her purgatory. She would not find solace until she used her demonic hand to rip out the throat of The Blade Lord. Only then would she receive a measure of the vengeance rightfully owed to her.

Before she could dwell further on the loss of her organic hand, the muffled sound of someone casually approaching drew her attention towards the sole entrance to her chamber. Silver light spilled into the room courtesy of the approaching Freylarkin who held a short silver chain, attached to which was a small Moonstone. The Moonstone danced gracefully in lockstep with its carrier, casting its weak silver light to dance across the jagged rock contours of the chamber's walls.

'Sitting alone in the dark again?'

'It helps me to focus my thoughts. Ah, I see you have brought more of your airborne companions for me to scry.' she said, whilst trying to push the ever-present pain of her clawed hand down into the depths of her soul.

'How much longer must we wait whilst you focus your thoughts Darlia?' asked Lileah pointedly. 'Our tireless manipulations of the Narlakai now bear fruit. Is it not time we used our monstrous puppets to slaughter The Blades and exile their benevolent shaper?'

Lileah was a petite thing, short in height and daintier than most Freylarkai. Poor diet and a life of deprivation were the likely cause of her gaunt features, though neither had diminished the pretty face that hid underneath the matted hair and layers of dirt. Yet despite her fragile appearance, Lileah held only contempt for the well-to-do inhabitants of Freylar. When she first encountered the urchin, shortly after her own imposed exile, she found Lileah surviving by clinging to the edge of Freylarkin society and the scraps left in its wake. The offer of more and the chance to exact revenge against those who had disowned her gave Lileah direction; they had a common enemy it seemed, and having a formidable telepath at her side was no bad thing. Over the passes Lileah had become like a younger sister to her; the two had become very close, all the while nurturing their common need to bring about the demise of Freylar in return for their poor treatment by its inhabitants. No one cared about their wellbeing or what their futures held, yet it did not matter since they had each other to draw strength from and to lean on during the bad times. Together they were able to shrug off the hurt society offered them with its cold shoulder and complete disinterest in whether they survived the next winter or not. The inhabitants of Freylar had cast them out and for that they would pay dearly, not least their revered master of war; Marcus' soul would be torn from its moorings by the spiteful abomination that was now her left hand, only then might the pain of its existence abate.

'Patience Lileah, for we may only have this one opportunity to punish those who exiled and abandoned us. I share your loathing for the inhabitants of Freylar; though they are not to be underestimated, else they will see to our permanent demise. I see a great many paths before us Lileah. Many lead to the future we seek, yet a handful do not. The correct paths are no longer as clear to me as they once were. Something else has taken up a prominent position on the stage of my own manipulation, something not of this world. That something clouds the future, making it difficult to accurately read.'

'What is this something you speak of Darlia?' Lileah asked, narrowing her eyes.

'Alarielle!' she replied.

'Her soul was taken from her during the ambush. I know this to be true, for my mind was linked to the Narlakin who devoured Alarielle's soul. It cannot be Alarielle. You speak of the impossible!'

'And yet I do not, for I have seen her. She is that something, but she is changed...somehow.'

Lileah took a moment's pause to allow her words to sink in, before rounding on her, clearly enraged by the unforeseen state of affairs.

'Damn it!' snapped Lileah, 'That ambush was supposed to distract Lothnar, break Nathaniel and thus destabilise The Blades. Instead, what thread of destiny have we set in motion by our failed efforts?'

'Do not see this as a failure sister. Lothnar remains distracted, with revenge clouding his judgement. Nathaniel too will be preoccupied with whatever force now controls his daughter's body.' she affirmed.

'So then, we proceed as per the original plan?' enquired Lileah whose temper now seemed to abate as quickly as it had flared into being.

'Yes. Ensure that the bait is ready.' she replied. 'Now then, let me see what your Sky-Skitters have yet to...'

It was sometime after the Peacekeepers had departed before he dared to emerge from the relative safety of the shadows concealing his presence. He had been lying on the cold hard floor for some time now, and it had drawn most of the heat from his body. His mouth was dry and his neck stiff from being doubled back whilst observing the woman's horrible fate. The mobile prison, which the woman's lifeless body had been unceremoniously thrown into, had also left the scene of the crime; the only evidence of her ever having existed was the slick dark red stain on the pavement, along with the awful memory of the sickening event which burned in his mind. The scraping sound of the woman's body being dragged in its sack across the pavement, along with the ensuing dull thud as she hit the interior of the vehicle, haunted his mind. They were awful reminders of the disgusting scene and they replayed relentlessly inside his head, threatening to break his spirit. Despite the injustice he had witnessed, logic and reason had not yet abandoned him. It would be some time before the hunting party circled back to the area during their ongoing patrols; he needed to use the opportunity to continue threading his way towards Kaitlin's sanctuary. Finally mobilising his body into action, he leapt to his feet and broke into a sprint, crossing the junction via the same route as the ill-fated woman. Careful not to stumble as she had, he mounted the pavement cautiously, offering only a cursory glance to the murder scene, before resuming his rapid pace across the metropolis. As was now second nature to him he continued to evade the metropolis' artificial light, slipping between every recess and shadow available, all the while maintaining good speed. It would not be long now before he laid eyes on Kaitlin's library. He offered a silent prayer, to no one in particular, that Kaitlin would still be holed up in her literary reliquary, burning the midnight oil.

'Trouble sleeping again?' he asked peering up from behind the stack of books which were his sole source of company – until now that was.

'My past life seems determined to haunt me yet again.' Rayna replied. 'May I sit with you?'

He raised his left arm and gestured to the rocking chair opposite. Many passes ago, in happier times, his wife would often sit quietly opposite him as they read together by the light of the moon. Alarielle had shown little interest in literature, thus his nocturnal habit had become a solitary affair since the loss of his wife; it seemed strange now to share his moonlight privacy with another.

'Do you read?' he enquired softly.

'I certainly used to, prior to my arrival in Freylar that is.' replied Rayna as she eased herself into the rocking chair opposite, lifting her feet off the cold floor.

'My late wife used to read a great many books, though Alarielle never showed an interest.' he said.

'And you read...poetry?' Rayna asked, clearly intrigued by his choice of literature.

'On occasion; it was my wife's passion. I dabbled after her release as a way of honouring her memory I suppose.' he replied.

'You do indeed honour her memory Nathaniel.' said Rayna with a warm smile. 'I'm afraid that poetry is wasted on me, though your battle doctrines would aid me greatly. That is if I were able to read in this feeble light, as you so effortlessly do.'

'My eyes serve me well after dusk, unlike your own, though you are not without means to create your own light. You are a light bringer after all.' he said.

'I'm not sure the glow of my skin would be sufficient in this instance.' said Rayna.

'But there is so much more to your ability than the radiant colour of your skin. You and your kin have the ability to manifest light from within. Moreover, once manifest, you can control and manipulate the light.' he explained.

Rayna turned her hands inwards and proceeded to study her palms. She clenched her fingers tightly then released them a few times as though expecting something to appear from within the balls of her fists. Having failed with her first experiment she tried cupping her hands together before releasing them, again with the hope that something might ensue. Again nothing came to pass. He watched Rayna's experiments with growing amusement; she possessed the curiosity of a child seeking new experiences, though more often than not found new frustrations instead. It would be difficult for him to train her in the use of her ability, since his own was very different. The Freylarkai took many passes to manifest and control their abilities, if indeed they did at all. There was every chance, he supposed, that Rayna would never develop her now dormant ability. He figured that Ragnar was best placed to assist Rayna in manifesting her ability, though he doubted the Captain's aptitude for teaching if not his willingness to help.

'I believe body movement is only part of the required process when summoning forth your inner light.' he said. 'When I renew one's flesh, I imagine the natural process of re-growth occurring at an accelerated rate for it to then physically take place. The same principal can likely be applied to your own latent ability, though I must admit I do not know how one imagines light into being.'

'Blind leading the blind eh?' Rayna said with an infectious grin.

He laughed heartily, unable to suppress his amusement, 'You certainly have a way with words. The Freylarkai are typically cautious and reserved in their dialect, yet you have an inoffensive way of cutting to the heart of matters with great joviality.'

'It's a shame I wasn't able to do the same with Lothnar.' replied Rayna.

'That was personal. His spite was directed as much towards me as was towards you.'

There followed a lull in the conversation, yet it was not an uncomfortable silence. Rayna turned her head towards the small window adjacent to them and stared vacantly through the grubby glass oval into the night sky. It was a clear summer's night bathed in crisp white moonlight. The sky was abyssal black though it teemed with the winking lights of distant stars, as Rayna had called them, some of which were visible through the canopy of the forest dwellings. To him and the rest of the Freylarkai they were the Night's Lights; however, Rayna had shattered their limited understanding of the phenomena, suggesting they were in fact distant iterations of their own sun. The notion was entertaining initially, but in the wake of the ever-growing rumour of the revelation from within the queen's private quarters, Rayna's science was fast becoming more convincing. Content simply to share the moment, despite the lack of conversation, he returned to his reading whilst Rayna continued to study the stars. He missed these moments which he had previously shared with his wife prior to her release; although it brought him happiness sharing his midnight sanctuary with another once more, it was also a painful reminder of his first great loss. This was not the first time that Rayna had inadvertently caused him such heartache, nor would it likely be the last. Her rebirth in his daughter's body had been difficult for him to adjust to, but even so he enjoyed her company; in a way the bizarre state of affairs had returned his daughter to him in the physical sense at least.

'A change of subject I know, but have you thought since about what was said in Mirielle's private quarters Nathaniel?' asked Rayna suddenly.

'I try not to.' he replied.

'I'm surprised,' replied Rayna. 'Does it not concern you that we could all be mere parasites living within a host which is haphazardly floating around incapable of defending itself against all those looking to harm it?'

'Please do not think me disinterested Rayna, however, the scope of the revelation is enormous and entirely beyond my control or understanding. I am content to leave that particular concern for others to angst over. Besides, simply living is a risk.' he explained.

Rayna relaxed into the arch of her chair and chewed her bottom lip as she digested his words. It was one of the many traits he admired about her; she considered the opinions of others, and information in general put to her, before finalising her own thoughts decisively. Marcus was the same. There were leaders, and then there were good leaders. Marcus was undeniably the latter; he habitually took the time required to understand all the considerations of a given debate, where feasible, before arriving at his ultimate decision. Marcus was also impossibly amiable; it was very difficult to be offended by Marcus even when at odds with his command. Rayna possessed a remarkably similar disposition on both accounts, though she was more open and candid with her dialect. Even so, she was by far the most interesting candidate he had come across since Marcus had secretly asked him to seek out an individual worthy of leading The Blades into the future. The potential for greatness was certainly there, though it was rough and needed refining. Whether or not the Freylarkai would follow an outworlder into battle was another story, though they might look more kindly upon The Guardian. Finding a way of encouraging Rayna to follow that path would, however, be tricky; her humility would not sit well with that mentality, though perhaps the role of the reluctant icon would yield its own merit. He was musing, however, and for the time being she had enough on her plate with Lothnar's challenge.

'I see your point.' replied Rayna, eventually.

Not wishing to kill off the conversation, he chose to steer their midnight social in a new direction pertaining to more current affairs.

'Your training is progressing well. Far beyond my expectations in fact.' he said smiling warmly.

'I didn't think The Teacher capable of such high praise! I am most fortunate.' she replied with a wry grin comparable to one of his own.

'Do not let my praise swell your over-enthusiastic ego Aspirant.' he said jovially in return, fully appreciating her grasp of his own dry sense of humour.

'In all seriousness though Nathaniel, do you believe I will be ready in time to receive Lothnar's challenge?' enquired Rayna.

'If you continue your strict daily training regime in the arena then yes, I believe that you will be ready...ready enough at least to put up a fight.'

'Though you do not believe it possible for me to best him in combat?'

'Not with martial prowess alone. If you wish to best Lothnar in combat then you will need to master that elusive ability of yours, along with your wraith wings.'

Rayna sighed deeply. He understood well her unspoken frustration. The act of wielding a physical weapon was tangible, and thus a skill she could develop through discipline and repetition. Learning to manifest that which currently did not exist, however, was a far more perplexing challenge.

'I fear that mastering either one may not come to pass since they are entirely unknown to me. How can I attempt to control things which do not exist?' she asked.

'You may need to seek out a fellow light bringer who will commit to assisting you in that regard, however, I may be able to help you get off the ground so to speak.' he said.

'How is it you hope to achieve the latter?' Rayna asked.

'You will find out soon enough.' he said grinning. 'We will make an early trip to the Eternal Falls tomorrow morning where all will become clear.'

Rather uncharacteristically, Rayna chose not to question him further on the matter. The perplexed look on her face suggested, however, that she would not see his unorthodox approach to taking flight coming until it was too late; that thought amused him greatly. Instead she made herself comfortable in the rocking chair and slowly closed her eyes as fatigue finally got the better of her.

'Sleep well child.' he said.

'Nathaniel, it's breathtaking up here. But how exactly is this going to help me summon forth my wraith wings?' she asked.

It had been an early start that morning; it was still dark when they had left their tree, though as always Nathaniel's eyes had guided them safely along the correct trail through the heart of the vale's forest towards the northern ridgeline. There the landscape rose in a sharp incline towards the vale's northern mountain range. The hike had been hard on their legs, so it had taken them some time to reach the base of the Eternal Falls. Their reward was a gruelling climb to the top of the falls, up an adjacent rock face slick with spray from the energetic falls. She had initially presumed the climb to be impossible, though Nathaniel soon convinced her otherwise having made the climb himself successfully numerous times before. In spite of the near vertical rise there were a good number of footholds and nooks to aid their ascent, which proved to be relatively trouble free despite her aching arms suggesting otherwise after reaching the summit. For her safety Nathaniel had insisted that she follow his lead, and in addition had tethered them to each other by rope during their ascent; a wise precaution given her unfamiliarity with the climb. Upon reaching the top of the falls, they were rewarded with a stunning view of the vale which was rendered all the more beautiful in the morning light that broke across the stunning landscape from the east as the sun greeted her fondly. She had a new-found love for the sun's warm caress as it seemed to enliven every part of her being with its touch, enhancing all of her senses; colours appeared all the more vibrant, her sense of touch became more sensitive and renewed strength coursed through her muscles. Her relationships with the light of dawn and the encroaching darkness of dusk had taken on a peculiar role reversal since her rebirth. The spectacular view from the summit of the Eternal Falls reminded her of the first time she had laid eyes on the vale when Kirika and Nathaniel flew her in across the river. That moment in time seemed distant to her now given everything that had happened since her arrival. Looking down into the heart of the domain brought everything to the fore once more; the ball of light, her rebirth, the revelation proclaimed by Mirielle, Lothnar's challenge, her training in the arena, the repressed memories of her past life and everything in between. So many fundamental changes in her life had happened in such a short space of time and yet, instead of them breaking her spirit, she had managed to endure the changes seeing each as a fresh challenge eagerly accepted.

'My apologies Rayna, I did not quite hear your question.' replied Nathaniel, half shouting.

They were less than three paces from the edge of the falls, on the western bank of the stream which fed them, cascading down the northern ridgeline into a pool at the base of the falls, before flowing onwards and ultimately joining up with the main river running the length of the vale. The stream was only a few of paces wide, though its current was strong, causing the water to race to the edge of the falls in a loud crescendo where it crashed against a single exposed rock. The rapid current then violently dropped away into the pool below, before snaking its way south through the forest. Reluctantly she turned away from the raw beauty of the stream so that she might better converse with Nathaniel over the raucous noise of the falls. The moment she came about Nathaniel shoulder charged her hard in the midriff, lifting her off the ground before dumping her cleanly into the stream. The unexpected impact partially knocked the wind out of her, leaving her gasping for breath whilst struggling to get to her feet in the waist height water. The current was far stronger than she expected, preventing her from righting herself quickly. She floundered around trying to edge towards the bank of the stream with no success; the icy cold water had her in its firm grasp and was determined to pull her over the edge of the falls along with it. Despite the impact, her training allowed her to recover quickly, well enough at least to rasp Nathaniel's name before he disappeared from view. She involuntarily rolled over on to her back, before being cast into a free fall as the momentum of the current forced her a good couple of paces away from the vertical sheer into an inelegant forward dive. The pool raced to meet her as gravity pulled her down towards its imminent embrace. Panic, adrenaline and various other stimuli flooded her mind and body as they collectively acknowledged their inevitable fate. Small rocks, worn by the relentless cascade of water, broke the surface of the pool infrequently here and there, heightening her fear of a painful impact. In that brief moment she tried with conviction to will her body to halt, as though simply believing an alternative outcome would make it so. She crashed violently into the pool. Her hearing became muffled with the sound of water pressing against her ears and her vision was impaired. A dull pain stabbed at her upper left arm. Rising quickly to the surface of the water, she snatched at the welcoming air for breath, still struggling to breathe after Nathaniel's earlier assault. With her hearing and vision restored, she regained her bearings before thrashing wildly towards the western edge of the pool. She hauled her body onto the shingle at the water's edge with supreme effort, the weight of her sodden clothes and the waning strength in her left arm threatening to pull her back into the water's dark embrace. She lay with her face flat to the shingle, regulating her breathing and seeking to regain her composure. Her red hair was slicked across her face, partially obscuring her vision, and her wet clothes clung tightly to every curve of her new body. The pain in her arm worsened; it began to throb now as though held in a vice like grip. As she turned her head slowly to investigate the cause of the pain, her peripheral vision was distracted by an iridescent ochre glow emanating from behind her shoulders. Protruding from her upper back were two ethereal geometric wraith wings, similar to those she had seen Kirika and other female Freylarkai use. Her wings shimmered, or rather gently pulsed, as her heavy breathing caused them to move ever so slightly. Whilst they were predominantly orange in colour, each was essentially pearlescent adjusting in hue with the changing direction of the morning light shining upon them; they seamlessly cycled from orange, to ochre, to yellow and all the colours imaginable in between, then back to orange. The effect was enchanting; it threatened to send her spiralling into a trance.

'Ah, so my little trick worked I see.' said Nathaniel dryly.

Enthralled by the light and colour of her wraith wings, she had failed to notice Nathaniel's silent rapid drop from the summit of the Eternal Falls. He had used his own wraith wings to slow his descent, rather like engaging an air brake. Now Nathaniel stood with his arms neatly folded a short distance across from her. The familiar grin was stretched across his face; clearly he was pleased with the outcome of his deviance.

'You...are a menace...Nathaniel!' she replied exhaling heavily.

Nathaniel laughed heartily at her words before replying, 'I have never been called that before Rayna, though I do have my tricks I grant you that. Best you devise some of your own if you are to succeed in besting Lothnar.'

Words temporarily escaped her, not least because of her ongoing laboured breathing and the painful throbbing in her left arm. Regardless of her personal views on Nathaniel's unorthodox training methods, the effectiveness of his approach towards her development was indisputable.

Whether the catalyst was anxiety, fear, or sheer determination to slow her descent, her wraith wings had at last made themselves known to her. The breakthrough had come at the expense of her arm, however, which ached more now that her attention was no longer pre-occupied with dying. Unable to articulate a suitable retort to Nathaniel's words, she shifted her gaze to inspect her injured arm. The upper part of her left arm had turned mauve in colour; a clear sign that it had sustained a heavy knock. In all likelihood she had clipped one of the rocks penetrating the surface of the pool during her fall. Although the skin had not broken, blood was starting to permeate through the battered skin indicating heavy bruising caused by ruptured blood vessels. She winced as the pain in her arm continued to swell, unrelenting in its torment.

'You were lucky you did not impact directly on the rocks.' said Nathaniel as he closed the distance between them before kneeling alongside her to better inspect her arm.

'Lucky you did not do Lothnar's job for him you mean.' she replied, finally with a worthy retort.

'Hold onto that humour of yours. You will still need it.' he said with a wry grin.

TWELVE
Endurance

He hated using Waystones. The feeling of one's body sliding from one location to another was disconcerting. He would much rather make the attempt at climbing to the apex of the Tri-Spires, though Mirielle would likely frown at such an outlandish undertaking. Instead he begrudgingly used the stones as was expected of him, though no one had insisted –not yet at least – that he be happy about it. Slowly his body began to feel his own once more; he was never particularly quick at regaining his composure when using the wretched means of transportation. There were many times when Marcus had heard him grumbling incessantly outside after particularly stressful encounters with the stones. On one occasion he had even gone so far as to threaten to put his axe through one of the things. Regardless of his personal loathing towards Waystones in general, they were the only practical means of ascending the Tri-Spires and therefore only occasionally did he agree to meet in Marcus' personal quarters; on this particular occasion the sensitive nature of their meeting had demanded it. No sooner had he walked two paces, the door leading to Marcus' personal chamber swung open, seemingly of its own accord.

'Damn it!' he growled, 'Am I that conspicuous?'

'Yes, you are. Come in old friend, I require your counsel.' came Marcus' commanding voice from the chamber beyond.

He quickened his pace which aided him in thrusting his formidable frame through the small single open door leading to Marcus' modest personal quarters. The chamber was sparsely furnished, but then Marcus was never one for ostentatious splendour or an affluent lifestyle; Marcus was a Blade first and foremost, and chose to live his life as such. The constant defence of the domain and the continued development of those Freylarkai making up the ranks of The Blades occupied Marcus' every waking cycle. As Captain of The Blades, he was supposed to release The Blade Lord of some of the burdens of command, though in truth he wondered if indeed that was actually ever the case. He was a Blade, and a fine one at that. He inspired his Blade brothers and sisters, both on and off the field of battle, though command, politics and administration were alien to him. Nathaniel would have been a more worthy candidate for the position, but Marcus had laboured the point that The Teacher was needed in the arena. Besides, the Captain of The Blades needed to be of Paladin or Valkyrie stock, which in itself left Marcus with precious few suitable candidates. Whilst each was a force to be reckoned with in their own unique way, none – himself included – fulfilled all the criteria required for the title of Captain. Ergo, he was the best of a bad bunch; he knew this to be the sad fact of the matter. He had reluctantly accepted the title of Captain because Marcus had asked it of him, though in truth he hoped that another would in time take his place – Nathanar perhaps, should Aleska ever decide to step down and make way for the order's youth. Nathanar was an exemplary Blade, one who had earned respect from his brothers and sisters in battle and who had commanded the Adepts on numerous successful missions. Nathanar's temperament was sound, his aptitude for administration good and he proved to be politically insightful. On paper Nathanar was an ideal candidate, though he had to agree with Marcus' assessment of the Freylarkin. Nathanar lacked something essential; like a perfect cooked meal left to go cold. There were those who believed that Nathanar had never truly been tested in battle. Until such time came to pass, one could never truly know if he would rise to the occasion, and solidify his status within The Blades, or instead break when faced with insurmountable odds. It was thus expected of Nathanar to enter the Trials; there Nathanar would prove his mettle against whichever Paladin or Valkyrie opposed the Freylarkin in the finals, but until that time none could be sure of Nathanar's suitability for future captaincy.

'I would have it known that I am very much still in my prime Marcus.' he said.

Marcus stared at him blankly for a moment before a wide smile broke across his face, 'Far be it for me to accuse a Freylarkin with an axe that he is no longer counted amongst the youth of Freylar.' said Marcus light-heartedly.

Marcus gestured towards the sparse writer's bench; it was his habitual perch when the two conversed privately in Marcus' quarters. Marcus himself always favoured the window sill for The Blade Lord loved to look down upon the vale whilst marshalling his thoughts. He leant against the bench folding his arms in his usual manner, ready to receive Marcus' words; there was little doubt they would concern some new crisis which threatened to encroach upon the domain of Freylar. Marcus took up his usual place, leaning against the arch of the chamber's solitary window with one foot resting on the sill. He did not speak immediately; Marcus' liked to build tension and suspense in his audience before delivering his sermons.

'I have received word from Lothnar.' he said, finally breaking their comfortable silence.

'So, what are the soul stealers up to? Nothing good presumably.' he replied.

'They are amassing their numbers.' said Marcus flatly.

'What? Since when did the Narlakai conceive the notion of mobilising for war? Surely their animal-like instinct is incapable of such grand designs?' he questioned.

'We do not know at this stage if that is indeed their objective, and if so whether we are the target of an invasion. With that said, we need to prepare for the possibility of war.'

'You mean Fate Weaver has yet to scry that particular strand of fate?' he asked sardonically.

Marcus chose to ignore his derogatory remark; indeed it was difficult to agitate The Blade Lord. Whilst it was never his intent to raise Marcus' choler, bitter loathing for Aleska, Kirika and the rest of their meddling kind more often than not clouded his better judgement.

'Lothnar has expanded his network of spies and now holds sway over the dire wolves. They are now our eyes and ears across the borderlands.'

'And should the Narlakai march on Freylar?' he asked, cutting to the heart of the matter.

'If that dark cycle should indeed come, then I would have that battle fought on a battlefield of my own choosing. Prepare The Blades Ragnar, I want them ready to march at a moment's notice should ill word be received from Lothnar.' Marcus commanded.

'Including the Aspirants?'

'All of them. If the Narlakai march on Freylar, I will not have that battle fought within the vale. The potential for civilian casualties is unacceptable.' said Marcus firmly.

'I will have Nathaniel sharpen The Blades to a point. His pet project will have to wait.' he replied.

'You mean Rayna?'

'Yes...that one!'

There was a momentary lull in their verbal exchange. Marcus seemed to be lost in thought whilst staring blankly down into the vale. It was not uncommon for The Blade Lord to break away mid-conversation; he respected the fact that Marcus took the time required to consider matters fully. Marcus never dallied, yet his decisions were neither rash nor uninformed.

'She is a Blade Aspirant and will be treated as such.' said Marcus firmly, finally breaking his silence.

'She is not ready.' he said pointedly.

'Are we ever? Is Nathanar ready? You know as well as I that we are each of us tested in battle. When faced with adversity do we break, or do we hold our ground despite seemingly insurmountable odds? The Guardian will prove herself worthy of that title, or be released trying. Besides, have you seen her fight in the arena?' asked Marcus raising a single eyebrow.

'Very well...and no, I have not. I confess that I have not made her development any concern of mine,' he replied. 'Should I?'

'Nathaniel probably thinks you should. He is unable to assist Rayna in manifesting her ability. Given the potential horrors we face, another capable light bringer would be of great use to The Blades. I do not ask that you instruct her, brother, only that you consider the possibility.'

Marcus possessed a silver tongue; The Blade Lord had a way of drawing the best out of any Freylarkin. He did not trust the outworlder, though he could find no fault with Marcus' logic on the matter. The Blades lacked a good stock of capable light bringers; they would require more if indeed a war with the Narlakai came to pass.

'I will observe first-hand if Nathaniel's teachings have thus far been in vain. If she is worthy, I shall consider your indirect request.' he said.

Marcus turned his gaze from the vale below towards him, before nodding once as a mark of respect. The Blade Lord then brought their discussion back on track.

'Find me a foothold to the north of the vale Ragnar, from which we can intercept the Narlakai should they indeed decide to invade Freylar.'

'As you command.' he said.

With their meeting concluded, he pushed himself forwards off the writer's bench and made his way towards the door. Marcus' concerns were now his own. His priority was to consult a local cartographer in order to tactically assess the landscape to the north of Freylar. Instead though, he found himself wanting something entirely different. Although Marcus had not directly asked that he review Rayna's development first-hand, his own commitment to doing so immediately began to nag at his mind. Until now he had given the outworlder little thought, despite Mirielle's absurd revelation, yet now he found himself wanting to sate his curiosity.

'Ragnar...' Marcus said rather meekly, as he neared the doorway. 'Make sure they are ready old friend, but keep word of these details between ourselves, Kirika and

Nathaniel in the meantime. I do not wish to incite panic or bickering at this stage over mere speculation.'

He grunted in acknowledgement then left Marcus' quarters, leaving The Blade Lord to continue his quiet contemplation. The Waystone which had brought him to Marcus awaited him outside the chamber; it mocked him silently from its stone pedestal in anticipation of the likely fraught return trip. He was unsure as to which angered him more; the threat of a Narlakai invasion or the inanimate crystal before him with its witch-like means of transportation.

The constant clash of blades still rang keenly in her ears. Anika had reassured her that before long she would no longer pay much attention to the sound of The Blades sparring, though for the time being at least every clang of metal and thud of wood continued to reverberate through her. She felt every impact along with every bead of sweat rolling down her forehead, exacerbated by the intense glare of the mid-cycle sun making her habitual practice all the more strenuous. Nathaniel had warned them all that there was no place for exhaustion in the arena; if one tired during a fight, they invariably lost that fight. So it was that Nathaniel actively promoted sparring during the intense heat forcing them to endure a torturous training regime lest their will be broken, followed by their likely prompt dismissal from the order. Nathaniel was a task master and showed little leniency, yet all of the Aspirants accepted this; there could be no room for weakness amongst The Blades, the continued defence of the domain demanded such. The Blades operated as a single militant order which stood as a bulwark against those who would seek to harm their domain; they were the domain's living armour, and like any set of mail the wearer could ill afford defects or chinks in that armour. Thus Nathaniel's hard-nosed training mantra was never questioned. Despite this, Nathaniel's training ethic was more than just axe to grindstone; he formed strong bonds with each of his students. Nathaniel wanted them to succeed, and thus he tested their limits. Moreover, Nathaniel was determined that each would return safely from their future assignments. The tragic loss of any Blade, regardless of rank, was a blow felt by the entire order. Nathaniel's raison d'être within the order was to ensure that each Aspirant reached a level of marshal prowess sufficient to defend them against the enemies of Freylar; he gave them a fighting chance.

'Anika, keep your guard up!' shouted Nathaniel.

'Yes Teacher!' replied Anika, channelling renewed strength through her left arm.

They had been sparring on and off since first light; both were now exhausted, though each continued without complaint to follow the will of The Teacher. It was Anika though who was beginning to tire from exhaustion; the Freylarkin's moves were no longer graceful and fluid, instead they had a mechanical jerk to them. Anika's movement became laboured as muscles began to tire. With her opponent struggling to counter her moves, she rushed Anika looking to wrong-foot the Aspirant with an abrupt flurry of forceful strikes. Anika maintained guard causing both of her falchions to glance off her opponent's shield. The first few blows amounted to little more than the patter of rain, though when Anika dipped her head she increased the power of her attacks; the rain became a torrent of hail causing her opponent to buckle at the knees. Anika hunkered down as the intensity of her blows escalated. Although her arms now felt like lead weights, the boldness of her brazen assault caused Anika to go to ground. No longer at risk from a counter attack, she closed on Anika and kicked the young Freylarkin's shield up and to the right with her left heel. Anika fell back onto her shield arm clearly daunted by the audacious move, though there was little chance for the defeated Freylarkin to contemplate the decisive move as she stepped in offering Anika the tip of her right falchion. Bested in combat, Anika loosened the grip on her sword allowing it to slip heavily from her right hand to the floor of the arena. The defeated Freylarkin tipped her head backwards a little, wary of the blade she now held in close proximity to Anika's exposed throat. Before she could look up to seek approval from The Teacher opposite, the heavy clapping of hands behind her drew her attention. Careful not to lose sight of her opponent and repeat mistakes of old, she moved deftly to Anika's right flank in order to observe the source of the clapping whilst maintaining watch over her fallen opponent.

'Enough for now, both of you.' said Nathaniel to her right.

She withdrew her right falchion swiftly and turned to face their newest audience member. Anika promptly retrieved her sword and rose to her feet, wearily, to stand by her side. She immediately recognised the hulking Freylarkin who stood opposite as Captain Ragnar, still clapping his enormous club-like hands. Numerous times she had witnessed the Captain of the Blades swinging his monstrous axe into the arena's wooden practice targets, though the Paladins and Valkyries rarely ventured towards the west gate where Nathaniel trained his Aspirants. This was the first time since beginning her training as a Blade Aspirant that a senior member of their order had approached her, aside from Nathaniel. Despite the seemingly reassuring clapping of his hands, she believed there to be more to the Captain's presence than simple praise.

'Captain Ragnar,' said Nathaniel taking up position between them. 'To what do we owe the pleasure of your company?'

'The girl has spirit I see,' boomed Ragnar. 'Your handiwork or a natural affinity?'

'Both I feel. Rayna is a rough diamond.' replied Nathaniel.

'Well, that rough diamond of yours requires assistance with her ability, so I hear.' replied Ragnar, cutting straight to the point.

'Indeed. She would benefit greatly from the tutelage of another of her kind. I myself cannot help her adequately with the manifestation of her latent ability.' Nathaniel explained.

Ragnar turned to face her so that he could take her measure; he was assessing whether or not she was worth devoting time to, that much was clear. There was nothing complicated about Ragnar, he was an open book and forthright with his words. Whilst she had not actively sought to win the Captain's approval with her earlier display, she nonetheless hoped that she had caught his attention.

'I will instruct you in the use of your ability girl. Meet me at the Eternal Falls at dusk. Do not disappoint me.' Ragnar said pointedly, before turning his attention back to Nathaniel. 'Nathaniel. A word in private.'

Nathaniel offered Ragnar a curt nod before both walked slowly towards a secluded part of the arena to converse privately. Once they were safely beyond earshot of their superiors, Anika wasted little time in discussing the encounter in an attempt to glean further information on the matter. Anika turned sharply towards her, wide eyed and full of curiosity.

'Captain Ragnar wants to instruct you personally! Wow, what an honour.' said Anika enthusiastically.

Anika was a spritely young Freylarkin, eager to please and full of wonder and excitement. She found it curious that such a cheerful individual would actively seek induction into a militant order. Anika was kind and courteous, if a little naive and immature. Although no slouch in combat, she found it difficult to picture a Freylarkin of Anika's disposition on a battlefield defending the realm against its enemies. Despite these prominent character traits, Anika also possessed great zeal, which stayed the Freylarkin's course regardless of the challenges ahead. She could only assume that Nathaniel had determined the zealot to be worthy of his time due to the devotion Anika demonstrated towards The Blades, both in and out of the arena.

'If you say so.' she replied with a half smile.

'Rayna, the Captain of The Blades is famed for his deeds on the battlefield. To be trained personally by him is a huge honour!' Anika pressed emphatically.

Again she smiled at the eager young Freylarkin, though this time she offered a casual wink of her right eye to her pious Blade sister.

'Rayna you tease.' said Anika, at last realising the pointlessness of her words.

'Only because you are my sister, and isn't that what sisters do?' she replied. 'Besides, I dare say that his interest in my development is not personal. I gather from Nathaniel that the order is short on light bringers. The Blade Lord likely played a part in all this.'

'You have a keen mind Rayna, and your skill with the blade has already surpassed my own.'

'I'm fortunate that Alarielle's body is well practiced in combat. The moves Nathaniel teaches us come readily to me.' she replied. 'I fear that I have cheated you.'

'I do not believe that to be so Rayna. You are The Guardian. Your deeds are your own.' insisted Anika.

Again she smiled. Anika's fervour was fierce. She had no desire to insult the Freylarkin's beliefs, regardless of her own self-reservations, as such she decided it best to steer the conversation in a different direction.

'At any rate, what do you suppose they're talking about over there?' she questioned, inclining her head towards Nathanial and Ragnar who stood some ten paces away.

'I do not know. Whatever the subject matter is, it must be important.' replied Anika.

'What makes you think that?' she asked averting her gaze from the two conspirators back to Anika.

'Since neither converse regularly with one another...at least not publically.'

'Are you sure?' she asked agitatedly.

'Of course I am sure.' replied Darlia tersely, clearly unimpressed by her apparent lack of respect. 'You should know well enough by now that I do not dabble in happenstance. This one's eyes have seen him skulking around the Black Thorn to the east, several cycles from now. He is in league with a pack of dire wolves, indeed he is their new alpha.'

'I do not question your mastery of your born ability sister, only the timing of the event.' she replied earnestly, eager to repent for her unintended transgression.

'Then be more specific with your words in future Lileah. Once Freylar is subservient to our rule, you will need to measure your words carefully when commanding those beneath your heel.' lectured Darlia.

Darlia was correct, as was usually the case. She knew well that Darlia held her best interests at heart, though there were times when she felt treated like a child in their relationship. As much as she wanted to punish those who cared not for her wellbeing, seizing control of the domain of Freylar was as much about proving her worth. She harboured a deep-seated need to prove herself to both Darlia and those who had shunned her existence. Darlia had been her benevolent guardian since the first cycle their collective misfortunes had brought them together. She yearned for the opportunity to repay Darlia's affections, beyond those of simple bedroom pleasures, by delivering the hand of The Blade Lord to her mistress. Such a token of gratitude would surely elevate her in Darlia's eyes; she would no longer be seen as the abandoned waif in need of protection, but instead the slayer of Freylar's most auspicious champion. Such an act would demoralise The Blades, scattering their order, and along with it Mirielle's rule.

'The Night's Lights were clear to me through the eyes of this Sky-Skitter, and it is they which gave me my bearings in the vast ocean of time. Now is our time Lileah, that much is clear to me. Shepherd the Narlakai under your sway past the Black Thorn immediately. When the light of dawn prohibits their advance move them instead through the under-pass. Deny Lothnar his fallback corridor and he will do the rest for us.'

She smiled at Darlia's words and the vehement manner of their delivery. They had waited long enough for the opportunity to lay siege to Freylar and its haughty inhabitants. Now, finally, their chance to correct past errors of judgement was within sight. No more would they bide their time cowering in the dark recesses of the Narlakai borderlands. Now was the time to step forth from their concealment and meet their arrogant kin in the flesh once more. Retribution would be their long awaited prize as a great reckoning would come to be settled in their favour, of that she had no doubt. Freylar's scriers were a force not to be taken lightly, but even they could not analyse and foresee every strand of destiny. The element of surprise was theirs; she was insignificant in the eyes of the Freylarkai and Darlia was no doubt perceived to be lost to time, if not dead after Marcus took Darlia's hand. Though she had not witnessed the horrific act in person, Darlia's retelling of how The Blade Lord left her lover clutching a gore splattered severed left wrist whilst screaming in agony only fuelled her hatred towards the Freylarkin. Mirielle had decreed that Darlia be banished for pushing the boundaries of a scriers' ability, to supposedly dangerous levels, and that an example be made of the accused to deter others of Darlia's disposition. Ever one to lead by example, Marcus carried out the official decree in person with ruthless efficiency. Marcus then turned his back on Darlia; a crumpled bloody ruin on the floor of Scrier's Post. Darlia had not suspected Mirielle capable of commanding such acts of barbarism, and thus had made no attempt to foresee the tragic event. Due to her lover's misplaced trust, Darlia was humiliated, ousted and subsequently left for dead by those Freylarkai subservient to Mirielle's rule, who were ignorant enough to believe that their elected queen knew better than one who could foretell the future.

'Once we are clear of Black Thorn, I will command the Narlakai to march on Freylar as previously discussed.' she replied gleefully.

'Indeed. You will then rejoin me at my side as we cast Mirielle's wretches into the abyss of their own arrogant making. There will be no coup de grâce for our misguided kin, instead only suffering as we burn their domain from the inside out before claiming the charred remains as our own.' Darlia proclaimed. 'Then, they will be forced to acknowledge our existence whilst they kneel beneath our heels.'

It filled her with immense joy knowing that now was the time of their long overdue reckoning. She had waited all too long for the opportunity to avenge Darlia's exile and her own shunned existence.

'I will bring you back a wolf's pelt sister, upon which we will celebrate our impending dominion over Freylar.'

Darlia rose purposefully from her place of contemplation on the floor of the chamber, releasing the Sky-Skitter before seeming to glide effortlessly across the uneven ground towards her. Darlia stepped intimately close, meeting her gaze, their faces a hair's breadth from one another, and then kissed her lips delicately. Her ecstasy increased immeasurably when Darlia's good hand brushed her inner right thigh, then slid under and up her short pleated skirt with the singular intention of motivating her further. Darlia worked her way along her right jaw line with caressing lips, then further up to playfully bite the lobe of her ear.

'Get it done Lileah.' Darlia whispered lovingly into her right ear.

'I will.' she moaned quietly in return. 'I will...'

THIRTEEN
Sanctuary

Kaitlin's library was discreetly located at the end of a long parade of nondescript buildings; the majority of the metropolis' structures were unremarkable, each borrowing the same tired formulaic design of those constructed before them. Whilst the modern design gave the metropolis a clean look, there was little character to be gleaned from such generic architecture. The metropolis had a sterile feel to it; it was clinical with no room for error or spontaneity. In his mind at least, Kaitlin's library should have been ostentatious in its appearance; the structure deserved the splendour and magnificence of an ornate chest containing wondrous hidden treasures, though instead it was little more than a boxy container. For both the middle and apex classes the metropolis provided a clean and comfortable way of life, however, to him that life seemed a hollow and stale existence. Although his own personal circumstances were miserable in the extreme, he possessed something the civilised inhabitants of the metropolis did not. His was a life of exhilaration and adventure. Every day brought with it fresh challenges, as he sought to survive undetected in a world intent on rejecting him at every opportunity.

His midnight parkour had successfully brought him to his benefactor's literary sanctuary. Even at such late hour weak light emanated through the glass panelling of the library; a safe bet that Kaitlin was still enraptured by a lengthy novel despite her body's certain need to sleep. Kaitlin devoured books as one might drink water, thus she spent much of her non-working life at her place of work simply reading. He admired her passion for the literary arts, though he often wished that Kaitlin would indulge in a life outside the prison of her own making. It was unlikely that she would share his view on the matter; Kaitlin had mentioned on more than one occasion that her books provided her freedom through imagination. As knowledgeable as Kaitlin was, however, most of her experiences were consumed through the writings of another; they were second hand at best, therefore how could Kaitlin fully appreciate life having not indulged in one directly herself. These were not issues he wished to discuss with Kaitlin for he valued her friendship too much to risk jeopardising it over a difference of opinion, besides, his own life failed to provide the framework for a meaningful debate. As he made his swift approach towards the main entrance of the building, he pulled forth from under his stained t-shirt a string of bio-keys which hung loosely around his neck; one of these keys would grant him access to the library. Having forsaken his own means of identification in a bid to remain undetected, he had acquired substitute bio-keys since the removal of his own implant. It was these proxies which he used frequently as fake digital aliases when infiltrating the metropolis, thus protecting his own identity. His own bio-key was long since destroyed, immediately following the crude surgery to remove it. The bio-key he sought now belonged to a Mr L. Cameron who was officially retired and enjoying his twilight years indulging in printed literature. The ugly truth of the matter, however, was that the original owner of the bio-key remained at their place of residence, decomposing inside a black sack stolen from a patrolling Peacekeeper; better to contain the rotting carcass than attempt to dispose of it. In exchange for procuring an alias of their own, his occasional hacker acquaintance Trix had re-engineered the bio-key for him so that it continued to relay healthy vitals. He figured that Mr L. Cameron had at least another decade to run before the authorities would question the elderly citizen's unblemished health record. Trix had also rigged the key to generate false tracking data to mask his actual location. So far as the authorities were concerned, Mr L. Cameron was a man of unyielding routine; a trait not uncommon amongst the elderly. In a single fluid motion he swiped Mr L. Cameron past the main entrance's key entry system causing the library's doors to part silently. He immediately slipped past the main doors into the library's foyer, which he then crossed rapidly into the library proper.

Despite being only dimly lit, there was light enough in the heart of the library to ascertain Kaitlin's whereabouts. Engrossed in yet another lengthy novel, Kaitlin failed to notice him enter despite her elevated position up on the library mezzanine. Not wishing to scare the life out of her by creeping up the twisted stairwell to her lofty hideout, he instead called out gently, hoping to attract her attention.

'Kaitlin it's me, Callum.'

He waited for a moment, hoping for some kind of acknowledgement, but Kaitlin had clearly not heard him. It was plain to him that Kaitlin was oblivious to the real world around her, as was often the case when she buried her head in a novel.

'Kaitlin!' he repeated, this time in a more audible tone.

Again Kaitlin continued to remain blissfully unaware of his presence. Whatever it was Kaitlin was currently reading, it had consumed her attention entirely. He reminded himself that it was of no use, for when Kaitlin ventured into her other world there was little or no distracting her. Kaitlin was no doubt off on some literary adventure within her own mind, far away from the normality of her mundane reality. Recognising the futility of his efforts he quickly crossed the length of the library, paying no attention to the expansive aisles of printed media which flanked his approach, then climbed the twisted steps up to Kaitlin's inner sanctum. Kaitlin was sat with her back towards him, partially slumped across a white, high-gloss rectangular bench, as was typical of the stark furnishings within the metropolis. Kaitlin's head rested against the inner forearm of her left arm, which was bent backwards leaving her hand free to fiddle with her long, straight, raven-black hair which spilled down onto the bench. The tight grip of Kaitlin's right hand claimed ownership of a thick paperback novel, responsible for spiriting her away from an otherwise drab normality. Kaitlin wore black-framed glasses, on account of her poor vision, a knee length, black, pencil skirt and a white, long-sleeved dress shirt with its cuffs pushed up.

'Ahem!'

Kaitlin flinched, clearly startled by the noise. She accidentally lost her thumbed position in her book as she turned round sharply to meet his gaze. Kaitlin's surprise quickly passed, giving way to a wan smile once she realised who had gotten the drop on her.

'Callum, you really must not scare me like that.' Kaitlin said warmly.

'I apologise. You were away with the fairies on another of your grand adventures.' he replied whilst offering a smile of his own in return.

'I must confess that I did not expect to see you here tonight. Please, come sit with me.' Kaitlin said ushering him to take a seat.

He walked around the bench and took a seat opposite his inquisitive host who was clearly eager to understand the reason for his unannounced visit. He glanced at the oversized novel titled Sarmation Tribes which Kaitlin had since discarded and pushed to one side. Kaitlin reached out enthusiastically and grasped his hands pulling him closer as if to suggest that their intimate conversation should be conducted in whispers. As was always the case, Kaitlin's simple touch was enough to arouse his interest. With her dress shirt pulled tightly across her well-proportioned breasts, as Kaitlin half leant across the bench towards him, his genitalia began to stir in hopeless anticipation.

'Callum, what are you doing here? You are lucky I have not yet gone home for the night. I did not expect to see you for at least another week.' said Kaitlin.

'Kaitlin, you're always here.' he replied, giving her a quick wink of his right eye.

'You tease. But seriously, what if someone else had been on duty...what then? You risk too much by coming here on a whim.' said Kaitlin in the manor one might expect from a teacher lecturing a student.

'I had to Kaitlin. I have not eaten in days and sources of food in the Wild are scarce now that winter approaches.' he explained. 'I'm ashamed to admit that this is my first winter since the Exodus, and I am ill prepared for its arrival now that the streets are on lock down. I didn't intend to burden you with my problems, but would you be able to spare me some non-perishables to tide me over whilst I work out a solution?' he asked.

Kaitlin squeezed his hands tightly in sympathy and nodded gently.

'Of course I will. In fact...I am on duty for the next few days, so you can stay here with me for a while.' Kaitlin said sympathetically.

'No way, I couldn't impose on you like that Kaitlin. I can be on my way soon enough.'

Kaitlin was a kind hearted individual and never one to turn a blind eye to those in need, though he had no intention of taking advantage of her good nature. He had planned to move on immediately once resupplied; he had no desire to trouble Kaitlin with his misfortunes.

'Nonsense, you will stay here with me. It will be an adventure. Besides, was it not you who told me to get a life of my own, in not so few words, when last you were here?' enquired Kaitlin offering a playful wink of her own.

'Yes, but not one with me in it! I'm Shadow class Kaitlin. If the Peacekeepers catch you harbouring me you will quickly disappear into one of their black sacks. It's too dangerous!' he protested. 'I can't ask this of you.'

'You are not asking Callum...I am insisting. In case it has slipped your attention, I am an adult capable of making my own informed decisions. Now, you are staying with me and that is the end of the matter.' said Kaitlin insistently, ending their debate.

Kaitlin was right about one thing at least; she was an adult, an attractive young woman in her late twenties no less. Whether Kaitlin realised the full extent of her good looks he did not know, though her feminine wiles always got the better of him. Kaitlin had a way of disarming his every defence simply by her presence. Initially he thought his affections towards Kaitlin to be driven entirely by lust, though as the years marched ever onwards he became more and more enamoured with her. In the Wild he would find himself frequently wondering after Kaitlin; what book was she currently reading, had she gone home for the evening and if so, aside from sleeping, what did she do there given that she lived alone. All were questions he idly contemplated when he was not pre-occupied with evading the Peacekeepers or searching for food and new clothing.

'Very well, you win as...' he began to reply when suddenly the entire mezzanine began to shake violently beneath them, as though invisible hands sought to tear it from its elevated moorings.

Nathaniel was shaking her abruptly; she had been gone again, ensconced within the lurid half-forgotten memories of her former life. In the space of a single moment, her new world snapped back into focus once more with blinding ferocity. She felt dizzy, and her head ached; she could feel pressure in her frontal lobe causing it to throb. Nathaniel released his grip on her; he stared blankly into her eyes, unsure what to say or do. Although a master of armed combat and physical healing, Nathaniel had no experience with trauma of one's soul. According to Nathaniel she was physically well, and yet her mind was a bed of open wounds which would require time to heal of their own volition. Some of those wounds would undoubtedly leave behind mental scars; constant reminders of her dark past burned deep into her psyche.

'I'm fine...well, kind of.' she said looking to try and put Nathaniel at ease.

'I do not know what course of action to take when you disappear within yourself like that.' said Nathaniel, clearly concerned by her troubled state of mind.

'This is not something you can aid me with Nathaniel. My past is my own. I alone must face the demons lurking in the dark recesses of my soul.'

'And if they consume your soul...what then?' Nathaniel asked with alarming sincerity.

'They won't!' she affirmed, shaking her head. 'They are little more than a passing gale. Let them have their fleeting moment of destruction, for when the storm breaks I will be the one left standing.'

She delivered her words with conviction, enough it seemed to relieve some of the tension in her mentor's strained visage. Although she was not strictly speaking his daughter, it was clear that Nathaniel cared greatly about her wellbeing. Despite Nathaniel's unrelenting training regime and his use of questionable techniques to develop her skills, these events and the potential risks associated with them were always calculated on his part. By contrast, her suppressed memories were entirely beyond his control and thus Nathaniel was unable to counsel her with regard to such matters, neither could he offer any practical assistance.

'I am glad to hear it!' replied Nathaniel. 'But on another matter, it might be prudent for you to start making your way to the Eternal Falls. I am certain the Captain of The Blades will not wait for your tardy appearance, if that is what you are thinking?' said Nathaniel with a wry grin.

'Shit. How is it the Freylarkai keep track of time without...no matter.' she replied, managing to exercise enough restraint to hold back a lengthy rant on the subject of time management.

'Without what, exactly? I do not understand your question Rayna.' replied Nathaniel.

'Hold that thought.' she said, hurrying towards the door of her room. 'I need to get to the falls before Ragnar, else I'll likely incur his wrath alongside Lothnar's'.

'Indeed. Tread carefully in your haste Rayna.'

'I will.'

His walk to the falls had been a good thing, for Rayna at least. He had supposed that with his indifferent attitude towards her development, Rayna might be caught by the rough edge of his tongue. After his leisurely stroll to the Eternal Falls, however, his temperament had softened; the calming influence of the falls coupled with the soothing balm of the surrounding nightlife in full song had mellowed his demeanour, albeit temporarily. Ordinarily he might have boiled over inside at the prospect of waiting on a Blade of lesser rank, but the warm air agreed with him and the soothing ambiance of the nightlife along with the distant crash of the falls had put him in a good mood. He would wait, though not for long. Fortunately for his one-time student, Rayna quickly made her presence known as she came bounding through the wood towards the large pool at the base of the falls with all the grace of a feral Ravnarkin chasing down its prey. Again he admired Rayna's spirit. Clearly she was aware that she was late for their rendezvous, yet Rayna's determination to rectify her tardiness was admirable. Given the speed at which Rayna hurtled through the undergrowth, she would reach him a little worse for wear.

'You are late!' he boomed as Rayna raced towards his position, stopping short by only a few paces.

'I...have...' Rayna began to speak whilst desperately gasping for breath.

'Well...what clever excuse do you have to offer me?' he asked, intrigued as to her response.

He was an intimidating Freylarkin, he knew that fact well; his physical bulk and gruff tone of voice often put Aspirants on edge. The truth of it was that he enjoyed watching them squirm in his presence. Whilst he did not actively seek to torment the order's newest recruits, to him the inevitable process was one of amusement. His need to toy with the Aspirants was much like a rite of passage. They all endured it at some point, there were no exceptions.

'I have...no excuse Captain. I am late, and that is all there is to say on the matter.' replied Rayna, whilst trying to regulate her breathing.

With his right hand he drew his fingers and thumb across his long beard – an act he subconsciously performed when engaged in thought, which was not often. He tried hard not to over-think the machinations of fate; perhaps his attitude towards fate was the root of his discord with Freylar's scriers who sought instead to manipulate it. Rayna could have offered him any number of convenient excuses for her tardiness; instead she was exceptionally frank regarding the matter. Ordinarily he might have considered such a response disrespectful, though given the number of fresh cuts and scrapes Rayna had acquired en-route he could see that her words were entirely genuine. Also, Rayna stood to attention before him; a sign of respect towards those of greater rank. Rayna seemed completely unflustered by his earlier comment; she would likely therefore not provide the entertainment he sought. Perhaps this one was not to be toyed with.

'At ease.' he ordered. 'We will be seated by the pool's edge for your training.'

Rayna followed the direction of his outstretched arm as instructed, though he was pleased to observe that she walked to his right side quickening her pace to match his long stride. Rayna had placed the pool to his left, and chose not to walk ahead thus exposing her back to him; these were encouraging signs of tactical awareness in his opinion. Whether her behaviour had adopted Nathaniel's teachings as a default state of being, or whether she simply did not trust him, the reason for Rayna's actions mattered not. What mattered was that Rayna maintained her guard outside of the arena. Perhaps Nathaniel's teachings had proven their worth after all, or maybe Rayna's former life had wrought such instinctive behaviour. Regardless of the cause, Rayna was unlike any normal Blade Aspirant he had tormented in the past for his own personal amusement. It was possible, he mused, that the evening would not be an entire waste of time after all.

'Sit.' he said, pointing to a patch of long grass along the bank of the pool. 'How far have you progressed with your ability?' he enquired, taking a seat of his own opposite.

He crossed his legs and made himself comfortable. Rayna chose to kneel instead; he supposed that her light agile frame would exert less pressure on her knees. He was aware of Lothnar's secret affections towards Alarielle prior to her release, indeed he himself found the Freylarkin pleasing to the eye. Although Rayna possessed all of Alarielle's physical attributes, she carried herself in a more confident manner than her predecessor. In his mind at least, Rayna's confidence made her all the more attractive. Kirika's influence over Rayna's style was also apparent.

Despite his loathing of Kirika, there was no denying the scrier's seductive dress sense, which she had clearly passed on to Rayna. Assuming Rayna's questionable past was to be taken at face value, he wondered how someone born of the opposite gender coped with such radical physical change. He could not imagine conducting himself well in such a scenario, indeed he was impressed by Rayna's ability to get on with life accepting her lot for what it was.

'Hold your hands outstretched before you, palms facing up, and close your eyes. Now is not the time to maintain your guard.' he directed.

Rayna nodded courteously acknowledging the latter part of his dialogue and did as he had instructed without hesitation.

'What am I to do now?' Rayna asked unwaveringly.

'Tell me what you see.' he replied.

'I see nothing. The light in the vale is fleeting and my eyes are closed. All I see is the dark.'

'Then you are not looking hard enough girl.' he replied curtly.

Immediately Rayna opened her eyes and fixed his gaze with her own. She had a determined look about her, like a dire wolf ready to charge its prey.

'I have a name Captain. I would ask that you kindly use it, regardless of seniority.' stated Rayna sternly.

'Ha! You impress me...Rayna. But do not overstep your bounds else I will cleave your head from its moorings.' he proclaimed.

'Understood, and should I do just that you are welcome to try...Captain.' Rayna replied, completely undaunted by his open threat.

He snorted derisively, though was unable to prevent the corner of his mouth from curling upwards. Rayna was confident and steadfast; both were traits he admired in any Freylarkin, more so in a female. Few stood their ground as well as Rayna against his rough edge. His initial lacklustre opinion of Rayna had now improved markedly. Slowly he began to understand fully why Marcus had suggested that he assist Rayna in developing her ability, and why Nathaniel was so keen to train her in the art of combat. He, like many others, had believed Nathaniel's motives to be those of a fool, looking to fill the hole in his life following the release of Alarielle's soul. On reflection, however, his presumptuous initial assessment of Nathaniel's motives potentially seemed now to be in error. Rayna's distinct personality intrigued him. Even after their brief encounters to date, he realised instinctively that Rayna was destined for more than the average lot of a rank and file member of The Blades; he saw now that Marcus was right to introduce him to her.

'Close your eyes. I will not tell you a third time.' he commanded gruffly.

Rayna closed her eyes as instructed; her face was one of pure concentration as she tried hard to seek out that which he would have her discover.

'I do not see anything Ragnar.' said Rayna.

'Of course you do, look harder. See the pin-prick of light in the furthest recesses of the darkness.'

'I...I see it!' replied Rayna. 'The light is barely visible.'

'Focus intently on the light. It is your inner light, an extension of yourself. See it double in size as you command it with your will alone.' he said.

The concentration etched across Rayna's face intensified. He noticed too that her arm muscles began to twitch as she sought to impose her will upon the new-found light.

'It grew!' replied Rayna excitedly. 'Ragnar...it's growing in size, intensifying too!'

'Good. You have control of it. Now exert your will. Bend and shape the light as you see fit, for it will obey you. It is a part of you. It is the light of your soul made manifest.'

'Ragnar, it's growing so fast. The light seems almost real to me now!' said Rayna clearly shocked by what she was witnessing.

'It is real...it always was. Open your eyes and observe now your inner light set free from the shackles of darkness.' he said.

Rayna opened her eyes; immediately she turned her head to the side averting her eyes from the brilliant light spilling forth from her upturned palms, each of which cupped white spheres that radiated forth pure intense light. As a light bringer himself he knew that the light would be cool to the touch, though he could appreciate Rayna's mounting apprehension as her hands began to subtly shake. He grabbed both of her forearms with his over-sized hands, seeking to reassure her that all was well. He was not a compassionate Freylarkin by nature, and yet instinctively he always sought to rally his brothers and sisters in times of need, steeling frayed nerves. This moment was like any other on the field of battle when Aspirants were inevitably called upon to be tested for the first time; uncertainty typically got the better of them, casting doubt in their minds. It was his task to set aside those doubts by bolstering their courage. Now he sought to do the same by rooting out Rayna's obvious trepidation.

'Do not fear it. This light is yours to control now. It is the light which you have previously caged within your soul, now reflected outwardly for others to see.' he said reassuringly.

'Ragnar, this is incredible. I can't begin to thank you for making this possible.' replied Rayna earnestly.

'Your gratitude is not required. What is required is that you control your ability and, in time, learn how to master it. You must learn how to fashion it into a weapon with which to blind your opponents, and understand how it can light your path when the darkness seeks to mask the world around you.' he said.

Without any prompting on his part, Rayna began to manipulate the spheres in her hands so that they elongated vertically from her palms like two shafts of light each tapering to a point. Slowly she rotated her palms inwardly gripping the base of the vertical columns, before continuing to shape the lights further by refining them into crude representations of the falchions Nathaniel had assigned to her.

'Excellent!' he boomed as he released his grip on her forearms.

Rayna's rate of development was astonishing. He had heard Nathaniel's talk of muscle memory and how it could be trained to allow one to fight instinctively. He drew his hand down the length of his fiery red beard musing as to whether the same was possible for a Freylarkin's ability. Eager to accelerate her development further still, he quickly stood up and thrust forwards his right arm. A colossal shaft of light of his own making immediately extended in both directions from his grasp. An enormous axe head of pure white light formed from the top end of the shaft illuminating the darkness of the night which had crept in around them. The light danced across the pool as he drew back his weapon ready to swing at his protégée.

'Defend yourself Rayna! Show me first-hand what The Teacher has wrought.' he said, offering her a coy smile for the first time since their inharmonious introduction beneath the arena.

He did not bother to wait for Rayna to acknowledge his challenge; instead he twisted his light-axe and gripped it tightly with both hands. In one fluid motion he brought the weapon round and high across the top of his head, before arcing it down towards where Rayna knelt. A wide trail of pale yellow light chased the flight of his axe as he directed it effortlessly towards where Rayna knelt. As the axe passed over his head threatening to cleave Rayna in two, she crossed her falchions then performed an upwards scissor like thrust kicking out her left leg thus allowing her to channel strength into the parry. His axe raced downwards, contacting with both falchions in a blinding flash of purest white light which exploded outwardly from the point of contact. Most Freylarkin would have been temporarily blinded by the effect, however, both were light bringers; their unique vision filtered out the worst of the crippling light. The explosive light forced him to recoil, though the blast also caused Rayna to fall backwards awkwardly to the ground. Despite being knocked down, Rayna was quick to recover to her vertical base after which she adopted an offensive stance. Although both weapons were ethereal in composition, like the wraith wings of a Freylarkin, their physical reaction to each other was vigorous.

'For non-corporeal weapons, that was...violent!' Rayna said breathing heavily.

'The light blades you wield are of little direct use against most of Freylar's enemies. With that said, they are devastating against the Narlakai, who have an aversion to light.' he explained. 'Learn to master them well, for our kind number few.'

'Nathaniel has enlightened me on those who would seek to destroy our domain. I had thought the Narlakai unlikely to ever attack Freylar given their disposition.' replied Rayna.

'That is true...for the most part.' he replied.

'What does that mean exactly Ragnar?'

'It means that you should get ready, and that I will train you...sister!'

FOURTEEN
Advance

He awoke to the deep throated growl of one of his lupine brethren standing in close proximity. The dire wolf could have easily torn out his throat whilst he slept were it not for the fact that he was their alpha, having bested their previous pack leader, and thus commanded their loyalty and respect. The dual with the pack's previous alpha was brief; only a handful of exchanges were made during the fight, and yet each unparried attack promised with it the release of one's soul. He suffered a nasty gash to his right leg during the combat, though fortunately for him the wound was not beyond his natural ability to heal. His lightning-quick reflexes allowed him to escape the worst of the damage, without which the dire wolf would have likely torn his leg off. A painful procedure to stitch the wound closed after the fight had been successful, in a crude fashion at least; a skilled renewalist would no doubt be able to finish his novice handiwork properly upon his return to the vale. In the meantime a makeshift leg splint aided his recovery by easing the pressure on his leg, and by ensuring that his efforts to dress his wound remained intact. His opponent was not so fortunate. Whilst lunging high for his head, he had deftly switched his favoured dirk to his left hand and reversed his grip on the blade before sinking it deep into the dire wolf's thick neck, showering them both in hot blood as they crashed to the floor locked in a lethal embrace. Both had struggled to right themselves as the blood from the wounded dire wolf made the ground slick beneath them. Indeed the dire wolf never did fully regain a vertical base. It fought valiantly, looking to protect its status as pack leader rather than vacate the position, though ultimately he was the victor. Since his ascension, none of the other wolves had thus far challenged his position of authority. The pack obeyed and he directed them in line with his own agenda. The dire wolf standing before him now, like many of the others, had been tasked with observing the Narlakai's movements, thus allowing him to develop a better understanding of their whereabouts. It was clear that they were amassing their numbers, yet the purpose of this still remained unclear. Idle speculation suggested that an invasion of Freylar was likely, but he was not sent to the borderlands to report back probable truths. He needed to be certain of the Narlakai's intent. He opened a fresh conduit to his mind and linked it directly to the dire wolf's own; his lupine brethren knew better than to disturb him whilst he slept; this one therefore clearly had an urgent tale to tell.

'Speak brother. Tell me what you have witnessed.' he communed telepathically to his eager subject.

The dire wolf's thoughts were primitive in construction, akin to that of a young Freylarkin. Even so, there was enough mental substance for him to accurately glean that which the adult dire wolf had witnessed during its patrols. A great shadow had risen from the cracked earth beyond the Black Thorn and was moving south towards Freylar. The shadow was amorphous, black as a winter's night and writhed with a sea of gangrenous tendrils which extended outwards from the core mass, which drifted purposefully towards its destination. Since he had never witnessed Narlakai moving in close formation, he could not be sure if the imagery painted poorly by the mind of the dire wolf was indeed that which he feared. Despite the poor mental rendition, the facts presented to him were compelling even in their raw state.

'Show me!'

'Out with Ragnar again?' he asked as he eased further back into his favoured rocking chair.

'Not tonight.' replied Rayna who promptly ensconced herself in the chair opposite. 'The Captain has other duties to attend to.'

Rayna rotated her right hand upwards and very slowly a small sphere of whitish-yellow light began to emerge from the palm of her upturned hand. The sphere was approximately the size of an apple. It rose steadily upwards before coming to rest a good pace above her head. The light emanating from the sphere was soft and inviting; the perfect accompaniment for his nocturnal literature. Rayna tended to turn in late, in the hope that tiredness would keep the worst of her repressed memories at bay, and so had taken to keeping him company after her lessons with Ragnar. On the first couple of occasions, Rayna chose to sit quietly, rocking gently in the chair opposite; he fancied the downtime did her good, allowing her to reflect on all she had learned. As time marched on, Rayna took to reading herself. To begin with she superficially scanned the texts he offered her, yet with each book Rayna consumed she became more engrossed. Now Rayna would immerse herself in heavy volumes on battle doctrine and strategy. Occasionally neither would speak to the other, and yet it was a comfortable silence which both of them readily enjoyed. Rayna also took the opportunity to practice her ability whilst they read. Initially Rayna was only capable of sustaining light enough for her to read for short periods of time; a reluctant candle provided a flickering yellow light after her ability had petered out for the night. Now though, Rayna was capable of filling the entire room with light up until she decided to turn in. Occasionally Rayna would have the light follow her into her room and remain lit until sleep spirited her soul away. The speed of her development was remarkable; Ragnar had even concurred as such. Rayna was relentless; be it morning, noon or late into the night, Rayna's capacity to learn was insatiable. Rayna devoured knowledge as though it nourished her, and she was ravenous. On one occasion he had questioned her on the matter, to which Rayna's response was 'I won't screw up again.' He never fully understood what Rayna meant by those words; her dialogue could be quite unique at times, a tell-tale sign that she was not native to Freylar.

'Kirika has also gone to ground of late, offering a similar reason. I'm guessing that you might know what these duties are.' said Rayna, seeking to tease further information from him on the subject.

'Might I now?' he replied with a single raised eyebrow, accompanied by one of his customary wry grins.

Rayna knew full well that he would not divulge information regarding sensitive matters concerning the safety of the domain, however, that did not stop her from attempting to glean valuable information from him. He decided it best to change the direction of their conversation, thus avoiding the possibility of Rayna cornering him with her inquisitive line of enquiry.

'You and Anika seem to be getting along well.' he said, swiftly changing the subject.

Rayna smiled and gave him a quick wink of her right eye acknowledging his diversionary tactic.

'Anika's positivity is refreshing, and she is extremely kind hearted. It would be difficult not to like her, however, I do find her zealous behaviour towards the order cause for possible concern.' replied Rayna.

'Hmm, I share your concern. Yet it is that behaviour which strengthens Anika's resolve. It allows her to stay the course of her training.'

'Yes, but that type of behaviour can also get you killed...I mean released.' said Rayna. 'There is a dangerously fine line between being goal-driven or determined versus the often single-minded impetus of a zealot.'

'The life of a Blade is a precarious one.' he replied. 'Besides, she has you to look out for her.'

'I am just an Aspirant Nathaniel. Anika will require a Blade of greater skill than my own to haul that fanatical backside of hers out of trouble should her headstrong nature seek it out.'

He laughed heartily, to which Rayna offered a coy half smile of her own. His daughter had always been quite reserved, often measuring the correctness of her opinions before rarely voicing them. By contrast Rayna told it how it was, yet she managed to do so in a jovial non-offensive manner. Whilst he still struggled to reconcile the loss of his daughter, Rayna's curious insertion into his life had helped to dull his pain. To say that she was a welcome distraction would have been unjust; Rayna was more than that, she had become like family to him. They had a connection to each other now which surpassed the fact that Rayna wore his daughter's visage and lodged with him. Whilst close proximity to Rayna and the need to protect what remained of his daughter had brought them closer together, it was their unexpectedly complimentary personalities which had cemented their relationship. In many ways he saw Rayna as his daughter's alter ego.

'I have something to give to you.' he said rather impulsively.

Rayna raised an eyebrow as he quickly rose from his chair to retrieve a narrow wooden box stood on its side, at a slight angle, amidst the piles of books heaped up behind where he had been sitting. The box had an ornate golden clasp, and was covered in a fine layer of dust, suggesting that some time had passed since last it was opened. Having found that which he sought, he passed the box to Rayna placing it squarely on her lap.

'That is for you to keep. I expect to see you make good use of it.' he said smiling warmly as he parted with the gift. 'Please, open it.'

Rayna studied the box curiously as he sunk back down into the comfort of his chair. She ran her fingers along the top of the box from the outer edges inwards, then promptly flicked the centre clasp upwards with her thumbs before folding back the lid. Inside was a falchion unlike no other; the weapon was beautifully crafted from a crystalline material similar to the Moonstones found throughout Freylar, yet the surface of the material bore no rough edges, giving it a slick, glassy appearance. The falchion emanated a dull silver light along with faint shadowy wisps, akin to smoke, which rose from the surface of the blade before quickly dispersing as though diluted by the air around them.

'The blade has been shaped from Dawnstone, amongst other things.' he said offering some explanation as to the weapon's curious nature.

'It's beautiful Nathaniel.' said Rayna in awe of the weapon. 'How did you come to own this blade?'

'It is one of a pair, though its twin is lost to me.' he explained. 'That is a tale for another time. Suffice to say that the two blades are unique to my knowledge. I have not seen or heard talk of others of their kind.'

'Nathaniel...I cannot take this. I am not deserving of such a weapon.' said Rayna who moved to pass the box back to him.

'Yes you can. The blade is called Shadow Caster, and it was not crafted to lie idly in a box. We have had our adventures together, the Caster and I, but now it is time for a new Freylarkin to wield it in battle.' he said doggedly.

Rayna grasped the falchion by the hilt then drew it forth from its place of rest. Whilst pulling Shadow Caster free of its wooden confines for closer inspection, translucent ephemeral smoke trailed from the flat of the blade as it passed silently through the air. The silvery-grey smouldering blade had an amorphous look to it, yet it felt solid enough in her grasp.

'Thank you Nathaniel.' said Rayna humbly. 'No one has ever gifted me something as precious as this before.'

'Do not be fooled by its deceiving appearance. That blade was shaped for battle, it will cut deep into your foes and weaken their resolve.' he said.

'And the Narlakai? Can it harm their form?' Rayna asked, eager to learn the capabilities of her new weapon.

'No more than those weapons forged of steel, though it will alert you to their presence.' he replied. 'The Narlakai are stimulated by their proximity to one another. Shadow Caster has the soul of such a monster imprisoned within it, thus it can sense their presence.'

Rayna stood up and moved towards the centre of the room so that she could try several practice swings to get a feel for the weight and reach of the blade. Judging by Rayna's favourable reaction, he supposed that she found the falchion lighter than perhaps expected. Dawnstone was incredibly lightweight, yet it was rarely ever seen in Freylar given its native home of Narlak.

'Nathaniel, this blade is exceptionally light. It feels more like an extension of my arm compared to my practice blades.' said Rayna excitedly.

'It will serve you well, more so given your lithe physique. Please do not take the following observation with disdain, but you are not perhaps...as strong as you once were prior to your...' he said, struggling to find the correct words to convey his train of thought without causing offence.

'Prior to my altered gender you mean?' said Rayna boldly, clearly enjoying his bashful awkwardness regarding her lot.

'Indeed.'

'It's in no way a taboo subject Nathaniel.' said Rayna plainly. 'You can ask me any questions which you may have.'

Rayna returned to her chair, then carefully placed Shadow Caster back in its box, which she placed neatly to one side on the floor.

'Changing sex has certainly been a shock for me, more so, I should imagine, given the sad circumstances under which the change occurred. I am not confident that I can adequately articulate my feelings on the subject, though it is what it is. My former life was a wreck, in part due to my own inaction though more so due to external influences over which I had little or no control. I cope by viewing what has happened in a positive light. Kirika has also aided me with the transition. I have been given another chance to attempt to live a life of worth, as opposed to one of survival. I will not squander the opportunity by despairing over my past misfortunes. There is little value in brooding over what has gone before, instead it makes more sense to plan what one will do next.'

'Hmm, wise counsel from one so young.' he replied thoughtfully. 'I admire your strength of character Rayna, it serves you well.'

They spoke very little for the remainder of the evening, content simply with each other's silent company as they continued their literary adventures; he with more of his late wife's poetry in hand whilst Rayna consumed further battle doctrine. It was early morning when Rayna finally decided to retire to her bed with the sphere of light she had manifested still in attendance. Although his nocturnal vision allowed him to continue reading after Rayna's departure, the loss of her company bothered him. He had become accustomed to reading alone after the release of his wife, yet now he found himself wanting more. The nights spent with Rayna had reminded him of the companionship he once enjoyed with his wife. Unable to concentrate in his solitude, he set down his latest captive piece of text and retired for the night.

It took them a good half cycle before either could lay eyes clearly on their target. His right leg was still healing, causing him to limp slightly as he walked. To make up some time he had employed the use of his wraith wings in part, though doing so was a risk; better to take advantage of cover from the cracked relief of the borderlands as opposed to skittering along at low altitude. Still, there was little choice in it. They needed to confirm the current situation with the Narlakai fast, and his injury only slowed them down. It was well into the night once they reached their destination, yet both were able to make out the great shadow spread thin across the horizon with their nocturnal vision. His companion snarled with contempt at what they were witnessing.

'Damn it! How did they get around us with such apparent ease.' he said aloud in a cursing tone.

They were several hundred paces from the writhing dark mass, yet even at this range it was clear as to both its composition and intent. The Narlakai were comparatively large, at nearly three paces in height with their tendrils outstretched, and yet he was witnessing at minimum a good thousand or so of the horrors drifting slowly towards Freylar in close formation. His heart sank at the sight. Pessimistic thoughts of atrocities to come flooded his mind as the ordeal with Alarielle raced to the fore once more. Freylar was ill-equipped to deal with an invasion of such nature. Whilst The Blades were a militant order to be reckoned with, their weapons were largely ineffective against the semi-gaseous forms of the Narlakai. Then there was the issue of numbers. Though few, the Narlakai still numbered more than his brothers and sisters in battle; low conception rates throughout Freylarian society meant that they habitually numbered fewer than other races. Due to their slow population growth, the Knights Thranis had taken to hunting the neighbouring Ravnarkai to the south in an attempt to stem the ferocious beasts' rate of expansion; The Hunt as they called it was part of their heritage, a tradition which went back some three thousand years. Culling the Ravnarkai was a dangerous affair, one which took its toll on the order. Their continuing crusade had cost them dearly over the passes. The Knights Thranis numbered approximately one tenth of The Blades who were Freylar's primary defence, yet without their sacrifice the vale would have been overrun long ago by the murderous Ravnarkai. By contrast, no one hunted the Narlakai.

The Narlakai had extended their front line making the task of out flanking the core mass extremely time consuming, yet they did not possess enough intellect to implement such a stratagem unaided. It became clear to him that other minds, possibly even aware of his own presence in the borderlands, were orchestrating the Narlakai movements; someone else was commanding them as a puppeteer would their marionettes. He needed to root out the hidden force at work, and to do that he needed to get closer. A glance skyward suggested there were no Sky-Skitters present; no doubt their sense of self-preservation had driven them away from the rolling shadow – that or they had all settled down for the night. He decided not to risk calling to the airborne messengers in the hope of potentially stirring one from slumber, thus the task of delivering his report fell to his lupine companion; four legs would be swifter than two, especially when one was lame. He wrote a brief coded message, utilising a cipher that only he and The Blade Lord conversed with privately, which he then entrusted to his companion for safe delivery.

'*Take this and deliver it to the Tri-Spires with all haste,*' he commanded telepathically to the dire wolf. '*Do not stop for any reason.*'

With his simple command successfully relayed, the dire wolf quickly disappeared into the night in a south-westerly direction. Although light on its feet, he estimated that it would take the dire wolf a good four cycles to reach the vale. In the interim the best he could hope to achieve was to learn more about the disturbing situation unfolding before him, though in order to glean further information he would need to shadow the mass. Moreover to try and determine the orchestrator behind the Narlakai's uncharacteristic advance upon Freylar he needed to get close, dangerously so. With swift and decisive movements he deftly traced an irregular path ever closer towards the advancing Narlakai as he sought to maximise his cover by hugging the limited dusty lumpy terrain available to him. Keeping low he limped between large groupings of rocks, fallen dead trunks and clumps of dried scrubland still clinging to the surface of the hostile landscape like parasites feeding on a dying host. The ground was hard and unforgiving; having spent a considerable amount of time scouting the borderlands he missed the comparatively soft footing of Freylar's grassy plains and dense woodland. Thoughts of Freylar with its verdant flora and crystal clear waters returned to him, reminding him of just how desolate and uninviting the borderlands actually were.

As he neared to within a couple of hundred paces of the Narlakai, his keen telepathic ability began to flare into being as it sensed the presence of another of his own kind; he had discovered the catalyst behind the Narlakai's apparent invasion of Freylar. Frantically he scanned the mass visually trying to lock onto the source of the presence, though whoever was responsible for agitating his telepathic senses was entirely obscured from sight. It frustrated him to know that another individual, presumably a Freylarkin, was in close proximity and yet he could neither track their absolute whereabouts nor determine their identity. It was a distinct possibility that the illusive presence was also now aware of his own existence, perhaps even his identity considering the telepathic mastery required to herd the vast numbers of Narlakai stretched out before him. Whilst he had suspected external forces at play, he had not anticipated happening across an individual of such power. It was extremely rare that he encountered a telepath capable of rivalling his own prowess, let alone completely surpassing it. Acknowledging the existence of such an individual was not easy for him, for to do so meant admitting their superior mastery of their shared ability. Initially he had sought to glean further information by shadowing his target, though there was now a real risk of him jeopardising the security of Freylar given the unknown capabilities of his newest rival. If the enemy was able to enter his mind forcibly and successfully extract information against his will, then that knowledge could be used to damning effect against any defence mounted by Freylar. He could ill afford to risk further exposure to the telepath, thus he decided to quickly withdraw to a safe distance well beyond the periphery of the individual's detection.

He cursed himself for releasing the dire wolf from his charge so soon, though his decision to do so had been made without the luxury of hindsight. Abandoning his surveillance to return to the pack was not an option; he needed to maintain a visual on the dark mass. He required other means of relaying his reports back to Freylar. Assuming his fortunes improved, he hoped to call a Sky-Skitter with the approach of dawn, thus enabling him to communicate the existence of the rogue telepath by airborne courier instead. In the meantime, all he could realistically do was track the Narlakai from a safe distance and observe their movements. Yet even that task proved to be less than straightforward. The Narlakai had already slipped through his dragnet once before and come dawn, when they would seek refuge from the sunlight in the cracks of the desolate landscape, there was every chance he would lose their scent again. He concluded that there had to be some means, hidden below the surface in all likelihood, by which the Narlakai could resume their ponderous advance long after the safety of night had abandoned them.

'Damn it! Who are you?' he cursed once more aloud to himself.

FIFTEEN
Serenity

His time spent with Kaitlin was magical. Through clever manipulation of staff rotas and extensive use of her charm to convince work colleagues to take their outstanding annual leave, Kaitlin managed to engineer the situation to their advantage, ensuring – for the most part at least – that they had the run of the library for themselves for almost three straight weeks. There were only a couple of occasions when he needed to be on his guard, during which time they played the roles of the unacquainted librarian and apex class citizen for the benefit of Kaitlin's peers. It was an amusing charade, one which they acted out flawlessly and with delicious amusement; like performing a play to an unsuspecting audience. A fresh change of well-tailored clothes, supplied by Kaitlin, and his invaluable bio-keys meant that Mr L. Cameron was now a staunch follower of the literary arts, according to the Infonet at least. During the day, he would immerse himself in fictional worlds created by talented authors long since laid to rest, so as not to interfere with Kaitlin's work duties. Come the evening, after the library had closed for the day, both he and Kaitlin would dine together prior to socialising at length well into the early hours. They would talk incessantly about everything and anything; they discussed the books they had each read, the current economic state, government policies, his unique way of life within the Wild along with anything else which took their fancy. Occasionally there were people in life who connected with one another effortlessly; his relationship with Kaitlin was exactly that, effortless. There were no secrets between them, each was perfectly candid with the other, though he never spoke of his increasing desire to be with her; he valued his relationship with Kaitlin, so he chose not to risk jeopardising what they had. When he had first sought Kaitlin's aid, his intent was purely to tide himself over whilst he got his self-sufficient lifestyle back on track. Now he found himself selfishly wanting more. A life of survival and constant hardship now seemed like a distant memory as he became increasingly satisfied with his comfortable, albeit temporary, lifestyle; and yet this new lifestyle of his could not last. Their ruse had no future for it was simply not sustainable. Yet despite the glaringly obvious truths, he still fancied himself a permanent resident of Kaitlin's library. He did not want their play-acting to come to an end, or their evening social soirees. The weekends were even more enticing. With public access to the library limited to the weekend mornings only, both he and Kaitlin had the run of the entire building during the afternoons. He realised that in essence they were two young adults playing house together, but he did not care. His time spent with Kaitlin was joyous and he did not wish it to end, though invariably nothing good ever lasted in his world.

It was the last Thursday of his stay with Kaitlin and both were settling in for the evening. Kaitlin had been particularly busy that day, as public attendance had been higher than usual. Empty plates lay strewn out before them from their evening meal which he habitually cooked. The act of cooking their evening meals was now a firm part of his daily routine; it was his way of saying thank you to his host, and the least he could do for Kaitlin given the kindness she had shown him. The library had a modest kitchen to the rear of the building strictly for staff use, but after hours it became his private culinary proving grounds. Whilst he never claimed to be good at cooking in general, he had become quite the chef during his stay with Kaitlin, of which she was most appreciative. After the long days spent attending to the library's general public and maintaining its continued order, Kaitlin was grateful for his efforts in the kitchen despite his initial bumpy start. Often she would crash out on one of the library's long stylish reading sofas and relax whilst taking in the delicious aromas which drifted in from the staff area. Though he still classed himself as a novice, he had successfully prepared a number of complex meals and enjoyed the challenge they provided. His main source of satisfaction though came from Kaitlin herself when she greedily devoured each and every meal laid before her, leaving behind nothing except for empty plates; the true measure of his success in the library's kitchen. That evening they had dined on a quick and easy meal he had prepared, and yet the contented look on Kaitlin's face after they had finished eating implied that his simple approach was well received. To accompany their meal Kaitlin had purchased a long-stemmed bottle containing a potent alcoholic drink, little of which now remained. He had no idea what the drink was made from, or indeed what it was called, however, the sweet creamy liqueur was incredibly easy to drink. In a short space of time they had both emptied the bottle; only a small amount of the intoxicating liquid remained in their glasses, which they cradled in their hands trying to eke out for as long as possible.

Without warning, Kaitlin gulped down the remainder of her drink then quickly abandoned her chair in favour of one of the library's long black reading sofas; she lay back on the sofa, allowing her right arm to hang off its edge after making herself comfortable. Her long white dress shirt pulled tightly across her breasts causing it to gape, revealing a glimpse of her pale pink lace bra. Even the alcohol in his system could not subdue his genitalia from complete arousal at the sight. Whether she realised it or not Kaitlin was a temptress.

'Have you ever been with a woman Callum?' asked Kaitlin grinning, widely as she lightly tapped the hard wood of the library's floor with the backs of her finger nails.

He was certain now that Kaitlin was indeed keenly aware of her own feminine wiles, though he could not tell whether the sweet liqueur was motivating her playful demeanour. At any rate her seductive pose, followed by her leading question, was enough to cause him to blush; any notion of reacting nonchalantly had been blown away by her sudden and direct line of enquiry. With a single question she had emotionally disarmed him, leaving him vulnerable and exposed. It frustrated him immensely that he found it difficult to articulate his feeling towards her.

'Err...once, though it was several years ago during the latter part of my time spent touring the metropolis' children's homes.' he attempted to explain coolly.

Kaitlin seemed to enjoy his unease, as he answered her question awkwardly, in much the same manner as an elder sister might tease their younger brother over matters of the heart. She was playing with him; that much was obvious. Whilst they spoke incessantly about a great many things, they had never once spoken of personal love interests.

'So how was it?' Kaitlin asked with a grin of amusement still etched across her face.

'You tease!' he replied.

'I know, and you rise to it so well.' replied Kaitlin, giggling at his expense.

'Well...if you must know, it was awkward.' he continued. 'Although she never let on, I'm pretty certain it was her first time as well. It was painful, for her that is...at least that's what I believed. Anyway, why are you asking me these questions Kaitlin? Surely you know how it goes.'

Kaitlin rolled her head away from him and stared absentmindedly towards the high ceiling of the library. For a moment she seemed to be lost in thought, cut off entirely from the world around her as she focused inwardly on a moment of private introspection. The act was not unknown to him, many times before Kaitlin had cut away abruptly mid-conversation whilst she took time out to marshal her thoughts. It was a trait he admired, being able to suddenly pause the moment and really think matters through before continuing one's journey through life; it was a mannerism he sought to emulate himself in time.

'I wouldn't know.' replied Kaitlin, after a good minute's silence. 'Perhaps you could educate me?' she continued, finally turning her head back towards him.

Kaitlin's mood had softened somewhat; her previously playful demeanour had now become one of self-contemplation in the wake of her own words. He could feel heat rising again in his face as he knowingly blushed once more. Despite his growing desire for Kaitlin, he had never once presumed that she might entertain feelings of her own towards him. He suddenly began to feel incredibly self-conscious. Perhaps their shared drink influenced Kaitlin's words, or maybe a fear of imminently returning to her normal lonely life had gotten the better of her. Either way, Kaitlin's casual proposal had caught him completely off guard. His secret desire to be with Kaitlin now seemed like an imminent reality and yet rather than being overwhelmed with excitement, instead he felt quite nervous about the prospect. He had wrongly assumed that a young woman of Kaitlin's natural good looks would have previously engaged in sexual relations with others; the thought of attempting to realise her, almost certainly unrealistic, first time expectations unnerved him. His desire for Kaitlin was stronger than ever, though he did not relish the thought of being her first time partner in the bedroom.

'Err...you've caught me off guard somewhat Kaitlin.' he said awkwardly before exhaling deeply. 'Is that what you truly want of me?'

'Yes.' replied Kaitlin resolutely.

'Very well, though perhaps we could wait until tomorrow evening.' he continued. 'I would rather, and I appreciate that this sounds incredibly cliché, that your first time was special and not a half-intoxicated sexual foray on that there sofa.'

'Callum, despite my lack of experience I am not a naive little girl.' replied Kaitlin flatly.

'Of that I'm very much aware. Though it may not matter to you, it matters a great deal to me. Tomorrow evening I shall enlighten you, as you put it, though I would prefer the experience to be more than a random encounter.' he said defiantly.

'Mea culpa. I never took you for a romantic.' replied Kaitlin with a childish grin.

'Hardly, but my first time was awkward and clumsy. I want you to have better memories than my own.'

There was no immediate response to his words, instead Kaitlin drifted once more into her own private head space as she considered his point of view. The devil on his shoulder screamed in his ear at his pathetic stalling, yet despite his burning desire his conscience would not allow him any other course of action. His life to date had been little more than the cumulative wreckage of a series of ever-worsening experiences, as such he remained adamant he would do right by Kaitlin; she deserved no less, though he began to muse as to whether his own expectations were themselves unrealistic.

'Thank you.' said Kaitlin finally deciding to rejoin their conversation. 'Is there anything you want me to do in readiness for tomorrow evening?'

'Actually there is one thing. Buy yourself something seductive.' he replied in an aloof manner.

Kaitlin's eyes widened following his words and her face flushed noticeably red. He smiled inwardly at her embarrassment, having finally turned the tables on his would-be lover. Kaitlin turned her head away quickly in a poor attempt to conceal her surprise embarrassment. Now he had found the correct way of countering Kaitlin's novice attempts at dominating him; the thought of teasing her further on the run up to their encounter amused him greatly. Regaining her composure, Kaitlin sat upright then called up a holographic access panel to the Infonet. Although Kaitlin broke the mould for the average young woman, nonetheless the female desire to shop for an occasion was stereotypically strong in her. It was abundantly clear to him that she would be otherwise engaged for the remainder of the evening, meaning that conversation would be limited, and so he chose to leave Kaitlin to it by quietly sloping off to resume his latest literary adventure.

It was strange to see her sleeping contently at such a late hour post dawn; typically Rayna's restless sleeping patterns ensured that she was up well before him in the mornings. He briefly considered waking her, though given the rarity of the situation he decided to allow Rayna to continue sleeping instead. Since commencing her studies in the arena, Rayna had taken no time out for rest as was expected of her given the enormous challenges she faced; he figured therefore that she was probably exhausted from her intensive training schedule, enough even perhaps to keep her harrowing repressed memories at bay. He closed the door to Rayna's room quietly then made his way downstairs. It was barely light outside, but he insisted that all Blade Aspirants in his charge commence their training early each cycle; he ensured that each Aspirant utilised their training cycles to their fullest so as to develop their skills to their maximum potential, especially now, given Lothnar's portent of a Narlakai advance. Wasting no time he grabbed a large handful of berries from a worn clay bowl sat upon the modest wooden table in the tree's ground floor living area; as was normally the case, he chose to consume his breakfast en-route to the arena in the mornings. After grabbing a few more items of fruit, he closed the door to their dwelling behind him quietly then set off towards the arena. He was anxious to catch up with Ragnar to see if there had been any further word from Lothnar on the Narlakai's amassed numbers. Although he understood the need to await further word from Lothnar on the matter, nonetheless the wait was frustrating. Standard protocol demanded that Lothnar maintain regular contact every three cycles in times of strife, thus a fresh report was imminent. With that in mind he picked up his pace through the dimly-lit wood, breaking into a light jog. He decided it prudent to seek out Ragnar at the Tri-Spires prior to entering the arena; if there was further word from Lothnar then he wanted to know immediately. Moreover, he wanted to see any further reports in their raw written state so that he could judge the potential severity of the situation for himself.

'Aleska, are you ok?' enquired Kirika politely.

'I am fine dear.' she lied, trying hard to conceal the worst of her pain. 'When you have lived as long as I have, it can take a little time to get going in the mornings.'

It was still early as they walked around the base of the Tri-Spires and down through the sprawl of alleys and outbuildings loosely connecting it to the arena below. As Kirika's mentor she insisted that they convene early morning every third cycle to catch up and discuss the young scrier's progress. There was a time when Kirika would meticulously inform her of the tasks assigned to her by Marcus, their progress and how she was advancing with her studies. As well as instructing Kirika on the advanced use of her ability, she would also provide counsel on the intricacies of subterfuge and politicking in general. As time continued its relentless march forwards, however, she became a crutch less utilised as her protégé began to stand tall on her own; it would not be long now before the young scrier stepped out from her shadow entirely. It wounded her ego accepting that she had all but passed over the reins to the next generation; she knew well that her time on the ruling council of Freylar grew short as a consequence. Now their morning walks were little more than social affairs during which they conversed openly in relative privacy.

'I hear that Rayna has settled in well. You have done a great job helping her to integrate with our society.' she said as they began to close on the arena's west gate.

'I am not so sure about that Aleska. Nathaniel has likely taught her far more than I.' replied Kirika humbly.

'You should not cast your efforts in such a poor light. Nathaniel would have taught her much about close combat, military strategy and more besides, but he is not the most sociable of individuals, nor is he fully in touch with the current youth of Freylar.' she said. 'He would have imparted little practical knowledge of use to Rayna beyond the field of battle.'

'And yet you seem to socialise with Nathaniel rather well.' Kirika teased playfully.

She smiled warmly at her protégé; it pleased her to know that they had broken down the formal relationship which once existed between them. She was confident that her efforts to create a close bond between them would ensure the relatively free flow of information down to her once she ultimately stepped down from the ruling council.

As their leisurely meandering brought them to the west gate proper, she spied Nathaniel approaching from the edge of the vale below. Without conscious intent, a wide smile formed across her face. She enjoyed The Teacher's company a great deal and found herself valuing their friendship increasingly more so with each pass. Kirika inclined her head towards Nathanial's approach, offering a childish grin in acknowledgement of her unvoiced thoughts. She chose to ignore Kirika's obvious good-natured teasing and instead cast her gaze back down towards the vale. It was then that she caught a glimpse of something else in the periphery of her vision. Something in the distance was cutting a diagonal path towards their position from the north-west. Whatever the creature was, it moved rapidly, bounding frenetically across the sloping base of the vale's southern ridgeline as it made its way ever closer. Kirika too had apparently noticed the cause of her momentary distraction, as had Nathaniel, who had promptly unfurled his wraith wings in an attempt to intercept the target before it could reach them.

'What is that?' asked Kirika in a worried tone.

'Dear, if *your* eyes cannot answer that question then there is little hope that my own will do so for you.' she replied. 'It looks to be a quadruped of some description, perhaps a wolf even.'

'Aleska, wolves do not venture into the vale. They shun our very existence.' said Kirika.

'I realise that Kirika, but what else could it be?'

Both of them fixed the creature with glaring eyes as it continued to head directly towards their position. Although clearly adept at traversing difficult terrain, the creature made numerous clumsy errors, suggesting that either its legs were tiring from exhaustion or it had instead sustained some form of injury. Despite its obvious handicap, the creature continued to make swift progress and threatened to reach them ahead of Nathaniel who was pushing hard up the mountain side. As the creature drew ever closer across the verdant slope of the southern ridgeline, their eyes quickly picked out its key distinguishing features the moment it snapped into focus. Large pointed ears, thick tail and a long muzzle confirmed her initial speculation to be partially true at least, however, its build was ferocious; it was certainly no ordinary wolf, it was more than double the size one would expect of such an animal.

'That is a dire wolf, I am certain of it!' she stated.

'Aleska, defend yourself.' said Kirika, hurriedly reaching for a dagger concealed beneath her dress strapped to her outer right thigh.

'Wait! This one appears to be mission bound.' she replied, quickly motioning Kirika to stand down.

Shortly after identifying the oversized canine it was upon them. Rather than charge head-long in, as initially feared, instead the dire wolf slowed its pace considerably prior to impact. It collapsed neatly before them, pressing itself flat to the ground whilst breathing heavily. Like a massive set of bellows, the dire wolf's lungs sucked up large volumes of air before exhaling noisily, producing a sound akin to that of waves rolling across a shore. The dire wolf was clearly exhausted from its journey, suggesting it had travelled a considerable distance to reach them. Cautiously she dropped to her knees before the exhausted lumbering wolf, at the mildly painful expense of her aging joints which sought to remind her of their advanced maturity. Trying to put the animal at ease, she cupped her arms around its wide neck and proceeded to massage its strained neck muscles. It was then that Nathaniel arrived, though fortunately he had the sense to sheath his blade, realising quickly that the dire wolf had not sought to harm them. For a Freylarkin of such pale complexion, Nathaniel was visibly flushed; sweat beaded across his forehead due to the exertion of his failed attempt to intercept the dire wolf.

'It does not appear to mean us any harm.' she said confirming the situation aloud.

'Agreed, but why is it here?' questioned Nathaniel in a raspy voice, seeking to regain his composure.

Assured that it meant them no harm, she began to feel round the lower neck of the dire wolf, following up on a hunch. Sure enough her hands contacted with the familiar smooth surface of a message scroll tied around the animal's neck. The tiny scrolls were tools of communication commonly used by Freylar's scouts to deliver reports back to the Tri-Spires. Typically Sky-Skitters were used to relay such communications, however, in times of need, scouts were known to improvise by using other suitable couriers; she had only seen a dire wolf used once before for such a task, as their savage nature often made them unsuitable.

'It delivers us a message.' she said, quickly unravelling the scroll and promptly passing it to Kirika. 'Here, you read it dear. Your eyes will serve us better than my own.'

Kirika took the scroll and proceeded to make attempt at deciphering its message, though she appeared to have difficulty translating the text.

'It is encoded with a cipher unknown to me. I will try and determine the origin of the message instead.' said Kirika.

Kirika closed her eyes and gently brushed her fingertips along the length of the scroll. Her conventional eyes had failed her, hence Kirika turned instead to the aid of her second sight to fill in the blanks of the mystery presented to them. Aleska observed judgementally as her greatest student masterfully delved into the past, tracing the origin of the scroll back to the hand which had placed the written message upon it.

'The message is from Lothnar.' said Kirika quickly reopening her eyes.

'Then it is likely intended for Marcus. I am scheduled to meet with him this afternoon. I can pass the message on to him then.' she replied.

'No! It must be delivered to him now.' said Nathaniel cutting in abruptly. 'There can be no delay.'

'And why is that Nathaniel?' she asked, seeking to tease further information from The Teacher.

'We will know the facts soon enough.' replied Nathaniel. 'Come with me, both of you. We need to deliver this report with all haste.'

Nathaniel was clearly withholding information; strange that he was aware of events entirely unknown to her. Ordinarily the situation would have been reversed, given her position on the ruling council; therefore she concluded that Lothnar's report pertained to events likely leading them towards a path of war. She could not tell if Kirika was a part of the loop either; their time together had been well spent and Kirika had become quite the politician over the passes. She had taught her future successor to guard her secrets well, perhaps even a little too well. For the first time since her ascension to the ruling council, almost a lifetime ago, she felt omitted. There was a time when Marcus would have included her in all matters, regardless of their significance, and yet that time was now fast coming to an end, or so it now seemed. Despite the obvious subterfuge, she was accepting of the fact and harboured no bitterness towards her fellow council members. It was time she forged the next chapter of her life, and in doing so stepped down from the council of her own volition.

'So be it, however, I ask that you tend to our deserving messenger here before we depart.' she said.

'Very well, though I trust that you will ensure that its temperament remains in check.' said Nathaniel. 'I am not comfortable with the prospect of an adult dire wolf wandering around Freylar.'

SIXTEEN
Gambit

Lothnar's report was clear; the Narlakai were marching on Freylar, yet despite the clarity of the words – after he had successfully deciphered them – he still needed to read the message scroll twice before its contents registered fully. After reading the report for the second time, he quickly summoned a council of war beneath the arena. There he promptly broke the disheartening news in full to his fellow Paladins, Valkyries and queen Mirielle, also in attendance, who sat in Lothnar's vacant seat at the large oval table before them. Most were obviously horrified by the likelihood of invasion, some visibly angry at the prospect; even Thandor's usual aloof demeanour had been replaced by one of both concern and disgust, and surprisingly he was the first to break the mounting tension in the chamber.

'Marcus, this report makes no sense.' said Thandor. 'To our knowledge the Narlakai have never previously demonstrated a desire for conquest. Why do so now?'

'Agreed, though I do not have an answer for you brother.' he replied candidly.

'They are nightmare horrors, driven by instinct and little more.' boomed Ragnar, bringing his heavy right fist down onto the table. 'Why waste time attempting to understand their motives? They are marching on Freylar. We must move now if we are to meet this threat in the field.'

'I agree that we cannot fight them in the vale, but if we establish their motive we can potentially end this threat without mass conflict.' replied Thandor.

'And what if they have simply exhausted their current food supply and are migrating to fresh pastures. What do you propose we do then Thandor, poke them with your rapier perhaps?' retorted Ragnar angrily.

'I could offer them your head. That might slow them down.' Thandor replied flatly.

'Enough!' he cried. 'We cannot meet this threat in the vale. I asked Ragnar to identify a battlefield of our own choosing, to the north of the vale, shortly after Lothnar first identified the Narlakai's swelling numbers'

'If we intercept the soul stealers at the edge of Bleak Moor, we can secure the high ground before they penetrate our domain.' Ragnar explained.

'And what numbers would we be committing to this campaign?' enquired Natalya.

'Everything!' he said resolutely. 'According to Lothnar's early reports, we are at a numerical disadvantage even if we commit the entirety of The Blades.'

'You mean to send the Aspirants into battle?' asked Mirielle, her voice betraying her obvious concern.

'We must.' replied Ragnar.

'Agreed,' Nathaniel said. 'It is what they are trained for my queen.'

'That will leave the vale entirely undefended,' said Thandor. 'Will the Knights Thranis not lend their support?'

'I intend to speak with them after this meeting is concluded, however, our relationship with the Knights Thranis remains damaged.' he replied. 'We cannot assume any aid will come from them. Bad blood aside, the Ravnarkai continue to warrant their crusade which of course is their primary concern.'

'Then we are alone in this...' Mirielle mused aloud.

There was a natural brief recess following their queen's poignant statement; indeed they were alone, and yet failure was unimaginable. Even Ragnar's anger abated whilst each Freylarkin who sat around the large wooden oval table quietly considered the ramifications of the decision they all knew had to be made. They could not afford to fight a skirmish within the confines of the vale; the loss of civilian life would be considerable. The Narlakai slipped easily between areas of cover like shadows dancing on the edge of one's periphery, so they needed to face their apparent invaders in the open where cover was sparse. Bleak Moor would serve them well in this regard, plus the height advantage that the terrain offered them would make assessing their opponent's movements more easily. Ragnar's choice of battlefield was tactically sound, though it would draw the main fighting force out of the vale; a wager they had little choice but to accept.

'I understand more than most the risk of leaving the vale undefended, indeed the very notion is anathema to me, but we have little choice but to do so. Therefore I plan to station a rearguard at Scrier's Post, consisting predominantly of Aspirants. Nathanar will command them, for it is high time his leadership was tested fully.' he proclaimed. 'Nathaniel, I would like you to accompany Nathanar as his second-in-command. Nathanar will benefit from your counsel and your presence will help put the Aspirants at ease.'

Nathaniel nodded respectfully. Whilst he suspected The Teacher yearned to stand on the frontline alongside The Blades of the war council, Nathaniel's skills would be utilised to better effect steeling the jangled nerves of the Aspirants during their first time in the field.

'If the Narlakai manage to flank the main force then the rearguard will see battle quickly enough.' he continued. 'Mirielle, I ask that you take refuge at the Cave of Wellbeing. Aleska will oversee operations there. The Tri-Spires will not be safe if our defence is breached.'

Mirielle too offered him a silent nod of confirmation, though the concerned look on her face told him that she was far from happy with the situation. Although service under Mirielle's rule had seen plenty of conflict for The Blades, the notion of defending against an imminent invasion was alien to her; understandably Mirielle feared for the safety of the Freylarkai and their domain.

'Knowing Lothnar, he will be shadowing the Narlakai as we speak, attempting to learn all he can about our enemy's strategy. I remain hopeful that he will find a weakness in their assault or indeed the motivation you seek Thandor.' he said.

'Agreed, and for Freylar's sake I pray that he learns of the truth behind the Narlakai's advance.' replied Thandor.

'You mean invasion?' Ragnar cut in.

'They have not invaded Freylar as yet Ragnar.' said Natalya.

'Semantics aside, when do you propose that we march Marcus?' asked Kirika.

'Immediately.' he replied.

She failed to recall the last time she had slept in – and to such a late hour too! It was well into mid-cycle by the time she fully awoke. Light from outside flooded her room, invigorating her body, and a cool breeze tickled her exposed skin through the single open window. For the first time since her arrival in Freylar she felt wholly content as she lay semi-naked on her bed, staring vacantly at the twisted wooden ceiling above. She was late for her training, and yet her serene state of being failed to register any concern regarding the fact. She knew well that Nathaniel would not react favourably to her late arrival in the arena, and yet he had allowed her to over-sleep. She rolled gently on to her left side and regarded the full length of her body; it was strange that she no longer felt uncomfortable with her new physique. She recalled the awkwardness of her first dress fitting with Larissa, and yet now such activities were a part of her way of life. Scavenging for food, planning one's sleeping arrangements and moving from one bolt-hole shelter to the next were no longer concerns of hers. Although living conditions amongst the forest dwellers were rudimentary, they were nonetheless comfortable; her lifestyle now, in comparison to her once fragile existence in the Wild, had improved markedly. Adapting to her new way of life had not been easy, despite Kirika's welcome aid in easing the transition, yet she had no regrets. The sphere of light had given her the chance of a fresh start, and she had taken it regardless of its guise; she had no qualms at having accepted its unique offer, though she craved to know more about the enigmatic entity. The truth revealed to her through Mirielle's enhanced sight on the cycle of her rebirth was inescapable; it tugged at the back of her mind, refusing to let go. Like an itch unable to be scratched, the sight of the sphere's lattice layers criss-crossing the sky haunted her soul. The revelation had caused her to frequently question the very nature of Freylar and its existence.

    Fully awake now, and with too many complex thoughts running through her head to ever return to sleep, she willed herself out of bed and set about her routine. After dressing herself and setting her hair in the manner Kirika had taught her, she grabbed Shadow Caster along with some fruit for her commute to the arena and set off. It was rare that she travelled to the arena during waking hours, typically she left early in the morning and returned late afternoon, and so it was unusual for her to witness Freylarkin life within the forest in full bloom. She had failed to appreciate just how many Freylarkai inhabited the forest and its bespoke dwellings, given most of her waking time was spent in the arena itself. She began to understand why it was that Kirika had become detached from the place of her childhood; it was easy to lose oneself in the hustle and bustle of life in and around the Tri-Spires. Nathaniel had chosen to ground himself in the heart of the forest, a notion which only now she began to fully appreciate, since life within the forest was abundant. All around her Freylarkai went about their routines, unperturbed by the surrounding verdant woodland. As she strolled leisurely through the forest she focused her attention on the ambient sounds of agriculturists working the surrounding land, artisans fashioning tools and household items with hot metal, as well as outdoor classes educating the youth of Freylar. The forest played host to a sizable hidden community which she had previously been largely unaware of. As she leisurely picked her way along the numerous forest trails she intermittently glimpsed the forest's natives as they curiously observed her presence, in most cases for the first time. It had slipped her mind entirely that those closer to Nathaniel's home had likely not seen a great deal of her, if they had seen her at all, since her arrival and that any local knowledge of her presence within the forest was likely based on hearsay alone; now her

unsuspecting neighbours had first-hand confirmation that
The Guardian lived amongst them.

Later that cycle, once she finally arrived at the base of
the arena, it rapidly became clear to her that an event of
great importance was sparking into life. The habitual clash
of sparring blades emanating from the arena had been
replaced by audible roll calls and frantic chatter. Stepping
into the arena proper, she bore witness to a logistical hive of
activity which saw weapons and armour rapidly being
distributed amongst her brothers and sisters. Initially she
supposed that the frenetic activity was the result of an
impromptu drill, designed to keep The Blades sharp, though
as she surveyed the organised chaos she spied most, if not
all, of the Paladins and Valkyries present. It quickly
became apparent to her that it was no drill she had casually
walked into the middle of, but instead The Blades were
urgently preparing for some form of major conflict. As she
stood in the eye of the storm, clueless as to the cause of the
goings-on around her, Anika came running towards her
dressed in full battle regalia.

'Where have you been Rayna?' said Anika in a mildly
scolding tone.

'Does that really matter right now Anika,' she replied
tersely, 'What's going on?'

'You just missed Marcus publically addressing The
Blades. It seems likely that the Narlakai intend to invade
Freylar!' replied Anika, clearly disgusted by the notion.
'Marcus has given the order for The Blades to march out
and intercept them, before they can reach our domain.'

In the short moments following Anika's grim overview
of events, her joyous mood rapidly turned towards darker
thoughts like a mid-summer's storm rolling in over the

horizon. The thought of an invasion was completely at odds with the majestic surroundings of Freylar; why would a race largely driven by instinct potentially seek to destroy their way of life she mused. Ragnar had recently hinted at the possibility during their first late evening training session; now his dark prophecy threatened to engulf Freylar.

'Where are we being stationed?' she enquired.

'The bulk of the Aspirants are being assigned to Nathanar's rearguard. We are to be stationed at Scrier's Post, to guard against the possibility of the main force being outflanked.' Anika replied. 'Nathaniel will be accompanying us.'

'And who will remain in the vale?' she asked.

'Operations to evacuate the vale will commence shortly. We are fully committed to the campaign.' said Anika.

'Hmm, because we are vastly outnumbered I'm sure. Marcus can't afford to send The Blades piecemeal to the enemy and can ill afford to fight a messy skirmish in the vale itself. This is a desperate gambit indeed. Where is the main force planning to make contact with the Narlakai?'

'At the edge of Bleak Moor.' said Nathaniel who had managed to approach them unnoticed amidst the background commotion. 'Did you enjoy your sleep?' he continued with a wry grin.

'Indeed I did, though perhaps I should have slept a while longer.' she replied jovially as Ragnar also made his approach.

'You had best prepare yourself Rayna, for you will be one of only two light bringers attached to the rearguard.' boomed Ragnar. 'The remainder will predominantly be assigned to the main force whilst one or two others accompany queen Mirielle's personal entourage.'

'Ragnar, can we not employ the services of civilian light bringers?' she enquired.

'They lack the required training to be of any real value in battle,' Ragnar replied.

'Indeed they could be a liability, and we dare not build our defence upon questionable foundations.' added Nathaniel.

'You mean to say that if they were broken in battle, they would damn others in the process?' she pressed.

'My books were not wasted on you I see.' replied Nathaniel.

'Enough chatter.' Ragnar broke in. 'The Blades will be marching out shortly. Rayna, get your armour on and join your fellow Aspirants. Nathanar will address you all shortly.'

Having barked his orders, Ragnar promptly turned and left them where they stood. Nathaniel gave her a small wink of his right eye then hurried to catch Ragnar up. All around Blades were furiously preparing weapons and armour in readiness for the campaign. Whilst the veterans of the order seemed driven by a singular united purpose, her fellow Aspirants by contrast appeared less so; indeed most of the Aspirants seemed to be disassociated from the world around them as though lost in the whirlwind of frenetic activity. It was then that doubt started to creep into her mind; sparring in the arena was one thing, engaging an enemy in battle was entirely different. Although she could not directly compare the experiences of her previous life, she knew well enough how crippling both fear and the need to survive could be. She began to fully appreciate

Nathaniel's view on the use of civilian Freylarkai for their abilities in times of crisis; how could the order rely on such individuals when its own less-experienced members were having a difficult time dealing with an impending call to arms. Her causal demeanour, as a likely result of over-confidence from her initial success in the arena, began to wane as she started to question her own mettle. Despite her own creeping reservations, Anika proved the exception to the Aspirants' general demeanour; the zealot in her had surfaced to the fore once more and was the driving force behind Anika's iron resolve. The remainder of the Aspirants, however, seemed to be aimlessly standing around waiting for Nathanar to rally them, which he did not. The unfocused attentions of the Aspirants reflected poorly on them, which would not do.

'Anika, follow me. Let's focus the minds of the rearguard shall we.' she said.

'Agreed, they are an embarrassment to the order.' Anika replied disdainfully.

She hurried towards the nearest armour stand where she selected hard leather armour in line with her lithe feminine build, along with a set of vambraces fashioned from a dull metallic alloy, leather cuisses and matching greaves. Anika helped her quickly don her chosen armour and adjusted it tightly following a well-practiced ritual. Both then marched directly towards the meandering Aspirants.

'You might want to cover your eyes.' she said mischievously to Anika who looked entirely bemused by her suggestion.

She outstretched her arms then cupped her hands allowing light to manifest within them like pools of pure white liquid, then in a single explosive act she clapped her hands violently together sending out an expanding wave of brilliant white light which ran down the centre of the rabble before them. Those facing her moaned as they immediately raised their hands attempting to block out the worst of the light, whilst others turned on their heels alarmed by the unexpected explosion of light. She grinned childishly as those Aspirants temporarily blinded by her light slowly began to focus on their unexpected tormentor. She had sought to gain their attention with a cheap trick, and now she had it. All she needed to do now was find the right words for her impromptu rally.

'We are on the cusp of war, and yet you roam this arena like lost infants. You are Blades, all of you, regardless of rank. You are the bulwark which shields Freylar from those who would see it fall to ruin. Yes, we are nervous. Yes, we are inexperienced. But act as such when you stand before the Narlakai and we shall all lose our souls to their eternal damnation.' she proclaimed, surprising even herself. 'Now, each of you, armour up and take your place alongside your fellow Blades. Nathanar commands us, and we shall not leave him wanting. I didn't get out of bed this morning simply to hand my soul to the Narlakai.'

Her unexpected rally stunned many into silence. Even non-Aspirants close enough to hear her sermons looked to her in curious bemusement. As her words began to take root inside her brothers and sisters, heads started to nod cautiously in agreement and were shortly followed by occasional cheers of affirmation. Regardless of her unorthodox delivery, the results were soon apparent as those already wearing their armour moved to stand in line before her, quickly forming disciplined ranks. Without any prompting on her part, Anika stepped from her side and began to walk the length of the unit now rapidly taking shape before them; Anika meticulously scrutinised each Aspirant in turn, ensuring the proper wearing of their chosen armour. Where one fell short of her expectations, Anika intervened, correcting any perceived deficiencies so that each Aspirant was fit for service to the order. It filled her with renewed hope to see her brothers and sisters come together in unison ready to face the imminent darkness which threatened to extinguish their very being. As the last few ranks moved into formation, she turned around to match the unit's facing. Satisfied with her inspection, Anika promptly returned to her side. Shortly thereafter, Nathanar, Marcus and Nathaniel made their approach at the front of the unit, facing them head-on. Nathaniel was sporting one of his familiar wry grins, though he also had a look of pride on his face.

'Good,' Marcus said warmly, 'Now stands before me a unit which I can use on the field of battle. You should each be proud of yourselves. It is an honour to defend both our domain and our queen in times such as this. Should the main force find itself outflanked during the engagement, responsibility will pass to yourselves to defend Freylar and its people. This is your duty, and one which you must each fulfil at any personal cost. Nathanar will command you now. I wish you all good fortune.'

Before Marcus turned to rejoin those more experienced within the order, he offered her a courteous nod followed by a curious smile. Although he spoke no words to her as such, Marcus' body language spoke for him and favourably so; knowing that she had pleased The Blade Lord helped enormously to put her at ease. Only Nathanar and Nathaniel remained before them now, each judging them according to their own assessment criteria. With command of the rearguard now officially assigned to Nathanar, the Blade Master stepped forward to address those under his command.

'Rayna, after that little demonstration I am inclined to elevate you to the position of sergeant for the purposes of this campaign. You will report to Nathaniel who is second in command of the rearguard. You will see to it that your fellow Aspirants are ready at all times, and that my orders are carried out swiftly. Are you ready for such responsibilities?' he asked in a soft but firm tone of voice.

'I am ready.' she replied, cutting straight to the point.

'Good,' replied Nathanar. 'Shortly we will march ahead of the main force to Scrier's Post, just as soon as Nathaniel and I have finalised arrangements. I want to make good time and ensure that the rearguard takes up a solid defensive position when we arrive at our station. Please ensure that the Aspirants are ready to march. Anika will assist you.'

Nathanar spoke softly once more and was nothing if not pleasant, though she wondered how their newly appointed commander would fair in the heat of battle; she could not imagine a Freylarkin of Nathanar's disposition barking orders across a war-torn battlefield. Despite her reservations, she was keenly aware that individuals often reacted very differently in combat situations, having read volumes on the subject courtesy of Nathaniel's modest library back at their tree. She mused as to whether Nathaniel had been stationed with the rearguard to monitor Nathanar's ability to command in the field, and yet it was equally probable that Marcus simply wished the Aspirants to have a friendly face alongside them during their first campaign. Still, regardless of whether or not Nathanar could command the rearguard effectively in the field, she had seen him sparring in the arena enough times to know that he was razor sharp in combat; knowing that their ranks included both The Teacher and an accomplished Blade Master made her feel more at ease.

'Understood.' she replied gently nodding her head.

Nathanar and Nathaniel took their leave and rejoined Marcus on the other side of the arena. Earlier that morning she had been enjoying a well-deserved rest from her routine practice and yet now she stood waiting to march towards a likely war; the absurdity of the situation would have given her cause enough to laugh, if not for the uncertainty of their fate. Perhaps she should have stayed in bed.

SEVENTEEN
Restless

It was late afternoon when the rearguard began their march to Scrier's Post; the primary force marched out shortly thereafter and could be observed to the south-east for some time, like a snaking shadow, until the fading light of the cycle saw fit to bid their kin farewell. When darkness finally descended upon them, it fell to Kryshar and Rayna to light their path at the head of the column; Kryshar was an experienced light bringer, though was newly inducted to The Blades as a rookie Aspirant. It concerned him greatly that only two light bringers were assigned to the rearguard, however, The Blades were stretched thin on resources, given the magnitude of their campaign, and Marcus could ill afford to leave the primary force lacking. Their march had been relatively trouble-free, aside from the occasional stumble by Aspirants failing to properly watch their footing during their ascent from the vale. After they had left the vale the landscape opened up considerably, bidding them farewell to the verdant flora they were accustomed to, which was instead gradually replaced by bleak scrubland and the occasional isolated copse. They had marched hard and fast through the night, as commanded by Nathanar, and made good their arrival at Scrier's Post just prior to dawn.

Scrier's Post was an isolated and lonely manor, resembling a chapel of sorts, as per its designer's original intent; it was built as a sanctuary for scriers seeking peace and isolation, allowing them to focus more clearly on the images presented to them via their second sight. There was a time when the sanctuary had been the destination of frequent pilgrimages by scriers across Freylar of varying ability, though more recent events of a regrettable nature had seen the allure of frequenting the landmark peter out entirely. Now the sanctuary stood as an abandoned reminder of the omnipresent dangers which threatened to consume those scriers unable to temper their thirst for knowledge. During its inception, Scrier's Post had been wrought from a raised bed of rock by shapers of old; thus it occupied a commanding elevated position over the predominantly barren landscape. Surrounding the grounds of the sanctuary was an organic-looking rock wall, some four paces in height; more evidence of talented shapers bending the laws of nature to suit their own agendas. The wall was entirely unbroken save for a single, black-gated archway towards the south of the property, through which they had passed upon their arrival. Since Scrier's Post had been left to fall into a state of neglect over the passes, the large imposing gate was seized firmly shut when first the rearguard attempted to breach the property. It had taken the combined will of several telekinetic Freylarkin to liberate the gate once more, thus granting them access to the derelict site. The grounds within the perimeter were fairly bland and unremarkable, though the sanctuary itself was a far more intriguing sight. The same techniques used to shape the Tri-Spires were also evident in the construction of the sanctuary; the entire structure appeared to grow out of its founding rock bed thus it had an organic look about it despite being crafted from stone. The sanctuary had a pitched roof, again fashioned from stone, around the base of which ran a low parapet. Long slit windows ran the height of either end of the structure, allowing light to enter the interior of the sanctuary, which in turn refracted through an enormous Moonstone; this was suspended from its high vaulted ceiling on a thick silver chain. The interior of the sanctuary was almost as bare as the surrounding grounds, save for the Moonstone and a crude flight of worn stone steps which ascended into the open roof space providing access to the external parapet above. At least the structure was watertight, for which they were extremely thankful given the sudden severe downturn in the weather; ominously dark clouds had started to gather from the north and were now beginning to roll in across the bleak horizon. Rayna had asked him, rather dryly, if the Freylarkai could also control the weather; the very notion had amused him greatly at the time.

Given the nocturnal behaviour of the Narlakai, Nathanar had ordered half of the rearguard to rest within the sanctuary during the morning whilst the remainder of the force dug in and looked to fortify their position. Scrier's Post was ill-suited to withstanding an attack, yet despite this fact the rearguard managed to secure adequate fire points behind the roof parapet which gave them a commanding view over the grounds and beyond. Due to the acute angles involved, those Freylarkin wielding bows would not be able to draw line of fire to enemies pressed hard against the outer wall of the perimeter. In order to reduce these blind spots, Nathanar ordered their only shaper to craft a handful of arrow slits through the perimeter wall; the preservation of historical landmarks was not chief amongst Nathanar's immediate concerns. Yet despite their meticulous preparations, they were not expecting to engage the enemy at all; it was still hoped that Marcus would command the primary force to victory against the Narlakai, regardless of their own inferior numbers. Come noon the rearguard changed shifts allowing the remainder of the force the opportunity to rest before the black of night descended on Scrier's Post. He tried to get some rest himself; however, recent events occupied his waking thoughts, refusing to grant him the small mercy of sleep as they clawed incessantly at his mind. He sat upright against the sanctuary's east wall, knowing too well that sleep would not come. Whilst he was a veteran of too many wars, nerves still managed to play their part during the build up to any mass confrontation. It was not his own fate which overly concerned him, but instead those under his charge. He wondered if any of the Aspirants littering the sanctuary floor truly slept themselves knowing the potential ill fate which silently stalked them. Finally convincing himself that sleep would indeed elude him, he quietly left the sanctuary and ventured outside in search of something else to occupy his thoughts. The light was starting to fade now as dusk began to settle around them. The rain had subsided, yet the ever-present drizzle continued to trace an irregular path down from the grey sky above, carried by a light wind which had now picked up. A wry grin momentarily flashed across his face as he amusingly acknowledged the way in which the weather which had chosen to mimic their gloomy mood. Droplets of rain spattered against his exposed arms where they promptly resumed their irregular descent, following the contours of the many scar lines running haphazardly across his skin. He disliked fighting in the rain since one could never be entirely sure of their footing. Although the disadvantage equally affected their enemies, he preferred to rely solely on skill rather than luck when battling opponents. Still actual fighting was never as practiced in the arena, and so he lectured the Aspirants well on the merits of being mindful of their surroundings.

Potentially fighting against the Narlakai was task enough for the green combatants, but doing so in the rain would worsen their chances of victory if indeed they were engaged in battle.

He paced the grounds observing the general demeanour of the rearguard; those who saw him nodded politely out of respect to their mentor. Most of the Aspirants he spied wore expressions of concern or anxiety, but more worryingly he noted a handful whose expressions were entirely vacant, suggesting that they could not fully come to terms with their current lot. He had seen the same look on countless faces throughout past campaigns; often said Freylarkin were the first to fall in any confrontation, though he hoped they would not share that fate, if indeed they were drawn into actual battle. Nathanar's presence had helped little to embolden the morale of the Aspirants. Whilst Nathanar was a poster boy for The Blades, maintaining an unblemished reputation, he lacked an edge with which to elevate himself in the eyes of his brothers and sisters. Despite being an able leader, and more than capable of commanding the rearguard in such dark times, they needed more than just a conformist commander; though Nathanar was an exemplary member of the order, they needed someone with determination, grit and a fiery spirit with which to tear through the darkness threatening to consume them. The rearguard needed more than just a model guide, instead they needed an icon; someone who would inspire them when faced with adversity. Hence the very reason Marcus had selected Ragnar as Captain of The Blades, despite his obvious shortfalls.

'Nathaniel, surely you should be resting?' shouted a distant voice.

Nathanar had seen him pacing the grounds like a restless caged animal, and now made his approach across the grounds towards him.

'We need you fully rested for the long night ahead of us brother.' said Nathanar, coming to stand before him.

Nathanar cut an impressive figure; for a Freylarkin Nathanar was considered quite tall, though he lacked Ragnar's broad physique, and possessed piercing blue eyes and straight raven-black hair which ended just below his jaw line. Like Marcus, Nathanar favoured the double-handed sword as his weapon of choice which, coupled with his long arms, gave him an enormous reach in battle.

'Sleep eludes me Nathanar. I seek to distract myself from thoughts of battle. Perhaps I could help to steady some of the Aspirants' jangled nerves.'

'That would certainly benefit our cause. They have a deep respect for you Nathaniel, as do I. They will listen more keenly to your words than my own.' said Nathanar rather openly.

'Give it time brother. They have yet to witness your deeds first-hand.' he replied. 'You are one of my finest students Nathanar, however, you need to work on inspiring those you command.'

'I am not sure that I have the flair for battlefield theatrics Nathaniel.' replied Nathanar.

'Not many do.' he said, contemplating his own words. 'Rayna seems to have piqued the interest of her peers. Elevating her to the position of sergeant was a wise move. Perhaps you should keep her by your side since doing so could be mutually beneficial.'

'I see the merit in your words Nathaniel.' Nathanar replied. 'I will think on it.'

A long uneasy silence followed Nathanar's acknowledgement of his suggestion. Nathanar seemed to have more to say, though he refrained from doing so. He could tell there was something troubling the young Blade Master's mind, though Nathanar was too polite and career cautious to raise matters of contention readily.

'Something bothers you Nathanar?' he asked, opting to give Nathanar the opportunity to unload his concerns.

'It is nothing Nathaniel.' Nathanar replied politely.

'Your face tells me otherwise, or have you forgotten that after all those passes training you in the arena I can read you like a book regardless of your political prowess.' he replied.

'I have not forgotten Teacher, though...'

'It is just the two of us Nathanar. Speak candidly if you will.'

Nathanar smiled, and in doing so seemed to relax a little; he had been notably tense since the rearguard began their march on Scrier's Post. Initially he had thought the cause of Nathanar's unease could be attributed to the natural stresses accompanying any position of command, yet as their march pushed on late into the night he had noted little change in his former protégé's concerned demeanour.

'My troubles stem from our numbers and resources Nathaniel.' replied Nathanar hesitantly. 'The invading Narlakai can be counted at more than double the numbers of the entire order. Then there is the issue of weapons. Most are ineffective against the Narlakai, and we have few light bringers to compensate.'

'You doubt our chances of victory over the Narlakai should it come to direct confrontation?' he enquired flatly.

'Yes.' replied Nathanar. 'Whilst I do not doubt The Blade Lord's tactics, I simply do not believe we have sufficient numbers to repel an invasion of Lothnar's reported magnitude.'

'I agree.' he replied, to Nathanar's obvious surprise. 'That is exactly why Marcus chose to evacuate the vale, and now you fully understand why it is that I cannot sleep.'

The mood between them had changed; he was naive to think that it would not. He had always enjoyed flirting with Kaitlin, yet her body language towards him now had matured; her sometimes coy, sometimes playful, demeanour had evolved into something entirely different. When Kaitlin regarded him now it was no longer through the eyes of a woman toying with her prey, now instead he felt as though she was studying him in anticipation of events to come later that day. That morning Kaitlin was up several hours before he had fully awoken; he had heard Kaitlin busying herself incessantly in the background as he faded in and out of consciousness, fighting a losing battle against his body which refused to rise at such early hour. Once he was finally up and about, it struck him rather unexpectedly that Kaitlin was preparing to leave the confines of the library; a rare occurrence given that she had few social dealings outside of her place of work. Such was her distraction that Kaitlin had not at first noticed that he had arisen, and so he startled her when at last she acknowledged his presence. Kaitlin explained to him that she had errands to run throughout the metropolis, including picking up several items of clothing she had ordered following their late evening promise. Now they sat opposite one another, making awkward small talk, as they finished off the breakfast he had prepared for them.

'So...is the library to close whilst you're out?' he enquired gingerly.

'If you do not mind, I was hoping that Mr L. Cameron might run it in my absence for a few hours.' replied Kaitlin.

'What, me?!' he blurted out suddenly.

'You know this place well enough by now Callum. I am sure you can cope for a short while in my absence.' replied Kaitlin flatly.

'Err, sure. If that's what you want.'

'It is.'

With their brief dialogue concluded, Kaitlin promptly rose from the breakfast bar in the kitchen and made her way towards the door.

'What time can I expect to see you return?' he called out after her.

'I should be back by lunch.' replied Kaitlin as she left the room.

After finishing his breakfast at his own leisurely pace, he wandered back into the main library. Kaitlin had left the building, leaving him alone; he had not been alone in almost three weeks. The thought of returning to his lonely, less privileged, former life now surfaced to the fore of his mind making his stomach churn. The last thing he wanted to do was return to the Wild, yet the thought of not doing so was an entirely selfish one. Remaining at the library was not an option. Moreover, his continued presence would place Kaitlin at even greater risk. Still, he had a library to run and now was not the time to contemplate his return to the Wild. Instead it was time for Mr L. Cameron to assist the resident librarian who, he would perhaps explain, had popped out for an emergency medical appointment or some such fanciful tale.

It was a busy morning at the library, during which he had spent most of his time attending to the incessant demands of its patrons. Few questioned his role of temporary assistant to Kaitlin, with the exception of the library's more regular attendees – most of whom he already knew on a first name basis. When he was not busy attending to the literary public, he spent most of his time filing returns and re-indexing the shelves. His busy time spent running the library in Kaitlin's absence saw the hours pass by at frightening speed. It was not until half past two in the afternoon when the work finally began to abate, yet Kaitlin still remained absent. Initially he gave Kaitlin's uncharacteristic tardiness little thought; it was not inconceivable that she had lost track of time, or perhaps had encountered congestion whilst travelling around the metropolis. Come five o'clock, when closing the library for the day, he started to become concerned with Kaitlin's continued absence. Later that evening, well after eight o'clock, he started to wonder if perhaps some ill fate had befallen her, either that or Kaitlin's nerves had gotten the better of her, causing her to give the library – more specifically him – a wide birth. He cursed himself for not having a means of communication with which to contact Kaitlin directly, then he realised that perhaps Mr L. Cameron did. Using the re-engineered bio-key he called up a holographic access panel to the Infonet. Since Mr L. Cameron had no previous direct personal dealings with Kaitlin, it was not possible for his alias to locate her bio-key implant via the Infonet. Although not a hacker himself, he had though learnt a number of useful tricks during his time spent with Trix throughout the early years of the Exodus. He promptly loaded up a modified search algorithm designed to penetrate the metropolis' central data core and conduct remote DNA searches against its database of bio-key holders; the algorithm simply required adequate search criteria to complete its task. If he could find a match then he would be able to access the information he needed directly from the database without ever establishing a peer-to-peer connection with Kaitlin's actual bio-key. It was a trick he had used previously to locate an unconnected individual, however, the software was not perfect; it could only conduct undetected searches for approximately ten seconds, and that was during the early years of the software's inception. Technological advances, which came with each passing year, no doubt saw the successful development and implementation of enhanced intruder prevention countermeasures; there was no guarantee that the outdated search algorithm could indeed run undetected for the theorised timeframe. He tried to pass the time by burying himself in another of the library's classic works of fiction, but continued thoughts of Kaitlin's unknown whereabouts soon lured him back to the access panel. Regardless of the risks involved, he had now managed to convince himself that determining Kaitlin's exact location warranted the illegal breach of security. He hurriedly grabbed one of Kaitlin's discarded dress shirts, left draped over one of the library's many sofas, then initiated a DNA scan of the garment via the holographic access panel. With the search criteria loaded into the algorithm, he immediately commenced an illegal search having decided that the ends justified the means. A record counter started to rapidly increment on the access panel before him as the algorithm executed its task. Six hundred, four thousand, eleven thousand; the algorithm interrogated the bio-key holders database with ease, but with so many inhabitants within the metropolis the search rate needed to increase. By his over-simplistic reckoning the search would have been conducted faster by name, though Trix had not coded the software to do so. Although the reasons for the decision were explained to him in detail, when Trix embarked on a techno rant he had a horrible tendency to switch off thus paying little or no attention. Four seconds, five seconds, six seconds; the search was talking too long. He was about to cancel the search when suddenly it ceased of its own volition, having identified a unique match. The software immediately severed its connection to the central data core, and displayed the results of the match on the access panel.

'What?' he said aloud. 'That cannot be...'

After he dispatched his report to Freylar, the dark mass continued its lumbering advance south. Tracking the Narlakai closely had been a challenge, more so given the injury to his leg. During the nights he struggled to maintain pace with the writhing mass as he limped awkwardly in the wake of its ponderous advance, ensuring that he remained undetected. When the sun rose in the mornings and the Narlakai dove back underground, seeking shelter from its harmful rays, tracking them became extremely difficult; it was impossible to predict whether the Narlakai would make significant gains beneath the surface, or instead advance only a few hundred paces. He was repeatedly forced to use his wraith wings to catch the Narlakai up after dusk which ushered in their advance proper once more. The further south they advanced, the less distance the Narlakai covered beneath the surface, as the once-cavernous sub-terrain began to close up; he made a mental note to explore the subterranean landscape of the Narlakai borderlands if he survived the impending confrontation with them. Whilst tracking their advance, he ensured at all times that he remained outside the reach of the telepath shepherding them. After their brief chance encounter, he had learnt enough to know that he would struggle against such a foe in a direct mental duel. He could ill afford to give up his location and the information stored in his mind, therefore he attempted to avoid further detection entirely. Still there would likely come a time, once both sides had played their hands, when he would be drawn into an engagement with the enigma; he hoped that he possessed the mental fortitude required to endure such an ordeal.

During the fourth night of tracking the enemy, shortly after catching up the dark mass once more, he was alarmed to discover that the front line had shortened in length yet it did not appear to be any denser in composition. Unnerved by the troubling discovery, he began to quickly scan the south-east horizon for signs of Narlakai having broken away from the main advance. Using his keen night vision he peered into the darkness, staring intently at the horizon, hoping to make out the remainder of the invasion force. There was nothing. Turning his attention to the south-west he resumed his visual scanning. It was not long before he spied a second detachment of Narlakai, approximately a third of the original force, which had taken a new direction.

'What are you up to...' he mused aloud.

As he crouched low watching the second Narlakai detachment drift slowly towards the south-west, dark thoughts began to manifest in his mind. Deep in pessimistic thought, it was then that he realised the imminent doom which he himself had played a part in visiting upon his kin; the main advance was nothing more than a distraction, a ruse designed to draw out The Blades leaving the vale largely undefended. If Marcus chose to intercept the Narlakai and commit The Blades to open battle, only a small invasion force would be necessary to sac the vale and release its civilian inhabitants. The insidious mind responsible for orchestrating the planned invasion had used him well; they had known that he would communicate the Narlakai's movements back to the vale. Now lines of communication were hindered, by both the spread of the Narlakai forces and the lack of Sky-Skitters choosing to approach the vicinity of the dark mass, and time was against him. It seemed doubtful therefore that he could alert Freylar to the cunning subterfuge unravelling before him.

'Bastards!' he uttered venomously under his breath.

With time running short, he needed to decide quickly where best to place himself. He had fought under The Blade Lord's banner for many passes and, knowing Marcus as he did, felt sure that their illustrious leader would march out to meet the threat of invasion head on. The Blades were a well-drilled, well disciplined, military order which needed to face its enemies in strategic open engagements; in a skirmish with the Narlakai, however, The Blades would surely lose. He affirmed to himself, therefore, that Marcus would not sit back idly awaiting potential conflict within the vale. With his decision made, he unfurled his wraith wings and flew directly towards the rogue detachment; the Narlakai would not breach the domain of Freylar unopposed, even if he stood alone. He hoped dearly that the enigmatic telepath remained with the primary force, and yet his instincts told him otherwise.

EIGHTEEN
Deception

Finally the need to cower and scheme in the shadows of their exile had come to an end. She had accurately predicted The Blade Lord's logical troop deployments through her continued scrying of future events and it had led them to this moment. Having abandoned two thirds of her flock to distract Marcus' primary force, Lileah now stood once more by her side with the remainder of the subservient Narlakai enslaved to their will. She rubbed the sodden flesh and metal fused together at her left wrist as they picked out Scrier's Post before them amidst the black of night; it was now Freylar's last bastion of hope, reduced to such by her masterful manipulation of events. This was the fulcrum upon which they had gambled everything. The deck was stacked in their favour; taking Scrier's Post would be formulaic, if not for the uncertainty of Alarielle's enigmatic successor, whose future she could not foretell with any degree of certainty.

'If you are unsure about Alarielle's puppeteer, then should we not avoid Scrier's Post entirely?' asked Lileah, who stood peering into the darkness.

'We need to release them quickly, so that they are not free to harry our advance on the vale. Besides, if we leave them they will alert The Blade Lord sooner than our schedule allows.' she explained patiently.

'You are assuming that they have already detected us Darlia.' Lileah replied.

'As I have told you before Lileah, I do not assume. They have already detected us. At any rate, I thought you wanted to destroy The Blades? This easy victory will crush their resolve.'

'True enough. Then how is it you foresee us taking Scrier's Post?' asked Lileah.

'Overrun them! The darkness conceals our approach, thus we can afford to rush their position.' she proclaimed vehemently. 'Send the Narlakai over the north-east wall and release them all.'

'As you command, so shall it be.' Lileah replied enthusiastically.

Lileah straightened, then took a few steps backwards before tilting her head back slightly, allowing the rain to run down her gaunt facial features. As the telepath communed with the grotesque, semi-gaseous, writhing forms flanking them, her eyes glazed over while Lileah poured her conscious thought into the primitive minds of their monstrous entourage. The whip-like gangrenous tendrils of the Narlakai flailed wildly into action followed by their renewed lumbering advance towards Scrier's Post. Although painfully slow to move, the Narlakai's purposeful movement would ensure that none fell by the wayside during their abominable charge. Indeed the prolonged sight of their horrific approach would likely rouse further dread amongst the inexperienced Aspirants who constituted the bulk of those defending Scrier's Post. An eerie sonorous moan began to sound from the black tide slowly pushing forwards before them, even though the Narlakai seemingly possessed no physical mouths to speak of. Although she despised the nightmarish horrors with every part of her being, she had no qualms manipulating the Narlakai into serving her own agenda. The Blades' illustrious leader had taken her hand; now she would take everything from him.

'Wake up!'

She flinched, startled by her sister Blade's fervent voice. It took her a moment to clear her head, and realise exactly where she was, whilst rubbing rheum from the corners of her eyes. Anika was standing over her, assuming the role of her gleeful tormentor; she had fallen asleep on the cold stone floor of the sanctuary, alongside a number of her fellow Aspirants who were also beginning to stir.

'Is it morning already?' she said, struggling to will her body back into action.

'Ha! Hardly...it is in fact well past dusk.' replied Anika. 'You can thank Nathanar for allowing you all to rest a while longer.'

'Oh good, well then...wake me in the morning.' she said playfully, feigning a return to sleep by closing her eyes.

'Perhaps you might grace us with your illustrious presence for what remains of the cycle, sergeant.' replied Anika, who gently drove a knee length buckled leather boot into her side.

'Maybe you should have the job, that way I can go back to sleep eh?' she said playfully.

'Get up Guardian, and show your fellow Aspirants how to use that fancy falchion of yours. It looks almost as black as my mood.' Anika said pointing to Shadow Caster.

The unusual comment prompted her to turn her head so that she could just see Shadow Caster, in her peripheral vision, which was sheathed in a scabbard across her back. The hilt of the weapon, which typically did not emanate the rest of the blade's characteristic wisp like smoke, now smouldered like freshly lit coal. With cat-like reflexes she was up on her feet. She promptly drew the alien weapon from its resting place, which caused it to trace an arc of dark smoke through the air. The entire length of the blade smouldered energetically as though the Narlakin soul trapped within it desperately sought escape from its imprisonment.

'What is it Rayna?' asked Anika whose facial expression had rapidly become one of concern.

'The Narlakai are here!' she proclaimed loudly. 'Get up! All of you, get up!' she shouted, causing her voice to echo slightly throughout the vaulted chamber of the sanctuary.

'How can you know such a thing?' asked Anika who was clearly alarmed by her sudden reaction to the weapon.

'Anika, I don't have time to explain. Trust me, and ready our brothers and sisters.'

She abandoned Anika by rapidly ascending the worn stone steps leading to the parapet above. There she encountered a number of rain-drenched sentries who had been posted along the perimeter of the roof. Holding Shadow Caster high in her right hand, she conjured a sphere of light in her left thus illuminating the entire length of the blade as it smouldered darkly in her grasp. Wasting no time, she hollered down to the remainder of the rearguard below who sought refuge from the rain as best they could.

'They're here, the Narlakai are here!' she cried, trying to cut through the dampening effect of the rain which sought desperately to silence her voice.

One by one Freylarkai sheltering along the perimeter wall moved towards the sanctuary, eager to hear her words more clearly over the downpour. Chief amongst them were Nathanar and Nathaniel who pushed their way through the massing Freylarkai to better hear her words.

'The Narlakai are here damn it! Ready yourselves.' she cried once more.

'Delay that!' proclaimed Nathanar. 'Sergeant, explain yourself. What proof do you have that the Narlakai are indeed upon us as you say?'

'She speaks the truth Nathanar!' Nathaniel interjected. 'That sword, Shadow Caster, contains the soul of a captured Narlakin. See now how it reacts to their growing presence.'

In the wake of Nathaniel's revelation, all eyes turned keenly towards Shadow Caster; heavy dark wisps of smoke continued to emanate from the smooth glasslike surface of the blade as the soul trapped within called to its approaching dark kin. Seeing the blade react as it did, concern began to spread rapidly across the faces of the onlookers as the general mood of the rearguard soured in an instant. Anika came bounding out of the sanctuary below flanked by a dozen or so Aspirants, each of whom joined the growing crowd of worried Freylarkai who now made up her captive audience.

'Sentries, what do your eyes see?' demanded Nathanar, whose soft voice struggled to cut through the rain towards the parapet.

'Nothing commander, there is nothing out there.' One of the sentries shouted back.

'Look harder!' Nathaniel hollered. 'Kryshar, assist them.'

The rearguard waited anxiously as the sentries scrutinised the horizon. Despite being selected by Nathanar for their enhanced night vision, darkness had now fully descended upon them which coupled with the increasingly heavy downpour made it hard for them to see much beyond a few hundred paces. At Nathaniel's command, Kryshar promptly joined them on the parapet. Pulling a fresh arrow from a quiver slung across her back, Kryshar grasped the shaft of the projectile firmly and proceeded to imbue it with light; a technique Ragnar had yet to instruct her in. Kryshar nocked the imbued arrow to her bow and released it at a forty-five degree angle to the north of Scrier's Post. The flare did little to improve her own poor vision, however, the sentries positioned along the parapet clearly benefited from Kryshar's aid.

'To the north!' shouted one of the sentries.

'Confirm, is it the Narlakai?' shouted Nathanar as loudly as he could.

'Yes!' replied another of the sentries. 'Approximately four hundred paces out, approaching our position from the north-east.'

'Blades, ready yourselves! Archers along the parapet now! Kryshar imbue their arrows. The rest of you, circle the sanctuary. Rayna, get down here with us.' barked Nathaniel sternly.

Her stomach churned at the realisation that the rearguard was about to engage the enemy. So far as she had understood the situation, none of them had realistically expected to be involved in the likely conflict. It was presumed that the primary force would meet the Narlakai on the edge of Bleak Moor. For the rearguard to be engaged now suggested one of two horrible outcomes; either the primary force had been out-flanked, or the Narlakai had already gone through Freylar's primary defence and were seeking to rout The Blades entirely. Missing every other step, she ran down the steps and out of the sanctuary to join those boots already on the ground. Blades wielding bows ran past her up to the parapet as she bounded out of the sanctuary. Despite Nathaniel's clear orders, confused Aspirants still loitered out of position likely paralysed with fear; Aspirants were rarely committed to battle, though The Blade Lord had been left with little choice but to deploy them.

'Circle now!' she shouted sternly to those flat footed Aspirants unlucky enough to incur her ire.

Those fear-ridden Aspirants who failed to react to her call were promptly herded into position by both herself and Anika, who diligently followed her lead. Nathanar stood on the northern circumference of the circle whilst Nathaniel bolstered the southern edge, opposite the gated archway; it was impossible to know for certain which section of the perimeter wall the Narlakai would attempt to breach first.

'Rayna, stand with me.' Nathanar cried over the worsening downpour.

Having shepherded the last of the lost Aspirants into position, she quickly moved to join Nathanar and Anika, who had also taken up position by their commander's side. For a seemingly innocent and inexperienced individual, Anika's focus on the task at hand was commendable. If Anika feared their imminent fate, the young Freylarkin certainly did not show it. Anika's commitment to The Blades and their success pushed all other concerns to one side regardless. She had previously expressed concern to Nathaniel regarding Anika, believing such zealous behaviour to be dangerous, and yet now it served the young Aspirant faultlessly. Glancing up over her shoulder she saw Kryshar working hard to imbue the projectiles of those Aspirants wielding bows along the sanctuary parapet. Despite being newly inducted into the order, Kryshar had been given immediate purpose which did not afford the green Aspirant time to consider the ramifications of their lot. The skilled light bringer visited each archer in turn in a round-robin fashion, ensuring that each had at least a single imbued arrow before revisiting them to work on additional shafts.

'Should the archers not be loosing their arrows by now?' asked Anika worriedly.

'Not yet. We have neither the visibility nor resources for speculative fire.' replied Nathanar coolly. 'Sentries,' he then cried up towards the sanctuary, 'I want a continued report on distance to the Narlakai.'

Despite her enhanced vision it was still difficult to make out the black mass before them; the driving rain coupled with the distance rendered the Narlakai invasion as little more than a murky smudge across the horizon, and yet it was a large smudge all the same. Lothnar's last report suggested that the advancing Narlakai numbered approximately three times that of the entire order, yet it was hard to confirm those numbers through the darkness. She had expected to see a wider frontage, though it was difficult to tell how many ranks deep the horde was in fact. Regardless of the actual numbers, her stomach churned at the sight and more specifically the thought of imminent battle. Although trained diligently in the art of combat, as was every Blade, open warfare did not suit her. They called her Fate Weaver since her talents lay in foretelling the future and reliving the past. Because her abilities were her primary focus, she was not counted amongst the order's battlefield elite despite her ascension to the ruling council; that honour belonged to the likes of Ragnar, Natalya, Thandor and The Blade Lord himself. When commanded into battle she favoured the relative safety of a bow, preferring to attack at range thus putting a measure of distance between herself and the enemy. When called to arms she had little interest in glory or conquest, instead she was happy to leave such endeavours to those more competent with the intricacies of close combat. Though she could never hope to rival Natalya's skill with a bow, she was nonetheless exceptionally competent as was expected of all the Paladins and Valkyries. As a member of The Blades she stood alongside her brothers and sisters ready to defend their domain, until their eventual release relieved them of that duty. Now virtually the entire order stood resolutely at her back whilst the rain beat mercilessly down upon them further adding to their misery.

She stood nervously at the front of the primary force, alongside her fellow Paladins and Valkyries, as part of the council of war – those Blades who formed the order's command group, led by The Blade Lord himself, who insisted on leading every campaign. Once the battle got underway, each of the Paladins and Valkyries would be expected to lead part of the force; she would no doubt command a regiment of archers as would Natalya. Aleska's absence felt strange, with her having been assigned to other duties; her venerable mentor had been tasked with leading Mirielle's personal entourage – which had been instructed to take shelter at the Cave of Wellbeing – as well as overseeing the successful civilian evacuation of the vale. It was difficult to tell if Aleska had personally requested the assignment, or if indeed The Blade Lord had issued the command by his own initiative.

'What are they doing?!' demanded Ragnar, clearly frustrated by his inability to regard the Narlakai first-hand on account of his poor vision in low light.

'The same thing as the last four times you asked. Nothing.' replied Thandor dryly.

'They march all the way to our front door, just to do nothing!' replied Ragnar tersely.

'Kirika,' Marcus said calling her closer, 'I need your second sight. This entire situation does not feel right, and I desperately need to understand why.'

'Marcus, battles are extremely difficult to accurately scry. The actions of any one individual can affect the...'

'I do not seek the intricacies of battle Kirika, rather I need to know if there will actually *be* a battle.' asked Marcus curiously.

'What? Where are you going with this Marcus?' asked Ragnar, cutting in impatiently.

'You suspect some kind of ruse perhaps?' Thandor questioned.

'Kirika, please, indulge me.' Marcus asked once more.

'Very well.' she replied. 'I need time to concentrate. These conditions are far from conducive.'

'To your witchery you mean.' interrupted Ragnar once more.

'Silence!' barked Marcus uncharacteristically. 'Kirika, please continue.'

Nothing. Every attempt to scry the as yet untold battle for Bleak Moor resulted in the same outcome; nothing, and yet Freylar would still fall. None of her visions made sense. How could Freylar fall to a non-event she wondered? All of her visions depicted the Narlakai horde remaining steadfast, how then was it that they would enter the vale and raze it to the ground? Unless...

'Oh no.' she said unintentionally aloud.

'Kirika, what have you foreseen?' asked Marcus.

'It is what I have not foreseen.' she replied. 'Marcus, we have each of us been deceived. The Narlakai opposing us have no intention of attacking, they are nothing more than a distraction.'

'How is it then that they intend to invade the vale if they remain here skulking before us?' asked Natalya.

'There must be a second detachment.' replied Marcus. 'They have succeeded in averting our eyes from Freylar's true threat.'

'Lothnar made no mention of a second detachment.' said Ragnar glowering angrily.

'If the Narlakai split their force shortly before making contact, Lothnar would have had little opportunity to contact us.' explained Marcus.

'Then where will this rogue detachment make contact?' Natalya questioned.

There was a long pause as each considered the question, with the obvious exception of Ragnar, who clearly remained irritated about having been caught off guard by a species with seemingly lesser intellect. Lothnar's reports of the approaching horde had focused their minds a little too keenly, it now seemed, blindsiding them to the real threat which as a consequence approached unseen. Fortunately The Blade Lord had always anticipated the possibility of a flanking manoeuvre and had therefore stationed the rearguard at Scrier's Post as a cautionary measure. However, with no immediate way of contacting Nathanar's command it was impossible to notify the rearguard of the new discovery and warn them of the imminent danger they faced.

'If we abandon our position we risk instigating that which we initially feared.' said Marcus eventually breaking their silence. 'We cannot commit the entirety of our limited resources on a hunch. Ragnar, have scouts double back to survey the south-east and south-west regions, and station telepaths along the way to maintain lines of communication.'

'It shall be done.' Ragnar growled.

'Also, dispatch a telepath to make contact with the rearguard and apprise them of the situation as a matter of urgency. The sooner we can make contact the better.' Marcus continued. 'Should they make contact with the Narlakai then I want to know about it immediately.'

The combination of sweat mixed with rain dripped from his forehead as he landed awkwardly on the ground, courtesy of his injured leg. He was exhausted and struggled to catch his breath; it had been a considerably long time since last he had truly pushed the boundaries of his airborne capabilities. Though not averse to flight itself, he nonetheless preferred tactile contact with the ground and the cover it offered him when operating in the field. By contrast he felt entirely exposed and uncomfortable when flying at low altitude, and thus he chose to do so infrequently. On the horizon stood the eerie silhouette of Scrier's Post, a long since abandoned haven for scriers of old, and before it the outflanking Narlakai vanguard which had broken away from its former host seeking to invade the vale unopposed. Despite his wounded leg continuing to slow him down, he was still able to move faster than the shambolic Narlakai before him. If his instincts served him well, as often they did, he would soon make contact with the damnable telepath, who he assumed to be at the centre of the writhing mass, manipulating the Narlakai as a puppeteer would its marionettes. Determined not to be the catalyst of Freylar's ruin, he clung onto the desperate hope of disabling the enigma herding the rogue Narlakai detachment; if he could disrupt its hold over the soul stealers then perhaps he could buy time enough for his brothers and sisters to learn of the deception and thus lend their aid, assuming the order was successful in defeating the remainder of the force. Such a venture was undoubtedly a fool's errand, and yet he felt ideally qualified for the near futile task, given that he had already been cast in the role of the fool courtesy of the unseen manipulations of another.

Drawing on what little remaining strength his tired body had left to give, he took flight once more seeking to bridge the narrowing gap between himself and the invading vanguard. As he resumed his erratic flight towards his intended target, the horizon suddenly lit up against its black canvas as thin traces of light arced down from the gloomy silhouette of Scrier's Post. The light rained down towards the advancing horde, spearing through the writhing mass, which moaned in response with an eerie sonorous chorus that made his stomach churn. Although a veteran of numerous campaigns, the sight of the Narlakai still appalled him regardless of their awful sound. He supposed that the reason for his deep-seated disgust towards their species was largely due to the manner in which they consumed their victims; the idea of losing one's soul to such nightmares was abhorrent to him, and as a result he would never forgive the Narlakai for taking Alarielle from him. There was also the matter of their grotesque alien appearance which made him feel uneasy for they shared nothing in common with the Freylarkai; to him the Narlakai epitomised the very essence of those fictional monsters depicted in stories of old, told over and again to scare young Freylarkai in order to facilitate their obedience. Hearing their horrid moans of pain as the distant light tore through their ranks did nothing to abate his hatred towards the nightmare horrors, if nothing else their torment spurred him onwards in the knowledge that he was now no longer alone in opposing their advance. Whoever now occupied Scrier's Post clearly sought to oppose the Narlakai vanguard and he was eager to aid them in their fight. He steeled himself ready for the enormous challenge to come, for soon he would make contact with the telepathic force which commanded the soul stealer's operations and was intent on Freylar's ruin.

NINETEEN
Contact

'Again!' shouted Nathanar weakly through the pouring rain.

She watched anxiously as shards of light rained down from the sanctuary parapet into the Narlakai host now beginning to swell along the outer north-east wall. Though each of Kryshar's arrows found their mark, they did little to slow the growing writhing mass of tendrils lapping at the perimeter wall. At Nathanar's command several of the Aspirants dropped down from the parapet, their landing eased by the use of their spectral wings, and promptly began firing at will from a short distance through the shaped arrow slits in the perimeter wall. At such close range their imbued arrows tore through the ranks of the Narlakai massing on the other side of the wall; awful sonorous moans filled the air in response to the point-blank attacks, momentarily drowning out the ambient sound of the torrential rain which continued to fall from the black sky above.

'Keep firing!' cried Nathanar.

Again the sky above them lit up with streaks of white light as more of the imbued arrows found their mark amongst the gathering soul stealers; once more the haunting sounds of pain resonated across the targeted ranks of the black tide crashing against the shoreline of Scrier's Post. Rather uncharacteristically of their species, the nightmare horrors responded by adapting their strategy in order to circumvent their unfavourable position by lapping round the circumference of the perimeter wall. The Narlakai quickly extended their front line, thus thinning their ranks and reducing line of sight to the Freylarkai stationed along the sanctuary parapet; the sudden change in formation afforded the Narlakai significantly better cover, shielding them from the worst of the potentially lethal projectiles. Though Nathanar seemingly lacked conviction in his orders due to his naturally soft voice, he nonetheless reacted well to the changing battlefield conditions and ordered more of the rearguard's archers down from the parapet to take up positions behind the arrow slits along the perimeter wall. Standing a couple of paces back from the makeshift arrow loops, more arrows were released by the Aspirants point-blank through their designated slits. Some of the arrows missed their mark splintering violently against the solid rock of the perimeter wall, though most found their target inciting further moans of pain from the nightmares concealed beyond. Kryshar too dropped down from the parapet before swiftly moving up to support the rearguard's archers by imbuing more of their arrows with light; without the aid of the light, The Blades' weapons would have little effect against the Narlakai. As though reacting instinctively to her presence, the crush of Narlakai directly behind the perimeter wall where Kryshar now knelt, suddenly rose up the outer side of the wall. Tendrils violently lapped over the top of the wall adjacent to Kryshar, permitting their tethered hosts to drag their semi-gaseous forms up to the apex of the wall. Desperate to pull back from her sudden attackers, Kryshar lost her footing on the waterlogged bedrock; she slipped awkwardly onto her back, where she froze, completely terrified and in awe of her alien attackers.

'Cover her now!' cried Nathanar to the remaining archers still stationed along the parapet, who had subsequently moved round to its north-east edge.

Arrows punched violently through the Narlakai who had successfully hoisted themselves on top of the perimeter wall; their hideous semi-gaseous forms began to rapidly dissipate shortly after contact with the light imbued projectiles. Two of the nightmares toppled backwards promptly disintegrating into a fine ash-like substance, as they fell away from the wall. The ash lingered in the air, like smoke drifting on a light breeze, whilst their gangrenous tendrils flopped to the ground where they writhed reflexively no longer tethered to their respective hosts. She had never seen a Narlakin before, having only heard their species described as abominations by members of the order, nor had she ever witnessed one's release; the sight was ghastly, and yet also strangely magnificent. The release of the two Narlakai ushered forth the emergence of numerous ghostly luminescent forms which appeared to rise from the falling ash of the vanquished horrors. Each form seemed to crudely represent another species; some were Freylarkin in appearance, whereas others appeared to be more animal-like. Shortly after manifesting themselves, however, the apparitions rapidly lost cohesion then elongated into thin traces of light which sped upwards into the night sky. Weathering the worst of the rearguard's abhorrent needles of light, a single Narlakin survived the volley and proceeded to haul its wounded form over the wall. It landed with a wet thud in a horrid heap adjacent to Kryshar, who was still losing her private battle with fear. Black gas seeped out of the invading Narlakin where it had been glanced a blow along its outer edge; none of the arrows had managed to hit close to the centre of the mass, as a result it was still able to press its advance.

'Archers, fall back!' cried Nathanar. 'Get back up to the parapet now!'

'Back now!' she cried, lending her voice to Nathanar's will. 'Kryshar move!'

The wounded Narlakin rose to its full height then opened a large vertical rift, not unlike some kind of ghastly maw, in its semi-gaseous body which appeared to draw in surrounding matter; the falling rain bent inwards towards the rift and pools of surface water leapt towards it as though pulled in by invisible forces. Kryshar screamed as her body began sliding towards the Narlakin's maw; gripped by fear the doomed Freylarkin remained paralysed, inadvertently bringing about her own ruin. The lone soul stealer wrapped several of its tendrils around Kryshar's limbs then raised the light bringer partially off the ground, drawing the petrified Freylarkin closer to its widening maw. The remaining Aspirants along the sanctuary parapet raced to nock their arrows, though most hesitated when drawing their bow, unsure of cleanly hitting their target. The few arrows that were released streaked towards Kryshar's attacker, though each failed to stop the Narlakin from completing its final horrible act as they glanced or flew wide of their target. The soul stealer appeared to momentarily inhale, causing it to grow marginally in size, whilst releasing a piercing screech that sent a shiver up her spine. Kryshar's rigid body suddenly went limp, causing the doomed Freylarkin's screams of terror to die abruptly. Kryshar's soul was torn violently from its physical moorings and pulled into the abhorrent rift.

'Bring it down!' she cried with conviction, pointing to the horror as it consumed its prize.

Those who had previously hesitated now released their arrows; one embedded itself into Kryshar's left shoulder, several flew wide, yet one managed to strike true puncturing the horror cleanly to the left of its maw. Immediately the Narlakin began to dissipate; its form slowly eroded away into the same ash-like substance as the others, and yet it continued to feed on Kryshar's soulless body, regardless of its own demise, as though driven by some kind of primal instinct. Before the Narlakin's semi-gaseous form completely eroded away, Kryshar's body dried and withered, completely desiccated by the horror's insatiable appetite for life. In the space of a few fleeting moments Kryshar's light had been entirely snuffed out, leaving behind the remains of a withered empty husk which folded in on itself as it became saturated by the rain. The sight of Kryshar's terrible release sent a shockwave of dread through those Aspirants unfortunate enough to bear witness to the young Freylarkin's untimely release. A cursory glance at her brothers and sisters told her immediately that they were not prepared for such a fight and that their nerves were clearly frayed; she quickly surmised that it would take little to break the Aspirants' resolve. Even Anika's eyes now contained a level of doubt which betrayed the zealot.

'Steel yourselves, for we are each of us about to be tested.' she cried hoping to focus the attentions of the Aspirants within earshot, so as not to afford their minds time to envisage scenes of further dread.

More luminescent forms rose from the parting ash left in the wake of the Narlakin's final release; she fancied that one of the apparitions was in fact Kryshar, now permitted to journey on to wherever it was that the Freylarkai's souls travelled to once released. She silently paid her respects to

Kryshar as the apparitions stretched into thin traces of light and sped upwards into the night joining their kin. The light of the departing souls momentarily lit up part of the north-east wall, revealing further breaches in progress as the Narlakai sought to clamber over the perimeter. Around them more wet thuds could be heard over the rain as further bundles of tendrils landed within the grounds. Those Aspirants, including Nathaniel, with particularly acute vision in low light rapidly acquired the fresh targets seeking to aid the rearguard's archers, all of whom had now ascended back up to the parapet.

'Nathanar, I regret that I have yet to learn how to imbue weapons with light.' she said, secretly cursing Ragnar for failing to train her in the technique.

'That is not important now,' replied Nathanar, 'Besides, it may very well be a moot point soon enough.'

'I don't understand.' she replied, wiping her drenched red hair away from her mouth.

'They are going to sweep over the perimeter wall and overrun us,' explained Nathanar bluntly. 'They have the numerical advantage for said stratagem, and we lack the resources to repel them.'

Anika scowled at Nathanar's pessimistic assessment of their situation. Numerous other Aspirants overheard their commander's dire prediction and immediately began to show signs of panic at the thought of their shared grim fate.

'Couldn't we fall back to the sanctuary and bottleneck their approach?' she questioned.

'The sanctuary will not accommodate us all, Rayna.' replied Nathanar dryly. 'I will not ask a third of the rearguard to sacrifice itself so that the remainder can improve its meagre chance of survival.'

'Perhaps Nathaniel can offer further counsel?' she implored.

'If that were true, he would have done so already.' Nathanar replied unsheathing his double-handed sword.

'I did not come to this world so that I could become food for those bastards!' she cried vehemently, openly casting aside the secrecy of her arrival.

'Then I suggest you fight well sister.' said Nathanar. 'Put that fervent light of yours to good use and perhaps we can make a fight of it.'

More arrows found their mark as the rearguard's archers picked out their gloomy targets, reducing them to little more than puddles of black filth containing detached writhing tendrils as the remains of the fallen Narlakai mixed with the heavy rain. Around them more streaks of light departed their world as unshackled souls ascended towards the next phase of their existence.

'I'll do better than that. Open the gate!' she cried, turning her back on Nathanar.

'What!?' replied Nathanar angrily, quickly turning to lay his left hand on her right shoulder.

She turned to meet his piercing gaze, 'You say they are going to overrun us, like water rushing to meet an insubstantial dam. If that is to be our lot, then open the bloody gate! Let the water in, and we will face it on our terms.'

'Thereby easing the pressure along the perimeter wall, is that your wager?' he demanded still grasping her shoulder firmly with his left hand. 'You seek a bottleneck of our own choosing.'

'Correct.'

'Then open the bloody gate, Guardian, and let us stem this black tide...together.'

Despite being asked to remain in Freylar, she was secretly pleased with the assignment Marcus had tasked her with. She was significantly more useful to the order managing the successful evacuation of the vale than taking a place alongside the other Paladins and Valkyries on the open battlefield. Though she could still fight when required, her martial ability had waned considerably over the last ten passes; her ability in the field was no longer representative of her title, that she knew and thus she understood fully The Blade Lord's need to assign her elsewhere. Although still comfortable commanding regiments of the order's finest into battle, confidence in one's ability was not enough on its own. True leadership could only be achieved by way of example. The Blades were first and foremost a militant order, she could not therefore lead whilst unable to demonstrate a level of martial skill beyond that of an Adept irrespective of her other talents; The Blades needed those of strong martial ability to lead them during their campaigns, more so than ever when facing foes such as the Narlakai. The order's commanders were required to inspire their brothers and sisters, and more importantly to provide hope when faced with adversity; neither of which she could realistically continue to offer as a senior member of the order, Nathaniel was the obvious exception. When Marcus assigned her to Mirielle's personal entourage, she welcomed the opportunity to lead the vale's successful evacuation.

Throughout the cave families huddled close together, each member hoping to reassure the other that Freylar's defenders would be successful in their campaign. All around her faces of concern told a familiar story; all had abandoned their homes at short notice, grabbed their loved ones and made the journey to what would hopefully be their salvation. The Cave of Wellbeing alone was far from adequate for the task of housing the vale's entire civilian population, however, the enormous network of living spaces, personal quarters, food stores and meditation chambers which extended deep below the ground away from the main sanctum offered the Freylarkai refugees the temporary sanctuary they required. The site as a whole was more than simply a place of healing or a bolt-hole for the renewalists; over the generations its underground labyrinth had been extended time and again by shapers burrowing ever deeper into the ground using their ability. It was the only plausible local site capable of temporarily accommodating the displaced Freylarkai during times of crisis, thus it was their first port of call following the hurried evacuation of the vale.

'Aleska, tell me plainly...have I failed them?' asked Mirielle sombrely as her gaze lingered on the downcast faces of the scared families around them.

'Of course not my queen.' she replied sympathetically. 'We could not have foreseen the arrival of this storm.'

'But could we have? Was it not I who tied your arms behind your backs, blinding your kind's second sight to such an outcome.' questioned Mirielle.

'Regardless of your past decisions, you know that we would have foretold this scenario if not for the intervention of another. You recall the one of whom I speak.'

'Perhaps, though she could not have done this alone.' replied Mirielle. 'I am unsure now as to whether I acted wisely in ordering her exile.'

'It was necessary. She was fast becoming a danger to both herself and others. One cannot control fate. At best we can prepare ourselves for its arrival.' she replied. 'Destiny always catches up with us eventually, no matter how much we may try to outmanoeuvre it.'

There was a brief pause in their conversation as Mirielle considered her words. It was unlike Mirielle to question her own decision making, though she appreciated that the current situation had placed their queen under a great deal of stress. Cracks in any leadership were almost inevitable when subject to invasion; the safety of their kin was always Mirielle's chief concern, as a result their queen rarely found time for herself. She pitied Mirielle due to the unrelenting burden of leadership which shackled their queen. In another life perhaps it would have been possible for
Mirielle to let down her guard, potentially allowing the obvious spark of attraction between their queen and The Blade Lord to ignite. As it was, however, Mirielle remained ever vigilant and often aloof during her rule as she routinely contemplated how best to lead the Freylarkai into the future. Mirielle allowed little time for personal social frivolity.

'Have you informed Kirika of your suspicion?' asked Mirielle, resuming their private discussion.

'Not yet. I believe that deep down, Kirika already suspects the same as I.' she replied.

'Who do you suppose is helping her?' asked Mirielle plainly.

'I do not know. I am not aware of any Freylarkai remaining loyal to her after the incident.' she replied. 'Though by now, I suspect that Lothnar will have uncovered the mystery for us.'

'You suspect, or you know?' replied Mirielle. 'Do not be coy with me Aleska, we have known each other far too long for that. I know well that your waning second sight is still uncannily accurate.'

She smiled warmly at Mirielle. Their queen had indeed known her for an awfully long time; she had counselled Mirielle closely when the enigmatic shaper first ascended to become Freylar's newest ruler, and then subsequently well into Mirielle's golden age of rule during the tens of passes that followed. Mirielle had been good for Freylar; their queen was a strong ruler and a wise decision maker, thus Mirielle had earned the respect of the Freylarkai which allowed her to unite them for the most part. A Freylarkin who posed a continued threat to the domain was swiftly exiled under Mirielle's rule; Mirielle would pass judgement, after consulting the ruling council to analyse the facts, and those considered a severe threat were swiftly exiled by The Blades. Whilst there were only a handful of exiles known to her, it concerned her that said individuals still enjoyed freedom beyond the domain of Freylar; she wondered whether or not she would have acted differently in Mirielle's position by showing reduced leniency.

'By now he will know.' she replied, not wanting to come across as too evasive.

'Well then, let us hope that he is able to communicate that knowledge to those who require it.' replied Mirielle.

'Let us hope so indeed my queen.' she replied.

'You know that you need not address me by my formal title Aleska. Surely your own venerable status on the ruling council and length of service under my rule has afforded you that small privilege, if nothing else.' noted Mirielle.

'Perhaps, nonetheless it is important that the civilian population observes your rule correctly during times of crisis. They look to you for unwavering guidance during times of uncertainty, and I do not seek to inadvertently undermine your rule with a privilege. It is important that you remain strong in your leadership and thus you are addressed correctly.' she replied fervently.

'Very well,' Mirielle replied with a warm smile of her own. 'But know this fact well Aleska. Though your time on the council grows ever shorter, my rule over Freylar would not have remained so if not for your wise counsel all these passes. Regardless of how this nightmare plays out, I wish to express my gratitude for your unrelenting support.'

'You honour me my queen.' she replied, 'And take solace in the knowledge that I believe that this nightmare will not end badly for Freylar.'

Mirielle held her gaze for some time following her bold choice of words; she could sense the desperate need for hope in the white abyss of Mirielle's vacant pupil-less eyes. Mirielle moved swiftly to stand intimately close before her then proceeded to grasp both of her hands. Freylar's most revered shaper then squinted slightly as though focusing intently on her seeing past the garment she wore, past flesh and bone, right through to her very soul; it was there that Mirielle found the source of her belief, deep within her soul. Whatever their queen had sacrificed for such enhanced sight, it enabled Mirielle to cut straight to the truth of all things.

'You know!' Mirielle whispered softly, quickly releasing her grasp.

'Yes.' she replied. 'The Guardian will save us.'

'Down on your knees!'

The pressure building inside his head was immense; it caused him to stumble to his knees whilst clutching his head, as though such an act would abate the searing pain shooting through his mind. His vision began to lose focus as the opposing telepath sought to overwhelm his psyche with their own, like unwanted noise drowning out one's own thoughts. He expected resistance, but not the overwhelming force now seeking to dominate his mind. He groaned loudly as he tried to push back against the hostile invader seeking to bury his conscious. The force responded in kind, pushing back with a renewed ferocity that burned through his mind causing him to scream in pain. Thin traces of watery blood wept from his eyes and his vision blurred causing his head to spin. He bit down hard, clenching his jaw, and forced his eyes shut attempting desperately to block out the sound of his own screams and instead focus his mind's eye on his attacker. He felt the damp ground contact with his forehead as he rocked forwards on his body, curling into a tight ball as his muscles tensed under the mental strain exerted upon him. Using mental exercises designed to calm the mind, drilled into him religiously as a young Freylarkin, he desperately sought calm within the eye of the storm currently laying waste to his psyche. Pushing all other concerns aside he focused solely on the telepath's voice, attempting once again to displace it from his mind.

'Stay down wretch!'

'Get out!' he cried.

'*Make me!*' the voice thundered in response, causing his muscles to further tighten.

He realised then the full extent of the power crushing down on him; he could not hope to best such a foe, at least not in a direct mental duel. Opening a fresh conduit to his mind, he projected his psyche outwards across the wet dark landscape towards Scrier's Post. As his astral projection raced towards Scrier's Post he began to sense the presence of the rogue Narlakai along with a fair number of Freylarkai, presumably having established a defensive position within the grounds. He jumped quickly between his kin, offering each a cursory scan as he formed the briefest of connections to them, trying to locate a Freylarkin of import. Though he discovered quickly that he had connected with members of The Blades, each mind he touched reeked of fear and despair; they were not veterans of the order, indeed far from it. But what then, he questioned. Surely not...Aspirants! The Blade Lord had deployed the Aspirants, likely fulfilling the role of a cautionary rearguard he surmised hastily. Time was now against him, forcing him to redouble his efforts. Like a frenzied animal frantically seeking shelter from a predator, he allowed his mind to dance wildly between the remaining Aspirants desperately seeking a suitable candidate. He needed to contact with someone of note, someone who could demand attention from the others, someone...Rayna!

TWENTY
Despair

By her command the Aspirants on the ground rallied towards the southern entrance where they formed a crescent shaped cordon around the gate. Gangrenous tendrils extended between the metal bars of the blackened gate, speculatively seeking out their prey, as their hosts sought with all futility to force their semi-gaseous bodies through the impossibly small gaps. More of the writhing nightmares could be heard flopping over the perimeter, landing with sickening wet thuds, as the press of Narlakai against the wall surrounding the grounds grew in height. The archers who had made it back up to the sanctuary parapet continued to send their dwindling shards of light towards the invading horrors, though their reduced rate of fire began to fail them. Those caught flat-footed on the ground, who were not part of the cordon, drew their blades hoping to hold back the invaders by means of close combat. Their inexperience against the Narlakai was painfully evident as they hacked wildly at their opponents, resorting to chance more than skill in attempting to land their blows. Moreover the notion of parrying became entirely reactionary, if not haphazard, as the engaged Aspirants struggled miserably to read their alien opponents. Tendrils lunged towards their targets, coiling rapidly round limbs and pulling several of the Aspirants down hard, before dragging them screaming towards their damnation to repeat Kryshar's abominable fate. Unable to stomach their imminent doom, Nathaniel broke away from the cordon to engage the enemy at their backs thus lending his support to the lost Aspirants.

'I will cover the rear,' shouted Nathaniel through the torrential rain. 'The rest of you focus on the hell about to be unleashed through that gate!'

Immediately after he broke rank, she could hear Nathaniel barking orders behind her as he sought to rally the Freylarkai stragglers. The Teacher had fought the Narlakai numerous times over the passes, so he knew well how best to tackle such foes. She glanced over her shoulder only to barely make out what must have been the dark outline of Nathaniel; she cursed her poor vision, made worse by the rain and her water soaked hair which she continuously pulled from her face. The black silhouette masterfully dodged its attackers with preternatural speed, before countering viciously with precision strikes of its own; severed tendrils flopped to the ground writhing to the now familiar sonorous moan of the injured Narlakai. Despite his martial prowess, without the aid of the light Nathaniel faced a tireless battle of attrition, given his inability to strike killer blows with mere metal alone. The semi-gaseous mass of the Narlakai was near impervious to conventional weapons of war, thus Nathaniel sought to incapacitate his foes by severing their vile appendages which he did with supreme efficiency. Seeing The Teacher at work repaired the broken spirits of the Aspirants caught in the fray who had all but given into despair; they quickly rallied alongside their mentor ready to receive further disordered charges from the Narlakai as more dropped over the perimeter wall.

'Open the gate!' yelled Nathanar, immediately drawing her attention back to her own pressing concerns. 'Force them to cluster!'

Wasting little time, the rearguard's telekinetics collectively wrestled the heavy metal gate open with their minds, immediately allowing the surge of Narlakai beyond to flood into the grounds. The thick dark forms pressed into the courtyard, using their tendrils to steady their advance as the rear ranks threatened to mount their advancing front line. Using the power of their minds once more, the rearguard's telekinetics erected invisible barriers to hold back the swelling black tide as best they could allowing the Aspirants to attack temporarily unopposed. The sea of amorphous black bodies and writhing tendrils before them was utterly abhorrent; never had she imagined bearing witness to such horrors, even in her worst dreams, yet now she stood face-to-face with their darkest nightmares made manifest. Pinned in place by unseen forces, the Narlakai moaned their awful chorus again. More of the soul stealing vertical rifts started to open up as they sought desperately to draw their prey closer. She responded in kind by extending her right hand, out of which rapidly grew a falchion composed entirely of white light. With her left hand she tightened her grip on Shadow Caster which now physically vibrated at such close proximity to its kin. Though the Narlakai appeared to lack eyes through which to see, it was clear that they sensed the presence of the cruel weapons she wielded vengefully; several of the forms reduced in size, trying to put some distance between themselves and her blades which were obviously anathema to their being.

'Bring them down!' shouted Nathanar.

Wasting no time, she leapt forwards, slashing the nearest Narlakin from right to left across its widening maw. The horror immediately disintegrated into ash leaving only its tendrils remaining; they flopped to the ground, useless without a host to manipulate them. The space left by the released Narlakin was immediately filled with another of the amorphous black clouds. She slashed again with both blades, sending the fresh nightmare to join its predecessor. More tendrils dropped to the water-soaked ground, writhing uncontrollably around her feet. Apparitions freed from the ash remains of the slain Narlakai lit up the area with their dull silver light, illuminating the outline of the black tide rolling in through the gate. The feeble light revealed an alarming number of black silhouettes pressing towards them. Again she slashed with her blades tearing through more of the Narlakai, releasing further traces of light to stream towards the sky. The tide moaned in response whilst edging ever closer; the telekinetics were starting to lose their hold over the soul stealers. Nathanar's enormous blade too tore violently through the dark ranks precariously fixed before them, but without the aid of the light he could only incapacitate his foes by severing their vile appendages, as Nathaniel had done; the ground beneath the Narlakai slithered repulsively with a life of its own as more orphaned tendrils flopped to the ground with sickening wet thuds. Anika and the remaining Aspirants also joined the combat slashing repeatedly at the Narlakai, doggedly following Nathanar's example, bringing their own sword arms to the fight as best they could.

'Our hold over them is weakening!' shouted one of the telekinetics to her left. 'We must end this now!' screamed another.

Holding absolutely nothing back, she buried her fears stepping defiantly into the black morass of Narlakai slashing with ever-widening arcs as she sought desperately to whittle their numbers down. Further horrid moans rose from the disintegrating black ash left in the wake of her devastating attacks; her falchion of light tore through the bloated bodies of the Narlakai with ease, visiting immediate ruin upon their hideous forms. Though Shadow Caster itself failed to damage their actual being, nonetheless the Narlakai withdrew from the weapon's touch almost as though it hurt them. She supposed the falchion's imprisoned soul incited fear amongst its kin; a reminder perhaps of a far worse fate, one clearly not wanting to be shared by the soul stealers.

'Rayna fall back!' cried a voice from behind her. 'Fall back now!'

Before she could put herself to motion, several large tendrils flicked violently upwards, connecting with her upper torso and across the left side of her face. The force of the abrupt simultaneous impacts swept her off the ground, before dropping her painfully onto her back causing the rear of her head to strike the ground hard. Shadow Caster loosened from her grasp upon impact, clattering wildly across the ground as it spun away from her reach into the night. Stunned by the impact of her harsh landing, she laid prone, struggling to blink her dazed vision into focus as the heavy rain splattered uncaringly across her grimacing face. Several other Aspirants were dragged up and over her head by long grotesque tendrils, only to be tossed unceremoniously into the abyssal rear ranks of the Narlakai continuing to push through the southern gate; the screams of the doomed Freylarkai faded rapidly into the background, consumed by the sound of battle and the worsening weather which continued to assault them. She tried to raise her dizzy head off the ground, however, stiff neck muscles and a throbbing pain at the back of her head thwarted her attempt. Her limbs ached, feeling tired and heavy, resisting her urgent desire to move; the feeling was not unfamiliar, though it seemed that her mysterious benefactor would not be present to save her a second time. Tendrils of light had been replaced by ones of darkness which rapidly coiled around her boots, before snaking upwards towards her thighs where they made contact with her ochre skin. The vile moist appendages caused her skin to crawl as they employed suction to attach themselves to her exposed thighs. They tugged at her body, causing her head to bump painfully across the contours of the uneven ground, as the tendrils slowly drew her back towards their host. The stars above began to recede, replaced by a black creeping shadow slowly obscuring them from her sight. Her world began to turn dark as a proverbial nightmare sought to drag her back towards a familiar feeling of despair, and yet...she was not afraid.

'I know you...' she whispered.

The result of the illicit search displayed on the holographic access panel before him burned into his retinas. There was no denying the integrity of the data; the DNA match was confirmed, there could be no cause for incorrect data retrieval. Unwilling to accept the result of the search, despite the conclusive findings, he immediately turned to the media hoping live streams would disprove his emerging fear. Scanning through the available broadcasts he focused his attention on activity local to the library's district, in particular news related feeds. Numerous data feeds covering various topics from building restorations to public demonstrations, births and growing energy concerns flicked rapidly across the screen as he briefly scanned their meta-content, dismissing each in turn. Finding nothing of interest he broadened his reach by analysing news feeds from other nearby districts. Political scandals, hostile business takeovers, celebrity gossip and the like were served up immediately via the access panel. None of the articles particularly interested him, with the exception of one; a single female member of the Shadow class who had been recently apprehended. Though few details were disseminated, it was reported that the unknown woman was due to be escorted out of the metropolis to join others of her kind. Reunited with her fellow Shadow class citizens she would have the opportunity to build a new life for herself – according to the report at least.

'Lies!' he said aloud, unable to contain his disgust.

Despite the complete lack of any imagery, he was certain the article referred to the woman he saw murdered brutally in cold blood by local Peacekeepers who had hunted her down for sport. Unable to stomach the article further, he swiftly moved on looking for anything else of note. Still he found nothing; perhaps his fear was unfounded he began to wonder. Regardless, he had to be certain and thus widened his search to include the metropolis' central district. The heart of the metropolis was a hive of corporate enterprise, government administration, entertainment services and retail outlets. Immediately a slew of fresh articles flicked across the access panel, replacing the others which disappeared rapidly from view. Again more of the same old news danced across his retinas, though there were also reports of civilian accidents and...

'No!'

He passed his left hand through the holographic access panel abruptly fixing a single poignant article before him; a young woman had been killed during the early hours of the afternoon whilst crossing a road. The article described how the woman had been hit by a vehicle as she hurriedly left a retail outlet, and that medical personnel called to the scene of the tragic accident had failed to resuscitate her. Time of death had been officially pronounced at nine minutes past two. The name of the victim was reported to be a Kaitlin Delarouse.

Feeling lightheaded, he stumbled backwards from the access panel. His mind seized up abruptly and pressure started to build inside his head. He glanced randomly around the room trying desperately to focus, but the increasing pressure numbed his senses. Misplacing his footing, he fell hard onto the floor, landing awkwardly on his right hip and yet there was no pain, only the growing numbness. He pushed himself upright, back onto his feet, half standing whilst trying again to focus. His breathing was laboured and all sense of balance eluded him. His body felt like a dead weight seeking to drag him back down onto the hard floor. Looking for support he veered towards an adjacent wall, driving his left shoulder hard into its unforgiving surface. He opened his mouth wanting to scream, yet there was no sound; the screams did not come. Instead tears began to stream down his cheeks as the grim reality started to penetrate his numb state. His vision became watery and a sickening feeling rose from his stomach. He slid his back down the wall burying his face into his thighs, curling into a tight ball like a wounded animal. There he remained, whimpering incessantly, as time ceased to be of any concern.

'Get up now!' echoed a terse, yet familiar, voice. *'You think cowering there mourning the loss of a love which*

never had the opportunity to blossom is going to help anyone? If so you are mistaken.'

'Who are you?' he replied aloud.

There were no others in the library. When closing for the day, he was sure to lock up as Kaitlin had instructed him. All entrances to the building were both alarmed and locked; if an uninvited guest had infiltrated the library, surely he would have been alerted to the fact. He momentarily glanced downwards at the string of bio-keys around his neck, immediately disproving his own theory; complete security was an illusion he reminded himself.

'You know who I am!' echoed the scolding ubiquitous voice. *'Is this sorry excuse for Alarielle's successor what awaits me in the arena? And yet, some call you The Guardian...pathetic!'*

'Lothnar...but...how can you be here?' he replied.

'More questions.' continued the distant echo. *'Stop wasting time and get up. The Blades are dying. You are supposed to be protecting them, light bringer!'* said the voice sardonically.

'I don't know how.'

'Then figure it out! You have a choice. Give into your despair, thus accepting the encroaching darkness, indefinitely, or...become something more than the loathsome body thief that you are.' lectured the scathing voice. *'There is a formidable telepath beyond the southern gate manipulating the Narlakai...kill it, as your kind would say.'*

Lothnar was attempting to provoke him, though he required no such goading in channelling his grief, manifest by the loss of Kaitlin, thus re-forging his wraith blade; he vowed then to use the vengeful weapon against Freylar's enemies. The hate burning inside him would no longer continue to stain his soul, turning it black with spite; instead he would make good his promise to Kirika, using his hatred to destroy those who sought harm to both himself and his adoptive kin.

'Get up now!' he screamed at himself.

Slowly her vision winked into partial focus. Raising her left hand she stretched out her fingers releasing a focused beam of light which shot forth from her palm. The shot was poorly aimed, on account of her poor sight, though it still managed to glance the monstrous shadow looming over her, causing it to reel back from her and release its grasp around her thighs. Biting down hard she rode the pain shooting through her back as she forced herself onto her feet. With her right hand she refashioned her light falchion; the press of Narlakai around her inhaled at the sight of the abhorrent weapon, fearful of the ruin it would visit upon their amorphous forms. The injured horror before her released a sonorous moan whilst part of its semi-gaseous body began to disintegrate where the light had penetrated its being. She felt the injured soul stealer tug at her soul, and yet the Narlakin had both retracted its tendrils and closed its ghastly maw.

'I know you.' she said once more. 'You stole something which belongs to me.'

Kaitlin had died because of her. It was because of her that Kaitlin had gone to the metropolis' central district. Overwhelmed by rapture, born from a promise she had given, Kaitlin had lost herself to the joy of expectation. Kaitlin's complete distraction had prompted the tragic incident and she was the indirect cause. Prior to now she had subconsciously buried the awful truth, refusing to accept her part in the horrible event. Now she had no defence against the sickening memory, which had resurfaced to torment her anew; she had been stripped bare and exposed to the undiluted facts as they were. In time she would learn to shoulder the burden of her ever-present guilt, though in the here and now there was only pain and sorrow. In that moment of realisation her heart broke, like a dam cracking open no longer able to contain the pressure upon it.

'Now...you will give it back!' she proclaimed vehemently.

Her pent-up self-loathing violently exploded into the world in a moment of pure rage, expressed as focused light directed towards her attacker. Brilliant white light lanced forth from her body burning intensely through the core of the injured Narlakin, which only moments prior stood menacingly over her. After disintegrating the nightmare instantly with its cruel caress, the beam of light continued its uninterrupted path obliterating each and every fresh horror in its path before contacting the perimeter wall with an explosive detonation. Those Narlakai caught within the blast radius were also promptly annihilated. Severed tendrils littered the ground, thrashing wildly across the soaked bedrock, whilst their former hosts were reduced to a thick ash which swirled through the air before mixing with the rain to form a vile black slick. The oily substance dropped to the floor, staining the ground like blotches of black ink. The abhorrent remains of the nightmares which had sought to engulf them promptly gave birth to a host of varying apparitions which rose simultaneously from the hell-stained ground. The ethereal forms of various different creatures, including several released Freylarkai, appeared as though summoned before her. Their combined feeble light dimly lit the carnage of war which surrounded them. Despite their losses, the Narlakai continued to flood through the southern gate at an alarming rate. With seemingly no end to the black tide swarming through the breach, the enemy's superior numbers threatened imminently to sweep the remaining Aspirants aside. Though she would never admit to it aloud, Nathanar's grim assessment of their plight held true.

As the apparitions left their world, ready to embark on the next phase of their existence, one of the host appeared reluctant to depart. The disinclined traveller loitering before her appeared to be a female Freylarkin, or rather it *had* been prior to its release. Lingering solemnly before her now, the apparition exerted an unseen force which tugged at her body, causing her breasts to gently heave. Inexplicably she felt connected to the disembodied soul hovering before her, unexpectedly drawn towards it as though it had once been a part of her. The apparition extended its arms outwards, beckoning her forth into its ghostly embrace, then without any warning it sped towards her at an alarming pace. Unable to evade the approaching apparition, it contacted with her body then faded rapidly from sight.

'*Who are you?*'
'What?'
'*Why is it you inhabit my body?*'
'I...what is this?'
'*Rayna... that is your name is it not?*'
'Yes, but...'
'*You are not native to Freylar.*'
'No, I was...'
'*I see...*'
'Alarielle, is that...'

'*Yes, I am she. My father trusts you...*'

'Alarielle, I did not intend...'

'*That matters not. Please, you must save him, do not let him share my fate.*'

'But, I do not possess the...'

'*Alone perhaps, but together we are stronger than you know.*'

'You would aid me?'

'*I would help my father. Besides...you have delivered me from damnation. I am indebted to you for my salvation.*'

'You owe me nothing!'

'*Sister with respect, you are wrong, I owe you everything.*'

'So what now...?'

'*Now...we destroy them!*'

TWENTY ONE
Retribution

'The Guardian lives!' cried the familiar voice of Anika from close proximity behind her.

'Rayna!' cried Nathanar, moving quickly to join her side. 'Our telekinetics are spent. We must fall back to the sanctuary, the Narlakai are outflanking us.'

'No, we need to charge them now.' she replied fervently.

'Rayna, such arrogance would surely end us.' replied Nathanar.

'There is a telepath beyond the southern gate herding the Narlakai. We must stop them!' she explained quickly.

'How can...'

'There's no time. Do you trust me?' she asked.

Nathanar's rain soaked face glared hard at her. All around them the screams of the dammed weakly penetrated the downpour. Each fresh cry for help slowly transformed Nathanar's unflinching gaze into a hate filled grimace; further persuasion on the matter was no longer required. Raising his double-handed sword high above his head in his right hand, Nathanar finally found his voice and with it the means to inspire those under his command.

'Blades, hear me! Beyond that gate lies the instrument of our ruin. To me brothers and sisters, and together we will charge the enemy's vile black heart and end this accursed invasion.'

'Form up!' followed a cry from Nathaniel who had since moved up to join them.

Quickly the remaining unengaged Aspirants withdrew from their positions, abandoning ground they had so desperately sought to hold. They formed up alongside Anika, who stood behind her and adjacent to Nathaniel; the spritely young Aspirant continued to preach fealty to the order as though it were an ongoing mantra. Anika's zeal rose to the fore inspiring others around her of a similar disposition. Though she questioned the zealous Aspirant's methods, their hour was dark; any means of rallying the Aspirants during their time of need were welcomed. With those still able rallied to his side, Nathanar levelled his immense sword at the southern gate, signalling readiness for their desperate charge.

'Together we are stronger. Now is not the time for self-doubt.'

'Agreed.' she said quietly under her breath.

Channelling all of her past regrets, frustrations, self-loathing, pent-up rage and determination, she once more re-forged the vengeful metaphor that was her wraith blade; a non-corporeal weapon of immense destruction, unseen by her enemies yet devastating to their existence. Coupled with Alarielle's own resolve and basic need for revenge, she willed every fibre of her being to unleash every lumen of energy she could ever hope to offer. At her command her entire body pulsed with the caress of pure white light. She focused the increasing amounts of light down the length of her left arm which she then directed squarely towards the southern gate.

'All of you close your eyes!' she cried.
'Retribution will be ours!'

Finally letting go of all of her hate and malice, directing it towards her foes, a large beam of pure white light exploded outwards from her right palm. The light lanced forwards with supreme ferocity, annihilating every Narlakin within three paces of its trajectory. The beam speared through the ranks of the soul stealers with its devastating touch, obliterating every Narlakin within its path, as it accelerated through the southern gate well beyond the perimeter wall. An awful deafening chorus rose from the enemy survivors, echoing out across Scrier's Post, in response to the devastating blow dealt to them.

'Charge!' cried Nathanar.

Nathanar's call to arms was promptly followed by similar outbursts from others behind them, including Anika's fervent cries.

Though the attack had taken much out of her, she willed her body forwards regardless with unrelenting determination; she broke into a sprint alongside Nathanar as they charged towards the southern gate through the thick mass of swirling black ash left in the wake of the newly-released Narlakai. The path before them was wide open, save for the ugly carpet of severed tendrils which littered the waterlogged ground. Both she and Nathanar led the charge; Nathanar tightly gripped his enormous double-handed sword before him, and she wielded dual falchions of light, having forged a second in the absence of Shadow Caster. The ground beneath them was treacherous, littered with writhing gangrenous tendrils and blotched with water-soaked ash, however, the widespread subdued light emanating from the mass apparitions released from their demonic confinement helped guide their advance. Though unable to tear her sight away from the approaching gate, she heard the unmistakable sound of weapons clattering against the ground as several of her brothers and sisters fell afoul of the slippery footing. Regardless of their losses, the rearguard's charge did not falter; they breached the perimeter wall with relative ease, passing through the southern gate, where they contacted more of the black horrors gauchely redressing their ranks. Beyond the shambling horrors stood two individuals, barely visible through the gaps in the flailing tendrils blocking their path.

'There!' rasped Nathanar. 'Run them down!'

Crashing into the vile black morass, wet tissue slapped at her face and exposed thighs as she bounded forwards, determined to maintain her momentum. Nathanar remained at her side using the razor sharp length of his blade to shield them against the worst of the impact. They pushed through the encroaching darkness, which sapped increasing amounts of their momentum with each advancing pace. More of the Narlakai's damnable vertical rifts began to manifest in the periphery of her vision, but regardless of the immediate dangers closing in on them she dug deep, finding new levels of grit and determination. In one final push to break through the thinning black tide, she used the last of her energy reserves to hurl both of her light falchions forwards, helping to clear the remaining path. Both weapons spun haphazardly through the black morass disintegrating every Narlakin they struck before fading out after six or seven paces; she was utterly spent.

Nathanar shouldered his way past the last of the Narlakai, whilst others around him fell to ash scalded by the last of her light. He was followed closely by Nathaniel, who had since overrun her; both veterans pulled free of the writhing black mass to face the true architects of Freylar's intended ruin. She tried desperately to pull herself free of the mass, but agile tendrils swiftly coiled themselves around her limbs, dragging her back towards the heart of the black abyss.

'No, do not let me go back!'

Behind her, screams rang out as the trailing Aspirants caught in the thick of the dark mass fought frantically to retain their souls. Glancing back over her shoulder she saw that Anika too had been caught in the nest of horrors; the fanatical young Aspirant swung her sword in short deadly arcs with reckless abandon, trying vehemently to hold back her attackers, and yet all around more of the sinister vertical maws were forming ready to devour fresh souls.

As the last strands of hope died in her heart, an agonising scream rang out, piercing their own desperate cries for help. Immediately the Narlakai released their hold on the remaining Aspirants, allowing their battered limp forms to fall to the ground like rag dolls abandoned in favour of something new. Inexplicably the Narlakai gently began to disperse, drifting languidly northwards as though an invisible force recalled them back to their home; in their wake lay the tired remnants of the once-proud rearguard, now reduced to a handful of surviving Freylarkai. A short distance away, a female Freylarkin, flanked by several seemingly still obedient Narlakai, hauled a wounded companion away from Scrier's Post in a north-westerly direction. The fleeing Freylarkin heaved her companion awkwardly under her right arm, her left hand apparently unsuited to the task on account of its grotesque claw-like appearance. Nathaniel ran immediately towards her, paying little attention to the withdrawing Narlakai, the renewalist in him desperately seeking out those in immediate need of his ability.

'Father!'

She quickly waved him by to attend to the others; her wounds were not serious and her strength would return in time. Nathanar then approached her slowly; he was physically exhausted from their ordeal and dragged his immense blood-stained sword beside him. He extended his free hand, using what little strength he had left to pull her upright.

'Thank you.' she said. 'It is done.'

'Albeit temporarily.' Nathanar replied wearily. 'It is likely that she will return.' he continued, casting a stern gaze in the direction of the fleeing Freylarkai.

'You mean the Freylarkin with the clawed hand?' she questioned.

'Yes.'

'Who is she?'

'You had best ask Kirika that question...'

'They are withdrawing.' said Thandor.

'What?!' rasped Ragnar, 'Surely your eyes deceive you Thandor.'

'They do not.' replied Thandor matter-of-factly.

'Thandor is correct. It would appear that this charade has come to an end.' agreed Marcus.

As he had feared, the bulk of the Blades forces had been lured out of the vale as a diversion.

His heart sank as his mind turned towards darker thoughts. Had the diversion succeeded in its task, he mused, yet surely not; a second detachment of Narlakai would not have had sufficient time to outflank their position and assault the vale, even if it had succeeded in evading the rearguard. Did this mean then that the enemy's plan had in fact faltered he wondered.

'*My lord!*' called the distant voice of a telepath suddenly. '*Message from Lothnar, by way of the telepathic bridge you ordered.*'

'Origin?!' he snapped aloud, turning his head to try and locate the messenger in person.

'What is it?' asked Ragnar, impatient as always.

He raised his hand to silence the Captain of The Blades. Both Kirika and Natalya approached, eager to learn the fate of their people.

'*South-west. Scrier's Post.*' the messenger communicated further.

'Please, your report.' he ordered.

'*Narlakai contact at Scrier's Post. Thwarted by the rearguard my lord.*'

'Survivors?'

'*Unknown. The fighting was fierce.*'

'Everyone, hear me now. We march on Scrier's Post, immediately!'

They failed to notice the silent approach of the Freylarkin stepping forth from the black recesses of the north-west perimeter wall. The emerging silhouette exhibited a nasty limp, yet despite their obvious handicap they approached swiftly revealing nothing of their identity until directly upon them. The Freylarkin was water-soaked on account of the torrential rain, which only now began to abate, and had a worn, grubby and earthy look about him.

'*Lothnar!*'

'Well met brother.' said Nathanar with a polite nod of respect to the veteran Paladin.

'Nathanar.' Lothnar replied.

Lothnar took a moment to assess the battlefield that was once Scrier's Post; the Paladin was clearly disheartened by what he saw.

'How many of you were stationed here?' asked Lothnar somewhat hesitantly.

'The Teacher, myself and every Blade Aspirant within the order.' replied Nathanar. 'We had two light bringers.'

Lothnar pressed both of his hands to his face. He shook his head slowly.

'This should have been avoided,' he said dejectedly. 'This is my fault.'

'No, it's not!' she said cutting in. 'If you had not contacted me when you did, we too would have perished.'

'Rayna, this could devastate the order.' Lothnar replied.

'Maybe...though perhaps instead it will serve to strengthen its resolve.'

A moment of reflection passed between them as each silently paid their respects to the recently departed. As was characteristic of the Narlakai's victims, there were no bodies. There would be no mass burning on the pyres. The selfless sacrifice of their brothers and sisters would instead be recounted through stories, etched forever in memory refusing to fade with time on account of the atrocity.

'What of the architect behind this?' Lothnar enquired, breaking their shared silence.

'She...the one previously shamed here, dragged her wounded telepathic companion away.' replied Nathanar.

Lothnar turned abruptly to face the rearguard's commander.

'Are you certain Nathanar?!'

'Yes.' replied Nathanar sternly. 'It was all I could do to run my sword through the flank of her wretched companion. They fled to the north-west. We were in no position to give chase.'

'I do not doubt your actions brother. Indeed I applaud them.' replied Lothnar.

'It is Rayna who deserves the applause.' replied Nathanar. 'If not for her, Scrier's Post would have fallen to the horrors.'

'Then I shall look forward to reading your official report.' replied Lothnar dryly. 'It should make for an interesting read.'

'In any case, we must contact the primary force and apprise them of our situation.' Nathanar continued. 'We cannot continue to hold this position should they decide to attack again.'

'I have already alerted the main force. No doubt they are already marching on Scrier's Post.' explained Lothnar.

'Good. That is reassuring to know.'

'Lothnar, if I may, I request that I have a word with yourself and Nathaniel in private at your earliest possible convenience.' she said, not wishing to delay the matter of Alarielle's soul.

'Very well, once The Teacher is done attending to the wounded you may have your word.'

'You forgot your first lesson.' he said with a thin smile as he passed Shadow Caster back to its rightful owner.

The alien weapon was calm now. In the absence of its kin the blade had returned to its habitual dormant state. He passed the weapon a short distance through the air, deftly causing its hilt to rotate in flight thus allowing Rayna to firmly grasp it.

'Never release one's grip on their weapon.' Rayna replied with a warm smile of her own.

'Indeed.' he replied. 'Now then, you wish to speak to Lothnar and myself?' he said nodding politely at the veteran Paladin also present.

'Yes, though I ask that each of you is patient with me,' implored Rayna. 'What I'm about to say will be difficult for you both to accept.'

Rayna's normally casual, yet also confident, disposition had been replaced by one of a far more serious demeanour; she looked apprehensive, which was most unlike her. He recalled when Rayna first met Lothnar, and accepted the Paladin's provoked challenge to dual in the arena, as well as her audience with queen Mirielle. During those stressful encounters Rayna had remained calm and collected, and yet now she seemed somewhat hesitant. Clearly she had been through the mill due to their recent confrontation with the Narlakai, though he felt certain that was not the cause of Rayna's apparent anxiety.

'Go on.' he replied, calmly folding his arms.

'The Narlakin which almost bested me this cycle was not like the others.' said Rayna gingerly.

'How so?' enquired Lothnar.

'There was a soul, trapped within it...' Rayna continued, clearly struggling to find the right words to explain her thoughts. 'One of great significance to you both.'

He felt the blood drain immediately from his face; he knew instantly who Rayna referred to. His eyes began to water as Rayna struggled with what needed to be said. Never once had he allowed himself the fool's hope of believing that his daughter's soul would be set free from its eternal damnation, though with the help of both Kirika and Rayna he had learnt to move on and accept his daughter's ill fate. Now the one who occupied his daughter's body threatened to turn his world upside down for a second time.

'Alarielle! Was it Alarielle?!' demanded Lothnar impatiently.

'...yes...it was...or rather, it is...' replied Rayna, whose eyes now mirrored his own.

'Rayna, I do not understand...'

'Patience Lothnar!' he rasped, unable to hide the raw emotion in his voice. 'Rayna, in your own time...'

'She is within me now Nathaniel. Alarielle chose not to move on with the others. Instead she stayed behind in me. She helped me to find the strength I needed to drive back the Narlakai. The strength I needed to save you, Nathaniel, her father. Even now I hear her soul, whispering to me...like a ghost.'

His heart broke and with it the strength in his legs abandoned him, forcing him down onto his knees; an entire legion of Narlakai had failed to lay him low during the battle for Scrier's Post, and yet now the sudden return of his daughter had done exactly that. Tears poured uncontrollably down his face, though he could not tell if they were born of joy or sorrow. Conflicting emotions assaulted his body, and his head began to swim. His daughter had returned to him, though now it seemed that Alarielle was destined to be a prisoner in her own body. In helping him, had his daughter exchanged one torment for an even greater one he wondered.

'Can I speak with her?' he asked meekly.

'Directly...in time perhaps, though I do not know for certain.' replied Rayna. 'But she can hear you, and I her.'

'Then, I need to know...and I mean no disrespect to you Rayna, but...is my daughter happy?' he asked hesitantly.

'Yes. Father, I love you.'

Rayna crouched before him then cupped her hands around his face, tilting his head towards her. She offered him a warm tearful smile; he knew then the answer he hoped for to be true.

'Your daughter loves you Nathaniel,' said Rayna sincerely. 'The fact that you go on is all the happiness she needs.'

Rayna reached for his hand and stood up slowly, inviting him to do the same. The strength in his legs returned, though he felt more than a little unsteady on them.

'We're a pair are we not?' said Rayna returning to form.

'Yes,' he laughed, still weeping, 'That we certainly are.'

Since his outburst, Lothnar had respectfully watched the events unfold in silence. Only now did the proud Freylarkin dare to approach any closer.

'Rayna...I have been hard on you,' said Lothnar, 'Yet it is difficult for me to accept your presence here in Freylar given the circumstance of your arrival.'

'I understand, even more so now....' replied Rayna.

'Though I cannot readily change my feelings towards you, know that you have earned a measure of my respect this cycle.' Lothnar continued.

'That is a start at least.' replied Rayna. 'But Lothnar, know now that I will defeat you in that arena.'

'See that you do my Blade sister, for you are now The Guardian of the soul I love...'

TWENTY TWO
Reflection

It was Saturday morning. Ordinarily the library would have been due to open that morning, but with the tragic loss of its primary curator the decision had been taken not to do so as a mark of respect. Kaitlin was widely known across the district and very much respected throughout the local community, a little known fact now evidenced by the carpet of flowers being laid outside the library's main entrance. Careful not to draw attention, he secretly peered through one of the library's windows at those who came to pay their respects. Although not an official wake as such, the library's loyal patrons used the opportunity to remember Kaitlin and her time spent managing the successful running of the traditional literary establishment. Given the library's elite patronage, the tributes being laid on the pavement outside the library were truly magnificent. He wished desperately to be able to contribute to the growing floral display alongside the mourners, though given his precarious presence within the metropolis doing so would have been entirely foolhardy. Instead he watched nosily from a safe distance as more individuals made their way towards the library to pay their respects to the recently departed.

The recent weeks had been amongst the best of his wretched existence; he cherished the memories of his time spent with Kaitlin. Now, however, his world was empty once more, perhaps more so than it had ever been.

'Better to have loved and lost than never to have loved at all.' he whispered to himself.

Hollow words, he thought, words that did nothing to abate the feeling of loneliness which stalked him, in much the same way that death tirelessly nipped at his heels; both were unavoidable given the nature of his miserable existence. Physically his heart was OK, though metaphorically speaking it had been shattered beyond repair. His cruel world had seen fit to deprive him of his sole source of happiness, thus plunging him into darkness once more, robbing him of the single source of light in his life. There was no justice in his world, only cruel intentions and endless torment. He was depressed, and he knew it. He wanted to punch the wall hard with his fists, though such fruitless behaviour would only leave him nursing bruised and bloodied knuckles if not broken fingers. Likewise he needed to tip over every table in the library whilst yelling crude profanities, and yet such reckless abandon would only draw attention to his presence. Instead he screamed silently within the confines of his own mind whilst struggling to come to terms with Kaitlin's passing. His was a harsh life; uncaring and hurtful. Now he just wanted to forget. He wanted to go home, back to the Wild.

That night he gathered up anything of use which would serve him well upon his return to the metropolis' artificial wilderness. He packed his new tailored clothes, which he had used for the Mr L. Cameron charade, along with various food supplies; his primary reason for abandoning the Wild in the first instance. He took nothing from Kaitlin's personal belongings; tempting though it was to acquire something by which to remember her, both his emotions and memories of Kaitlin were raw and he knew he would not be able to endure the constant reminder of her passing. Besides, they belonged to Kaitlin; by his moral code of ethics he did not feel entitled to her personal effects. Once he was finished packing for his return to normality, he made lupine had served him well and had proven itself to be most competent. Perhaps he could use its help, he considered. Certainly the dire wolf would be more than capable of keeping pace as well as tracking prey, plus it would have the advantage of being able to infiltrate places where he could not. Though regardless of the obvious tactical advantages, he would no doubt welcome the fellowship; more often than not, his was a lonely path travelled by few. He decided then that the company would likely do him good.

'Yes, I believe I will.' he said.

'Well then, you can be the one to inform Aleska.' said Ragnar.

'What do you mean?' he replied curiously.

'She has become quite fond of your lupine brother since delivering word of the invasion.' explained Ragnar. 'She even named that one.'

'Will I like this name?'

'Krisis!' said Ragnar nodding towards the dire wolf.

The hulking black wolf immediately rose from its place of slumber and approached them both. It stood patiently beside them, awaiting instructions from its Strider masters.

'Heh, I guess its naming was appropriate.' he replied. 'It is as good as any other. Well then, Krisis and I will be leaving shortly.'

'*You will assist me in tracking down our prey.*'

The dire wolf shifted its balance slightly, acknowledging his order. Together they would track down those directly responsible for the demise of the Aspirants. Though he had promised Ragnar that he would make no attempt at seeking vengeance alone, fortune smiled upon him and it had raven black fur and slanted yellow eyes; he was no longer alone.

'I forgot how much I love this view. From up here, little appears to have changed.' she said glancing down at the vale.

The climb had been hard on them, yet it had done them good to scale the falls, both physically and mentally, given the sense of achievement that came from reaching the summit. They chose to fly across the powerful stream feeding the falls, and subsequently hiked a short distance eastwards so that they could better converse over the thunderous sound of the falls. Upon reaching their destination she had invited Rayna to sit towards the edge of the precipice, allowing them to fully admire the vale's natural beauty. Her eyes drifted towards the Tri-Spires on the opposite side of the vale; from their high vantage point the heart of Freylar's rule seemed so small and insignificant.

'That reminds me,' she said, pulling out a smooth Moonstone hidden within the folds of her long dress. 'Queen Mirielle asked me to give this to you. It is intended as a sign of gratitude for your service at Scrier's Post. The queen has issued one to each of the surviving Aspirants.'

She handed the polished, teardrop-shaped stone to Rayna, whilst quietly scolding herself for not having done so sooner. Rayna immediately began to study the Moonstone closely, like a child fascinated with a new toy, poring over all its details.

'But it's too smooth. Surely this is no Moonstone Kirika?' noted Rayna inquisitively.

'The queen shaped each one in person. Though the raw material used was that of Moonstone, its shape represents the tears shed by the Aspirants in the wake of the horrific attack on Scrier's Post.'

'It's beautiful Kirika, and very much appreciated. Please thank Mirielle for me. However, you did not bring me all the way out here just to present me with a shiny trinket.'

She smiled weakly casting her gaze towards the distant horizon of the southern ridgeline. She knew the words well, having practised them repeatedly before their meeting, and yet now they obstinately stuck in the back of her throat refusing to be spoken when needed most. Typically she had no qualms in discussing the matter, though she cherished her unblemished, innocent relationship with Rayna; the information she had to impart would only muddy affairs. It frustrated her that she had little say regarding her direct involvement in the matter; given a choice, she would have gladly distanced herself from its stain on her family name.

'Have you heard the news regarding Nathanar?' she asked changing the subject; avoiding the true reason for their clandestine meeting.

'He has ascended to the rank of Paladin within the order, has he not?' replied Rayna.

'Indeed he has.' she replied. 'Aleska chose to step down from her position on the council, and has formally retired her service to The Blades. There will be an official ceremony for both in due course.'

'I am pleased for Nathanar, as well as for you I might add.' replied Rayna with a curious grin.

'How so?' she replied, quickly turning to face Rayna.

'Well...with your mentor stepping down from the council, one would assume that you now have more freedom to grow into your role as ruling council member?' explained Rayna.

'True. I forget how astute you can be. Your candid demeanour serves you well by distracting others from fully realising what truly goes on inside your head.' she replied.

'Damn...you've discovered my little trick.' replied Rayna with a quick laugh.

'And let us not forget your own accolade.'

'Which is?'

'Come now, you know of what I speak sister.' she replied.

'Ah, you refer to my own ascension to the lofty rank of Blade Novice?' replied Rayna.

'You mean to say that Nathaniel has not yet discussed the matter with you?' she enquired.

'What matter?' questioned Rayna. 'Now you have lost me entirely.'

'Sister dearest, Nathanar has repeatedly spoken most highly of your actions at Scrier's Post.' she said. 'He has been lobbying for your ascension to the rank of Blade Adept, a request which has since been sanctioned by The Blade Lord himself!'

It was rare to see Rayna stunned into silence; the Freylarkin's insatiable curiosity and drive gave Rayna little cause to remain quiet for any length of time. She found it odd that Nathaniel had not already passed word to Rayna of the promotion, though he had been rather preoccupied as of late with the decimation of the Aspirants' ranks. The loss had hit The Blades hard, more so given the detriment to the order at the grass roots level. The tragedy would likely cause potential new recruits to think twice about joining The Blades in future, nevertheless, the order had faced its share of adversity in the past; it would continue to operate as Freylar's primary means of defence, regardless of the pressures placed upon it.

'I am not sure if this news pleases you.' she replied, looking to rouse Rayna from her visual paralysis.

'Yes, yes, I am pleased...it's just that...' replied Rayna who struggled to convey her thoughts on the matter.

'It is just what exactly?' she asked, beaming curiously.

'Things are moving so fast,' replied Rayna. 'If I blink, I may stumble and fall.'

'Perhaps that is true, but...knowing you as I do, should you indeed fall it will not take you long to get back on your feet.' she replied.

'Your faith in me is appreciated, though all this talk of praise and adulation is not why you have brought me here Kirika.' replied Rayna. 'Speak plainly sister. No more dancing around what must be said. What is it that weighs so heavily on your soul?'

There was no avoiding the subject any further. Despite desperately wanting to distance herself from the truth behind the recent invasion of Freylar, she knew well that she would never be entirely absolved of the root cause of the attack. Ragnar already held a dim view of her, given her ability to scry, and recent events would only increase his disdain towards her. Scrier's were not to everyone's liking, some believed them to be untrustworthy and manipulative; this latest travesty would only worsen public opinion. She often secretly wondered if her lot would have been improved without her ability, though surely without it she would have never been elevated to her current role.

'I have been avoiding this matter for some time now, since what I have to tell you will not cast me in a favourable light.' she said reluctantly.

'Would this matter be why Ragnar regards you so unfavourably?' Rayna enquired.

'In part yes.' she replied.

'...and the reason for his hostility is?'

'Is that I know who orchestrated the attack on Freylar!' she replied.

'You mean the Freylarkin with the clawed hand?!' replied Rayna now staring intently at her.

'Yes...that one.'

'But how is it that you know this individual, Kirika?'

She paused for a brief moment, hoping dearly that the truth owed to Rayna would not sour their relationship.

'I know this Freylarkin because regrettably...she is family to me. Her name is Darlia. She is my sister.'

– www.thechroniclesoffreylar.com –

DRAMATIS PERSONAE

Ruling Council of Freylar
Aleska, Valkyrie
Kirika 'Fate Weaver', Valkyrie
Marcus 'The Blade Lord', Paladin –
Commander of The Blades
Mirielle, Queen

The Blades
Anika, Blade Aspirant
Kryshar, Blade Aspirant
Lothnar, Paladin
Natalya, Valkyrie
Nathanar, Blade Master
Nathaniel 'The Teacher', Blade Master
Ragnar, Paladin –
Captain of The Blades
Rayna 'The Guardian', Blade Aspirant
Thandor, Paladin

Civilian Freylarkai
Larissa, Dressmaker

Deceased Freylarkai
Alarielle, Blade Adept

Exiled Freylarkai
Darlia
Lileah

Orders
Knights Thranis
The Blades

Races
Freylarkai
Narlakai
Ravnarkai

Dire Wolves
Krisis

Humans
Callum 'Fox'
Kaitlin Delarouse
'Trix'